JANIECE HOPPER

CRACKED BAT

Suzanne,
Dance Your Spirit
Always!
Janiece

Ten Pentacles
Monroe, Washington

Published by Ten Pentacles
Monroe, WA
Please visit us at **tenpentacles.com**

Publisher's Note
This book and its cover quotes are works of fiction. Names,
deities, characters, places, occurrences, products, and events are
the products of the author's imagination or are used fictitiously.
Any resemblance to actual persons, living or dead, businesses,
events, circumstances, products, or places is coincidental.

Ten Pentacles is not liable for any life, spiritual, emotional,
physical, or Karmic occurrences that result from anyone reading
or not reading this book, but we wish you well.

ISBN 13: 978-0-9814777-0-1
Library of Congress Control Number: 2008900948

Original Cover Art by Melinda Peeples at tg-peeps
Cover Design by Rhonda Dicksion at Indigo Dog Design

Intuit-Lit is a trademark of Ten Pentacles, Monroe, Washington
98272
The Nia Technique is a trademark of Nia Technique, Inc.
Portland, Oregon 97205.
* This paperback book was printed in the United States of
America. The paper used is 30% post consumer product made
with no chlorine. It is approved by the Forest Stewardship
Council.

Dedicated to the real Shune,
and the fine art of
divine scavenging,
in solidarity with women
who refuse to forfeit
due to pain

Chapter One

Books can be shelved or packed away, but little girls shouldn't be. Linnea Perrault had this sense embedded in her flesh. With a delicate rose tattooed across her ankle, she shoved her foot into a damp snow boot, apologized to her daughter, and dashed after Dan. "I had a feeling something was wrong all day. Why didn't she call me?"

Her husband shrugged, backing their weather-beaten sedan out of the icy driveway. "She said she needed to see you immediately."

Linnea bit her full lip, tasting candy cane gloss. Neither of them said another word until he pulled alongside the frosted chain link fence that enclosed June's yard. He motioned for her to get out.

She widened her dark green eyes. "You have plenty of time to come inside."

"I'm stuck on Step Two," he said. "I can't deal with anyone else's problems right now. I've got to figure out how to connect with a power greater than myself, one that can restore my sanity, or at least keep me sober." He turned the corners of his mouth up, crinkling the black knit ski cap over his brow, eerily rearranging his features so that he looked like a gargoyle.

1

Disturbed, she adopted a gentle teasing tone. "Dan, you believe in a power greater than yourself. Love."

"Nope. I don't. Lack of faith is a distinguishing characteristic of an alcoholic, my dear."

Stepping out onto the curb, Linnea shuddered, but not from the chilly air rising off the slush at her feet. "How am I supposed to get back?"

Dan shrugged. "Walk?"

Walk through this neighborhood by herself at night, in the snow, no less. Could resisting whiskey fog his mind that much?

He leaned over and pulled her door shut. He was off, driving to an AA meeting across town where he wasn't likely to meet anyone they knew.

The stench of cat litter and cheap beer emanated from the trash can beside her. The cold fingernails of self-doubt dug into her rib cage, clutching at her heart. She excoriated herself for missing his addiction for an entire year. Why hadn't she been able to tell he'd been drinking whiskey in the garage while she blithely read bedtime stories to Megan or sat up late working on *The Edge*?

Of course, he had functioned so well, unlike her family members. Sure, he could sleep through a thunderstorm or Fourth of July fireworks, and often flagged during sex, but she was usually so exhausted herself she figured it was normal for this stage in their lives. True, he'd been sinking into a morose funk more frequently, but she assumed it was from stress. There were always rumors that Coffeestalk was going to open a shop on Spinning Wheel Bluff.

When the car disappeared completely, she steeled her shoulders, thinking longingly of the ebony leather-bound book she'd dropped in the foyer when he whisked her out the door. She hadn't taken the time to pick up *Grimm's Fairy Tales*, to put it where it would not be stepped on. She didn't yet know that books and bodies have something in common, that they both hold stories the mind refuses to remember. She only wished she was home, ignorantly sitting on the edge of Megan's bed reading *Snow White*, waiting for the polls to close.

***

She sat scrutinizing June on a faded, under-stuffed couch, surrounded by overweight cats. The last time she and Megan counted, there were seven of them, all strays brought by kind folks who just knew June would give them a good home. Nicotine had staved the pounds off for years, but June's nightly pastry was gaining on her. "Mom, what did the doctor say?"

"He gave me a clean bill of health."

Linnea had spent many teenage evenings on this very couch with her mother, bonding over refined sugar while the house crumbled around them. "How's your glucose?"

"It's fine. You shouldn't be so paranoid."

As mice skittered across the grungy, brown carpet beneath them, Linnea drew her knees tightly to her chest. Some of the cats watched the rodents, but idly. Others dozed contentedly.

"This is surreal," she said. "These cats should be ashamed of themselves."

"You have a hole in your sock."

Linnea would have liked a much thicker layer of acrylic between her feet and this particular floor. She nodded ruefully. "I'm running low. My good pair is in the wash."

"Your husband ought to buy you some new ones." June poured cream into a freshly-brewed cup of Dan's renowned Miller's Blend. He was always giving her coffee beans, single vacuum-packed bags of decorative brown paper with his signature gold seal. Her freezer was full of them, but she made instant when she was alone. It was too much trouble to grind beans for one person. "Socks are cheap. Business is good."

"Money's tight." Besides, detox made Dan too disorientated to discuss anything, let alone footwear. Linnea eyed two mice frolicking across an old edition of *The Edge* that had slipped off the battered coffee table before them. *The Edge* would have to report earned income this year to the Internal Revenue Service, but not much.

June sighed. "I wish *I* could buy a new floor. Eat your Danish, dear. You look thin."

"Good thing he likes a woman with hips to hold on to," Linnea muttered, obediently taking a bite of Bavarian cream.

A heavy tabby struggled to pull its ample hindquarters up onto the coffee table. It nosed around the gilded china pitcher. June crooned, "Whiskers likes Great-Grandma's antique tea set, don't you?"

"Get down!" Linnea commanded, to no avail. As a mother, she felt nauseous watching animals tiptoe on tables and countertops. Covertly, she checked her fork for the caked-on cat food the dishwasher often couldn't scour away.

"Clean enough for you?" June tried to appear amused.

She nodded, nonchalantly peeking at the pastry for either feline pelt, or signs of filched corners. Not from the beloved pets, but from the grown sons who mooched off June. Early in her marriage, Linnea had ceased to call her brothers by name, preferring to think of them in fairy tale terms, first brother, second, and third. Like wolf pups, they'd devour their mother's dessert and her retirement, for that matter, without a care.

But her childhood home was unusually calm this evening. No television blaring about terrorism. No pounding stereo threatening to implode the dilapidated rambler. The splintered doors down the hall hung open, so she knew that no one was passed out behind them.

"Why did you want to see me tonight?" she asked gently. "I can't stay long."

"*Your* father called."

Linnea wrinkled her brow, wrestling with the incongruity between the words and June's manner. When her ex-husband called, things usually got ugly.

"Your *biological* father."

"My real dad?" Her heart doubled over on itself.

"His voice sounds exactly the same as it did twenty-eight years ago. I always knew he'd be sorry about leaving. He's back in town. He wants to see you. He wants…a relationship."

A mouse ran straight up the brick wall. When its tiny body reached the coarse-grained crown molding, it fell backwards. Crazed from unnatural acrobatics, the mammal twisted on the way down and cracked on the hearth.

The telephone rang shrilly. June snatched the receiver to her ear. Covering the mouthpiece, she whispered, "It's the parole officer. They found my poor Jaime."

Linnea's heart unfolded from its defensive crouch. Churning blood escaped from all four chambers. Adrenaline urged her to flee. She had no desire to find out why Brother Number One was in trouble again. She stepped into her soggy snow boots and slipped outside.

The dark clouds overhead seemed indecisive about

which form of precipitation to dump upon Puget Sound, but the air was fraught with the tension of a storm about to strike. Sacrificing her common sense to the lull in the weather, she began to walk home through the ice-glazed streets. Crack dealers worked out of several rentals on the blocks between Mom's house and Pilchuck's main artery.

Her feet crunched frozen concrete all the way to the main drag and then began a deeply imprinted sojourn toward the beach. When she was young, the neighborhood had been safer to traverse, but the house had been far more treacherous. Gunter Hendricks had lived there then. He was, as her mother would say, the biological father, of the boys. He'd adopted her upon marrying June. Linnea learned to call him Daddy, looking up to him like Jack looked up to the giant at the top of the beanstalk. She'd often imagined that Evergreen Way was a vine she could slide down while he rampaged through the house and yard, yelling for blood behind her.

Back then, her legs had frequently hurried her to the water, but the desire to get away had also been strong enough to propel her though a scholarship program to a full ride at the state school where she could live in student housing. She'd met Dan in her junior year while they were in barista training for Coffeestalk. She'd planned to be an English teacher, but she'd never started the credential program. Her desire to do so evaporated like the steam rising off cappuccino the first evening they closed the store downtown by themselves.

"No one pours as beautifully as you do," he had remarked, taking her in with a gaze that implied he was attracted to much more than the tilt of her wrist. "You are the epitome of grace and gorgeous to boot. Someday, you will be the Queen of Coffee."

She had laughed, savoring his compliments like crème de la crème, staying long after they'd locked the door to the outside world. He went about reconciling the till, with various beans planted under his tongue. After hours, he'd blend grinds, striving to cultivate his own eclectic coffee as an artist struggles to mix the most resplendent color. Linnea was entranced by his passion. Dan's mellow golden and rich brown brews worked on her heart like love potions. She was also intrigued by the rebellious aspect of his business plan. Like David against Goliath, yes, and like Jack against the Giant, he was determined to open a small shop of his own, despite the corporate domination of the coffee business.

They were married the summer she graduated with her B.A. in English. Taking what they learned from their corporate employer, they gambled on gentrification, leasing a small building on the bluff overlooking Spinning Wheel Bay. They opened The Mill the year road work forced all of the local college traffic past their front door.

Linnea reached the skin-scraping concrete divide that separated the road from the pulp and paper factory. Still limber at thirty-two, she shimmied over it. Out of habit, she stuck to the outside of the parking lot. She didn't want to run into any of June's co-workers, smoking outside.

A chaotically spinning snowflake nearly blinded her, bludgeoning the bridge of her nose. She marched on toward the edge of the water, toward Tower Island, accessible only by ferry. How dark the sparsely-inhabited place was on a winter's evening.

I have a life now, one that I created for myself. Why would I want to deal with a deadbeat dad now that I'm a damned good mother? Her misty breath wafted over Puget Sound. The dark salt water had not frozen, but it was surprisingly still,

7

devoid of life energy, like June's eyes had been tonight until she'd mentioned her first love. "I always knew he'd be sorry about leaving."

What if he is really sorry? What if he's been agonizing over it for years? How can I deny anyone the peace and joy of knowing his own child?

It wasn't that she'd never imagined facing him. After Megan was born, she'd even considered looking him up herself, but she'd never gone beyond casting the idle thought.

Her stomach contracted. Her daddy was back in town, but all she wanted to do was crawl between her own flannel sheets and sleep. It was nigh-impossible to run on a rocky, snow-covered beach, and it would have been easier to climb Rapunzel's tower than take the stairwell in snow boots, but Linnea did. She wanted to get home. Chelsea was there with Megan, but suddenly Linnea couldn't bear the thought of her four-year-old waking up to find her parents gone.

Chapter Two

"What's wrong?" Chelsea nearly knocked a bowl of cherry pits off her desk with her bottle of cranberry juice when Linnea burst into the office. "Is your mom sick?"

Panting from exertion, eyes watering from the warmth of the room, she shook her head, chiding herself for alarming her friend unnecessarily. Chelsea had lost her mother to breast cancer the previous year. "No, she's fine. Thanks for being here for Megan. I'm sorry I took so long. Did the bond pass?"

"By 1,967 votes. Despite the snow."

"Thank God!" Gratification was a welcome counterbalance to the fear and shame Linnea was struggling to suppress.

Chelsea clasped her hands over her head victoriously. "Hail to the power!"

Linnea copied her gesture. "Of a press that stands up for children's health, education, and responsible land use in one fell swoop."

The women grinned, coming together in a high five.

The children who lived in Spinning Wheel Bluff were bussed to a school across town. When some of them got sick from lead in the pipes and untreated asbestos in the building, their parents formed an advocacy group and contacted *The Edge*. Experts determined that it was cheaper to build a new school from scratch instead of trying to fix the problems, but there was no money to buy more land, let alone pay for construction.

Meanwhile, the owner of the Spinners, the local baseball team, died and his granddaughter put the team up for sale. Realizing that the school district still owned the land the old stadium was built on, Linnea met with the parents' group. The very day a corporation in California made an offer on the team, *The Edge* published the parents' proposal to tear down the stadium, put a bond before the voters, and build a new school as soon as the Spinners left. They printed the rallying call over and over again. Despite a few letters to the editor protesting the end of the baseball era, the campaign had obviously been a success.

Linnea glanced around the home-based office, proud of the work they did. The diaper service and organic grocer ads Chelsea had pasted into the current edition of *The Edge* were on her desk. "They look great."

A *Consume Your Colors* graph was propped against the printer. From the looks of the fruit nearby, her partner was embarking on a red week.

Chelsea twisted a strand of her shoulder-length auburn hair around her finger. Tentatively, she said, "I called Dad to talk about the retirement article."

"Your dad?" Linnea echoed hollowly, sinking into her chair. Suddenly the three letters in one little word overwhelmed her. *Dad.* Her legs seized from running in her boots. She pulled them off and rubbed her calves, annoyed to see the widening hole in her sock.

"He told me not to write it yet. He thinks he might stay

with the baseball team awhile longer. He's going to a meeting Wednesday morning to find out more."

"That's weird." She was happy to turn her mind from her own worries. "Would he go to California with the Spinners?"

Chelsea shrugged. "He might, to get some sunshine." She laid her long, elegant fingers on Linnea's arm. "You look beat. I'll take this to the printer in the morning, so you can sleep in some. I'm here for you when you're ready to talk. I'll never forget how you helped me when my mom passed away, not to mention all the mashed potatoes you made to get me through a few nasty break-ups."

Tears welled up in Linnea's eyes. How could Chelsea even begin to understand her situation when she had a gem like Larry Clark for a dad? After she lost her marketing job two and half years ago, he'd remodeled her childhood room and added a bathroom. She still lived there, keeping him company while he mourned his wife of forty years. "Don't be nice to me. It makes me cry."

"You goof," Chelsea rolled her hazelnut brown eyes. She gathered up her laptop. "Go to bed."

Linnea saw her to the front door and stood staring at the black book on the ground. Alone, she felt ice cold and fearful. Shivering, she went straight to bed, not bothering to wash her face or brush her teeth. She'd just gotten warm, burrowing beneath multiple layers of blankets, when Dan whipped them off to slide into bed beside her.

"Sleeping Beauty," he whispered as winter air washed over her, "I'm home."

She tugged the linens urgently, grasping for elusive warmth and a reason to keep from revealing her mother's news to him until she'd made up her mind how she felt about it. She found just the anomaly she needed. "You don't smell like mouthwash."

"I'm not trying to cover anything up anymore," he said, contrite.

Last fall, when the Freshbreath ran out before grocery day, he'd come to bed mid-week smelling an awful lot like her brothers' indiscriminate belches. She'd been surprised. "Have you been drinking?"

"Don't make a big deal out of it," he'd snapped. "I had to counteract all the caffeine I had today."

Now, Linnea rolled to face him, smiling encouragingly. "How was your meeting?"

"The discussion was good." He hesitated. "But my sponsor fell off the wagon today. Can you believe it? Apparently, I have no hope of recovering unless I find someone who's worked all the steps and can *stay* sober."

She propped herself on an elbow. "Is there anyone else in the group who can help?"

"I don't think so." He lay flat on his back, staring at the ceiling. The digital light of the alarm clock illuminated his disturbing expression.

She had never anticipated a kink like this in his progress. But she should have. They both had lots of relatives who drank to excess. The fact was, none of them had been able to quit. But then again, no one had really tried as hard as Dan.

"I haven't met anyone with much to offer me yet. There are some guys there who've been working the program for years, but they'd already bottomed out long before they started. They lost their families and their jobs first. I don't see how they can advise me about how to stay sober and live up to my responsibilities."

Linnea didn't respond. She succumbed to the vision of herself she'd seen in recurring dreams ever since he revealed his drinking problem. In it, she sat cross-legged on the sidewalk, leaning against the brick wall of the bus station downtown. She was dirty and disheveled, unshod. Cold air rushed through the tattered soles of her unsubstantial socks. Megan whimpered in her lap. Both of them begged disdainful passersby for spare change or scraps of food.

Dan turned toward her to see if she was listening. "You look shell-shocked. Didn't the school bond pass?"

She studied his face. Could he handle her problems even though he was stuck on Step Two?

Suddenly, a scream sprang from Megan's room with the force of a panther seizing its prey, assaulting them both.

Linnea was beside their daughter before his feet even hit the floor. "What's wrong, sweetie?" She placed her hand on Megan's forehead, scanning for evidence of pain.

The child sat upright in her bed, her small body rigid. Her green eyes were glazed over, glimmering in the nightlight. Linnea could feel the four-year-old's distress resonating in every cell of her own being. The little girl's chest heaved up and down in dread. She didn't seem to see her parents.

"What is it?" Dan asked anxiously. "Tell Daddy."

"Nightmare." Linnea pronounced. Mothers at the gym had discussed night terrors. She pulled Megan onto her lap and rocked, softening her belly so she could sink into safety. "Her body clock is off."

"What do you mean?"

"She went to bed earlier than she's used to. She was worn out from playing in the snow."

He scowled. "She looks likes she'd going to hyperventilate. What are we supposed to do? Should I get a paper bag?"

"Give her a minute." Linnea kissed the top of Megan's head, hugging her gently, gyrating in a circular motion.

"Okay. Sixty seconds. If she doesn't snap out of it by then, I'm calling 911."

Linnea sighed. He counted under his breath. At forty, Megan finally broke through her terror, sobbing, "There was a monster stomping on the roof, trying to crash through to get me."

"That was just the rain," Linnea crooned.

"There's no monster."

Megan's sobs ceased. She folded her arms across her chest to glare at them. "I want Dwarfy," she demanded. "Right now."

"Go get him, Dan."

"Who?" He furrowed his brow.

"Her garden dwarf. He's in the dining room. We bought him at Mulberries today when I went to solicit their ad for bare root roses. She fell in love with him at first sight."

Dan carried the gnome back upstairs much like he'd taken dirty diapers to the hamper before potty-training succeeded. The little girl flung her arm over Dwarfy's solid torso, resting her nose against his pointy red hat. She closed her once-wild eyes contentedly.

"Why was he in *my* chair?" Dan whispered. "He's ugly."

Linnea scowled at him, but Megan didn't hear the disparaging comment. The little girl had fallen into a natural sleep almost as soon as she inhaled the scent of Mulberries' rose potpourri clinging to him.

Linnea's own heart was still pounding from distress, but she smiled fondly at the peaceful child. "She's been lugging him around all day, all fifteen pounds of polyresin. At least he'll be easy to keep clean."

"He needs a shave. We've got to do something about her taste, Linnea."

"Well, I was going to read *Snow White and the Seven Dwarves* tonight and introduce her to the idea of a handsome prince. But I had to go to my mother's." *To find out about my father.* "And it wasn't really an emergency."

"So she exaggerated." He shrugged, trundling off to bed. From the window, Linnea saw the light in the apartment over the garage come on. Her cousin, Clary Sage, had just moved in. Her baby, Serengeti, was crying and Clary Sage was caring for her alone. *No way. I'm not gonna do it.* Linnea climbed back into bed and pushed her cold feet against the heat radiating from Dan's bare legs. *I do not want to have a relationship with Rick Andersen. A man who wasn't there, like Dan is here.*

Commuters need java at ungodly hours, so Dan always left early in the mornings. But when Linnea woke shortly after dawn, she wasn't alone. Rolling over, her elbow hit something hard. With his obsidian black eyes wide open, Dwarfy smiled warmly at her. Behind him, Megan dozed. Her little body nestled in the depression Dan's manly one had left behind. Her pink cheek lay on his pillow.

Extracting herself from the linen cautiously, Linnea tiptoed downstairs. She made a pot of Miller's Blend, retrieved *Grimm's Fairy Tales* from the floor, and carried both her cup and the book back up to the bedroom.

Sipping in bed, she basked in the luxury of having the best coffee on the West Coast at her fingertips. She was lucky to be married to a man as accomplished as Dan. How could she let his alcoholism or withdrawal-driven crankiness overshadow his positive attributes? Maybe she should bake him a batch of his favorite chocolate chip cookies. No. He had all the baked goods a guy could wish for at The Mill. She could give him a foot rub or a massage when he got home.

Comforting touch, but that's what *she* wanted. She wanted to make love, too. She wanted both in equal measure, but these days, he wouldn't stay in one place long enough for either. If he did, he was sound asleep within seconds.

Megan opened her eyes, smiling blissfully at her new love. Linnea read the story to both of them. Despite Dan's appraisal, she didn't think Dwarfy was ugly at all.

"My dwarf is different from Snow White's." Megan declared.

"How?"

"He's the one that *I* need."

Linnea chuckled warmly, kissed her daughter on the nose, and hustled to get them breakfast. Afterwards, she checked for an email from *The Edge's* printer. A new message appeared on her screen.

Linnea,

Your mother gave me your email address. I thought it would be less intrusive to contact you this way. I don't want to interfere with your life, but I want the opportunity to get to know you...on your terms. Are you willing to meet me?

Sincerely,
Rick Andersen

There it was. Andersen. The name with which she'd been born and baptized. But when June had married Gunter Hendricks a few short weeks after meeting him, the surname and the father who had given it to her was erased from Linnea's four-year-old records and daily vocabulary. Later, she'd never known what to do about the family trees teachers so enthusiastically assigned in school. She had desperately wanted to be a good child, an honest one. Writing Gunter Hendricks on the father's branch had always made her feel like a liar, but that's what the adults wanted her to do. The name Andersen had always unnerved her, casting her adrift in feelings for which she had few words. It felt like a mortal sin of the Dark Ages just to look at it, let alone to say or write it. But sinners finagle indulgences, don't they? They learn to mutate transgressions.

There was one Andersen to whom she had clung unabashedly: Hans Christian. She'd loved his fairy tales so much that she often wondered if he were a blood relative and she a descendent with a receptive gene. She felt that he had created stories just for her. Hang in there, Ugly Duckling. One day, my dear, you will be a swan.

She needed to seek out and hold onto Hans now. She had a volume containing his tales in her closet, probably in the same box as she'd found the Grimms' collection last night. She was willing to unpack the books for Megan's benefit, but not to unearth the heartbreak associated with them.

Rick Andersen is just a name. The I.D. tag on the courier who carried my second X chromosome. An anonymous sperm donor. He's nothing to me.

She stifled her fear and anger. Such emotions weren't necessary. She wasn't about to let a perfect stranger interrupt her happily-ever-after, now that she almost had it. She was just waiting on AA to work. Besides, she decided, rereading the screen, this was not a message from a man who was suffering. He didn't need her to alleviate the agony of his soul, if he even had one. It was formal and polite. She carefully positioned her fingers on the keyboard. Thank God, he hadn't called her on the telephone. She wasn't sure why, but she was terrified to hear his voice. She typed:

No.
Thank you.

hit the send button, and closed her email. She sat back in her chair, satisfied. Crisis resolved.

Clary Sage entered the office, balancing baby Serengeti on her hip. Linnea beamed at the bright-eyed baby, dressed in a pink crocheted sweater that Megan had worn.

"We're taking the bus over to see Hommy." Clary Sage's short blonde hair shimmered beneath the full spectrum lighting. "I'm so grateful you're letting us live here, but I've decided to marry him. I would like to wake up in his arms every morning."

Clary Sage had moved in on Friday. In three days, the marriage had been a no-go twice. Linnea wasn't sure how to respond. "Be careful. The snow is gone, but sidewalks are slippery."

"He's a fine man. He's getting an engineering degree. He's got a job parking cars at Claudio's, and he's terribly worried about his family and friends back home. He was never in the Taliban, you know. He's handsome. I mean, are you prejudiced against him or something?"

Linnea was stunned. Why was Clary Sage so passionately defending him against her? Then again, people often perceived her as privileged. In fact, so many people she met assumed that she'd attended Ivy League college, vacationed abroad, and knew the difference between foreign cheeses that she often let herself forget she'd been raised by low-level pulp and paper mill managers. "If I have anything against him, it's because he's so much older than you are, Clary Sage. I think he took advantage of your kindness and your innocence."

"No, he didn't. He loves me for those things."

"Forget how good-looking you think he is. Do you really and truly love him?"

She blanched. "I think so...I don't know. I just don't want to be swayed by the news or other people's prejudice." She stared at her almost petulantly, like a child wanting a withheld teddy bear.

Linnea drew a deep breath. "Okay, I'll give it to you straight up. I'm afraid he'll stifle you. He's already talked you out of enrolling for classes this quarter even though you qualified for the grant and free, high-quality childcare."

"That's just because he's devoted to Islam."

"Clary Sage, the prophet Muhammad actually encouraged women to get an education. His first wife owned her own business and his second one was an authority on history, medicine, and poetry."

Linnea had written a full page article about women's roles in Islam when *The Edge* covered the opening of Pilchuck's first mosque. *God, it feels good to be so clear-headed this morning, after last night's confusion.*

"He said I should be focusing on the baby."

Linnea leaned forward. "What do you think?"

Clary Sage looked at Serengeti sadly. "I think I could take good care of her and take a class or two. I want to do what's best. I just don't know what that is."

Linnea was glad she and Dan had room for Clary Sage

and Serengeti in their home, even if it was another financial pressure they didn't need. And she could postpone her plans to move *The Edge*'s office into the apartment over the garage indefinitely. "No one is rushing you to make up your mind. Weigh your options and be very careful out there."

* * *

Megan tottered downstairs, laboriously balancing Dwarfy's mossy green base and black boots on the tops of her untied pink sneakers. "Dwarfy wants to fingerpaint with me today, Mommy."

Mary had a little lamb. If Dwarfy followed Megan to school, there would undoubtedly be chaos in the cubby hall. And there were social conventions that being forced to observe in this case would be downright cruel to her enchanted child.

"Oh, sweetie," She smiled sympathetically, cupping her daughter's cheek with her palm. "You two would have fun together in the splish-splash room, but I don't think you should take him with you."

Megan's face fell. Before tears followed, she added gently, "Dwarfy can go with us when we go to the library, but he's too special to take to school. You know the school rule about sharing."

The little girl's eyes grew wide. "Dwarfy's mine! Just mine." Megan flung her arms around his shoulders and squeezed him tightly as she whispered in his molded ear. "You stay here while I go to work. You can play *Fairy Tale Lotto* on the computer until I get back." She sat him down in front of the monitor in the living room.

Linnea took her to preschool. At the gym, she increased the resistance on the elliptical and pushed herself hard. At home, she'd just pulled a load of Dan's boxer shorts and undershirts from the dryer when June called.

"Are you going to see him?" she asked immediately.

There was no need to explain who *him* was. "No."

"Why not?"

"I can probably count on one hand the number of times you've mentioned him to me since he left. Every time you do, you lower your voice as if you're talking about the devil. I just don't have a good feeling about it."

"Oh, Linnea," June chided. "A woman always lowers her voice when revealing her husband's extramarital affairs or telling a child that her daddy wanted her to be aborted."

Linnea felt confused. "But why do you want me to see him now? Are you sure he's not evil anymore?"

She laughed. "Linnea, don't be so paranoid. He was never evil. Mixed-up, maybe. He sure sounds good on the phone now. I always knew he'd turn out, that he'd grow up. I told him the day he left that he'd be sorry about leaving you. But if you aren't ready to see him, honey, I understand."

Paranoid? Ready? "Mom," she said trying not to sound upset, "I've got a million things to do before I go get Megan."

She hung up, started a new load of laundry, unloaded the dishwasher, finished folding Dan's underwear, and forced herself to think about the casserole she was going to make for dinner. While she worked on the article about the library fundraiser, a second email popped up on her screen.

Linnea,

Please reconsider. Your mother told me about little

Megan. I'm sure there are some issues that might still affect you and your family because of what I did so long ago. I want to give you a chance to deal with them. I have been sober for ten years. I've taken all the steps to be healthy but this one. I am sorry for what happened to you and I want to make amends for everything. I'll pay for any counseling you need. Please do this for your little girl and Dan.

Hopefully yours,
Rick

She stared at the reasonable words on the screen, anxiety inflaming her sinuses. She printed the message. Struggling with her coat, she hurried for the beach, nearly overcome with obliterating adrenaline.

As fog dripped from the cliff edge above her, she sat on the rise belonging to the *Aurora*, Captain Pillar's nineteenth-century steamship, and inhaled the essential oil of wet wood. The bridge deck had lodged there since the 1902 accident when the craft had run aground on the rocks. When Linnea was younger and oblivious to the dangers of transients, rot, and decay, she had often found solace on the splintered floor of the *Aurora*.

Hot tears streamed down her pale cheeks. As she reread the message, chronically fatigued, but proverbial hope recharged within her, rising from her heart like the air bubbles stemming from the nutrient-rich creatures concealed deep within the sand. *I don't need counseling. But he knows he was wrong and he wants to make up for it. He wants to do something for my family, for me. Maybe he really has changed.*

All she'd ever really known about Rick Andersen was one day he was there and the next, he wasn't. Granted,

June's guarded explanation for his departure had once included a short story about attending a party with him where he drank too much. Yet Linnea had never pictured him as an alcoholic – let alone as someone who worked through a Twelve Step program and recovered.

Maybe he could inspire Dan to stay sober. Maybe the Universe was sending him to help, to reward her for always being so good no matter what her cruel stepfather said or did, no matter what her mother asked of her. Maybe her father was the living proof that love is the higher power that heals addiction. Linnea rocked back and forth along with the soothing rhythm of the tide, waves of gratitude swelling within her body. Maybe his return would erase any chance that Dan would do to Megan what Rick had done to her.

A seagull with cock-eyed silver markings landed beside her. When she smiled happily, it minced toward her as if lured by the silver flash of a clam's tender belly. With its saffron bill, the bird greedily snatched her water bottle. Lifting it off the ground, he fluttered toward the bay, but soon let the disappointing catch drop into the surf.

She watched the transparent bottle bob upon the gray water. She remembered combing the beach as a little girl and finding a wine bottle with a twist-on lid. She'd had a paper napkin in her pocket. With a magenta crayon and crooked letters, she'd written, *Daddy, please come back for me.*

She'd stuffed the scrap into the bottle, tightened the top with all her might, prayed it would bypass Tower Island on its way out to sea, and tossed it into the water.

She must have watched too many re-runs of *Gilligan's Island,* because she was far too confident that she would get a response. She never did. It took a year before she gave up hoping that he stood waiting behind every knock on the door. It took another for her to stop watching for bottles containing his reply. Eventually, not only had she given up on him coming back, she'd forgotten that she'd ever wanted him until now.

As the seagull landed beside her once more, she saw her little girl self on her knees in her bedroom late at night, begging a grandfatherly God to bring Daddy back to her. The seagull sifted through the gravel. Surely, any scavenger willing to dig deep would be fed. Surely any daughter ready to resurrect a love long thought dead and thus deeply buried would eventually be found. Trudging home from the shore, Linnea felt like a piece of driftwood, battered by the sea.

Chapter Three

When she reached the front porch, she found a package addressed to her. She opened it, reading the handwritten note taped to protective tissue paper inside.

Please don't have cold feet.
Rick

Beneath the wrapping, she found an assortment of bobby, knee, and slipper socks in an array of baby soft pastels, classic tweeds, and bright colors. Rubbing burnt orange chenille to her cheek, she stroked purple cashmere. *I've never had anything made of cashmere. He must have good taste.*

She burrowed through the bounty to see what else he'd sent. A rainbow-striped pair of knee-his with spaces for each individual toe reminded her of lollipops and carousels. *And a sense of humor, too.* All told, there was at least a month's worth of socks in the surprise package.

Had June told him about her holey sock? It felt wonderful to imagine her parents discussing her needs, planning something that would make her happy. She and

Dan did that all the time for Megan, but no one had ever done it for her, as far as she could tell. She hugged herself, giddily, suddenly strung out on socks.

She returned to her keyboard and typed,

O.K. I'd like to meet at my house. How about tomorrow morning at 9:30?

Megan will be at preschool then. I'll just have to make sure Clary Sage isn't home.

Rick Andersen must have been waiting beside his laptop at the hotel because she got an immediate response.

The Universe is good! 9:30 is perfect. I won't impose long.

Rick

"The Universe is good!" she gasped. "He thinks like me!" Email was so much faster than a message in a bottle. She slipped on a new pair of socks and went to pick up her own little girl.

* * *

"It was the strangest thing," she told Dan over the bits of bagel and stray poppy seeds left on their plates from lunch, "to do something normal, to discuss the auction with the other mothers while waiting in the playground, or to talk with Miss Cindy about sending crackers for snack next week. By the time the auction rolls around or I bring the saltines, I'll have met him. I mean, I feel like I did when I was pregnant. I'd look at the expiration dates on the orange juice and think, by the time this expires, I'll have the baby." Dan stared at her as if she were sprouting

26

a moustache.

She waited for him to say something, but he just shoved another potato chip into his mouth. Maybe he was in shock.

More buoyant by the moment, she rose to clear the dishes, glancing at Megan playing a computer game in the living room with her dwarf in the chair beside her. "I mean, this feels like the day we got married. I couldn't believe other people were going grocery shopping or washing the car. I thought everyone in the whole world should stop and eat cake with us." She beamed at him. "What do you think about all this?"

"I think I should have gotten you some socks for Christmas," he said cautiously.

"Why?" She admired the cashmere on her feet. "I've got plenty of socks now."

"I'm sorry, but this is kind of weird. Out of order. People aren't supposed to get married and have kids before they meet their parents. Are you sure you want to do this?"

She felt like the summer sun, although it was the darkest time of year. The most delightful warmth and affection radiated from deep within her. She dumped the crumbs off Megan's reindeer placemat into the trash. "Yes."

He stepped behind Linnea at the sink, wrapping his arms around her waist, resting his chin upon her shoulder. "You sure are in a good mood."

Happiness made her light-headed. She pressed her hips backwards, deliberately tucking her tailbone between his solid thighs. They hadn't made love once in the past three months, sacrificing their last bit of free time to AA.

"I was going to haul the Christmas ornaments back up

to the attic before I head to The Mill this afternoon," he said in a low voice, bending his knees to tilt his pelvis up into the rise of her jeans. "but do you know what I want to do right now?"

Seductively, she pressed down into his warmth. "Yeah. Why?"

"For one thing, you're glowing." The rigid tip of his tongue probed her collarbone. "And you taste like…honey."

"Honeysuckle." June had given her lotion for Christmas.

He buried his face in her neck. "And I want to…"

"Daddy!" Megan called imperiously at their feet. "The computer's locked up."

Dan sighed. "Tonight," he whispered in Linnea's ear, "I'll skip my meeting."

She wondered if missing a meeting would set him back, but a little love would be good for both of them. She answered by slowly circling her hips against his. Dan groaned and tore himself away.

Just as Linnea finished sweeping, Clary Sage struggled over the threshold of the kitchen door. She carried both Serengeti and her unzipped diaper bag. A long cardboard box, bulging between the handles, caught on the oak frame. "Hommy gave me a gift."

"Too bad it doesn't fold up into your wallet." Linnea stopped short. She had sensed how uneasy Clary Sage felt using their laundry detergent over the weekend even though she and Dan had assured her that they didn't mind sharing. She reached for the baby so her cousin could get inside. "You seem ambivalent about it, at best. What did he give you?"

Clary Sage set her bag on the counter and opened the

package. "It's a burka." She pulled a long black swathe of fabric out of the box. "Hommy wants to take us home to visit his family. He said I should starting wearing this. You know, to get used to it before we go."

"Clary Sage! You can't go to Afghanistan right now. Are you crazy? There's a war on."

"But he said there is no fighting in his village, and we won't stay long. He promised we could swing by Tunisia on the way back to the States and go to the Serengeti Nature Reserve for our honeymoon. Wouldn't that be cool? I've wanted to go there ever since I was Megan's age. I can't wait to see the zebras, the gazelles, and the giraffes in the wild."

"And all the lions and the vultures," Linnea added, tightening her grip on the baby.

Clary Sage slipped the veil over her head just as Chelsea walked in the kitchen door. "Oh, my God! Is *that* your bridal veil?"

Linnea felt a scream building inside the baby clinging to her. "No," she answered for Clary Sage in the most soothing voice she could muster. "She's just trying on a burka." But it was too late. As the black form reached out for her, Serengeti burst into terrified wails.

Linnea held her so close that she could feel the infant's heart racing. "Take it off!" she urged.

Clary Sage pulled the fabric away from her face. The baby stopped crying, but continued to shudder. A palpable sense of relief filled the room once the head covering was back in its box and the lid replaced. Linnea handed Serengeti to Clary Sage. She held her close.

Chelsea looked concerned. "Did he say you have to wear that?"

"The people in his village believe women should draw

their veils over their tits and not display their beauty."

"That's not the most accurate translation from the Quran there is." Linnea glanced at Chelsea. How could they discourage this diplomatically?

"Well, it does take the pressure off me to lose the baby fat," Clary Sage quipped, heading toward the stairs to her apartment. "Besides, veiling started out as an upper class fashion. I think Hommy's family is actually quite well off."

Chelsea waited until she was out of the room. "God, is he a fundamentalist?"

"I don't know. I should have him over for dinner soon, but entertaining Hommy seems awfully daunting."

"And how much weight does she have left to lose anyway? Six pounds?"

Linnea shook her head.

Chelsea shrugged. "The good news is everything went well at the printers. I've got my dad's van out front." Larry never drove the van himself, but paid the registration and insurance so they could use it to pick up and deliver their papers.

"Your dad's great." *And soon, I'll meet my father. He has to be pretty special, too. He's willing to pay for therapy and, for all he knows, I could need it for the rest of my life.*

"Where'd you get those purple socks?"

* * *

Later, on her first All Father's Eve, Linnea tried to write an article. She'd scribbled some notes about how important it was for a married couple to share the same values. She'd even gotten as far as the title, "Multicultural Marriage," and then stopped, stymied because she wanted to argue against Clary Sage marrying Hommy for a variety of reasons, but she was afraid her piece would sound racist.

She glanced up. Dan sat on the sofa with Megan in his lap, watching a Fairy Tale Tikes movie. Crossing her heart, Megan held his big arms around her waist by cupping his elbows in her upturned palms. Whenever she giggled at the screen, he absent-mindedly kissed the back of her head. His eyes were glazed over, so Linnea knew his mind was a thousand miles away from the storyline, but his body was right there with her.

She was glad her daughter had an affectionate father. Aside from the fumbling advances of greenhorn teenage boyfriends, Dan was the only man she could ever remember touching her lovingly. Linnea glanced at Clary Sage sitting in the rocking chair, bottle-feeding Serengeti as absorbed in *Sleeping Beauty* as Megan was. Linnea cringed at the thought of her young cousin in Hommy's arms. *She's too young to be a mother. She's not ready to make a lifetime commitment to the hijab.*

At the baby shower Aunt Jean had thrown just before moving to California, leaving her daughter and granddaughter with nowhere to stay, someone had asked Clary Sage how on earth she'd ever met Hommy. She'd found him, she explained, sitting all alone in a back corner of the pizza parlor where she once worked. He looked sexy in his grungy safari jacket. She watched his expression grow more and more melancholy as other diners cast dirty or distrustful looks his way. She felt sorry for him.

Sympathy tears another sister asunder. Despairing of ever being objective on this matter, Linnea deleted the scant beginning of her article and left her office to wander upstairs, wondering what to wear when she met Rick.

Which colors did he like? What looked best on her in the dead of winter? She had a rose turtleneck that looked fresh, but any shade of pink would make her feel too vulnerable for this. Blue or green set off her eyes and would compliment the red highlights in her wavy golden hair.

She tried a sapphire cardigan on, scanning the mirror critically. *I'm so pale in January*. For the first time, she realized how odd it was that Snow White's mother would have wished for a daughter as white as snow.

After refolding her options and settling on her usual blue jeans and a black sweater, she dug through the box from which she'd taken *Grimm's Fairy Tales* the previous evening. Among scraps of poetry she'd collected since her early teens, she found a book with white leather binding. At first glance, it could have been taken for the sort of Bible one gives to girls making First Communion or Confirmation, but it wasn't: It was her old Hans Christian Andersen book. The cover was yellowing, but she thought she could freshen it up with shoe polish.

She held the book between her palms, feeling its heft, remembering its magic. Within moments, memories of her fourth birthday party burst forth from the crevices of her cranium like candy from a splitting piñata.

It had been her special day. Eager to get on with it, she'd stood impatiently while June tied the blue sash around the waist of her white dress.

Linnea could still feel the cruel plastic barrette tugging at her unruly hair. The elastic of her lacy tights conspired with glossy, over-buckled sandals to constrain her while the sweet anticipation of her daddy's arrival hung in the frenzied air, as tangible to her as the tantalizing promise of pink-frosted cupcakes.

Her party came and went, replete with Pin-the-Tail-on-the-Donkey and a hot potato to pass in aluminum foil. When it came time to make her secret wish, Linnea scrunched her eyes shut, whispered her plea, and blew out the candles. But he'd never come. Cake magic didn't really work.

After the party was over, and the guests were all gone, there was a timid knock on the door to the apartment. An extra sense told Linnea it wasn't him, even before June opened the door. She was delighted though to see his beautiful teenage sister standing on the welcome mat with a present for her. The book she now held in her hands was the one tangible thing, the one belonging that she had that she could associate with her biological father and it hadn't even come from him. He'd known nothing of it, but a gift from his kid sister had been close enough to his spirit for her to treasure.

Now, clutching it close to her gut, Linnea crawled into bed, still wearing her jogging suit, and pulled the thick down comforter over her head. *What if he doesn't come? What if he does? What if I like him and he disappears again?*

She lay there with the heavy book pressing into her solar plexus and stomach, ignoring the crushing sensation. Suddenly, she sprang up, running to the bathroom, retching great gasps of hot air. It felt very familiar. When she was four, she'd vomited her cupcakes shortly after her party.

"Linnea?" Dan sang in baritone, entering the bedroom, hoping she'd disappeared to slip into the red teddy he'd given her last year for the holidays, when he was still interested. He peeked in the open door. "Are you all right?" he asked, frowning at the sight of her.

She nodded, still bending over the toilet, still struggling to extract herself from the whirling scene in her memory. June had been crying while she had been throwing up in her bed. There was something about neither of them owning a spare sheet. And without the check Rick was supposed to bring, there hadn't been enough cash to take the soiled linens to the laundromat. There'd been birthday expenses, and then Linnea saw her wet rag doll sheet hanging crinkled in the foreground of a cracked tile shower.

She blinked several times, struggling to bring herself back to the present. She'd never accessed a memory from before Gunter entered her life. Going back so far was disorientating. She drew a deep, shuddering breath. "What's Megan doing?"

"Sleeping with that ugly little man."

Linnea smiled half-heartedly. "I'm not going to throw up."

"Is this about your dad?"

She swallowed hard, nodding.

"You don't owe him anything. You don't have to go through with it." Dan spread his arms out like a magician's assistant. The "Ta-da!" was implicit. "You've got me."

She hurled herself into his open chest. "You won't leave me?"

"Not in a million years."

He braced the base of her neck with his fingertips, covering her mouth with his own. She softened her lips. His tongue met hers. She tucked her cashmere-covered toes between his feet, leaning into his groin. He pulled back, scanned her face, checking. His eyes twitched with desire.

"I felt like a child a minute ago," she whispered, still pressing into him.

He reached for the zipper on her athletic jacket. "You feel like a woman to me." He lowered his hand to her waist. His fingers swept up over the skin, beneath her lacy camisole. His breath grew ragged.

She sighed deeply, burying her face in his hair, inhaling French Roast. Her thighs melted, succumbing to the heat of his lower body. He seized the waistband of her panties, pulling her to their mattress.

After making love like the famished, he stayed close for a change, stroking the curve of her buttocks while she burrowed her face in his neck. His fingers wandered down to the sweet spot on her inner thigh. She hummed huskily. She mouthed his earlobe, trying for more, whispering, "This is exactly what I wished for this morning."

The phone rang, startling them. "Let them leave a message," he said. "I forgot how good this feels."

Linnea groaned. "I don't want Megan to wake up." Twisting away from his touch, she snatched up the receiver before the second ring and held it to her ear.

"Why didn't you tell me you decided to see him?" June asked instantly.

For a split second, guilt and panic exploded in her belly. She felt the urge to bolt. "How do you know?"

"He just had a check delivered to me. Get this, twenty-five thousand dollars!"

Linnea sat up suddenly. "For what?"

"Back child support. I guess he doesn't want to meet you as a dead-beat dad."

Sex had lightened the heaviness in her heart, but this announcement lifted it right out of her. "That's great. You should put the money in a CD, for your retirement."

"Oh, don't you worry about me, honey. I'll put it all to good use. I just have a few debts to pay off first."

Foreboding filled Linnea, but she said good-bye gracefully and hung up.

After hearing the news, Dan said, "I thought child support was supposed to go to the kid."

Linnea jerked the comforter over her naked body. "I don't mind that he gave my child support to her. God knows she needs it." She felt a sharp pain in her pelvis. An unformed question about her own restitution welled from deep within her. She tightened away from it as quickly as she'd pulled away from Dan to answer her mother's call. "It's her money to do with as she pleases. I'm glad he paid her. He must be really responsible now."

"Or extremely rich."

Linnea imagined all the sacrifices Rick must have made over the years to accumulate so much cash. She saw the generic over-the-counter medications, the knock-off clothing, and the dutiful deposits at the bank. "At some point, he realized that I was more important than other things."

Dan frowned. "Even if he did, didn't you print an article a while back saying a college-educated woman sacrifices at least ten times that amount to be a stay-at-home mother until her kid starts school?"

Why is he trying to ruin this? "Yeah, but that's in today's money. There's been a lot of inflation since we were babies. And besides, he did give me up to Gunter, so technically, he wasn't even liable for my support."

"Don't make excuses for him until you meet him." He laid his hand upon hers as if to keep her from springing away. He gazed wistfully at the bedspread clasped over her bare breasts, but she turned out the light and lay down with her back to him.

She knew that her mother would use what should have been spent raising her to pay off the bondsman for one of her brothers' DUI's. *But I don't care about any of that. If he paid that much for the admission ticket, he'll show.*

Chapter Four

Linnea stood in the corner of her office, hidden from view to anyone arriving outside the bay window. She imagined Rick judging her by sizing up her re-sided home with its original tongue-and- groove porch and welcoming wreath on the front door. They had finished painting the cedar planks antique green last spring, adding a cream and dark red trim during the summer. She was certain the white picket fence, their fair-sized city lawn, and the swing set would testify to her life's success.

Her body was conditioned to be on the elliptical machine at the gym this time of day. Even so, she was still surprised at how desperately her legs clamored to run. Her stomach inched up, huddling against her heart, as if her vital organs didn't quite trust her ribs to support them during the encounter.

Linnea didn't want anyone but Dan and June to know about this meeting, in case it didn't work out. She remembered a girl from high school who played the psychiatrist's nurse in the drama department's production of *Harvey*. When her role was announced, Kelli dragged Linnea to the phone booth at the fish and chip bar across the street from Pilchuck High. From there, she called her long-gone dad, begging him to attend a performance. He wasn't interested and told her so. The star of the spring play slid down the greasy plexiglass wall dividing them from finger-licking gawkers. Huddled beneath a dripping awning, she cried.

Half under the shelter, with rain sliding down the gap between her tailbone and the waistband of her jeans, Linnea had knelt beside Kelli, awkwardly trying to comfort her. All the while, she'd felt relieved, even a little bit smug, that she'd long since gotten over Rick's lack of parental investment.

College-bound Kelli had been fighting morning sickness by the time the cast bowed for their last standing ovation. She nearly vomited on the fluffy white slippers of Linnea's costume.

The low hum of a car's engine reverberated around the street corner, rumbled along the Perraults' front walk, and ceased. A parking brake creaked. The air was still and silent. She imagined the driver checking the house number against a note in his hand.

A car door opened and shut. She took a deep breath, listening to the spry click of well-heeled shoes on the front steps, waiting for the knock she'd longed to hear years earlier. When it came, it was strong, steady. He wanted to be with her.

Childlike joy and excitement welled right up through her core, overflowing into every part of her being. Linnea opened the door, greeting her father with a warm smile.

In the split second that followed, she was swept away by a surge of tiny details. Rick's lips were thin, unlike hers, which were almost too full for her narrow face, but his upper one matched hers, dipping and curving like the top of a Valentine heart. His head was oval like hers, but the set of his jaw squared it off. His eyebrows were bushy. Hers were delicate, but both pairs arched up at the outer edges. She was startled by the bronze tint of his tan, but she was completely taken aback by the pores on his face and the prickly hair follicles on his chin.

He's real. She had spent most of her life scanning large crowds for Rick. Now, she realized she wouldn't have been able to point him out in one. Her mental image of him had been far more ghostly than she'd suspected.

Like mirrors, hungry to recognize self on the outside, Rick's intense blue eyes seized hers. "I would have known you anywhere," he said, striding forward, embracing her tightly.

His long-suppressed desire to hold her snaked its way through the sinewy tissues of his arms. Her body softened into him, but as he reclaimed her, his squeeze became increasingly constricting. She stiffened, suddenly worried that this stranger might actually be a serial killer who posed as the long-lost fathers of girls and strangled them on their doorsteps.

Trapped in his arms, she stood stock-still, breathing shallowly while the unfamiliar man clung to her, trembling. He was nearly as tall as Dan. Almost as fit, too, but he couldn't compete with a guy who arm-curled 150 pounds of raw coffee beans on a bi-hourly basis.

Rick finally released her, but before she could catch her breath, he changed his mind. Once again, he pinned her arms against her sides. His body heat penetrated her clothing. Linnea's muscles recoiled as he cleaved to her.

Relax. He can't be suffocating you. You can still smell him. The scent of aftershave, nervous perspiration, and his black leather coat, hung about them. Dan always smelled good, too, exotic and earthy like the Brazilian soil from which his coffee came. Except when he over-roasted the beans and the smell of burnt hulls clung to his hair.

"Yes!" Rick stepped back for another view. "You are definitely my daughter. I recognize the little girl you used to be."

Still tingling from the pressure of his hug, and reeling from the shock of being held in his actual three-dimensional arms, Linnea felt fragile and tearful. Just as Cinderella must have been unnerved by the sudden appearance of her fairy godmother and the transformation of animals and vegetables into ball-going accoutrements, Linnea's nervous system was overwrought. At least there had been a tangible pumpkin sitting on the ground before Cinderella got inside the coach.

"Do you recognize me?" he asked.

She cocked her head. "I have only one memory of you."

"What is it?" He kept grinning broadly, repeatedly taking her in from head to toe.

"I remember you and Gunter outside the condominium shaking your fists at each other." Towering over her Daddy, the soon-to-be Stepfather had leaned forward. Animosity rose up through his neck, toxic as the mercury of a thermometer, flooding his face with crimson dye and erupting in words too terrible to recall.

Back then, Linnea had sent Rick heart waves of love, white light that could give the quavering man a luminous skeleton, but he must have blocked it. He allowed Gunter's threatening fist and the poison spewing from his tongue to bleach him into opalescence. Linnea watched her daddy turn, without a farewell wave or a backward glance for her, and flee, evaporating into the oblivion beyond the parking lot.

She'd known then that something was terribly wrong. How could a big daddy be afraid of the man his little girl lived with?

"I wish that wasn't it," Rick said. "I was supposed to take you out that day, but I'd been drinking and didn't show up until hours past the court-appointed time. Your mother wouldn't let you go with me that late. Good move on her part, but I hung around arguing until Gunter drove me off. Now, I'm sorry I put him in that position, but I used to hate that man."

There would time to talk about him later. "Come in." Linnea stepped aside with a sweeping gesture. "Welcome to the life I can barely keep up with."

He took in the downstairs, the fresh flowers, the casual furniture, the new floor, and the old millwork. He admired her college diploma with honors on the wall of her office, but all the time, he kept an eye on her. They sat side by side in the kitchen over coffee, muffins, and photo albums.

Rick finished admiring the fourth album of Megan. "The pictures of you begin when you got married. Don't you have any from when you were growing up?"

"No."

Rick arched his brows questioningly.

"Mom never took many. She was always so busy with all the babies."

"But that's not fair."

"And," she interrupted, instinctively refusing to let him judge June, "my childhood isn't really something I want to remember."

His jaw tightened. "Why not?"

Linnea looked down at her hands, twisting involuntarily in her lap.

"Tell me," he whispered.

Her tongue seemed too heavy, her tonsils swollen. "Gunter hated me."

Rick sighed, as if he'd received confirmation of something he'd been hoping to avoid. "Was he abusive?"

Spine-wrenching, tailbone shame coursed up to her neck. It always did when she let herself remember. "It was tough, but he's gone now. He left my mom with all those adolescent boys right after I moved into the dorm."

"I guess I don't have to make amends to him, then. I've thought about it."

Linnea's stomach doused the inside of her torso with acid. Struggling not to double over, she said soothingly, "You don't have to. I kept tabs myself. All the cooking, cleaning, yard work, and free babysitting I did more than compensated him for my keep. As soon as I was old enough, I worked to buy all my own things."

Rick was silent. She could not fathom what he felt.

"Linnea," he finally said, laying his hand upon hers, "I don't know everything you've gone through in your life because of me, but I'm sorry for whatever it was. I want you to believe I thought I was doing the best thing for you when I left. All I heard was that you had little brothers and lots of pets. I thought you were happy, and I was glad you had a real family. It just wouldn't have worked if I'd stayed. Gunter and I despised each other. Neither of us was mature enough to cooperate on a custody agreement."

Linnea had always assumed the one time she remembered seeing the daddies together had been the only time they'd met. The skin does not think in sentences, but her questions sprouted subcutaneously. How could he have abandoned her to a man he loathed? Didn't he realize that if her stepfather was too immature to work out a custody plan, he would be incapable of being kind to her?

She stiffened her entire body against her wondering. Her father was contrite and he was fifty-seven now. There was no need to make him feel worse by asking about the workings of his twenty-something mind. "When I was growing up, I had a friend who had to travel back and forth between her parents' houses. She kept forgetting stuff she needed, like her gym shoes or her library books. She always wanted one home." Linnea stopped herself. It probably wasn't healthy to reassure him that much. She bit her lower lip.

Biting his bottom lip, too, Rick carried his cup to the microwave. He reheated his tepid coffee for thirty seconds and rejoined her at the table. "Do you know much about alcoholism?"

She shrugged. "My brothers have drinking problems, as Mom would say. Her brothers are the alcoholics." Linnea looked down at the napkin she had twisted in her lap. The words seared her already raw throat, "Dan, too."

Rick glanced around the kitchen and adjoining rooms as if he'd see signs of domestic violence on the walls. "How bad is he?"

"Not. I didn't even realize it until about three months ago."

Enchiladas with rice and beans had been a staple in her house for years, but she hadn't been able to stomach them during the last ninety days. She'd just dished up the plates, when the printer called with a question about the next day's edition. She asked Dan to turn the stove down and took the call. When the leftover rice began to smoke because he'd ignored her, she dashed over and removed the pot.

"Are you trying to burn the house down?" she asked.

"What kind of question is that?" he snapped. "I work my ass off so we can afford this damn place."

Linnea was taken aback. "Calm down." He never used such coarse language at home before. She glanced at Megan. "I was only joking."

"Well, I don't appreciate that kind of humor." He sulked through the rest of their meal.

As soon as Megan finished eating, Linnea put a DVD in for her to watch. "Dan," she said, rejoining him at the table. "You've been really uptight lately. I know work is stressful, but it's not fair that you get to be furious while I have to stay calm so Megan won't be afraid."

"It *is* fair, Linnea. You are naturally a calm person. I was the one born with a short fuse. I inherited my temper from my family."

That was one of the sorriest excuses, she could imagine anyone making. "Your family is a bunch of drunks," she snapped, stomping to the sink. After she filled the dishpan with hot water, she looked up to glare at him. He was sobbing over his salad.

"I am an alcoholic. I'm out of control, and I don't know where to turn."

That had been one of the worst moments of her life. She hadn't given herself time to think about why.

With tears in her eyes, she told Rick, "I called Alcoholics' Anonymous as soon as he admitted it. He spoke to a woman on the phone who told him about the meeting across town. He grabbed his keys and went. I'm really proud of him for that. He's been going every night since, except last night."

"Why not last night?"

Linnea's throat burned as she blushed. "Uh, I needed

him."

"Of course, you did." Rick ducked his head slightly, looking at her tenderly.

"I should have noticed sooner, but he hid it brilliantly."

"I know something about that." Rick replied. She didn't know him well enough to recognize whether his tone was smug or sage. She chose to think he was speaking from a place of transcendent wisdom. After a moment, he exhaled sharply and cracked his knuckles. "If someone wants to quit drinking, they can. It's hard to break the habit. It's hell, really, but the program works. I'd be happy to talk to Dan about it, honey. I've sponsored a few guys. I can give him some advice and a little pep talk, if he wants it."

Linnea put her elbow on the table, resting her cheek in her palm. It felt so good to enlist someone else in her cause, to take a little of the load off. She'd intended to be completely supportive of Dan, but each time he left for a meeting, she got a visceral reminder of how much drinking had become front and center in his life.

Deep down, she was devastated that the interplay between her husband and his liquor, his craving, their secretive coming together, and the drama of their parting was obviously more compelling to him than her love and their family. While his nightly attendance at AA certainly promised a future payoff, there was no telling how long he'd be stuck on Step Two. As soon as she sensed the ache in her chest and the churning in her belly, she stiffened. Rick had come back and so would Dan. She just needed to keep the faith.

Rick gently tapped her nose with his finger. It was a playful bid, it seemed, to comfort and cheer her. She smiled.

He drew back, startled. "I'd forgotten until just now that I used to do that when you were little. It always made you smile back then, too."

With an unexpected surge of jealousy, Linnea leaned forward. "Do you have any other kids?"

"You were the only one for me."

It hadn't mattered to her until that very moment; but she felt intensely relieved he'd had no other children although he'd been married and divorced three times since leaving June. He quickly assured her that he was on good terms with all of his ex-wives, even the last one, who was an unbelievable hypochondriac with hefty medical expenses.

"A woman's standard of living usually declines dramatically after a divorce," Linnea said, silently worried about his track record.

Abruptly changing the subject, Rick pulled pictures of his vacation house on Kauai from the inside pocket of his jacket. "Have you ever been to Hawaii?"

She shook her head. "I've never had a vacation like that. Dan went to Buenos Aires once to set up a contract with a supplier, but he didn't stay long."

"That settles it. We'll have to go. You can see there's plenty of room for the three of you at my place. We'll have a family vacation."

Secluded beach. Digging Frisbees from out of the hibiscus. If only they could go. But there was the remodeling debt to repay and premium hikes in the insurance Dan paid for his employees. Besides, Rick didn't know them enough to be serious about the invitation. "That sounds wonderful," she said casually.

Images of palm trees swayed in her mind while he went on to mention something about real estate and the stock market. She realized he was being vague about his wealth. *He doesn't want to brag, but he's no slouch.* She couldn't help being glad that he didn't live in a single-wide trailer, like her Uncle Ron, Clary Sage's dad. She got up to reheat her coffee in the microwave for thirty seconds.

She had read accounts of people who had watched their whole lives flash before their eyes, within seconds, straddling life and death, preparing to meet their Maker. It had never occurred to her, though, how exhausting it would be to exhume the elements of one's whole existence. Without the divine intervention that accompanies imminent death, two hours wasn't nearly enough to compress all of her accomplishments and cares into the package of self she wanted to present to her father.

But over one pot of coffee, they'd still spoken more than she and Gunter had in the entire twelve years they'd lived under the same roof. On that note alone, Rick was quite a step up in the communication department.

He admired the tile she and Dan had installed in the kitchen. They discussed *The Edge* and The Mill. "I'm so proud of you," Rick said, "but no matter what, I'd love you. I'd love you if you were a motel maid with five illegitimate children."

That didn't quite ring true to Linnea, but she gave him credit for trying to express unconditional love, even if he did it clumsily. "Now that's a daughter who would need a bit of counseling."

"You don't?"

"No, thank you. But I did apply to the Shady Inn before I got my scholarship," she said mischievously. "I really did."

His eyes were soft, shining with affection. "Geez, honey. I'd like to take you out to lunch, but I have to go to a meeting this afternoon. Would you like to see me again?"

"Of course, I want to see you again." She felt as comfortable with him as if she had known him once upon a time. "I want you to meet Dan and Megan as soon as possible."

"I'd like that, sweetheart. I really would." He paused delicately, obviously attempting to avoid being intrusive. "I don't want to pressure you, but I would like for us to have a relationship. I'd like us to have a friendship."

The unexpected longing churning rising inside of Linnea was too intense for friendship. To her surprise, she blurted, "I have friends. What I don't have is a father."

His smile seemed to extend well past his face. He wrapped his arm around her shoulders and pulled her close. "Well, you have one now, honey. I swear to God I'll never leave you again. I've learned my lesson. I know now that ninety-nine percent of life is showing up."

He was caring and sincere. The girl voted most likely to retain her composure lost it in his embrace.

"Let it out." he whispered into her ear as tears streamed from her eyes. "Let it all go."

After she'd cried long enough to give herself a rollicking case of heartburn, but not nearly long enough to rid her body of all the feelings suddenly insisting upon acknowledgement, he looked at his watch. "I need to meet someone about a business opportunity here in Pilchuck." Cautiously, he added, "Would you be okay with your dear old dad moving back to town?"

She sat straight up. Poor June would be a wreck, worrying about running into him at the mall. "Wh…what kind of an opportunity?"

"Oh, let me see if it works out before I tell you." Gently, he brushed a tear from her cheek. "I'm so sad to leave you now."

Linnea sniffled, chucking her emotional turmoil into the hinterlands of her psyche like June dropped off dry-cleaning to pick up later when she could afford it. "It's okay. I have to go get Megan at preschool pretty soon and deliver the paper this afternoon. Oh! I forgot to thank you for the socks."

"Did you like them?"

"Very much. Did Mom tell you I needed some?"

He shrugged. "No, we didn't talk about you at all."

"So you just knew?"

"I had so much fun buying them. There's a lot I've never had the chance to do for you that I'd like to do now."

Linnea's spirit unfolded like the pure white petals of a daisy, eager to reveal its golden face to the benevolent sun.

"Can we meet for dinner tonight?" He asked. "You, me, Dan, and Megan?"

"I'd like that, Dad."

He clasped her to his chest, kissing the top of her head. He slowly pulled himself away. "I'll meet you all here at five."

He dashed out the door. Linnea crossed her fingers behind her back, hoping that he was telling the truth. She had a lot to tell Chelsea and Clary Sage. Like imaginary friends, invisible fathers were always difficult to explain.

Chapter Five

For the next few hours, she wondered if she'd ever see him again. She vowed she wouldn't sit on the bench in the foyer, tapping her foot against the floor. If he didn't come back, she'd just make grilled cheese for dinner and go to bed. Scolding herself for being irrational, Linnea was still greatly relieved when, just as he'd promised, her father returned at five o'clock.

He hugged her effusively and met Dan with a steady handshake. "I can see she's been in good hands," he said. "Thanks for taking care of her."

Dan thrust his chest forward, like a rooster, eyeing him warily. "I'm the one who has been in good hands."

"Good match, then." Rick smiled approvingly.

Dan let his diaphragm drop to its natural height. With Megan clinging to her thigh, Linnea beamed at all of them.

Rick knelt. "Hi, Megan!" He reached into his pocket, producing a small plastic doll with long blue hair. "Look who I met wandering around downtown. He asked me if I knew any little girls who could give him a home. I met your dwarf this morning and thought you might have room in your heart for a troll."

She giggled, reaching for the disarmingly homely toy.

"Those were popular with my friends' kids when you were young," Rick said to Linnea. "I remember wondering if you had one."

She shook her head. She never wanted one. She'd been afraid of the odd, or the unusual. If she expressed an interest in anything outside of what he considered acceptable, Gunter made fun of her. Megan was different. She studied the troll's face. His ugliness was no reflection on her. She laughed aloud.

Rick rose to his feet with a pained expression. "You used to laugh just like that."

"She still does." Dan placed his arm around her shoulder.

Rick's jaw tensed almost imperceptibly. "So where are we going for dinner? My treat."

"I don't know," Linnea said. "We hardly ever eat out." It was an expense they couldn't justify.

Rick arched his eyebrow at Dan. "We can remedy that. Name the best restaurant in town."

"Claudio's!" She chose a locally celebrated seafood restaurant on the water. As she zipped Megan into her coat and tied her shoes, Rick stepped out onto the porch to make a few quick calls on his cell phone. Imagine eating somewhere expensive enough to require reservations.

* * *

Rick drove his own car, following the Perraults to Claudio's. As they pulled in front of the entrance, a Middle-Eastern valet approached the car.

"Is that Hommy?" Linnea whispered.

"Don't you recognize him?" Dan asked.

"I only saw him once, from a distance." How could she have forgotten that Hommy worked here? Why was she so nervous about seeing him? "Let's not do valet parking."

"We're already here." Dan scowled at her. He set the car in park and got out quickly.

The valet immediately slid into the driver's seat. Linnea scanned his profile, searching for a resemblance to Serengeti. *He doesn't look anything like her.*

Unaware that his forty-something face was being compared to a five-month-old's, he glanced at her impatiently. "I've got more cars coming."

Dan unbuckled Megan from the back. "Dwarfy has to come in, too, Daddy," she said.

"No! Linnea?"

Pretending not to be as perturbed by Hommy as she felt, Linnea picked her purse up off the floor and got out of the car, "Yes, Dwarfy has to come in, too. He's quiet. He won't eat much and even if he does, my Dad's paying for dinner."

Dan rolled his eyes. Uneasily, Linnea watched their car disappear around the building "Why didn't you just give him the car key instead of the whole key ring?"

"Don't be so paranoid," he hissed.

He was right. It would be silly to let anxiety overshadow the evening ahead.

Inside the restaurant, they were hailed as the Andersen party which was pleasantly disconcerting. "This is the first time I've ever done anything under your name," she whispered.

Rick took her elbow. "Having you do something under my name is a dream come true."

She kissed him on the cheek. Side by side, they glided after the hostess toward a choice booth overlooking Puget Sound. Hastily, Dan tucked Dwarfy under his arm. Grabbing Megan's hand, he hustled her after them.

Rick studied the dessert menu first. "I used to take you out for ice cream all the time. You used to be a vanilla kid."

She was delighted that he remembered that, even if she couldn't. "Not any more. I'm a chocolate girl now. My absolute favorite kind of ice cream is double-malted chocolate-crunch."

"Really?" Rick raised his eyebrows, obviously pleased. "That's my favorite, too. Must be genetic."

"I like vanilla," Megan said.

"Still genetic." Rick chuckled, ruffling her curls.

Dan used one of the crayons that came with the child-friendly menu to point out the window toward the northern end of their panoramic view. "There's The Mill."

"Spinning Wheel Bluff has changed a lot for the better," Rick said. "I read about The Mill in a Pilchuck Chamber of Commerce brochure at the hotel. You can be mighty proud of yourself, Dan. Have you ever thought of branching out, of opening a few more shops in strategic locations?"

Incredulity distorted Dan's smile. "Sure, *we*'ve thought about it, but I already work long hours as it is. Linnea and I decided a long time ago that it's more important for me to be around while our family is young than it is to open another store."

"Admirable. I can see you both have good values."

Linnea was pleased. *He must really be sorry that he left me.*

"Of course," Rick continued smoothly, "if you increased your volume, you could still expand your business while remaining in one location."

Linnea laughed. "The shop is busy enough as it is, Dad. You can't pack any more volume in there most days."

"What's your annual advertising budget?"

"He gets free advertising in *The Edge*." A shudder ran down Linnea's spine. She'd never felt anything quite like it before. She shifted uneasily.

"And trade journals have given me a lot of positive press," Dan put in, "but we're mostly a word-of-mouth operation."

"How about we take Megan and Dwarfy out for coffee tomorrow?" Rick asked Linnea. "I'd like to see this local legend in action."

She nodded eagerly, surprised to see the hostess leading Chelsea and Larry right to their table.

Rick's chuckle belied his feigned astonishment. "Well, look who's here!"

The men clasped hands conspiratorially. Larry's brown eyes shone. His glossy gray hair was meticulously trimmed.

"Sit down! Sit down," Rick urged.

The men grinned as smug as teenagers pulling a successful prank. Linnea and Chelsea exchanged puzzled glances. "You know each other?" Linnea asked.

"We grew up together," Rick answered.

"Our dads worked the pulp and paper mills and our mothers played bingo at the church."

Rick held out his hand to Chelsea. "It's a pleasure to meet my daughter's partner in crime. I'm tickled at this coincidence. Your dad and I used to be in cahoots the way you two are now

"Dad," Chelsea asked, "Have you known all this time that Linnea was Rick's daughter?"

"Yes. I knew the second I met her. I told you that I had known her dad."

Chelsea narrowed her eyes at him. "But you made it sound like you'd met him at a party or something casual like that. Why didn't you tell me you'd been close friends?"

"We just met again this afternoon," Rick said.

How nice for him to run into an old friend just after a lovely reunion with her. The waitress interrupted to take their orders. Linnea had always been a light drinker, and she hadn't had a drop of alcohol since Dan had revealed his secret. Sympathetic sobriety, she called it, but tonight her compassion was all for her own over-stimulated nerves. "Does anyone mind if I have a glass of wine?"

"Doesn't bother me at all, honey," Rick said, "I'm glad to see my girl can handle her booze."

Dan grimaced. For a second, Linnea questioned her selfishness, wondering if she was making a mistake, tempting him. But this was her party. She requested her favorite Riesling. Chelsea, less sympathetic to the teetotalers, pulled out her *Consume Your Colors* chart and decided upon a strawberry daiquiri. She ordered tomato soup and salmon with a red pepper sauce.

Larry motioned for the waitress to stop writing. "Have lobster with the rest of us instead, Chels. It's red."

"I have to consume the color Dad, and I don't want to eat the shell."

Megan requested chicken strips with extra fries for the dwarf. Borrowing a red crayon from Megan's pile to color a space in her dietary log, Chelsea whispered to Dan, "How's Linnea doing?"

"It took me at least a month to get her to smile at me the way she smiles at him after three hours," he murmured back.

"Stop it," Chelsea chided. "Can't you see how Megan looks at you?"

Linnea pretended she hadn't heard them, but she felt

even fonder of them both. Happily, she asked the fathers, "Where did you two reunite this afternoon?"

"At the Spinners' headquarters," Rick said. "God, I've always loved the Spinners of this world. Something about the independent streak of the unaffiliated really appeals to me. I bet you can understand that, Dan. You assert your independence from the big guy with your own excellent brand of coffee, don't you?"

He nodded. "That's right. You get me."

"Of course, I get you. What's more, I like you. But back to the story, Larry and I used to sneak in to see games when we were kids. We'd hide out under the bleachers and watch all nine innings and then some. Before long, the coach noticed us and we were enlisted as bat boys. That was something. Everything was grand until the day he was promoted to the dug-out and actually got paid for being there. Do you remember what I said when that happened, Larry?"

He looked at Rick blankly. "Can't say that I do."

"I remember as clearly as if it were yesterday. I was so jealous, so incredibly pissed off, I swore to you that one day I would own the Spinners."

Larry pursed his lips. Linnea sensed something about Rick's revelation was incongruous to him.

"I keep my promises." Rick stared intently into Linnea's eyes, as if daring her to contradict him. "When I give my word, I follow through. True to the promise I made almost fifty years ago, I bought the Spinners this afternoon. Fortunately for me, Larry has agreed to stay on to manage the team for another year or so."

What he thought was a delightful surprise actually felt deceptive to her. "But," she spluttered, "the Spinners have already been sold to a corporation in California."

"I am that corporation. I've decided to keep the team in Pilchuck. I want to be close to you."

He's that wealthy? He wants to be with me. Me! Me! Me! He really, truly loves me. No, wait. "But you can't do that. "The school district is going to demolish the stadium this spring."

"No, they aren't." Rick said slowly. "The Spinners still have two years on their lease. The district has to honor it."

The waitress set their drinks and a basket of buttered garlic bread before them.

Linnea hadn't even had a sip of her drink and her head was already spinning. "The construction bond just passed. It will expire if they don't break ground on the new school within six months."

"Not my problem." Rick sipped his iced tea.

Linnea sat stunned. She didn't know him, did she? And he didn't know her. He couldn't know how many hours and hours she'd worked on that campaign.

"The district can put the bond up again, if they want, when our lease runs out." Larry said, trying to make peace.

Rick spread extra butter on his bread. "Until then, the stadium is ours."

Linnea felt as if she were calling to him over a long stretch of gray fog. "But this hurts the children. They will have to go to that toxic school well past the time we've planned. That's more exposure. Megan will have to go there." The neighborhood kids got off the bus across the street from her house, but she wasn't about to let her breast-fed, cloth-diapered baby go off to be the one kindergarten canary that finally succumbed to the gas. "I'll have to home-school her."

"Do you have any idea how much money the school

district spent to pass the bond?" Chelsea added. "They can't afford to re-run a campaign like that. It's a waste of money that should be spent on the kids."

Rick swallowed a mouthful. "Whoa! After we get through implementing our plans, the Spinners will be making money hand over fist. I'll donate tax-deductible cash back to the district." He glanced at Megan. She was making the troll traverse the maze on her menu. "As for the little princess here, we can send her to the best private school in town."

"But what about the other children?" Linnea asked.

The lobster arrived. The waitress removed their shells amidst uncomfortable silence.

As soon as the server carried the buttery platter away, Linnea said, "This puts *The Edge* in a really awkward position."

"Yeah." Chelsea took a swig of her cocktail. "Here we've been advocating for the destruction of the stadium and the passage of the bond, and now our fathers are teaming up to prevent the school from being built."

Linnea wished Rick had given her some indication of his plans to buy the team before launching them. "Can't you just move the Spinners to California and come visit me?"

He looked annoyed. "There's been some re-zoning that affected the land I was going to build a new stadium on down there. But here's something you can take to the bank. I've directed everyone involved to keep mum so *The Edge* can be the paper to break the story."

Some consolation. "It's not good for the community to have the children bused out of the village every day to a risky site. It feels like Hamelin in the aftermath."

That spooky image had kept recurring to her throughout the whole bond battle, in fact, *The Edge* had hired a drama student to play the flute at their fundraisers. The banner across the limber troubadour's chest read, "Time to Pay the Piper." In the back, it said, "Bring the children home."

Though her stomach fluttered uneasily, Linnea bit into her lobster. It was really good. She took a second perfect bite and began to savor private school as an option for Megan. Her preschool continued on through the elementary grades. Linnea had always wanted to keep her there, but had never seriously considered it because of the tuition hike once the kids reached full-time enrollment. The Perraults could barely afford preschool three mornings per week. Still, she had an obligation to her community. "The school district has to build a new school. They will refuse to renew your lease when it expires."

"Fine," Rick said. "We only need two years."

Linnea's solar plexus slid into her shoes. *Then what happens? Dad disappears?*

"Haven't you heard about Pete Stealer?" Rick asked.

"Yeah," Dan said eagerly. "He had a 300 batting average with twenty-eight home runs last year. He was MVP for the entire independent league."

"He'll be even better this season," Larry promised.

Rick smiled as broadly as if he had batted that well himself. "The Spinners have him under contract for the next four years, but if we handle the kid right this season, we'll be able to sell his contract out to the majors for millions of dollars by next spring. Pete just needs a little more experience and a lot more promotion."

Linnea just stared at him. He was talking gibberish.

"After taking into account what I've spent to buy the team, by the time we clinch his deal, we'll have made at least two million dollars, probably three. Not bad for one year's work. Just think about what we'll all get. Larry here gets a hefty signing bonus from me and a raise that will help augment his upcoming retirement. Although after we get through grooming Petey, Larry will be lured up to the majors with him for a stunning second career." Rick made a gesture toward Chelsea, drawing her in, "Wouldn't you like to see your dad in the show, wowing the whole nation with his managerial talent?"

"He could have pulled it off years ago, if he hadn't been so determined to stay close to home while I was growing up."

Larry sat up taller. "I was never interested in all that spit and polish. And I'm ready to retire. I'm only staying on this year to make the transition easier for everyone involved."

Rick winked at Chelsea. "He has a straight shot at the big time now. Fame and fortune. And Dan, what would it do for business if The Mill were the sole hot beverage provider at Spinners' games? What if The Mill had its own sign right over the scoreboard at no expense to you?"

Dan's jaw quivered slightly, betraying his poker face. Excitement shone in his eyes. Rick beamed triumphantly around the table. "Megan gets private school. And you, Linnea, get the best seat in the ballpark right behind home plate, right beside your dad, with all the free hot dogs you can eat."

But I never eat processed meat. And this whole set-up is so unnecessarily self-serving.

He spread his arms wide, including them all in his bounty. "If we get all this in one fell swoop, who cares if the school district refuses to renew our contract when it's up?"

"What about the players?" Dan asked.

"We sell the team, dissolve it, or find another tax base willing to build a stadium. Let's worry about two years in two years." Rick dropped a sugar cube into his iced tea, stirring it vigorously. Linnea watched its sweetness disintegrate, wondering how he had sold them on all this so quickly. He took a long sip, nearly draining his glass. "But what really matters most to me is showing my daughter that she can trust her dad. I promised myself, when I gave up the bottle, that I'd get my little girl back. So here I am, doing exactly what I said I would. Let's eat and," he smiled broadly at her, "be sure to save room for your super-deluxe, double-malted chocolate crunch ice cream. Daddy's buying."

Despite her nagging, lingering questions, Linnea decided to think about it later, enjoy her meal now, and look forward to dessert. Her grueling public service campaign had been for naught, but she was getting a dad.

Chapter Six

Linnea sat on the edge of her daughter's bed that night, rubbing her back. An odd scuffling sound reverberated through the ceiling. "That's the monster, Mommy." Megan whispered, scrunching closer to the turquoise tunic of her reclining dwarf.

Immediately, Linnea called Dan to the room. "Something is making a strange noise…"

"I forgot to tell you," he interrupted. "I found a small colony of bats up there when I put the Christmas boxes away."

"Bats!" Linnea gasped. Warm-blooded bodies hanging upside down, swaddled in dark wings, only moving when the rest of the world was unconscious. Her skin crawled.

"Are they worse than monsters?" Megan gripped her hand frantically.

In his most reassuring voice, Dan said, "They are small animals, like mice. But they have wings, so they can fly. They like to sleep all winter. My guess is they think our attic is a toasty home."

"Are they bad?"

"No, silly," he said affectionately. "They're good. They

like to eat mosquitoes."

She chortled. "They *are* good. Mosquitoes like to eat me."

Linnea wanted to be reassured, too. "Why aren't they hibernating now?"

He shrugged. "Something woke them up." He kissed both of them and left the room.

Linnea tried to ignore her heart palpitations. "Are you okay, sweetie?"

"Mommy, I've got Dwarfy. He watches out for me while I'm sleeping."

Touched, even bolstered herself, by Megan's faith, Linnea joined Dan in their bedroom. Pulling her sweater off, she asked, "What do you think of my dad?"

"I have to admit, I had my doubts about him at first, but it's obvious that he's really pulled himself together. I respect that. Giving us the hot beverage contract is a really nice way for him to start making amends to you."

She stepped out of her slacks. "I can't say I agree with his politics."

"It is a bummer about the school. You and Chelsea worked your tail ends off over that." He burrowed under the comforter.

"He seems a little self-centered. Probably because he doesn't have much practice caring for anybody else." But he had come looking for her, so he must be yearning to love. As his only child, she was the best person in the world to teach him how to do it. The request to serve Spirit, couched in a Catholic hymn she had often sung as an adolescent, resounded in her skull: *Let it be me Lord. Let it be me.*

"I'm glad it's all working out for you."

"Thanks for being here." Linnea stuffed her clothes in a

hamper.

"But I really need to go back to my meeting tomorrow."

"I'm sorry you had to skip two nights in a row, but I've needed your support through all this. I probably never really stopped loving him. I guess I just stuck my feelings somewhere deep inside and forgot about them." She waited for a reaction. Dan's lids were drooping, but she couldn't let him check out on her yet. "What about the bats?"

"Megan's not scared," he mumbled. "Don't be so paranoid."

Hours later, she was startled awake by a masculine voice calling her name from the doorway. She lay perfectly still. If she didn't move, whoever wanted her attention might drift away. Suddenly, Gunter was whispering in her ear. "The bat in the attic is going to fly down to sit on your back and bite your neck with its sharp teeth. Tonight, it will suck out your blood."

"No," she heard herself say in a little girl's voice, "I will roll over so it can't sit on my back." The words came so easily. She'd said them before.

"Then it will sit on your chest and bite the front of your neck."

So, there was nowhere to turn. Dread clutched her throat, but she managed to gurgle, "I'll scream."

"You can't do that. Bats sense the vibrations in your throat and lap up your voice faster than you can utter a sound. You should just be quiet and let it have what it wants."

"I'll run to Mommy."

"If you come out of this room, I'll pull down your pants and give you the worst spanking you've ever had.

That will hurt way more than any bat bite." He grinned hideously. "And after that, I'll make you sleep outside where hundreds of bats can get you."

Gunter disappeared. There had been a bat in the cabin he and June rented the year she was seven. Linnea saw herself lying in a hide-away bed in a strange room, feverishly praying for the beast to stay away or for her daddy to come get her. She had startled herself awake each time her tired muscles hinted at letting down their guard. She remembered lying with the Hans Christian Andersen book beneath her pillow. Somehow it had kept the bat at bay when she was a frightened little girl. It was on her nightstand now. Perhaps it could ease her adult anxiety. Tucking it under her flannel pillowcase, she hoped its magic still worked.

She reached for Dan's hand. He rolled over, pulling away, doggedly holding onto slumber and refusing to be disturbed by her whimpering.

* * *

In the morning, Linnea found Clary Sage in the family room, using the burka to play peek-a-boo with Serengeti. "Good idea! A game will help her get used to you wearing a veil. Although I have to say, it's beyond me why any one with a face like yours would want to hide it."

Clary Sage giggled. "Thanks, but burkas are just temporary, you know. After George Bush gets done bringing democracy to the Middle East, women will stop wearing them."

"I wouldn't bank on it."

Clary Sage was silent for a moment. "How was dinner? Has he changed?"

"He has." Linnea plugged in the toaster. *Damn! What am I going to say to all the people who helped us get the school bond passed?* "He's coming over after I interview the mayor and write it up. Will you be home in the afternoon? I want you to meet him."

"I'll be here then, but would you watch Serengeti for me for an hour or so before lunch?"

Linnea tensed. She didn't want this to become a habit. But she wanted a second child someday, after AA worked. She could use the practice juggling Megan, a baby, the paper, and all the other things she needed to get done in a day. *Thank God, I didn't get pregnant before I knew what Dan was really doing in the garage.* "I can do it today. Where are you going?"

"To see Hommy, but I'm going to wear the burka, and Serengeti just can't cope with that yet."

"I thought it was for your trip. Does Hommy expect you to wear to veil every time you visit him?"

"I don't think *he* does, but the way his roommate looks at me makes me feel creepy. Their neighbor, Dr. Jafairi, is fine, but I feel safer being around the other guy when I have the burka to hide behind."

"Hmm. Then, by all means, leave the baby with me when you go over there."

* * *

While Clary Sage practiced managing the burka with ease before her date, Linnea typed up her article about the mayor. Megan sat at her feet reading library books about bats. Linnea was surprised to find the ugly creatures somewhat endearing.

"See there," Megan said, pointing, "mommy bats wrap their babies in their wings to carry them where they need to go."

The telephone rang. Linnea picked up the receiver, still editing.

"How was dinner last night?" June asked.

"Fabulous!" Linnea found she was suddenly grateful her mother had encouraged the reunion. "He's still handsome. I see why you fell for him when you were young."

"Me, and all his mistresses."

Linnea didn't bring up what a quandary he'd created for *The Edge*, or how difficult she'd found it to endure congratulations for passing the bond from villagers she met at City Hall and in the library earlier in that morning. She did tell June about Rick's plans for the Spinners, cautioning her to keep it quiet until she could figure out a way to make it public.

"But I don't want him to move back to Pilchuck," she wailed. "What will I say if I run into him at the grocery store?"

"Don't worry, Mom. He's easy to talk to."

"Then he really must have changed." June sounded triumphant. Her faith in his eventual redemption had been rewarded. "I bet he's glad now that I didn't have an abortion when I was pregnant with you."

* * *

Linnea was still disturbed by her mother's last comment when Clary Sage left, but small children are distracting. She buckled Serengeti into Megan's old high chair and began peeling the baby's banana. Someone knocked at the door. She hurried to open it. Clary Sage had probably forgotten her bus pass.

Her womanizing, abortion-wanting father stood outside the front door instead. Despite her editorial upheaval, she was happy to see him again. Her DNA seemed to be dancing, celebrating their reunion on the cellular level. She was so glad he'd become a new man.

She greeted him with a grin. "So you're still real."

"I've always been real. Ready to go out to lunch?"

Discomfited by his timing, she said, "I thought you were coming later. I just made lunch. Would you like me to make you a sandwich?"

Rick entered the foyer. "Thank you. What a treat." He proffered a small rectangular box. "I brought truffles...for dessert."

"Oooh!" Linnea took the black and white box from him. He was too early. She still had to call the county to compare ordinances before she could finish the piece she was writing.

"Only the best chocolate for you." Rick hung his coat on a hook. "What kind do you usually eat?"

"I don't buy any, so I can't eat it." Linnea beckoned him to follow her into the kitchen. "But I do have a terrible sweet tooth, and when I just can't resist, I dip into the chocolate chips in the pantry."

He wrinkled his nose at the idea of semi-sweet. "You're pretty trim. You can afford to eat a truffle or two, now and then. Hey, who is this lovely baby?"

"Serengeti," Megan piped up.

Rick gave a silly wave and an exaggerated bow. "How's the troll?"

"Hi!" Megan giggled. "I don't know your name."

Rick hesitated, glancing at Linnea.

Let's just call the kettle black. "This is Grandpa Rick," Linnea said.

Megan's eyes grew wide. "Grandpa Rick, like Grandma June?"

"Exactly like that. Thank you," Rick added huskily to Linnea.

Shit! I don't know if I should have done that. "You are her grandpa. She might as well call you that. Serengeti here is my cousin Clary Sage's baby. You wouldn't know her. She's only nineteen, but you might remember my Uncle Ron and Aunt Jean? They're divorced now."

"I remember Ron. We used to party. Nice guy."

"Maybe." Ron was a loser. Clary Sage was a teenager who, sensibly enough, never wanted to go home which is probably why she'd gotten mixed up with Hommy who did. "Clary Sage lives with us now, in the apartment over the garage."

He sucked the inside of his cheek. "Does she pay rent?"

"Just utilities." She offered Serengeti the spoon. "She's trying to save up for a car. Serengeti's father doesn't contribute much."

"I'm surprised Dan doesn't insist on some monthly payment or on leasing it out to someone who can pay market value. He should take advantage of opportunities to make your life better, to treat you to Claudio's once in awhile. I'm looking at buying investment property in this area myself. Rent is only going to go up around here."

Linnea explained the situation in full as she made a sandwich for him and fed the baby.

"She's a cute little tike," he remarked. "Too bad her parents are so irresponsible. You used to put banana up your nose, too."

"All babies put bananas up their noses." After his remark about irresponsible parents, she wasn't about to give him credit for remembering such a generic detail. But she wasn't going to hold one insensitive comment against the man. *At least this old dog is working on some new tricks.*

After lunch, she excused herself to take Serengeti upstairs. After a few minutes, Rick followed, sauntering into the master suite where Linnea sat on the bed, gently changing the resistant baby's shirt. "You have a decent view of the water from here."

Rick ignored the sloping piles of binders, trade journals, and coffee reviews stacked around Dan's computer. He pulled the office chair out of the alcove and sat where he could watch Linnea and take in the scenery simultaneously. "Whenever I'm troubled, I head to the beach, or at least to the bathtub."

"Me, too." She liked that they had that in common.

"It's genetic. But your patience with kids obviously isn't. How did you learn it?"

I remember how it felt when adults were impatient with me. "Patience isn't the right word. Patience makes it sound like children are irritating and have to be tolerated. I like kids. I understand how they think and feel."

"Are you going to have any more?"

"Possibly." *It's very strange to be sitting in here talking about intimate things with a man I met only yesterday. It doesn't seem to bother him at all. Of course, he's been in a lot of women's bedrooms before. Maybe he's so comfortable because it's his daughter's room, but I'm not a little girl.*

The bumps beneath the Matisse coverlet were the purple cashmere socks Dan had pulled from her feet during the other night's lovemaking. She suspected her lacy panties were still crammed down there as well. This was definitely weird. She hoped she wasn't blushing.

If she was, he didn't seem to notice. "Hommy sounds suspicious to me. He's too old to be involved with Clary Sage. I can assure you, I'm not at all attracted to younger women. If I do get married again, I promise I'll marry someone around my own age."

She nodded, wondering why he'd felt the need to

reassure her of that.

He pulled a glistening heart-shaped locket out of his shirt pocket. The gold was first-class, thick, impeccably cast, obviously crafted and commissioned by men who did not care to conserve either precious metal or money. It was something a rich woman would wear.

"This is for you. May I help put it on?" Barely waiting for her to lift her curly locks or nod assent, he deftly clasped the gold chain around her neck.

"Thanks, Dad." She let her hair fall back around her shoulders, unsure of what else to say. Besides the socks and the little box of chocolate, the necklace was the first gift her father had ever given her. It was obviously extremely expensive, and a little out of alignment with her sense of style, but it was special. If he'd given her a locket as a little girl, she'd have put his photo inside, but now Dan and Megan were closest to her heart.

"You look a lot like your mother did when she was young. Prettier, though."

Once again, she didn't know what to say. After Rick accepted Megan's invitation to see her books downstairs, Linnea handed the baby a toy. She remembered June handing her a doll, towels, plates filled with food, laundry to put away. Her mother had been there her whole life. Linnea took a slightly misshapen ring from her sparsely filled jewelry box. The gold band was thin, and the ruby in the center was really just red glass. June had given her the hand-me down the day she got her first period. She slipped the ring onto her finger and, wearing gifts from both of her parents, carried Serengeti down to the first floor.

She found Megan cuddled up to Rick on the sofa, cajoling him to read the caption under a picture of thousands of bats clustered in a cave. He looked decidedly queasy. With a bit of misgiving about leaving them, she decided to try loading the dishwater before Serengeti got fussy. She buckled her into the infant carrier on the counter the moment Clary Sage stumbled through the back door, sporting a pulpy purple bruise just above her cheekbone.

Linnea gasped. The tissue around her own eye throbbed with a sudden infusion of empathetic inflammation. "Did he hit you?"

Chagrin added a pink overlay to Clary Sage's complexion. "I misjudge distance wearing a burka. I bumped into a door jamb."

She's usually quite graceful. I hope she's telling me the truth. Linnea grabbed Megan's boo-boo ice pack from the freezer. She lifted the terrycloth bunny to the wound. "Hold this on your face. My dad's in the other room."

"Can I meet him later?"

Linnea nodded. Clary Sage grabbed the handle of the infant carrier and fled up to the apartment with Serengeti.

Suddenly, the instinct to check on her daughter overwhelmed Linnea. Leaving the dishwasher door open with the top rack full of clean cups, she hurried into the family room. Megan was reading in her own way, confidently interpreting text from the pictures. Rick watched her incredulously. Megan looked up, smiling at her brightly. All was well. Linnea relaxed, but Rick seemed restless in the house, like a dog kenneled by the drudgery of domesticity. "Let's go for a walk," he suggested.

Megan wanted to take Dwarfy with them, but Linnea was able to convince her to leave him in the foyer to make sure no one woke up the bats in the attic while they were away. The three generations made their way through well-tended residential streets, heading toward The Mill. Once they were outdoors, Rick's tension eased.

It was overcast and chilly. By the time they reached the cafe, Linnea was ready for a steaming mocha, but Rick said, "Would you like to walk down to the beach? I want to avoid the crowd a little longer. I like having you to myself…and Megan, of course."

Flattered, Linnea agreed. It was exhilarating to be the apple of a daddy's eye. While Megan threw pebbles out into the water and played tag with the gray tide, they wandered over to the old *Aurora*. The breeze ruffled his hair. He read the historical marker with a wry smile. "Do you know how the Andersens ended up in Pilchuck?"

She shook her head. "Mom never told me anything about your family. When I was twelve, a lady at church told me that your parents moved out of town."

"Would you like to meet them? They'd love to see you and my sister, well, she'd be just tickled."

Linnea had always wanted to thank her aunt for the fairy tales that had sustained her, but she wanted to be secure in her relationship with Rick before his relatives came into it. After all, she'd grown up believing that they were crazy.

On Easter Sunday when she was eight, she had watched the kids across the street leave in their station wagon. They were going to an Easter egg hunt at their paternal grandparents' home. Every year they came back, bragging. The plastic eggs they found there were stuffed with dollars. Linnea could have used some cash herself, because the Easter Bunny hadn't brought her a *Nancy Drew* book like she'd asked, even though she'd made it a point to tell her mother where she could buy one, in case the bunny needed guidance.

So there she was, picking artificial grass out of the shag carpet in her brothers' room so the little beasties wouldn't choke on it, ruminating on the role of grandparents, cautiously pumping June for information.

"Did I ever go to my real dad's family for Easter?"

Concentrating on the diaper change at hand and musing over how long to keep the ham in the oven, June was inadvertently forthcoming, for a change. "His family is crazy." She dumped a wadded diaper into the stinky pail. "His mother always insisted upon having red carpet in the living room even though it showed the lint. Worse than that, she never liked Catholics. I know she'd hate my new shag."

Twenty-four years later, the comments about the carpet still seemed a bit odd, but now Linnea realized that her mother's message had been tainted with pain. June's sense of rejection had leached through Linnea's psyche like the red dye bled pink on her hard-boiled breakfast that morning. The sad fact of her childhood was, that from choice of flooring to faith, if your perceptions differed, a whole lot of disowning had to go down.

Lack of cash or the idealized girl detective aside, Linnea grew up secretly resisting this. The Edge's success proved plenty of people embraced alternative views, but she wasn't up to inviting any potentially unsupportive people into her life. One resurrection of a vanished relative per year was plenty. "Let's wait awhile," she said to Rick.

"Whenever you're ready. For now, I'll just tell you how we ended up in this two-bit town." He sank onto the shipwreck, gesturing for her to sit beside him. "See, this heap of dead wood sailed out of San Francisco way back in 1900. My great-grandfather, Zachariah Andersen, was in Captain Pillar's crew, heading to the Klondike Gold Rush in Alaska. They'd made it this far north when a rough storm struck out at sea. Pillar decided to bring the ship into this bay to wait out the weather. As they sailed around what later became known as Tower Island, the chain on his steering wheel broke. He spun the wheel frantically, but he lost control of his ship and ran it ashore here."

"I knew that's how Spinning Wheel Bay was named," Linnea said. "He spun and he spun, but he couldn't stop the collision. I didn't know that my great-great grandfather was on board."

"A lot of the crew joined others passing through on their way north, but Zach decided to stay here with his captain. I don't know what possessed him. He got a job at the sawmill to tide him over until they were ready to sail again. But in the meantime, Pillar fell in love with a local girl. Some say she bewitched him to make him give up a life at sea. He married her, left the ship marooned right here on the beach, and just for the hell of it, organized the local loggers and fishermen into a recreational baseball club which eventually became the Northwest Independent League."

"And you just bought the Spinners from his granddaughter. It's as if you are completing the circle."

Rick nodded. "She's a sweet old lady. She said she knew I was meant to have the team."

"It might not just be sweetness that made her say that." Linnea said. A man at the senior center had once told her about a little girl who wandered away from her family during a parish picnic at St. Frances' in the early sixties. The whole congregation had been hysterical. But within minutes, the first old lady Pillar had called the Pilchuck police chief from her home on Tower Island. From a forty-minute ferry ride away, she suggested he check the rose garden at the   cemetery across the highway from the church.

The old man had rubbed the age spots on his forearm as he recalled guiding law enforcement through the graveyard at dusk. That night had been the highlight of his career. They found that sweet little angel just where Mrs. Pillar said they would. She was wrapped in a stranger's pink shawl, sucking her thumb, sleeping peacefully beneath a statue of the Virgin Mary. Linnea smiled. "Local legend has it that the Pillar ladies have natural psychic ability."

"Well, that might explain the hex that fell on Zach at Pillar's wedding. He fell in love with the bride's cousin, Mavis. He got her pregnant and married her. Instead of following his dream of striking it rich in Alaska, he ended up working at the saw mill for the rest of his life, staying on after it became the pulp and paper factory. His son worked there, and his son worked there, and even I worked there for about two weeks. But do you know what really gets me about it?"

Ecstatic to learn that she shared ancestry with the intriguing Pillar ladies, Linnea shook her head.

"It has always bugged the hell out of me that Pillar was one of the richest sons-of-bitches on the West Coast when he ran aground here. He could have easily afforded to skip that last run to the Klondike for a little nooky, but Zach should have gone on. My life would have been so different so much better if only he'd stuck to his original plan."

"He was loyal to his captain and then he fell in love," Linnea spoke softly as if by decreasing the volume of her voice he wouldn't realize how vehemently she disagreed with him. "I think that's nice."

Rick raised his brows. "How nice is this? Just after his first kid was born, Zach got a letter from one of his original shipmates, bragging that he'd made a fortune in Alaska." He shook his head in disgust. "He should have been in on that action."

A cold breeze cut right through her clothing. "*We* might not have been born if he had been."

"The Andersens were pulp-and-paper poor, white trash in Pilchuck. When I was a schoolboy, Pillar's great-grandson was in my class. Every time he came to school bragging about his baseball team, his pony, his vacation, or his car, I swore to myself that one day, I'd be rich, too."

Linnea shivered. Rick wrapped his arm around her in an effort to warm her. She wanted to pull away from his embrace.

"That's why I ultimately had to leave Pilchuck," he said. "Back then, the only way to make a living around here was to work in the factory or fish, and neither job paid what I was worth. I realized I had to leave. There was no way I could keep my promise to myself and stay here."

Her stomach tightened. *What about the vow you made to my mother?* "So you left this area because you made a promise to yourself that you'd do whatever it took to make a fortune?"

He grinned. "Yeah. But I've returned because I also swore to myself that I'd get you back. It's taken a long time, but I've done it."

Megan joyfully tossed stone after stone out into the waves. Linnea glanced sideways at Rick, but his handsome profile made her want to cry. Was their reconciliation already signed, sealed, and delivered? If so, she had missed something.

She stood up quickly, stepping forward as if making

sure Megan wasn't too close to the water's edge. *Be calm for her. Be happy for her.* "Would you have come back for me if you hadn't made it big, if you couldn't buy the team?"

"I don't know." Rick stood as if he had a cramp in his back. Clearly, the conversation was over, and it was time to move on. "I never considered it. It was always a package deal to me."

Her DNA had already stopped its delirious unfolding, opening to her father. Now, her uncertain cells began to recoil from the reunion. *Okay. This is heavy emotional stuff...and he's not very good at communicating with sensitivity because...he's a jerk. No!*

Her mind searched for a better explanation. Maybe he'd meant to say it was a package deal because he had to be like King Midas: he'd had to turn everything into gold first to figure out how much he missed his daughter. After he got rich, he realized his wealth meant nothing without her. Her cells and her DNA could live with that. "Let's go get some coffee, Dad. Megan's probably cold."

Chapter Seven

The Mill sat on the corner of a busy village street, its wide-paned windows overlooking Spinning Wheel Bay on three sides. Mothers in athletic garb pulled mission tables together. Constantly eying the clock so they wouldn't be late picking children up from school, they discussed articles in *The Edge* over lattes while sharing the fat grams in a scone with work-out buddies. College students thumped heavy backpacks onto the dark wood floor near the battered leather sofa, ordered their favorite drip, and focused on flirting.

Many came to The Mill to work, creating their own cubicles within the communal space. Sipping java from gold mugs, men in yarn beanie hats telecommuted via laptops. Professionals conferred in suits, and delivery truck drivers stopped in regularly. Throughout the day, the burnished roaster standing in the back of the shop in the center of a stone plaza roasted batch after batch of coffee beans. A pound a minute.

Dan prepared Linnea's mocha and a drip. She and Rick sat so they could watch Megan measuring cooled beans into golden canisters. He said, "You should get her a puppy. A dog is better than an attic full of creepy bats. I wish I'd had a pet as a kid, but my parents wouldn't let me. Is there anyone around here that sells purebred Golden Retrievers? I always wanted one of those."

Why was Rick's revelation irritating her? She glanced at Dan, willing him to come interrupt the conversation. He and the baristas whirled around one another, caught in a daily dance of grinding, percolating, and gossiping with the long line of customers at the counter. The espresso machine hissed loudly.

"I don't want a dog," she said. "Gunter got a Saint Bernard when I was Megan's age." Gunter used to say that he had always wanted a woman, a dog, and all the ice cream he could eat. A daughter had never been on his list. "Its name was Brutus. He used to sit on me and slobber. I would yell for Mom to come get him off."

He chuckled. "That must have been funny."

Yeah, it had been funny for about ten seconds, and then what she'd thought was play had turned into something else. The dog had pressed her vertebrae to the ground, forcing the thin skin covering her spine to spread out on the cold concrete. Far heavier than she, the beast overwhelmed her resistance with a possessive squat. He panted heavily, a few inches above her neck. Thick drool overflowed his flabby black jowls. The sickening stickiness dripped downward into the hollow above her clavicle.

Her heart beat as rapidly as he breathed. The dog rubbed his underbelly against her front ribs. His hindquarters pinned her legs. Struggling against his disturbing gyrations, she caught an alarming glimpse of his pubescent penis dribbling on her jeans. She yelled for all she was worth, but the stupid-head dog remained smugly on top of her. She screamed and screamed.

Eventually, Gunter came out of the kitchen. June did not.

"Get him off me!" she pleaded.

He smirked, getting a beer from the outside refrigerator.

"Please help me," she begged.

He turned on his heel, disappearing into the house. She curled her parched lips back into a disgusted grimace, turning her head to the side. She dug her incisors into the dog's front leg. His nasty fur tasted like canine spit and wet grass. But the bite made Brutus shift, just enough for her to slip out from under him and run.

She slammed the garage door so the enormous dog could not follow her into the side yard. She was so mad she didn't even take her pink cowboy boots off as she stomped through the back door into the house and down the hall. She muttered disparagingly about the mean new daddy and his stupid new dog.

Passing their bedroom, she saw him lying on top of June, just as Brutus had pinned her. He licked June's neck with his long pink tongue, pressing her into the plush maroon bedspread.

"Stop it!" June exclaimed. "Stop, please stop!"

Gunter shoved his knees between hers. Linnea saw Mom's feet move as if she were trying to escape, but her stupid-head new husband was too heavy.

With lightening speed, she leapt up onto the bed, kicking Gunter. "I'm gonna kick you with my big boots!" she bellowed, pummeling him again and again until he grabbed her inner thigh and pinched, twisting her leg out from under her so that she crumpled onto the floor.

June laughed and he grinned as if he'd won a Herculean victory. Shame-faced and confused, Linnea was alarmed when Gunter ordered her to her room. She couldn't bear to leave her mother alone with that man, especially since she seemed completely unaware of how creepy he was. Linnea dragged her feet across the hall. The door closed quickly behind her, its draft chilling her backside. She shivered involuntarily, hearing the flip-lock fall. Moments later, the parents were laughing again.

"I think pets make people more responsible," Rick was saying now. "If my folks had only let me have a dog as a kid, I'm sure I would have been a much more responsible parent when I had you." He broke off the corner of his marionberry scone. "What's wrong? You look upset."

"I'm not upset," she lied. The bergamot wafting from the tea of the networking realtor next to her stung her sinus tissue. Brutus had been a regular torment until the Pilchuck Society for Prevention of Cruelty to Animals came by one day. They cited Gunter for having such a large dog on a small lot and fined him for failing to consider the dog's best interests. They sent Brutus to a kinder, more suitable home in the country where he could be free to run and play.

Linnea's nostrils flared.

"Look, honey," Rick said. "If you are upset...or angry, I can take it. Lay it on me. Here," he pushed his hot cup of coffee toward her, "just pick this up and throw it at me."

The realtor snapped her laptop shut and hurried to a table clear across the shop.

"I know I deserve it. Go ahead." He leaned back in his chair, like a do-gooder volunteer in the charity dunking booth.

She eyed his leather jacket. She couldn't ruin it. Damn it! She didn't want to be angry with him. She resorted to the shallowest of breathing, denying oxygen to the fire in her eyes. Shrouding her face in a veil of gaiety, she said, "I'm not angry. I just don't want a dog."

"No dog," Rick agreed, instantly at ease. He popped a piece of scone into his mouth. "I have a cat in Hawaii. Do you like cats?"

As a child, she'd had a black one whose sandpaper tongue provided the only comforting touch available after an incident with Gunter. She always figured it thought of her as Salty Girl. "Mom has seven."

Rick whistled. "That's good company. I miss my cat terribly. In fact, when we go next month, I'll bring her back with us."

She wondered if her anger had obscured something he'd just said. "When we go? Where?"

"To Kauai, of course. I've got a call into my travel agent now. How long can you and Dan get away?"

Linnea panicked at his assumption of her affluence. "Dad, we can't afford to fly to Hawaii right now."

"The whole trip is on me. You won't have to spend a cent. Of course, if we visit the Kona Coast, Dan could write some of it off on his taxes, right?"

She hadn't been on an airplane since before September 11, 2001. "Of course I want to go, but is it safe? What about all the cut-backs in maintenance? Airline security? I have Megan to consider."

"I won't let anything happen to you. To either of you."

For a moment, she let herself bask in unfamiliar parental largess, his empty locket warm against her chest. It felt wonderful. Megan took gifts from Linnea and Dan as easily as she embraced a sunny day. Now, it was Linnea's turn to take and Rick's turn to give. She stared down at her hands so that her father, her public, *The Edge*'s readers, and Dan's customers would not see her eyes welling up with love and joy at the justice of it all. As she twisted her wrist, the red glass ring glittered in the dull winter light passing through the window.

"I want to show you a good time," Rick said. "I think you need it. And when Dan starts doing business with the Spinners, he'll be able to take you on trips and buy you your own car himself."

Slamming a chair down beside her, Dan said pointedly, "We choose to have one car. It's a political statement."

"That's really noble. I'm impressed, but my lawyers are writing our contract as we speak. It's a good deal, Dan. Twenty-five home games, two thousand adults per game, and an average of sixty degrees Fahrenheit each evening. Hot coffee ought to sell better than ice cream or sno-cones, eh?"

Dan was clearly calculating in his head. "We'll need another roaster to keep up."

"There goes my new car," she teased, "and probably the whole first season's profit."

Rick eyed the packed café. "Where would you put a second roaster if you got one?"

"Below." Dan leaned forward excitedly. "We can tap into the existing gas line and route it downstairs."

"Which is where we used to live," she told Rick. "When we started out, we couldn't afford the rent on two places. We already had a kitchen here, so we put a shower in downstairs and slept on an air mattress for two years."

"Wow, you two really were bohemian. You have great values."

She wasn't used to having her values judged as if they were accessories. "We did what we had to."

Rick scanned the café. "Couldn't you just trade up for a

bigger roaster?"

"Then we'd have to nitro-flush," Dan said disdainfully.

Rick appeared confused, so Linnea explained. "If you use a big roaster, you have to use water to cool the beans before you take them out. Otherwise, they'd be so hot, they'd ignite. If you have to water the beans, you also have to flush them with nitrogen to remove the oxygen from the water. Otherwise, the beans degrade too fast. The process tends to make the coffee taste flat."

"I roast small batches, so I never have to nitro-flush," Dan said proudly. "And I never want to. The Big Green had to start flushing when they began expanding."

"He means Coffeestalk. They roast mind-boggling big batches at a time. They've always been a threat to us. They have shops all over Pilchuck, but they just haven't made it to Spinning Wheel Bluff yet."

"That reminds me," Dan said, "an L.C. mechanic was in this morning. He says L.C. is taking his newest billboard ads down because of your paper."

"Really?" She was excited. "All of them?"

He glowered. "I wish you'd keep me posted about things like this. I hate not knowing what's happening whenever the customers mention *The Edge* to me."

"Dan!" His sobering-up mood swings still unnerved her. "I've been telling you about the response to my editorial for two weeks."

"Who's L.C.?" Rick inquired, like a diplomat pushing peace.

"Luxury Cars, Incorporated. The owner is Lionel Cox. Get it? Those are also his initials? Cox just put up five huge billboards in the greater Pilchuck area. On the ads, his face is double the size of the Opulence sedans he sells. I wrote an editorial suggesting that most consumers care more about the quality of the product they buy than what the person who sells it looks like. *The Edge* was swamped with letters agreeing with me."

"I didn't know that," Dan grumbled. Sometimes it seemed that only interest he had in her writing was to ascertain that his weekly coupon had been given a prominent spot in the current edition.

"Yes, you did," she said firmly. "I told you." She was embarrassed he'd carry on like this. Lowering her voice, she said, "If you would read *The Edge* occasionally, you might know what the customers are talking about."

"In case you forgot, I'm having a personal crisis and I'm busy." Illustrating his point, he gestured toward a barista who was having trouble. "If you'll excuse me." He hurried away to adjust the spout on the espresso machine.

Rick took a long, satisfied swig of his dark-roasted drip. "You know, Linnea, you are a lot smarter and a great deal more powerful than you look."

It had been a long time since anyone had complimented her. On one hand, Linnea was deeply gratified he noticed her accomplishments. On the other, it was difficult to feel smart and powerful around someone who constantly reminded her of how she'd felt as a four-year-old.

Megan skipped over to them waving an extra-large gingerbread cookie. The sleigh bell tied to The Mill's front door jingled merrily. Linnea turned her head in time to see Dwarfy sail in, floating four feet above the ground.

Peeking out from behind the pointed garnet cap, Chelsea winked mischievously. "Guess who wants to share that cookie with you?" she set him down beside the delighted child. "I stopped by the office for some paperwork, and he told me you'd all be here. He was lonely." She slid into a chair, flashing a peace sign at the barista. The girl nodded, pulling two golden mugs from beneath the counter. "Did you hear about the billboards?"

Linnea nodded. "I love our readers." Damn it. She still had to tell them the bond they had passed wouldn't be honored. She had so much love, gratitude, hurt, and confusion swirling around in her mind that she knew it was foolish to add any more stimulant to the mix. Nonetheless, she quickly drained her mug to loosen the lump in her throat and then lowered it slowly, cautiously, as if an emptied cup could implode on its own volition.

A stranger was crossing the stone floor silently, heading right toward her. The moment his sable eyes met Linnea's, an intense pang of wistfulness shot through her. She smiled shyly. He smiled back as if she were the only other person in the room.

"This is Shane Carpenter," Chelsea said. "He lives in Arizona, but he'll be here until next September, lightening the caseload at Knight's Physical Therapy."

A steady life force radiated from him. Linnea could feel it. She was intrigued.

Rick smirked slightly. "Is that Knights? As in Jedi?"

Shane was not ruffled a bit, but given her attraction to his energy, Linnea found her father's quip highly offensive. People in the United Kingdom claimed Jedi as their religion during the census. *He could be one.* "Welcome to Spinning Wheel Bluff and The Mill," she said warmly. "Remember, since your office is so close, you can call the café for delivery if you are ever too busy to get away."

He smiled warmly at her. "Thank you. That's good to know."

Chelsea said, "Knights just bought a series of ads to introduce him to the clientele. I brought him over here to get hooked on Mill mochas, so he knows where to get a fix from day one."

Rick sucked his cheek in slightly. "Are you interested in working for the Spinners? We could use an on-call physical therapist this season."

"Thank you for the offer." Shane inclined his head slightly. "But I only want to work a few days a week while I'm out here. I generally prefer to set my own hours, and I don't like to be on call."

Chelsea unobtrusively set a mocha in front of him. Shane nodded his appreciation and took a sip.

"Oh, I see," Rick sounded disappointed. "Well, of course we'd pay a generous retainer fee and substantial overtime if we needed you beyond the regular workday."

"Dad, he doesn't want to."

Shane wiped his mouth with a napkin. "I'm just not interested. Some injuries take their own sweet time to heal, and I don't want to be pushing folks back into the playing field before it's appropriate. That usually leads to more and sometimes permanent damage."

Rick nodded curtly. He folded his arms across his chest and leaned back in his chair. Unperturbed, Shane went on, "Besides, I'll be leaving town before the baseball season ends. My spa in Sedona is scheduled to open in September."

"I've heard Sedona is a hot spot for healing," Linnea said. "Something about an energy vortex, right?"

Shane's eyes twinkled at her. "I've heard the same about this area. I intend to check it out."

Her curiosity was piqued, but her memory was triggered. "Thanks for reminding me, I still need to contact the county about a zoning issue. Thanks for the walk, Dad. Finish up, Megan. We have to get home so I can write my article." Linnea excused herself and went outside to make the call on her cell phone. From the other side of the window, she kept an eye on her daughter.

Megan broke off a piece of her gingerbread and set it on a napkin in front of her dwarf. She broke off a second piece and set it down beside Shane's mocha. He nodded the subtlest of thanks. Then, with an uncharacteristically coy wink at him, Megan ate the rest of the cookie herself.

Chapter Eight

Friday evening, Dan went to his AA meeting. Clary Sage watched the evening news and folded laundry in the family room. Linnea and Chelsea sat at the dining room table, staring glumly at old editions of *The Edge.*

"I feel guilty." Linnea stirred her hot chocolate, "He's forcing the children to keep going to that decrepit old school."

"It's not your fault."

"It doesn't seem like anyone can stop him from doing what he wants to do."

"That's why my dad says it's a good thing the people at the Spinners' headquarters *like* the changes he's making."

Linnea's chest felt tight. "We have to act now. The *Pilchuck Times* will find out soon. I'll write it up in an editorial as a fairy tale family reunion story, explain the problem, and confess my ambiguity about this whole situation. Our readers will understand that, if I'm open. And *The Edge* can still advocate getting the old school cleaned up so kids and teachers don't get sick."

"But if the district has to put that much money into

renovating the old building, they might give up on ever building a new school in the village."

Linnea pressed her solar plexus into the table as if that would help her exhale. *What if everyone thinks I've been seduced by his money and don't care about Spinning Wheel Bluff anymore?*

"Maybe you and Rick could get on a talk show," Chelsea said encouragingly. "People eat this type of thing up. We'd better start working ahead, though, because there's no way I can do the paper by myself during the weeks you're sunning your Snow White complexion in Kauai."

Ah, Kauai. At least, there she wouldn't have to answer to anybody for loving her dad.

Chelsea pulled her nutritional chart from her purse. "I need to eat one more red thing by eight o'clock."

Certain her friend's dietary obsession was a false front for her fear of breast cancer, Linnea always tried to keep up with the color Chelsea was on and took care to stock her shelves accordingly, but she'd neglected to go to the store since Rick's return. "Sorry. All I've got is a red pepper in the fridge."

Chelsea went to the kitchen and returned with the pepper and a paring knife. "Hey, is your dad going to book an extra seat on the plane for Dwarfy? If you try to stuff him in an overhead compartment, he's likely to tumble out and crush someone."

A strange squeaking startled them. Turning toward the foyer, Linnea caught sight of little bare feet slowly feeling their way across the carpeted steps. Megan clutched the oak rail with one hand, covering her eyes with the other. "Eek! Eek! Eeky Eek!"

Linnea dashed toward the stairs. "What's the matter?"

"I'm trying to echolocate a drink of water," Megan said, parting two fingers to peer at her, "like bats."

They'd read that bats detect both their dinner and direction by emitting high-frequency sounds that bounce off potential prey and obstacles. Amused, she asked. "And how's it going?"

"The cups aren't calling me back." Megan dropped her arms, frustration knitting her fawn-brown eyebrows together.

"Well...water calls me." Linnea gestured for her to come down. "Try calling the water instead."

Megan clenched her eyes shut, making strange caterwauls as she tiptoed through the family room toward the kitchen. Following to make sure she didn't bump into anything, Linnea heard the television newscaster say, "Several women were gunned down in Afghanistan today when the Taliban raided an illegal literacy program in the back room of a medical clinic."

Turning, she caught sight of a three-second image of women in full black burkas fleeing a stone building. A member of the Taliban followed, firing a machine gun at them. One fell to the ground. The hatred in the murderer's eyes seemed strangely familiar.

Clary Sage clicked the remote off, but Megan had already removed her blinders. "Bats, Mommy."

An image of the fallen woman's soul transforming into a bat and soaring far away from her body alighted from the recesses of Linnea's retina. "Bats out of Afghanistan," she whispered.

"I'm a bat," Megan said. "Eek, eek, eek!"

Upset by the news on T.V., Linnea calmly helped her daughter in the kitchen, tucked her back into bed, and returned downstairs. All the while, she felt an urgency, a need to get to work, to write, to do something, however minimal, that could help make the world a better place.

Clary Sage sat cross-legged by a pile of towels. The bruise on her pale cheek appeared more turgid than it had seemed over supper. "Do you have any ibuprofen? I have a terrible headache all of a sudden and your bottle in the kitchen is empty."

She shouldn't have let it run out. "I'm sorry. I was going to buy some next time I went grocery shopping."

Clary Sage sighed. "I guess I'll just go to bed, then."

"I bet the drugstore is still open. Do you feel able to walk over and get some? I'd go for you, but I've really got to get back to work."

Clary Sage hesitated. "I can probably get by without it."

"Here." Linnea pulled her purse from the hook by the front door. "Take my credit card. Buy a big bottle."

Clary Sage took the plastic, gratefully. "Fresh air would do me good." She put on her coat and shoes, and left.

Linnea found she couldn't concentrate on her article about edible landscape and global warming. Instead, she reread her old piece about the Pilchuck mosque, scanning her page on notable Islamic women. With a bright pink highlighter, she marked the bit about the sixth-century female founder of the Sufi element of Islam, Rabia al-Adawiyya, who had been a poet and mystic. She also underlined information about the Prophet Muhammad's progressive, egalitarian marriages. She would give it to Clary Sage to give her talking points to convince Hommy to let her start college. Let her!

She worked doggedly, surprised by how shaken she still was by the news report. After all, it wasn't the first time she'd seen someone killed on television. For quite awhile, the only sound she heard was the passing of cars on the road outside, the scratch of Chelsea's sketching pen, and the clattering of her own keyboard. When the phone on her desk rang suddenly, she answered with trembling hands.

The warm, friendly voice on the other end of the line quickly made her relax. "Hello. This is Sandy Pullyplug down at the Dent-a-Drug." The woman chuckled. "I've been working this job for over a year now and it still cracks me up to say that. Anyway, listen, I've got a young lady down here at the counter using your credit card. She's buying some pain reliever for that shiner of hers and a little essential oil that I recommend to calm her nerves and help her remember who she really is. Is that okay with you?"

"It's fine. She can get whatever she needs."

"Blessed Be! I'll fix her right up. You're the editor of *The Edge*, right? Loved that piece about the billboards. I'm the one who wrote in saying they looked like the propaganda Saddam Hussein hung up all over Iraq. My friends and I were pleased as punch you actually printed it, and a little surprised."

So that was why the name was so familiar. "That was a good letter and it helped. L.C. took its billboards down today."

"Yeah, well, I called L.C., too. Said I'd been planning to buy a car from them, but decided to skip it after reading your paper."

People are good. "Send us another letter sometime."

"I'll do that."

Clary Sage returned from Dent-a-Drug, her eyes sparkling like jewels. Her bruise appeared less swollen.

Her forehead shone with the residue of a thin oil, which also glowed at the base of her neck. "Doesn't this smell good?"

Chelsea squinted suspiciously at the injury. "What is that stuff?"

"Wait! Don't tell me." Linnea sniffed. "I know what it is...it's clary sage!"

She beamed. "I never knew clary sage was an herb. I thought my mom and dad just got drunk one night and made up a stupid name to punish me for being born. I'm going to go to bed now, to get some rest before Serengeti needs another bottle."

I'm glad that made her feel better, but she is so easily influenced. Like a lamb among wolves, really. I'd better watch out for her.

They worked another hour before the phone rang once more. "Hi there. This is Sandy again. Sorry to call so late, but do tell your friend the Nia Technique class begins at 10:30 on Sunday. She can bring the baby if she needs to."

"Nia?" Linnea didn't want to pry into Clary Sage's business, but she wasn't sure she'd heard right.

"Neuromuscular Integrative Action. The program combines creative dance with martial and healing arts. Mind-body-spirit. My daughter, Robin, teaches it. Got her training from Debbie and Carlos Rosas themselves, down in Portland, you know. I'm sure you agree it's better for Clary Sage to dance her spirit instead of shrouding her soul."

What had Clary Sage told this woman? Linnea grabbed the mosque-opening article and scribbled the start time in the margin.

"Oh, and I also want to say my friends and I love that bit you wrote asking why, if men evolved to be the hunters, they can't find anything in the refrigerator... even when it's right in front of their faces. What a hoot!"

Dan entered the kitchen just as she hung up. "Linnea!" he called "Where's the mustard?"

* * *

Later, in their bedroom Dan said, "I was surprised when your dad showed up at my AA meeting tonight. He walked right in, sat down, and said, 'I'm Rick and I'm an alcoholic.' He's joining our group so he can support me. He's sponsored a lot of people in the past. He said I could call him anytime I felt the urge to drink."

Dan seemed so relieved. "I'm glad, honey." She patted his arm encouragingly, sending telepathic gratitude to Rick, hoping it would infuse his hotel room downtown.

"He shared some personal information with the group. I can't tell you what he said, confidentiality and all, but I can tell you, you would have hated the stuff he used to do." He sat on the edge of the bed, looking her squarely in the face. "Even he said it's a damn good thing he didn't raise you. You wouldn't have turned out at all."

June and Gunter had disliked him so much there'd never been room for her to express herself regarding Rick, but she needed to say something now. "It really hurts that he wasn't able to pull himself together when I was a little girl who needed a daddy." She choked up, looking into Dan eyes, longing for him to stroke her hair, rub her back, or hold her.

He stiffened. "He couldn't have done that. He was a jerk in those days."

Her grief was acute; her generosity authentic. "But I'm glad he can be a mentor for you. She pasted a blissful smile upon her face and forced it to stick, even as she drifted off to sleep. Like an enchanted princess who succumbs to a slumbering spell, she could only weep in her dreams.

* * *

In the morning, Rick called, asking Linnea to join him on an errand or two. Dan was spending the rainy day at home to caulk the bathrooms and give his assistant manager some practice manning the café alone before their trip to Hawaii. Leaving Megan with him, Linnea happily climbed into Rick's rental coupe. She wiped the wet soles of her shoes on the floor mat just as a thoroughbred at the tracks paws the ground behind the starting gate. She was ready to make up some lost time.

They passed out of the village. He drove with one fingertip resting on the steering wheel. As he accelerated, he turned to smile at her. She quickly averted her gaze to appraise the traffic ahead of them, but did not command him to pay attention to the road while he was driving. Dan would not have escaped a reprimand.

Rick swerved to avoid rear-ending the station wagon in front of them. While he fumbled with the windshield wipers, she glanced sideways at him again. She had printed a very tongue-in-cheek Highway of Life section in the paper last year. Readers had written in, each revealing how her man's driving style compared with the way he made love. One guy habitually sped and cut other drivers off. His partner noted he was always where he wanted to go long before she even settled into her seat. Another woman's husband constantly tailgated the car in front of him. In bed, she was frequently rammed by his careless elbows and knees. Watching Rick at the wheel, Linnea decided it was no wonder that he had been divorced so often. She censored her imagination quickly.

"Here we are," he said grandly as they turned into L.C.'s parking lot.

"What are we doing here?"

"I need to return this rental today, and now that I'm home to stay, I need to get myself a car."

"Here?" She wasn't sure why she was so incredulous. He owned a baseball team and a spacious beach house in Hawaii. Of course, he would buy a car from L.C.

She amused herself by peering into the luxurious interior of a sporty convertible while he engaged in a low-toned conversation with a sales representative. Soon, he gestured for her to follow them to a full-size, onyx, German-made, Opulence.

Rick didn't even glance at the sticker in the window. "I'll take it."

She couldn't help it. She was impressed.

The salesman handed Rick a key and opened the door for Linnea. Rick nodded, gesturing for her to get in. As she slipped onto the sensuous leather upholstery, he hopped in on the driver's side.

"Return my rental and draw up the paperwork," he told the attendant. "We'll be back after lunch to sign. And be sure to let L.C. know I'm buying this car because he took all of his billboards down, just like *The Edge* suggested."

"Thank you, Dad!" She let the last word linger on her tongue, so they could both enjoy it.

He winked at her and started the engine. What a far cry from the sticky vinyl in the unreliable clunker June had driven during her childhood! Linnea couldn't resist the temptation to stroke the smooth mahogany of the dash.

"This is fun." She giggled, trying to read the price on the outward facing driver's side sticker. The January gloom didn't help to illuminate it, but she could see six digits before the decimal point. "Are you really buying this?"

"Did you want me to get something else?"

"I kind of liked the green Jag." she teased.

"You'd look incredible driving it. It matches your eyes beautifully. If you're a very good girl this year, maybe Santa Claus will bring it to you for Christmas."

"Like I could afford the insurance." She furrowed her brow. "I'd rather have a mini-van and start a college fund for Megan, if you're offering to play Kris Kringle on that scale. But really, Dad, this car costs as much as my mortgage."

He shrugged. "I'm lucky. I can afford what I want. What do you think about that?" He bit his lower lip, as if a lot were riding on her answer, and he didn't want to give away what it was.

Linnea felt the locket around her neck. "I think," she said slowly, "that I could have gone all through college, and even earned a Ph.D., for less than this car costs."

Rick's eyes widened. "Is that what you want, a Ph.D.?"

She shrugged, remembering the gut-wrenching stress she'd experienced trying to get the scholarship that paid for her undergraduate work. Her little brothers had pounded on her bedroom door, wanting her attention as she wrestled with algebra. She'd pushed her desk and chair in front of it to keep them out so she could concentrate. She grappled with abstract equations while Gunter, lying on the floor in front of the television, bellowed from the front room for her to bring him bowls of black cherry ice cream.

"God," Rick said, "You really are smarter than you look. If you want a Ph.D., honey, I'll pay for you to go back to school."

Retroactive wistfulness hit her once again. Where was

he when she was a high school senior assigned to work the bar because the seedy restaurant manager knew the customers would buy more when they saw her at the tap? She'd endured horrendous comments for six months until her scholarship awards were announced. Why did she have to go through all that for a lower level degree, if her Dad was going to come back to town later and hand her a Ph.D. on a silver platter? Linnea banished her warehoused memories.

She made herself smile gratefully. "I don't think this is the right time for that."

"Later, then." Rick smiled proudly at her. "Just tell me when."

He could afford whatever he wanted and that meant, that as his beloved daughter, she could afford to relax. She didn't even think to ask him where they were going. He drove the Opulence toward the shoreline. Linnea let herself succumb to the sensations of wealth. She enjoyed the unruffled ride in the luxurious car, especially after he tuned the radio to a smooth jazz station without knowing it was her favorite.

"It's genetic," she told him giddily.

Soon enough, however, he pulled up to a beachfront building on a busy thoroughfare not far from the center of Spinning Wheel Village. The black wrought-iron gates leading into the yard matched the glossy exterior of his new car. The home's Mediterranean architecture and white stucco was unusual for the Northwest, appearing even more out of place as the dreary sky overhead grew increasingly blacker and the whitecaps pounding across Puget Sound in the background grew grayer. A *Sale Pending* sticker was slapped across the realtor's sign bobbing in the breeze beside Linnea's window.

"Home sweet home," he said.

Linnea bit her bottom lip to keep her jaw from dropping. "You're buying this, too?"

Rick smiled at her with misty eyes. "I think we could have some great family barbecues here, don't you?"

"More like royal family balls." She saw herself in a shimmering gold gown, greeting guests at the front door. *Oh no, you don't, Linnea. He's putting Spinning Wheel Bay children at risk. Don't you dare get caught up in his lifestyle.* But the little girl inside her was jumping up and down, pirouetting with the pleasure of planning a big party. She blurted, "Can we go inside?"

"Of course, Cinderella. The realtor is waiting for us. Wait until you see the fireplace. I can't wait to hang Megan's stocking there next Christmas."

During the tour, the laughter of the overly-solicitous saleslady echoed over palatial marble floors and bounced off granite countertops. Linnea found the sound far more unnerving than Megan's attempts at echolocation had been. Her earlier elation collapsed. She withdrew to stand alone, watching her breath form condensation on the cold wall-size window overlooking the rollicking shore, barely listening to Rick and the realtor discuss the gold-plated faucets in the kitchen.

She had the vaguest memory of watching her exhalations turn to mist while staring out the window of another empty house. Even her father's background banter with a fawning woman seemed awfully familiar. As she tried to tie a memory to her sense of déjà vu, a seagull landed on the variegated gray-brown gravel leading to the water's edge. Fluttering its wings slightly, it beguiled her. "Want to fly away?" it seemed to be saying.

Planting her feet on hard stone, Linnea gripped the cold windowsill. "No. I'm hanging out with my dad today."

Chapter Nine

Rick drove into the crowded lot of a strip mall across town from Spinning Wheel Bluff and parked in front of a new delicatessen. "Since German is the order of the day, I say we give this German deli a spin. I've heard nothing but rave reviews about this place."

Linnea nodded, admiring the high-peaked gables and the blue scalloped trim. The rose mauling on the stenciled boxes lining the outside windows of the eatery reminded her of Mulberries, Dwarfy's original home. The owners of the deli had filled the planters with silk geraniums as red as the dwarf's cap, hoping to ward off mid-winter gloom.

Inside, the deli smelled of spicy pastrami, dill pickles, and fresh rye, which threatened to inflame her sinuses. She ignored the sensation, avoiding the potato chips that a little boy was spilling on the hardwood floor, and admired the tempting variety of red meats and orange cheeses displayed in the glass counter. She studied the daily specials scrawled across the chalkboard over the cash register while Rick skimmed a paper menu.

The blonde, broad-faced owner behind the counter greeted them enthusiastically. "You're the editor of *The*

Edge! I recognize you from the picture by your column. I totally agree that we need to support the public library."

Linnea enjoyed the recognition in front of her father.

"I didn't realize people all the way over here read *The Edge*," he interrupted. "I thought it was a neighborhood phenomenon."

After she took their order, the woman exclaimed, "Linnea! I've got something that would be perfect to donate to your Fairy Tales for Tots campaign. Give me a minute. I'll bring it out to see if you can use it." She handed Rick his change and vanished.

Rick pulled a chair out for Linnea at a small table draped in red-and-white checked cloth. "I give to charitable causes myself," he said, pushing her chair in after she sat down. "Every year, I send money to a boarding school in Mexico to care for kids who don't have parents of their own. They write to me each December, addressing their letters to Father Christmas. I make it a point to answer all of them. I've done it for about fifteen years."

Linnea's mind wandered to the socio-political realm, to orphans in Iraq and abandoned children in Afghanistan who were preyed upon by the Taliban. Poor things. Like the incongruous crack of a jolly Santa's whip on tender reindeer hide, a question suddenly lashed out of her lagging consciousness. *Why didn't you ever write to me or send me a box of school supplies?*

Before the welt of abandonment rose within her, she censured herself. She'd had plenty of school supplies in the United States. No need to begrudge the Mexican beneficiaries of her father's gifts.

She stirred her sparkling water with a red straw. Scrying in its crimson swirl, she had a vision of herself as a child, wearing a crisp white shirt embroidered with bright Tyrolean flowers and green corduroy jeans. She was waiting for her meal at a German deli just like this one. At the time, she hadn't wanted to order a sandwich for reasons peculiar to her six-year-old mind. "Why do we have to eat here?" she'd asked anxiously, washing hands in the restroom.

"Because Cousin Greta is visiting," June explained. "She's making Gunter, I mean Daddy, miss German food. He didn't grow up in America, you know. He was born in The Netherlands and raised in Germany where she still lives."

This Cousin Greta was an interesting woman. Platinum blonde, she wore a real rabbit fur coat that smelled strongly of cigarette smoke. The light brown hair on her legs splayed like flattened cow licks beneath the constricting nylons she wore under a tight black leather skirt.

Linnea sat beside Gunter at the table. His buttocks and thighs spread beyond the seat of his chair into her space. The scent of rye in the restaurant made her nose itch terribly. While he heaped stinky sauerkraut onto his plate, she tried to stifle the sneeze that might call attention to herself, that might make him force her to eat some of that nasty stuff, too. Thank goodness, June had remembered her allergy.

"You'll like it," June promised, pushing pastrami on white toward her.

"Too bad if you don't," Gunter said. "I paid for it. You're gonna it get down your throat."

The pastrami was spicy, but she liked it. It was the first time Linnea had ever seen shredded lettuce on a sandwich, but somehow it was better that way than as loose leaves in a salad. She relaxed as she ate, entertaining herself trying to understand the talk around her. Gunter had reverted to speaking German with tall, heavy-boned Greta, while June fussed over the baby.

As he ate more and more, he grew happier and happier. Linnea always felt much better when Gunter was in a good mood. She smiled.

"Hey, where are you?" Rick asked. "Our lunch is ready." He set Linnea's red plastic basket upon her paper placemat.

For the first time she could remember, her real father was serving her something to eat. Dan had prepared Megan's meals hundreds of times. Granted, Rick had just ordered a stranger to make it for her and carried it to the table. He hadn't spent four minutes and forty-one seconds babysitting a temperamental toaster to ensure the even browning Megan required, but he'd paid for what Linnea wanted. She smiled, deeply contented.

He settled into his seat opposite her, happily. "So what do you want to do in Kauai? Where do you want to go? Your wish is my command."

"Well, what *can* we do there?" Linnea realized she sounded like a child, asking what was permissible. Well, maybe she was. He was paying for all of it.

"Snorkel, boat, sunbathe on a secluded beach, go horseback riding, or hike. We could eat out at fabulous restaurants and go dancing. We'll have to get you a grass skirt, sign you up for hula lessons, and make sure you have a fresh lei to wear every day."

She nearly shivered with delight. What luxury. *He must really love me.* "The lei sounds a little excessive, but I've always wanted to take dancing lessons. The closest I've ever gotten is aerobics at the Y."

Rick looked disturbed. "All little girls should have dance lessons."

"Megan just started ballet. She's so cute out there, leaping and pirouetting in her pink leotard." Linnea thought of Clary Sage starting her Nia class.

"Here I am, finally." The owner was at her elbow. "Getting these made in the States has been a challenge, but I've finally found the right chocolatier." She handed her a gold box. "Look. Won't these be perfect for a fundraiser to put fairy tales into the hands of needy children?"

As she stared through a clear plastic lid at a solid white chocolate letter L, her vision grew blurry. Her hands began to tremble. She'd seen a glittering box just like this before.

On that day long ago, she had smiled at her second Daddy's congenial engorgement. Cousin Greta had remarked, "She's a pretty little thing, Gunter." Pointing to the hutch on the wall, she suggested, "Buy her a sweet."

Linnea turned around to see what she meant: a display of dark, milk, and white chocolate letters, each in their own boxes, faced out on wrought-iron shelves. Gunter and Greta got dark chocolate G's. June chose a box with a white chocolate J inside. The white chocolate letters were gorgeous.

"I want a white one, too, please," Linnea said eagerly. "It's more vanilla."

He grunted impatiently. "There aren't any white L's. So be quiet and get a brown one."

She knew from experience that Gunter was not always truthful about the availability of the things she wanted. She climbed down from her chair and stood before the hutch, searching for the desired candy.

"How about an E?" June suggested. "For your middle name, Elizabeth."

"It has to be for her first name," Gunter said gruffly. "That's the tradition."

"Who ever said that?" Greta whispered. "*Mein Gott,* it's just *schokolade* for a child. Give her what she wants. The shape of it doesn't matter."

Gunter said to his wife, "Make her take the L that's there."

Linnea heard the dangerous note in his voice, but her mind was focused on what she wanted. She'd just recognized something in the alphabetical array on the shelves, and a brilliant idea was forming in her brain.

"I'll have the A," she announced triumphantly. Confident that she had her mother and Greta's backing, she prepared to present the perfect argument. "When I was born, my last name was Andersen." She met her stepfather's glower with a joyful grin. "I can have the white chocolate A for Andersen."

Before she even registered what was happening, Gunter had grabbed her by one of the French braids plaited tightly to her skull and jerked. With her ear drawn to her shoulder, her neck doubled over dangerously.

Fear flooded her senses. Gunter's tight grip and terrifying gaze spewed poison all over her body. Tears sprung from a deep well within her, desperately trying to wash it off, but the chaotic vibrations of his rage continued, penetrating her skin.

"Don't EVER mention that asshole's name again," he bellowed.

The hot spice of the sausage on his breath transported his hostility up her quavering nostrils. Hatred scalded the interior of her skull.

"Your daddy didn't want you, little girl. So you don't deserve squat." The way he said "girl" sounded like obscenity. "A little piece of shit like you doesn't deserve to get what you want."

Linnea looked toward her mother. June sat white-faced and silenty, apparently, unbelievably, colluding with him. Gunter yanked Linnea's golden hair again. "Look at *me* when I talk to you, you little bitch."

June pulled the first baby brother's high chair a little closer to herself, rotating it away from the scene that was somehow acceptable for the child locked into it, but not for the other to witness. Linnea suddenly knew with every ounce of her being, every spasm of her bowed neck, that her life had taken a wrong turn.

"Don't look to your mother," Gunter yelled. "Look at me." He twisted her vertebrae. She thought the tyrannical ogre would snap her head off if she did not obey immediately. She fixed her eyes on him as he'd insisted, but refused to accept all he said. It was true, her daddy didn't want her, but there was nothing about being a girl that should keep her from having white chocolate. So strong was the force of her will against his that her eyes felt like a magnet repelling another of the opposite pole.

"Don't look at me like *that*," he hissed viciously.

Gunter's fist rose well outside her peripheral vision. She only felt its crushing descent, the first of countless blows to her tender cheek.

Now, while she was still caught in this long-forgotten memory, the friendly owner of the deli asked, "May I donate some for the auction?"

Linnea felt her jaw twitching oddly. She forced her lips into the shape of a gracious smile, expertly shrouding her feelings behind the invisible burka of a pleasant face. "Yes, please," she said, with only the slightest catch in her constricted throat. "These are perfect for Fairy Tales for

Tots."

The woman gestured toward the white chocolate L. "You may have that one, as a gift from me. My grandparents were Dutch, you know. They told me I couldn't open a German deli without keeping these on hand. I'll send a case or two over to your office as soon as I get another shipment in." The woman walked off, obviously pleased to be supporting a favorite cause.

As if the L for Linnea had triggered his memory, too, Rick said, "You know, sweetie, I'll be meeting with my lawyer again this week. I've already asked him once, and he said it would be a simple procedure to change your name retroactively."

Blindsided, Linnea stared at him disbelievingly.

"We could go in and erase Hendricks from your birth certificate and all school records. There's even a way to void your adoption. Would you like to do that? Would you like to become an Andersen girl again?"

Horrified at the prospect of reclaiming that name, Linnea grabbed her purse. Like Cinderella fleeing the ball when the clock struck midnight, she raced out the door. Knocking a window box askew, she darted around the corner of the building. In the alley, with rusting dumpsters and heaps of old junk, she leaned against the German façade and shook like a tiny mouse hiding from a raptor.

She'd done nearly the same thing as a child. She'd run into the hallway outside the toilets and cried. While her parents enjoyed their coffee and chocolate letters, smoky-smelling Greta had joined her. Kneeling beside her, she pulled a book from her handbag. "Here, I just bought this book up at the counter for you. It is a book of fairy tales that the wise women from long ago gave the Brothers Grimm. The stories are written in German and English."

Still sobbing, Linnea reached for the book. Like good fairies with their tales of old, her Andersen aunt and her Cousin Greta had tried to soften the evil spell cast by the daddies. But even then, Linnea realized that it would be up to her to figure out how to break free of the humiliation, if that was even possible.

Altering the maiden name on her legal records twenty-eight years after Rick had given her away to Gunter could not re-write her story. How could he think he could simply erase what she had endured? All Linnea wanted at that moment was to go home to her husband and her child. To her little girl who wasn't afraid of bats and who believed in the power of a garden dwarf.

Rick pulled up to the alley in the Opulence. "How about a ride, Princess?" He leaned out the window. "Even though you don't like my ideas, it's still a lot warmer in here than it is out there."

Linnea got into his splendid coach. She slammed the door hard on purpose. "Don't call me Princess. My name is Linnea Perrault."

Rick nodded without saying a word.

At home that afternoon, Linnea discovered that, despite her distress while leaving the deli, she'd slipped the gold box into her purse. She put the candy on a plate.

"L," Megan announced proudly. "What's it for, Mommy?"

"Love." Linnea shared the creamy white sweet with her daughter. It was as wonderful as she'd known it would be way back when she was six.

Chapter Ten

As winter transitioned into spring, Linnea struggled to balance euphoria and doubt. Her feelings continued to swing back and forth, like the bobbleheads on the dolls Rick ordered to give away during baseball season. She often found herself worrying about what would happen in two years.

She spent a lot of time with Rick. He dropped by her house for frequent visits, and often took her and Megan to lunch whenever he could get away from overhauling the Spinners' organization. Like children with weekend dads who take them to amusement parks, Linnea was beginning to associate her long-lost father with fun, extra whipped cream on the mocha, a jazz CD featuring the piece she'd admired on the radio, a beautifully bound collection of poetry by Emily Dickinson or a new novel that she glanced at through the window of the bookstore. There was no longer any need to put her name on the library's waiting list. Yet despite being drawn to his pleasure principle, she found herself frequently suppressing difficult memories and postponing hard questions, waiting to bring them up until after she and Rick had established a solid enough relationship to deal with them.

June called daily to relate how her life had changed now that her first love was back in town. Once she said, "I saw a black Opulence in my rear-view window pulling in behind me at the gas station! Thank goodness, I pulled away from the pump before he saw me." Another time, she reported, "I almost ran into him at the market, but I turned away, pretending to read labels, so he wouldn't notice me and stop to talk. I just don't know what I'd say if he did."

"Mom?" Linnea asked gently, "If you are so afraid to speak to him, why have you encouraged me to have a relationship with the man?"

"I can't believe how self-centered you can be," June snapped. "He broke *my* heart a long time ago."

Letters to the editor expressed disappointment that the new school was stalled. Some were even sarcastic with regard to the Spinners staying in town. But overall, Linnea's readers seemed to be as enchanted with the prodigal father story as she was and wished them both well. *Everyone loves a happy ending.*

She'd made little progress on her article about cross-cultural relationships. She'd created a hypothetical couple and she'd even managed to type, "If a person's point-of-view and resulting behavior are the byproducts of their cultural and political processes, then cultures that denigrate and diminish the feminine or the caring associated with it are very likely to produce violent men who demean and limit their wives and daughters."

She realized that's exactly how she'd always explained Gunter's behavior to herself. He'd brought his post-war Nazi upbringing to the United States and dumped it on her. *The Edge*'s readers could have handled her exploring the topic, but Linnea deleted her work, anyway. The *Pilchuck Times* would have gleefully accused her of stereotyping Germans and Muslims and men and women, for that matter.

Speaking of stereotypes and women, she'd never been much of a shopper. Other priorities had prevented it, but now, Linnea enjoyed visiting local stores with Rick, helping him decorate and furnish his new home. One day, a delivery truck pulled in front of her house, and the movers began unloading a dresser for Megan, a crate of dishes, and a carved oak table with chairs for the dining room.

She was elated, but upon glancing out the window Dan yelled, "Linnea, most people bring chips and dip when they come over to watch a game. Not a top-dollar, high-definition television *and* a new cabinet to keep it in!" He slammed the door on their new entertainment center. "Now there won't be a single room in this house without an extravagant gift from your father in it."

Linnea scowled at the hutch, still vibrating from the force of Dan's wrath. Could he have broken the T.V. screen? "You didn't complain when he brought those. This delivery is *my* commission for advising him on house wares. He said I deserve the dining room set I want, not what we culled out from our bulk order of furniture for The Mill."

He pointed an accusatory finger at the black and white Spinners jogging suit she wore. He eyed the spider logo as if he was tempted to pluck it off her right shoulder and flush it down the toilet. "You've never worn team apparel before."

Why would her shirt irritate him so much? Was it possible he was sneaking alcohol again? "Please don't do this, Dan." she struggled to articulate why her father's spending gave her a deep sense of ease about expenses. "I'm not being seduced by his wealth, sweetie. Money has always been tight. I try not to worry about it or let fear guide my choices, but I've always been afraid of being poor, afraid that something terrible would happen and there wouldn't be enough money to take care of essentials, and…"

She broke off. Hadn't June married Gunter because of poverty? "I guess I just figure that if it's easy for him to buy us a T.V. that we only watch three times a year, he wouldn't flinch at buying us a bag of groceries if we were starving." She smiled hopefully. Surely he could understand that?

Dan glared at her. "I've always kept food on the table. Even if was just peanut butter and jelly in the old days." He sighed heavily. "But Rick does owe you something. I guess peace of mind is expensive." He grabbed his keys, pausing to salute the movers as they passed on the front steps.

* * *

Clary Sage became fast friends with her Nia teacher. Robin was a young single mother, too. Her little girl, Susie, was just a few months older than Serengeti. Early one morning, Clary Sage came into the kitchen. "Are you all right?"

Slightly befuddled, Linnea stared at her over the rim of her coffee mug. "Bad dream," she muttered. She'd spent hours stuck in her begging at the bus stop nightmare and hoped a double shot of Red Sky Morning would rouse her from the residual depression.

"Gosh, when I was over at Sandy's house the other day, some of her friends were there. They were all talking about these spider dreams they've been having. None of them are scary, really. Just a lot of web repair and new weaving going on. But, isn't it interesting how totally different women can be having the same dream?" She took a deep breath. "Anyway, I have an announcement to make. I've decided to join a Wiccan circle. Sandy is one of the leaders."

That jolted Linnea awake. "You're going to be a witch?"

Clary Sage's face lit up. "You could come, too. You don't go to church anymore, do you?"

"I haven't been since the priest chose an Easter Vigil reading proclaiming all menstruating women are defiled. How can I teach my daughter to listen to lies?"

"Come to a meeting with Robin and me," Clary Sage pleaded. "We celebrate getting our periods."

"I'm so tempted." She had written an article about Wicca last Halloween and had always wanted to learn more. But right now, her mother and Dan were still adjusting to her having a dad in her life. A new spiritual practice might be too much. When they thought of witches, they thought of the old hag in Hansel and Gretel. They didn't understand that witches were the healers, the wise women, long before the Christians and the physicians lobbies got organized. "I don't suppose you've mentioned this to Hommy?"

Clary Sage crinkled her nose. "We aren't married. He can't tell me what I can or can't do."

"Even if you were married, he shouldn't dictate your life to you." Linnea bit her bottom lip. What had she just been telling herself about not freaking her husband out or alarming her mother? She'd have to think about the dictation of life later. At least, the dark ages of dating

Hommy seemed to be over. She could set her article about relationships like Clary Sage's aside. Thank goodness. She took another caffeine-saturated swig. "When do your meetings begin?"

***

By early March, when the Perraults and Rick were ready to leave for Kauai, Clary Sage had stopped seeing Hommy completely. They no longer even spoke on the telephone. Linnea and Dan didn't worry about leaving the house in Clary Sage's care while they went on their first real vacation ever.

At Sea-Tac airport, Rick strode toward them, grinning. He waved five boarding passes. "They wouldn't discount the dwarf, so I get first dibs on his in-flight pretzels and complimentary beverage."

Linnea kissed him on the cheek. "It's really sweet of you to get him his own seat. Thank you."

"I'm glad I could do it. I know Megan's not about to check him, and she can't keep him on her little lap all that way." Rick wrapped his arm around Linnea's shoulders, turning her toward their boarding gate. "All set for the time of your life?"

"I will be when we get there." She smiled, trying to quell her concerns about airline security.

"Don't worry, sweetheart," Rick whispered. "We're in for a lifetime of smooth sailing and highflying. I won't let anything bad happen to you."

Linnea lifted Dwarfy onto the gray conveyor belt and explained boarding procedures to Megan. Megan waved as cheerfully to her companion as if he were going on the kiddie roller coaster at the Seattle Center, but anxiety gripped Linnea when the resinous beloved disappeared through the black plastic flaps of the X-ray tunnel. "Now, just watch, sweetie, in a second, he'll come out on the other side. Maybe he'll tell you what's in Grandpa's luggage."

Once Dwarfy was back in Megan's arms, his mouth to her waiting ear, Megan smiled mischievously at her. "He says *you* have a box of animal crackers in your purse for me."

Linnea found herself frowning in consternation at Dwarfy for revealing the surprise. She had tucked the animal crackers beneath her camera. Bemused, she peeked into her red leather bag. They were still hidden from human sight.

On the plane, she drew deep, cleansing breaths, although there didn't seem to be enough fresh air to be had in the compartment for everyone on board. Fearing take-off, she dug her nails into Dan's palm while gently stroking the back of Megan's hand. Across the aisle, Rick fussed with his air vents and window shades. Linnea resorted to the soothing mental Hail Mary's of her youth. Surely, the *mother* of Jesus wouldn't fault her reasons for falling away from the church, would she?

Just as the flight attendants were about to bar the door, a dark-skinned, Middle Eastern man hurried on board, panting. The new passenger seemed anxious. He lifted *The Wall Street Journal* Rick had placed on the empty aisle seat beside him and waved it uncertainly in the air. "Yours?"

Reaching for his paper as if offering his hand to an unfamiliar dog, Rick surveyed the stranger from his shiny black shoes to his glossy black crew cut. "Got any luggage to stow?"

"No." The newcomer dropped into his seat and tucked his chin to his chest, mouthing something about Allah.

Arching his neck to look over the man's bowed head, Rick made eye contact with Dan across the walkway.

Dan raised his brows slightly and nodded as if to say yes, we could take him. Rick's eyes widened as he shrank back against his window. Beads of perspiration bubbled across his brow as he tried to focus on the headlines, but he dropped the paper. With trembling hands, he unbuckled his maroon seatbelt hastily and stood. "Linnea, wouldn't you prefer my window seat? It is such a pretty day."

Stymied, Linnea could only gape at her forsworn protector. "Move away from Megan?"

As the seatbelt sign flashed in the front of the plane, flight attendants rushed down the aisle, slamming the doors of overhead compartments. "Sit down now," one barked at Rick.

Obediently, he sank weakly into his seat, shrugging and smiling. "Let me know if you want a bird's-eye-view later."

Linnea wished he could have worn his mask for her just a little longer. She had put on a brave face for Megan, despite the fact that they were all about to die from a mechanical failure, a tragedy that could have been easily averted if someone who was supposed to be responsible had been more careful. Yet, Rick's fear made him seem vulnerable, more real, more like her. She sent heart waves of love to both her parent and her precious child. When she turned to kiss Megan's forehead, she caught Dwarfy's twinkling eye. Somehow, his bearded smile let her know, without a doubt, that they'd all reach their destination.

***

Awakening in his classic plantation house the next morning, Linnea stretched out on the richly padded mattress pretending to be a princess. She breathed in the heady fragrance of the mokihana lei draped over the arm of a rattan loveseat, listening to the low hum of masculine voices emanating from the lanai. Dan and Rick were already awake. Their conversational pauses were punctuated by the rollicking surf on the shore nearby. Delighting in the plumeria print of her quilt and the matching curtains, she wondered if Rick had chosen them with her in mind. Dreamily, she gazed at the shadow of a palm tree swaying gently across the white-washed walls of her room.

She sat up, kicking her tropical pink toenails over the side of the bed. She wrapped herself in her white travel robe, twisting her tousled hair up with a white terry band. She dug a bag of coffee out of her carry-on bag and joined the men beside the pool.

Both Dan and Rick wore Spinners T-shirts that were more wrinkled than the morning paper crumpled between them. Rick's well-padded cat purred in his lap. As if making up for weeks of lost time, Rick petted her vigorously. A hurricane of orange and white cat hair billowed about him, but he didn't seem to notice that he was sitting in the eye of a silky storm.

Enthroned upon a bright pink inner tube, Megan floated in the sapphire blue pool, sporting an oversized Spinners shirt over her red polka-dot bikini. Dwarfy stood guard, smiling at her from atop the diving board.

"Did you put sunscreen on her?" Linnea asked.

Dan sighed melodramatically. "She barely held still long enough for me to put her floaties on. She's got the shirt over her, and she's only been in the water for a few minutes. She wanted to take the dude in with her, but I told her he was allergic to chlorine."

Linnea scowled at him for not protecting Megan's fair skin. "Those floaties are so twisted they're cutting off the circulation in her arms." Awkwardly, she leaned over the pool, grabbed Megan's toe and pulled her to the edge. Megan giggled, staying perfectly still as she straightened the floaties.

Dan sighed loudly.

Soothingly, Linnea said, "I know you want Kona while we're here, but I've brought C Night to get us started this morning."

He rubbed his thumb and forefinger over the stubble on the sides of his chin. "Good thinking," he mumbled apologetically.

"It's mild, but invigorating." She headed toward the coffee maker on the patio bar, knowing she sounded like a commercial. She poured the grind into the basket, cajoling, "Don't grimace, Dan. I milled it minutes before we left for the airport yesterday. It's still good." For her father's benefit, she added, "This coffee wakes you up when your body clock is off without giving you an acidic stomach. I invented it when Megan was a baby. She had croup, and we had to nebulize her around the clock for a few days."

It was obvious from her father's blank stare that he had never heard of croup or a nebulizer. A peevish part of Linnea wanted Rick to suffer from ignorance and confusion for not being around when he was supposed to be. She wanted Rick to love her at least a fraction of how much she loved Megan, to feel some of the fear and panic that had gripped her the night she drove through misty streets toward the hospital with her precious toddler gasping for breath in the backseat. Part of her wanted him to understand how her own chest had constricted when Megan coughed.

Dan didn't give him time to feel remorse or empathy.

"After that, whenever our customers came in, saying they had sick kids, we'd roast a batch of Linnea's recipe and deliver a bag to them at home. We started calling it the Croup Night Special."

Linnea searched for cups. "But a college girl who used to babysit in the village got wind of it and came in asking for a drip when she had to study for finals. By the next afternoon, we had throngs of kids coming in asking for Cram Night Special. C's the standard abbreviation."

Rick sucked his cheek in, nodding approvingly. "Good marketing. Everyone thinks you made it to serve their needs. It surprises me every time I realize how smart you are."

She wanted to take what he said as a compliment. It took her a moment to twist it in her mind and sufficiently turn it into a good one.

Rick smiled at her with paternal pride. "Say good morning to Babe Ruth, Linnea. You don't want to hurt her feelings by ignoring her, do you? She's a sensitive little girl."

The golden sun was shining down. The glorious warm sand and the frothy white surf were calling her to come play. Linnea reminded herself that her relationship with Rick was unusually good for her family. "Good morning, Babe Ruth," she said to the cat on her way inside for the sunscreen.

* * *

For the next ten days, Rick kept the promise he'd made in the German deli: every morning, he had a fresh lei delivered, so that it was waiting for her when she woke up. Years of missed Christmas mornings seemed almost inconsequential as the glorious fragrance wafted from the silky petals across her shoulders.

They all went sightseeing, snorkeling, and sailing. They ate at fabulous ocean-view restaurants and attended tourist-minded attractions, including luaus with hula dancing. Linnea hadn't intended to purchase a muumuu, because she couldn't imagine wearing one in Pilchuck, but after the first few days on the island, she was lulled into a booth at an open-air market in Lihue. She couldn't decide between the deep blue gown with white lilies, the turquoise green splashed with coral hibiscus, or the simple white one. Rick scooped them all up and out of her arms, laid them on the table, and whipped out his wallet. Suddenly, irrationally, it felt as if he had always taken her to buy schools clothes when she was a child. Sure, the adult Linnea felt like a royalty when the vendor handed her a bulging bag, but having a father wasn't about going shopping. Was it? Having a father was about having someone who made sure you got what you needed when you needed it.

Some days, her favorite days, the four of them stayed home, and she savored the time simply spent together. Secluded at the end of a long, tree-lined, gravel road with views of rainbow-wound mountains and the magnificent turquoise ocean, Rick's incredibly private property was magical. In a leafy stand of glorious guava trees and bright tropical flowers, mother and daughter played hide-and-seek with local peacocks. Her father's lush garden embraced them, holding them in its green arms.

When the water beckoned, Linnea and Megan sunbathed and built sand castles on the sun-drenched beach. A long sandbar gave them ample room to wade and swim. One morning, leaving Megan and Dan with a wide array of pails and scoops, Rick and Linnea swam past the edge of the sandbar to a small raft buoyed a distance from shore. Linnea clung to the side to catch her breath, letting her tired legs dangle in the clear water. Dan and Megan seemed tiny. The few boats she could see were a long distance off. She turned toward Rick who held onto the other end of the float. "This is paradise."

"It doesn't get any better," he declared.

Linnea was about to nod, but a strong wave enveloped her legs and pelvis. Such an erratic assault by the water could have been terrifying, yet she felt enveloped by loving kindness. A bottle-nosed dolphin breached, suddenly baptizing her with sea spray. It cavorted closely around them. She could have reached out to touch mammalian flippers, but she didn't.

Wearing a naturally wide smile, the dolphin's joy and playfulness sent a charge of happiness through Linnea. She felt nothing but unity with the entire universe. Her body radiated with the dolphin's ultrasonic song.

Like the wick descending into a pool of molten candle wax, the desire to shed her human skin and take up a life at sea flickered within her. She dared to believe a deeper connection with the creature was possible and wished for it. Slowly, almost teasingly, the dolphin approached. Wiggling from side to side, it lifted its head and nosed her. Bestowed with a loving liquid gaze, Linnea nearly melted into the wetness around them. The dolphin clicked softly. As it slipped beneath the surface, a slow wave rocked over her shoulders. Pleasant chills circulated up and down her spine. It was as the planet herself had sent the dolphin to her. "Thank you," she whispered to the ripples in sea. *I love you, too.*

When she turned to Rick, his mouth was twisted with inexplicable emotion. He shook his head and pushed off the raft, diving into the marine depths. Assuming he'd been deeply touched by the encounter, Linnea gave him some space and watched him swim toward shore.

When his wake subsided, she flipped over. Alternately clicking like a dolphin and humming like a happy woman, she backstroked all the way to the beach.

On the last day of their trip, Linnea and Rick walked through the foliage to a majestic waterfall on the edge of his property. They sat side by side on a flat obsidian stone, dipping their feet into the pool at the base of the waterfall.

"It's so great having you here, honey."

"Dad, this has been an absolutely wonderful trip. Thank you so much for everything. Dan and I really appreciate it."

"I'm glad I'm in a position to be able to share with you. We'll come back here again soon." He plucked a snow-white gardenia from the plant beside them. Gently, he tucked the stem behind Linnea's ear. "You could have had your honeymoon here. I never told you this, but Larry forwarded a copy of your engagement announcement to me when the *Pilchuck Times* printed it. I couldn't believe my eyes when I opened the envelope. In my mind, you'd been an adorable little girl and then suddenly, you were this striking young woman. I called your mother. I told her I wanted you to have the finest wedding possible. I offered to pay for all of it. I wanted to be there. I wanted to be the one to walk you down the aisle and give you away."

She felt incinerating pain boil up from deep within her belly, like flames licking at her heart. She wanted to cry, "You'd already given me away!" but she didn't. She had settled for Uncle Ron that day, and he was already staggering at eleven o'clock in the morning. "Larry is a great guy."

Rick removed his Spinners baseball cap and twirled it

around his finger. "But your mother said that you didn't want to see me." He crushed the hat in his hands. "Was that true?"

"I was getting married. I was finished with fathers." And she had been. She remembered telling June, "Dan is the only man I'll ever need now."

The tears in Rick's eyes made them sparkle like the dew drops on the emerald leaves around them. "But you aren't now?"

Linnea shook her head, whispering, "I'm not finished. I love you."

"I'm glad. I'd been sober for awhile at that point, but on your wedding day, I got so drunk that my buddies had to take me to the emergency room. I wanted to be dancing with you. Instead, I nearly died from alcohol poisoning. That's the last time I ever touched a drop of liquor. I wish I could have been part of all the special occasions in your life. Your birthdays, your Christmases, your graduations."

Linnea imagined him vomiting in a toilet stall while she tossed her budget- conscious grocery store bouquet off the brick steps of the university chapel. Poor man. "I wish you'd been there for all those special days, too. I really do."

"Well, you're stuck with me now. I'll be there for all the special times to come in your life and in Megan's. I'll never let anyone or anything keep me from you again." He replaced his cap upon his silver-streaked hair. "I've told you this before, but if there is anything you ever need to say to me or want to ask me about the past, it's okay. It really is. Don't hold back. Understand?"

What good would it do to say anything about the past now? Why spoil the special time we have left to be together in this lifetime? "Right now, I just want to thank you again for everything, especially for giving Dan the contract. He's had such a hard time lately, but he hasn't even needed to go to AA since we came to Hawaii." Linnea's mind worked rapidly. "Maybe a little help with the business was all he needed."

Rick gazed at her sympathetically. "Don't kid yourself, honey. Admitting he can't control his drinking is tough on a man. It's a real notch off the ego. The best way for him to build himself up right now is to focus on building his business. I'm glad I can help him help himself stay sober." He gently touched the tip of her nose. "I can tell how much you love your family, sweetie. I'm so glad I can help with Megan's education, too, so she can have what you want for her."

"It means more than anything to me to make sure she has a happy childhood. We can only afford the tuition because of you, because of the coffee contract."

"Forget about the contract. I want to pay for her school myself."

His words made her feel more secure than she had ever felt in her life. He understood how much she wanted her daughter to go to a safe school that actually smelled good, where the air was fresh, the water clean, and she had room to move and play. Megan deserved to spend her schooldays surrounded by lots of fine books and plenty of art supplies. *But all children deserve that. And all of Spinning Wheel Bluff's kids could have had that, if you didn't need to fulfill your boyish fantasy.*

"Enough seriousness, you." He had a twinkle in his blue eyes. "Let's go back to the house and have some more macadamia nuts and a big glass of that guava juice you've become so fond of."

As they walked back toward the lanai, she was certain

that her childhood dreams had come true. *I just need a little more time to bring him around to caring about the common good. I'll find a way.* Now that her happily-ever-after had arrived, the wait and the heartbreak to manifest it didn't seem quite so bad.

* * *

That afternoon, overflowing with love, gratitude, and faith in all things fairy tale, Linnea carried a small tray of drinks down to the beach below the white clapboard house. Dan stretched out on a chaise lounge beneath a lone umbrella.

She knelt to kiss him on the mouth. "Megan's asleep." She handed him a glass "From the looks of things, it's going to be a long nap."

"Mai tais?" Dan stared at her incredulously.

"Right. Like I'm going to sabotage your sobriety. It's straight juice for you and only a drop of rum for me. I found a bottle of it in the back of the cupboard. Dad must keep it for company."

"Where is he?" Dan squinted around her shiny, spandex-clad hip as if he expected to see Rick hurrying down the trail behind her, wearing Spinners athletic socks and flip-flops.

"He went into Lihue on business." She bent down to nibble his ear lobe. "So we're all alone...on this secluded beach."

Dan set his glass on the ground, twisting the base deep into the sand, and rose to his feet, instantly knocking his hastily stabilized beverage over. With the sun overhead warming their oiled skin, he stepped close. The salty breeze tickled her thighs while Dan traced the moon-white curves rising over her low-slung halter top. "A woman like you needs a little protection in a place like this," he whispered.

"Can you give me any?" she asked in a low, sultry tone, slipping her free hand under his waistband.

He chuckled, seizing her hips. He gently backed Linnea toward a group of glistening black boulders. She set her Mai Tai on the first rock and slowly pulled his swim trunks down to his ankles. He dropped to his knees and, cradling the base of her neck with one hand, inched her into the stony alcove. Grinning eagerly, he untied the Hawaiian print knot behind her neck and tossed her top into a nearby hibiscus bush. In the soft, deep shelter of obsidian shade, beneath the brilliant blue sky, he removed the rest of her suit.

The capricious wind scoured their bare skin with fine grains of sand while sprinkling rosy hibiscus petals upon their naked flesh. Where the fertile earth joined the fluid sea, their mouths and bodies melded upon the shore.

* * *

Rick grilled shrimp on the lanai that evening. Even at the end of such an extravagant vacation, Linnea couldn't believe how touching it was to watch him actually cook for her. While he added the finishing touches to their plates, she turned her misty eyes toward the gray clouds building in the distance over the increasingly choppy sea. She told herself she shouldn't be turning a little barbecue into such a sentimental occasion. Matter-of-factly, she said, "I guess this storm is telling us it's time to go back to Seattle."

Her father set a plate in the middle of the glass table. She snatched a steaming shrimp right off the serving platter and plunged it into her mouth. Sex had made her hungry enough to forget her manners. "This lime and chili marinade is to die for." She grabbed another piece and bit into it eagerly. Megan glanced down at the empty plate before her and stared at her mother with wonder. She was used to being served first. Guiltily, Linnea gave her some food.

Chewing ravenously, Linnea glimpsed the housekeeper through the panoramic window. Watching Winnie unwrap a vacuum cleaner cord, she felt a small twinge of guilt. Rick had mentioned the woman worked evenings so her husband could watch their young children. Winnie lived on this island, but there was no vacation for her.

"I'm going to stay on here a little longer," Rick said unexpectedly. "Can you fly back by yourselves tomorrow?"

Linnea wondered about how much his change of plans would add to his airfare. "Of course we can fly back by ourselves, Dad."

"Good." he waved to the pool man. "I've got another guest coming in. Do you mind moving Megan into your room tonight?"

"We don't mind at all." Linnea shook her head to emphasize her acquiescence. Sand sprayed out of her hair, falling all over the lanai and sprinkling into her lap. Dan caught her eye. They burst out laughing. Their last afternoon in Hawaii had been well spent.

Rick crinkled his brow. "What's so funny?"

Dan hastily covered his mouth with a napkin, "Who's coming?"

His choice of words brought a round of giggles from Linnea. She knew she was acting like a seventh grader, but she felt so happy that she just couldn't help it.

"Our multi-million dollar man, otherwise known as Pete Stealer."

Linnea stopped laughing. Her shrimp fell from her

fork onto the patio floor.

Rick evidently took her sudden seriousness for extreme interest. "Larry emailed me earlier. He said Pete just returned to Pilchuck from an exhibition tour in South America. Apparently, the trip took a lot out of him. I'm flying our boy down here for two weeks to rest up before spring training. We're gearing up earlier than usual this year and, if all our dreams are to come true, our star player must be primed."

She laid her empty fork down beside her plate. "Actually, I'm not that hungry. I'll go move Megan's stuff now, to make it easier for Winnie." She pushed her chair away from the table and stepped over Babe Ruth who was now devouring her fallen entree.

Rick said to Dan, "As soon as you get back to Pilchuck, you'd better order The Mill banners and the big sign to hang over the scoreboard. We want everything in place by the time we start players' orientation."

Megan's room in the house had become a collecting ground for a variety of garishly colored swimming paraphernalia, blow-up beach toys, damp towels, hula dancer dolls, shells, and stones. Uncertain why she was feeling so strange, Linnea piled the things to leave behind in one corner of the spacious room while laying an open suitcase in another. The sea breeze blew strongly through the open window, but it didn't help to clear her suddenly stuffy head. She packed Megan's bags, leaving out nightclothes and a traveling outfit. She moved it all into the room she shared with Dan, then returned for Dwarfy.

Why did it bother her so much that her father was preparing to host someone else? She had no right to be so perturbed. She should be grateful for what she had been given, for what Rick had given Dan and Megan. So what if he invited someone else to his exclusive retreat on the heels of their special time together? He was deeply invested in Pete's career and it made sense to let Pete recuperate here. It was a good business decision, but why did an absolute stranger qualify for four more days than she did?

Judging herself harshly for such petty thoughts, Linnea dragged all of Megan's fluorescent flotation devices to the large walk-in closet at the end of the hall. Opening the door, she found herself peering into a wicker basket stuffed with ice packs and flax-filled heating pads. The items on the broad shelves before her made Linnea realize how sore her upper back felt. *Maybe we were too kinky on the beach.* She touched a blanket folded neatly next to the basket. Her eyes fell on a wooden box of essential oils.

She opened the compartmentalized box, feeling like a spy. She twisted the lid off a vial of clary sage, inhaling the soothing scent. She hadn't thought much about Clary Sage and Serengeti while in Hawaii. Now, she missed them. *This stuff must belong to my dad's last wife. The hypochondriac.*

It was rude to snoop through her stuff, but she was curious about this other woman. Guiltily, she unzipped a cosmetic case stashed near the oils. Valium and a variety of other prescription drugs used to numb pain were crammed inside. As she stared at her stepmother's little helpers, Linnea's neck suddenly felt weak, weary from holding up her head. She was tempted to borrow one of the pills, but opted to tuck her daughter in and go to sleep herself instead. By the time, baseball's rising star arrived, she and Megan were in Dreamland. Dan met Pete before turning in, but the Perraults left for the Lihue airport the next morning long before he opened his eyes in her paradise.

Chapter Eleven

The Perraults' jet touched down at dusk, descending from an orange twilight sky into dreary gray Northwest drizzle. By the time they disembarked and had driven north to Pilchuck, icy March sleet hinted at hail.

Within hours, Chelsea and Linnea sat at their desks with their chairs turned toward each other, warming their stockinged feet in front of an oscillating space heater. Linnea was still resentful about Pete, but she didn't mention it. "Sounds like you all had a good trip." Chelsea peeled an orange. "How did Dan do?"

"He relaxed and stayed sober, but he kept muttering on the plane, 'I need a drink.' He was just kidding, I'm sure." *Get over it, Linnea. Learn to take a joke.* The problem was, he hadn't sounded lighthearted at all. He'd sounded dead serious.

"He'll probably feel better after he gets back in the swing of going to meetings." Chelsea said reassuringly. She grinned impishly. "By the way, I met someone while you were gone."

Linnea playfully kicked her foot. "You could have told me that first, instead of listening to me go on and on about the dolphin."

"Hey, I happen to like dolphins a lot, really. Anyway, I took Dad back to the stadium last week after he dropped his car off at the shop. Jeff is a paramedic. He was there doing a safety check with fire chief. We got to talking and he asked me out for dinner that night."

I wouldn't have gone with him, Linnea thought. If I were single again, I wouldn't have anything to do with a guy unless I already knew he had a systemic reaction to the *thought* of alcohol.

"We ended up at his apartment for dessert. Double-malted chocolate-crunch."

Linnea hoped Rick's housekeeper would find the ice cream she'd left in her dad's freezer and take it home for her kids. She sure didn't want Pete eating *her* double-malted chocolate-crunch. She chided herself for being so childish about the whole thing. Why was this bothering her so much? "You look really happy. When are you seeing him again?"

"I'm going over to his apartment this evening. It may be the last time I see him there. He's looking around for a new place to rent. He lives in the Stadium Sights complex."

The way Chelsea's brown eyes bore into hers, Linnea felt that she should know more about Stadium Sights than she did. "That brick apartment building with the white trim?"

"That's the one. Your father just bought it to house the players."

That was a big move not to have shared with her. "He never told me that."

"Probably because he feels bad about it, and he should. He's raising the rent a lot for the current tenants to make up the team's rent. Jeff and his neighbors are pretty riled up about it, but apparently, there's not much they can do. Dad says it's good for the ball club. The guys can afford to leave their odd jobs now and really focus on baseball."

"But why didn't he tell me?"

"He was probably afraid you'd write a scathing article about rent manipulation. You've got a pretty good track record on that account."

Linnea stared at her friend. He had plenty of money. He didn't need to make the Spinners a top-notch team. Why would he drive people out of their homes by gouging them on rent? What could he possibly gain?

Chelsea studied Linnea's face carefully. "Surely he told you about Pete."

"Yeah. The boy is tired." Linnea barely masked the sarcasm in her voice. What was her problem? Giving him a rest was good business.

Chelsea hesitated as if hating to be the one breaking more bad news. "He was getting stoned in the alley behind a bar on Evergreen last weekend. Someone called Dad. I drove over there with him. He was back inside by the time we arrived. Guess who he was dancing with? Clary Sage."

Linnea was disturbed. Clary Sage was too young to be in a bar. "While he was high?"

Chelsea shrugged. "Yeah, but she left with Robin right after we got there. He took off with a college girl." Chelsea stopped suddenly and grimaced. "He reminds me of someone I used to know."

"The hockey player?"

Chelsea hit the print key on her computer, signaling the need for them to start work. "You'll like Jeff. He's gentle and soft-spoken, but he's a take-charge kind of guy, too. You should have seen him running the evacuation drill. You know, managing twenty-five rough-and-tumble baseball players is a lot like babysitting. Dad should have retired last season. He's not up to keeping tabs on Pete."

"So that's what my father is doing now." A gray wave of exhaustion washed over her. "He's watching over his multi-million dollar baby."

Chelsea scanned the print-out. "Dad told Pete that if the press finds out about his drug use, it could hinder his chance at the majors."

"Yeah, you actually have to make it to the majors before its okay to abuse drugs." Linnea's diaphragm twisted like shelving paper. She could barely breathe. Her entire chest burned.

Chelsea glanced up. "What's wrong?"

She tried, but she couldn't put a positive spin on it. "I understand that my father is protecting his investment, but he's also rewarding a perfect stranger for getting stoned. He's treating a guy he barely knows to *my* vacation."

Chelsea sighed. "I told them not to send him there. I thought they would listen to my advice."

Linnea saw sympathy in her eyes. She didn't want to need it. "Hey, where are the new ads and the article you started on the Spinners' opening gala?"

* * *

Linnea took two pieces of sourdough and passed the bread basket to Dan. She laid one slice on Dwarfy's plate and the other on Megan's. Dwarfy sat across from Megan, smiling. His resin suit was still as spiffy as it had been the first day they'd met at Mulberries.

She scanned Dan out of the corner of her eye. He seemed a little tense, but available. "I have good news and bad news," she announced.

Dan shoved a whole slice of bread into his mouth and looked at her expectantly.

"The good news is Shane bought another large ad. He wants us to run it for the next six weeks."

"Who's Shane?" Dan mumbled with a full mouth.

How could anyone forget him? "You met him at The Mill. He's a physical therapist."

He shrugged. "I meet a lot of people at The Mill. You can't expect me to remember everyone. What's the bad news?"

"We either have to bump The Mill's promo or add a whole page to the paper."

Dan chewed thoughtfully. "That's not bad news. Just ask your dad to run a three-quarters page promo for the Spinners. He can afford it. Then you can put The Mill's ad on his page."

Linnea tried to keep the impatience out of her tone. "You know how this works. Adding a whole page to the paper means two more sides of writing *and* two more pages of ads. We can't afford to reformat like that on such short notice, and we simply don't have the time."

"Jesus!" he snapped. "Are you telling me one piece of paper costs that much?"

Megan glanced up.

His short-temperedness frightened Linnea, but she remained calm. "I feel bad about it. Of course, I want to advertise The Mill, but everyone who reads *The Edge* gets their coffee there, anyway."

Dan glared at her. "Fine."

Megan was watching them intently. He noticed, but went on, "You can't afford to run my ad, but see, I couldn't afford to take a family vacation for ten days, and I did it anyway. It's going to take me ten weeks to get the books and inventory back in order."

"You probably have jet lag, sweetie." She hesitated. "You might feel a lot better in the morning if you get some extra rest. Maybe you could stay home and go to bed early tonight. Aren't there any meetings you could go to during the day tomorrow?"

In a low, strained voice, he said, "If I don't go to a meeting tonight, I'm going to go out and down a six-pack."

Linnea stiffened in the face of his threat. She'd made a mistake. *Okay, go to your meeting. But damn it, Dan! Can't you control yourself? Now Megan is going to ask what a six-pack is.* She made her voice playful. "Why would you do a thing like that?"

"Well," he said coldly, refusing to take her parental cue, "I was reading *The Pilchuck Times* today. You know, the *other* paper? And since someone *paid* to run a beer ad in there, I think I ought to support them, don't you?"

She felt as if he'd punched her in the solar plexus. Fatherhood affords fringe benefits to men who want the last word. She smiled brightly at Megan. "What would Dwarfy like for dessert?"

After she did the dinner dishes, she dialed her father's number in Kauai. Winnie answered the phone. Linnea told her to take the ice cream in the freezer home that very night and give it to her kids.

When Rick returned from Kauai two weeks later, he brought a bewildered Babe Ruth to keep him company in the mansion and a case of guava juice and a jar of macadamia nuts for Linnea. He also booked airline tickets for the family to have another Hawaiian vacation after the play-offs, which made Linnea feel guilty for being disgruntled about Pete's stay on the island.

She decided that if she kept really busy, she could wait until baseball season ended for Dan to relax and be nice again. With the Fairy Tales for Tots auction and Megan's school's fundraiser approaching, she threw herself into a frenzy of activity. She was desperate for AA to start working, but Rick told her it took lots of time to make progress. She didn't want to seem impatient or reveal her fear that he was sneaking a drink now and then, so as the spring passed, she didn't ask Dan what step he was on. Like a heavy pendulum, his scowls and irritability struck her down like clockwork, always coming at her just after she forgave and forgot his last descent into snarldom. But, she didn't keep track. She focused on promoting the paper's auction and was excited when the day approached.

"Why didn't you call me back?" June asked when Linnea answered her cell phone late one evening.

"It's eleven p.m., Mom."

"I called you at eleven a.m. *yesterday*."

"Chelsea and I are downtown at the library, decorating for the auction." Linnea continued to drape Christmas lights around the children's section. She wore several strands slung across the back of her shoulders like an illuminated winter scarf. "I couldn't call you back yesterday because I was trying to find organic whole-wheat hotdog buns for the Spinners' opening gala."

"You're doing too much. Why did you schedule Fairy Tales for Tots on the same weekend as the first baseball game of the season?"

"I booked the auctioneer last fall."

"Why doesn't your father just hire someone to handle his big deal? Aren't there event coordinators?"

Linnea was irritated. "It's just a picnic before the first

game, with a little entertainment. I simply planned the food and scheduled the performers."

"If I run into him, I'm going to tell him he shouldn't have asked you to do it." Playing Keep Away from Rick was wearing on June, especially since she had retired from the pulp and paper mill two weeks earlier and was getting out a lot more. "In fact, I'm going to tell him that he's completely unreasonable."

Linnea sighed, but she was too tired and distracted to defend him.

"I wanted to let you know I won't be coming to your auction Friday night."

No surprise there. "Because my dad will be here?"

"No, I've decided to celebrate my retirement by going to California to visit your Aunt Jean. I always liked her more than Ron. She just broke up with the man she moved down there to live with. She's got a small house of her own now, with enough room for me. She said I could stay as long as I want. It's a good time for me to get away. All the boys are in jail now, so I can't do much of anything for them until they get out. I'm leaving tomorrow."

Linnea was surprised. Her mother usually debated for ages before taking any form of action. "So suddenly?"

"I called to tell you about it yesterday." June sounded triumphant. "You just didn't call me back."

Chelsea swayed on a ladder, struggling to hang an abundant trailing fern from the wide ceiling beam. Water from the cachepot spilled into her face. She swore softly. The first string of lights Linnea had taped on a bookshelf fell onto the story time rug.

Linnea rummaged through a large box, looking for tape with more reliable adhesive. "So Clary Sage is living with me while you are staying in her mother's house? Did

Jean ask about her?"

"No, but I'm sure she will. What should I tell her?"

Linnea hesitated, but concern urged her on. "Tell her Hommy's back in the picture. They didn't talk for months. He never came to see the baby, but he called Clary Sage yesterday, and now she has that old vacant look in her eyes again."

"Oh, poor man. Maybe he really loves them."

Frustrated, Linnea snapped, "His student visa is up in September."

"Oh, Linnea. You're so suspicious. But I'll tell Jean what's going on."

"If she called and…"

"Offered a mother's wisdom. I'll tell her. Well, I've got to finish packing. You'll take good care of the cats for me?"

The cats? Silently, Linnea echoed Chelsea's overflowing cache box curse. "Mom, my ob-gyn says I shouldn't be changing litter boxes."

June sighed with exasperation. "When are you going to hurry up and have this pie-in-the-sky second child, anyway, so I can go on vacation? I haven't had any leisure for decades, you know. I just want to take a little trip to California. *I'll* probably never see Kauai."

Linnea's temples constricted with guilt. "Dan and I will be glad to take care of your cats." she said soothingly. It was a white lie. He would be highly annoyed, but Mom wasn't likely to be gone that long. "When will you be back?"

"I'm not sure. The shortest sentence was ninety days. I'll call you from California and let you know when I'm coming home."

After they hung up, Linnea called her own house. Unexpectedly, Dan answered. "You're home? Didn't you go to your meeting?"

"Why are you asking?" He snarled. "Don't you trust me?"

"Of course, I trust you." Linnea decided not to mention the cats. "I'm just checking in."

"I've got to stay sober for myself, you know."

She kept her tone conciliatory. "I'm checking in on *Megan*."

"Not for you. Not for Megan. For myself. Nobody should quit drinking for someone else."

Linnea's whole body trembled. The strings of lights swayed, the bulbs brushing against her bare arms. "Shouldn't somebody quit drinking if other people have to share their lives with him?"

Dan hung up on her.

Linnea had barely snapped her phone closed, questioning how she'd foiled his recovery, when Rick sauntered into the building carrying a cardboard cup holder.

"Hey, beautiful." He offered her a cream-colored paper cup with steaming rising from the mouth spout. "I know it's a competitor's, but we're all the way across town, and you need some caffeine. "Ha! You're glowing."

The Pilchuck Times would be elated to print, "Cheating Editor Electrocuted in the Act." They'd run a full color spread of her lying on the read-aloud rug like a fallen Christmas tree, wrapped in a sparking muffler. The cup stamped with Zoka's logo would still be in her hand. The coroner would confirm, she'd been with another man's mocha. Locals would start a public safety campaign reminding the citizenry not to mix liquids with electricity, all the while whispering behind Dan's back, gleefully gossiping about how his wife had succumbed to whipped cream wanderlust.

She extricated herself from the sparkling cords and took the cup. "Thanks." At least, it wasn't a Coffeestalk drink.

"I brought Chelsea some, too. I like her, though I must say her dad's been a pain in the ass lately, nagging at me about handrails and lighting. I'm not that crazy about that paramedic boyfriend of hers, either. Did you know that soul bro she's dating is organizing the Stadium Sights' Renters Association to boycott Spinners games?"

Maybe he was just too rich to remember the basics. Linnea took it upon herself to remind him. "People care about safety and affordable housing."

"I guess they do. The lights look nice, honey." Rick eyed her cup. "How's the brew?"

She wished he'd gotten her the next size up. "It was really sweet of you to bring it at this hour, Dad."

"Anything for my little girl. I know you are some kind of coffee connoisseur, but to be completely honest with you, I can't tell the difference between most brands." He smiled with such a disarming air of humility and confession that she laughed.

Linnea liked confiding in her father. "I actually like this one as well as any other."

Rick winked at her. "That'll be our little secret."

It felt like a betrayal of Dan's art to share this particular bit of information with Rick, but the intimacy felt soothing to her beleaguered soul.

"It's just between us," he assured her.

Chapter Twelve

From her hard plastic seat next to Clary Sage, Linnea sensed Dan's excitement about his sales in the coffee booth. He bustled behind the counter, grinning. It was truly gratifying to look across the green turf to see The Mill's grinder motif on a huge banner right below the scoreboard. The gold lettering gleamed.

Last night's Fairy Tales for Tots had been extremely successful as well. Rick had brought Pete Stealer to the auction. Like the third base coach during a game, he had given Pete signals during the bidding, causing him to raise his auction paddle on cue. Discretely, they'd worked together, escalating bids and buying quite a bit themselves. Now, she would be able to order a few hundred fairy tale picture books for the library and several for individual children various social agencies had identified as needing them.

Sitting behind home plate, she drew her first deep breath in weeks. Now that the auction was over, she could get some rest and attend to things she'd been neglecting, like her make-up.

"Are you sure my lips don't look too purplish?" She

had used the last of her usual rose right before the auction and hadn't taken time to buy herself more. She felt self-conscious wearing Clary Sage's unusual shade.

"Plum suits you." She bounced Serengeti on her lap. "Look, there's Pete. He is so fine in those player's pants. At the picnic, he asked me to a movie."

Linnea watched him stretch his quads along the sideline. He spit in the dirt. She wrinkled her nose. "Be careful with him. Rumor has it he uses drugs."

"But it was awfully nice of him to support Fairy Tales for Tots."

Linnea didn't mind that Rick had orchestrated Pete's purchases to promote the baseball player's image in the community. "Would you like to help me distribute the stories? There's nothing quite like giving just the right book to just the right person."

Chelsea slid into the seat beside Linnea, shivering in her sweatshirt. "Now I remember why I gave up coming to these things years ago. It's too damn cold to sit out here and watch nine or more innings."

Linnea zipped her jacket to her chin. "At least the king of the hot drink is happy."

Larry exited the Spinners' locker room through the dugout, carrying a large paper cup. He'd been spending twelve hours a day outdoors, working the Spinners harder than previous teams ever dreamed of, but Larry was pale, even his lips lacked color. He touched the brim of his cap at them like he was giving a player a batting signal. Chelsea giggled and Linnea smiled, knowing what his sign language conveyed. He'd been bringing his daughter a cup of hot chocolate at the start of every game since she was six.

"Did you get me a double shot of chocolate?" Chelsea

asked on cue.

"Shoot! Larry drooped sadly. "I forgot. Sorry, Chels. This is just water to go with my new blood pressure medication."

Since when has he needed blood pressure medication?

Chelsea frowned. "You've been working too hard."

"Just a little hypertension." He started to say more, but he glanced at Linnea. He smiled ruefully and turned back toward the dugout. In a loud, gruff voice, he shouted. "Play ball!"

"He needs to retire and rest." Chelsea said.

"Then he should." Linnea watched him walk up to Pete and pat him on the buttocks in a routine sort of way.

"No fair!" Clary Sage said. "I want to do that."

June's old lecture on acting like a lady rushed into Linnea's mind, but she stopped herself from inflicting it on Clary Sage.

The clouds overhead continued to build and a fine mist formed in the crisp air. Chelsea stood up. "If you'll excuse me, I'm going to go sit with Jeff in the cab of the ambulance. It's warmer there."

Linnea liked to watch baseball, but she was even more delighted to have two hours to do nothing but sit still. She was also glad to be supporting her father...to actually have one... wherever he was. She scanned the stadium, finally spotting him in the stands above the first baseline, surrounded by beer-bellied, middle-aged men. She could tell he was having a great time, probably once again rehashing the story about his boyhood promise to buy the Spinners.

Spinny the Spider used his third right arm for the opening pitch. It must have been a lucky leg because the game began exactly as if Rick's childhood passion had preprogrammed it: at the bottom of the first inning, Pete Stealer made two home runs. Before long, the neon board was displaying a score of zero to twelve.

"Ain't life grand?" Rick asked, sliding into the seat beside her. "I've got my best girl and a winning team." Dan followed him, carrying Dwarfy for Megan.

"The booth is hopping." Dan sank into a seat right behind Linnea. "So, I can't stay long."

She twisted around, smiling. "That sounds like an upscale problem, Honey."

The team mascot walked past them, hawking black licorice and cotton candy. Serengeti squealed, reaching for Spinny's fuzzy arm and waving a black toy in her other hand.

"This baby has the strangest taste," Rick remarked. "Spiders and bats."

Linnea barely heard him. Puzzled, she watched Megan lugging Dwarfy across the aisle to talk to a man on the other side. *Oh, it's Shane.* Megan hadn't seen him since that one day at The Mill, but that didn't seem to detour her from tugging on his hand. She chattered away. He nodded, evidently taking her seriously. He didn't seem to mind a little girl and her Beloved interrupting his concentration on the field. Linnea's heart went out to him. *But I should go get her in a second.*

The visiting team's mascot, a fat white turkey, waddled out onto the field. As the bird unrolled a life-size picture of a scantily-clad pin-up girl, the announcer said, "This gobbler has plenty of breast meat." The bird waggled his tail feathers and began pecking the woman's image with his beak. Spinny ran out on the field, arms flailing. He and the turkey had a tug-of-war over the woman's picture. The crowed roared with laughter and applauded, spitting out their sunflower shells. When the battle was over, the spider was triumphant. He held the woman over his head.

The announcer declared, "Spinny takes her home tonight. After all, he's the one with the sticky stuff." The turkey strutted off the field, flapping his wings angrily, leaving a trail of feathers behind. The crowd stomped its feet in approval.

Linnea was perturbed. Old Captain Pillar had never let things get raunchy. Nope, singing *Take* Me *out to the Ballgame* during the seventh inning stretch was as loose as the entertainment ever got. She turned to the woman at her side to complain, but Clary Sage quickly excused herself.

"I'm going over to talk to Sandy. I'll be back." As Clary Sage hurried away with Serengeti slung over her hip, the baby dropped the hard plastic bat she'd been mouthing.

Automatically, Linnea stretched over to pick it up. As she sank down into her seat again, Rick's hand went right along with her. He cradled her buttock with his hot palm, his fingers digging into her thin summer-weight jeans, fondling her flesh. Horror exploded within her. Her glut muscles contracted hard, resisting his probing. Panic surged up her spine, lodging in the base of her skull where sensation and the terrible sense she was making of them collided. Her skeletal structure shuddered with inarticulate shame. Her joints locked down, desperately holding off a barrage of nerve endings as her faith in her father was decimated.

As the heat drew away and Linnea's bottom made contract with the contoured plastic again, she grasped for the safer haven of self-doubt. Her perception simply had to be wrong. After all, she'd hardly slept in several days. As Pete stepped up to swing again, she imagined writing an editorial entitled, "The Butt of Baseball," an exposé on how hard seating made one's behind imagine it was sitting on things that weren't there.

With a crisp whack, splinters of wood shattered over home plate. Pete's foul flew high overhead, to the right of them. She lost sight of it in the disorientating glare of stadium lights refracting through fog. The ball plummeted at over ninety miles an hour, pummeling into her skull. A sharp crack reverberated throughout Linnea's cranium.

The most intense irritation she'd ever known seared through her cerebrospinal fluid. Rage and revulsion overcame her. Her head hitched to the right, like the dugout gates, hanging crookedly from metal hinges. She was dizzier than she'd ever been before, even after several games of Ring-Around-the Rosy with Megan.

Linnea's eyes were sliding up into her forehead, but Dan's panicked expression floating over her was so peculiar that she tried to take it in. "What happened?" she mumbled crossly. She was too sleepy to wait for an answer. Dan wrapped his arm around her. Stark white circles swirled across the backs of her eyelids. Trauma waves coursed through her body. She wanted to throw up.

"Stay with me, Linnea," Dan whispered. She felt his fear pulsing through his arm. "Stay awake."

Overwhelmed by the vacuum in her head and a body too full of vibration, she smelled the coffee in his hair, but not even the scent of espresso could rouse her now. The weight in her head sucked her into a soupy darkness.

"Dan." She struggled to infuse her weak voice with reassurance. "Make sure Megan's not scared. Tell her I'm okay."

"Her lips are purple," Rick shouted.

His brashness pounded on her ear drum, beating its

way through her inflamed brain. A convulsion squeezed her belly, sending burning acid up her throat. His voice made her body want to vomit.

"Be quiet," Linnea whispered.

Jeff's voice was close to her ear. "Linnea? Can you open your eyes?" The black hole in her brain was drawing her in. She wanted to go.

"Come on, sweetie, try," Chelsea urged.

Linnea opened them just enough to see the sheen of a paramedic's badge through her upper lashes. Her lids were way too heavy. She closed them again.

* * *

No one was waiting for her to wake up, except Dwarfy. He sat on the sterile counter beyond her feet, greeting her with his steadfast grin and twinkling black eyes. She found herself enthroned upon an overly elevated and frighteningly narrow hospital bed.

Cold air from the overhead register rustled the dull sheet hastily draped over her. The polka-dotted hospital gown she wore was unsubstantial. With an ice pack for her throbbing royal crown, Linnea was chilled to the bone. She shivered. Ice cubes in the plastic sack above her brow clinked together, slipping about like chipped fragments of thought.

Where was she, and why? She remembered Serengeti dropping the toy bat. She remembered picking it up, and then turning to watch the ball spin away from her through the night sky. But what had happened after that?

"She's awake!" Jeff strode through the doorway. "You sure got your bell rung last night."

Chelsea followed him in. "They say every time a bell rings, an angel gets her wings."

"Who are *they*?" Linnea's voice cracked.

Chelsea dropped down into the chair beside the bed. "Sandy says what happened last night wasn't an accident at all. She says wings sprouted out of that baseball and forced it to land on your head."

A floodgate of anxiety pounded up against the base of her skull. She cleared her throat. "What an odd thing to say. And why would an angel abuse me?"

They stared into her pupils. Jeff excused himself to go find a doctor.

She felt abandoned. "Where is everyone?"

"Dan left a little while ago to open The Mill. Clary Sage has Megan at home. Megan was worried about you, but Shane brought her over to the ambulance after they loaded you and asked Jeff to explain they were taking you to the hospital to be checked. Sweet little girl. She made us bring Dwarfy to keep you company. They did a CAT scan on you while you were unconscious. The doctors say you have a concussion."

"Where is my dad? Isn't he worried about me?"

"Our fathers came by after the game. They didn't stay long because they had to make sure the team got to bed on time."

Linnea was crushed. *Did they have to tuck the players in? Stand guard against their bogeymen?* "Thank you for being here when I woke up."

Chelsea patted her hand. "Dwarfy's been here, too."

Jeff returned with a doctor, who examined her quickly. He began the discharge process and rushed through home care instructions. Her head ached too much to concentrate on his rapid speech, but she figured she could read the patient care papers as soon as it didn't take quite so much effort to focus her eyes. Rick arrived just as she was about to get out of bed.

"You look like hell." He strolled toward her with his hand behind his back. "How are you feeling?"

Relieved that he'd come, she said, "Sore."

He frowned, searching her face. Inexplicably, she was suddenly repelled by the very person she'd wanted to see.

"I got a present for you," he said. "Hold out your hands and close your eyes."

Linnea complied. The light from the fluorescent lamp overhead was too jarring to keep her eyelids open for very long, anyway. Rick placed a heavy object into her outstretched palm. She knew what it was before she peeked. Fury prickled its way up her arm.

"I had to fight for it," he said proudly. "Right after you were hit, a pack of ten-year-olds ran over. One of them snagged the ball, and they all split. While you were getting oxygen, I chased them down and wrestled the ball away from the brat who had it. By the time I got back to our seats, you were being strapped down in the ambulance."

She could barely stand the feel of rawhide against her skin. "You didn't really wrestle with a child for it, did you?"

"Nah. I offered him a trade. I gave him a ball autographed by Pete."

"My head really hurts," she said. "I feel like throwing up."

Rick seemed disappointed that she wasn't more excited about his gift. "Didn't anyone ever teach you to play baseball when you were a kid? To watch the ball? To catch it if it came toward you? Didn't Gunter ever take you to a game?"

Linnea tried to shake her head, but her neck protested. "Of course not. He only took the boys a few times."

"Well, I can tell you, if I'd raised you, you would know

better than to look away from the ball, ever."

Her scalp began to spasm. She let the ball roll onto the stark sheet. The swollen tissue within her cranium shifted, slipping and buckling like white leather punctured by blood thread. She groaned, squeezing the sides of her face, trying to shore her head up.

He didn't notice. "Man, Dan should have caught that ball when it came down. He was right behind you. I can't believe he didn't even try to stop it."

She had an overwhelming urge to chuck the ball right through the window, but instead of breaking glass, she took a deep breath and set it on the nightstand. "I was just about to get dressed." She wanted him to leave the room. For some reason, she wanted to have real clothes and cosmetics on around him. Her lips were parched. *Damn! The only make-up I have in my purse is purple lipstick.*

"I'm glad you are all right, honey." He patted her knee. "A baseball to the head can be serious. That's why you should never, ever take your eye off the ball. But hey! We won the game! The Turkeys were toast. Pete was a batting machine. Looks like my motivational strategy for him was a success, eh? Nothing like the taste of guava juice to make a man strive for the finer things in life."

Tropical sun would do nothing for her now. She needed to go home, pull down the shades, and crawl beneath her own blankets, to draw them as tightly around her pain as the bats in the attic wrapped their wings around diurnal slumber. She was glad Rick had to hurry off to the ballpark to put his players on their bus.

Dan arrived, pale and wan. "I just hated leaving you here. Let's go home and get things back to normal. Quickly, he slung Dwarfy over his shoulder. Her locket fell from around the dwarf's neck. Two rings slipped off his upturned thumb.

"That's my jewelry?" *Who removed it? Who undressed me? What happened while I was unconscious?* Intense fear cascaded through her as she realized how helpless she'd been.

He bent to retrieve her treasures from the mottled tile floor. "I had Mr. Ugly here hold this stuff for you. You can't wear jewelry in the microwave."

"I was in a microwave?"

Dan scowled at her momentarily. Then he smiled indulgently. "You have to take your jewelry off when you have a CAT scan," he explained gently. He was being so ostentatiously patient with her, Linnea figured the emergency room physician had advised him not to expect coherence for awhile. He pointed toward the nightstand. "Is that the ball that hit you?"

"Dad just brought it over. Can you believe it? I say leave the damn thing here."

"You can't do that."

Did he mean she couldn't leave the ball behind, or that she couldn't curse it? Linnea was perplexed as he jammed the offending object into the kangaroo pouch of his sweatshirt.

"It hurt me. I don't want it in our house. Why do I have to keep it? Why do you want it?"

He shook his head as if her questions were absolutely absurd and turned his back on her as the nurse brought a wheelchair into the room. He followed them through the corridors in silence. After their medical attendant left them in the parking lot, he said, "You scared me last night. I told Rick I'd be lost without you. I'd start drinking again." He tossed Dwarfy into the trunk.

She was aghast at his carelessness. "You can't just

throw him in there like that."

"Throw who in where?" He slammed the lid.

"Dwarfy. He has to sit in the back with a seatbelt. Megan will be crushed if we bring him home rolling around in the trunk. It's not safe."

He rolled his eyes. Sighing impatiently, he liberated his daughter's Beloved from the deep cavern.

"So what did he say?"

"Who?" Dan asked, fumbling to get the belt around Dwarfy's girth.

"Dad. When you said you'd miss me."

"He said he'd lived years without you."

Did he mean it wasn't that difficult? "What else?"

Dan shrugged.

On the main road heading toward Spinning Wheel Bluff, he glanced sideways. "Rick should have replaced the high nets around the field before the season started. Someone took the old, rotten ones down last fall. Jeff says he and Larry have been after him to get new ones up for weeks. It's your dad's fault the ball hit you."

Her still-chilled body stiffened. "He must have thought it was safe the way it was. Obviously not, but thank goodness the ball didn't hit Megan or Serengeti. It could have killed a child. I'm so glad it fell on me instead. I can handle myself being hurt far better than I could have stood watching a child suffer."

Dan didn't seem to hear her. "The good news is that the coffee stand at the games is more lucrative than I thought it would be. We made almost enough to cover your CAT scan last night, though I think Rick should pay for it, since he was negligent. What do you want for lunch? I'll call for take-out."

"I just want toast." She leaned against the headrest. It

was simply too much effort for her neck keep holding her head in place.

"How about we get something from that German deli? The chocolate letters they donated to the auction were delicious. Wouldn't a chocolate L make you feel better?"

Her scalp convulsed so strongly, she almost gagged. "Why does it have to be an L?"

He spoke to her like he was speaking to Megan, "For your first name, silly."

She felt a surge of annoyance at him. "Who said it has to be for that?"

Dan's tone implied her surliness was both unfounded and shockingly unfair. "I don't know. I guess it doesn't have to be a L. You can have a Z, if that's what you really want."

"I just want dungeon food. Bread and water. Did you, by any chance, feed Mom's cats this morning?"

"Shit!" He made a violent U-turn. The fluid in her scalp sloshed from side to side. She moaned from the pain, but he didn't seem to notice.

* * *

Heavily dosed on anti-inflammatory medications, Linnea slept until late Sunday morning. When she did manage to get up, her head ached horribly. Normal daylight was overwhelming and even the steady hum of the refrigerator irritated her.

She wore dark sunglasses and earplugs around the house as she struggled to write an article on a possible teacher's strike in Pilchuck. One of the issues was workplace safety at the school Spinning Wheel Bluff children attended. She'd barely managed to type one paragraph before giving up. Her neck couldn't stand the strain of holding her head in front of the monitor.

In the afternoon, she peeled off the glasses and peered into her bathroom mirror. Her right pupil continued to alternate between dilating to an alarmingly large diameter and constricting to peculiarly small one, a shift a second.

Dan stepped in to set the empty laundry hamper in the corner. Loudly, he said something like, "Mirror, mirror on the wall. Tell me who's the fairest one of all."

"Look at my eye," she said.

Almost hypnotized by the rapid fluctuations in her reflection, he mumbled something incomprehensible.

Linnea frowned at him. "What did you say?"

Dan gestured impatiently for her to remove her earplugs. "Your care instructions said you should be back to normal by now. I think we should go to the emergency room."

She stiffened. The hospital was too cold and lonely. "But it's too expensive."

"There's another home game, Wednesday. I'll sell extra coffee to pay for the bill."

"But I don't want head trauma that requires *two* emergency room visits." The very idea made her anxious. Two visits smacked of serious injury, possibly even brain damage, permanent impairment. She needed her intellect to survive.

"Your eye is freaking me out. I'll go tell Clary Sage we're leaving."

* * *

The triage nurse warned them that their wait would be long. Linnea changed into another vexing examination gown. She and Dan slumped on a cot behind a drab burgundy curtain. Through the camera lens of an embedded reporter, they half-heartedly, almost mindlessly, joined a United States military invasion of a small town in Iraq.

An hour later, an emergency room doctor breezed into their small space, pulling their attention back to Pilchuck. Linnea stared at his face. She knew him. He'd recited the Quran, beautifully, at the mosque opening. He lived in the Stadium Sights complex next door to Hommy. She assumed he was from Afghanistan, too.

Dr. Jafairi smiled at her kindly. "What happened?"

Dan spoke up. "It was the top of the inning. Thirteen to one, with the Spinners in the lead. A pop fly fell on her head. I don't think it was that bad. I mean, at least it wasn't a line drive, but her eye keeps doing that weird thing."

"Tell me, what is this inning?" Dr. Jafairi frowned.

"Part of a baseball game," Linnea explained. "My dad owns the Spinners."

Rick, she realized with a jolt, was the man who had just raised the rent on the doctor. In fact, this trained professional, who probably had to repeat and repay for medical school in order to earn a second license in the United States, probably had a bone to pick with him. She drew a shallow breath and cast her lot to the Universe. Dr. Jafairi seemed conscientious. Surely, she could trust him to do his best, no matter who her father was.

Dan pointed to her temple to illustrate. "A pop fly fell on her head."

"What is this pop fly?" The doctor scowled at Dan impatiently.

Dan scowled back. "When the ball goes straight up into the air, it's called a pop fly."

"Oh! A baseball fell on her head!" Suddenly, the doctor was all business. Dr. Jafairi began to examine her fluctuating pupils.

"It fell at about ninety miles an hour," Dan added, "but

like I said, it wasn't a line drive."

"So what if it wasn't a line drive?" Linnea snapped. "It hurts just as much."

Dr. Jafairi had her follow his finger back and forth across her perceptual field. He ran a long cotton swab up and down her arms and legs, asking if the sensations differed on either side of her body. She felt no difference.

"You are okay," he said soothingly. "We do these tests back home in my village near Basra."

Basra! Linnea blanched. Here, she'd been hoping he'd overlook the fact that her father was Rick Andersen. She hadn't even considered that he'd have to overlook the fact that her country had invaded his home town.

He smiled at her reassuringly. "These test work just as well as CAT scans. Indeed, some of the old ways are the wisest."

Wanting to bask in his kindness, Linnea was relieved that another physician had at least declared her healthy enough to resume her life. If she could have just detached her head from her neck to carry its weight home in her arms, she would have felt like getting up and going.

"Please be sure to check with your family practitioner soon," he said before racing off to another patient, "but I am certain your eye is only flexing its muscle. It will equilibrate on its own time."

* * *

On Monday, the Perrault family physician directed her to train her eyes on his pointer finger and follow its movements. He was satisfied with her by now very experienced performance. "My neck hurts, too," she said. "I can barely bend or turn it."

"Spending a night in a hospital bed will do that to you," Dr. Mescar said. "Imagine what would have happened if you'd had to spend two or three nights there." He scribbled on his prescription pad. "I've ordered you a muscle relaxant. Take it as noted. You should feel better in a few days."

By Tuesday afternoon, she was able to quit wearing sunglasses in the house.

Chelsea still had to do all of the computer work, however. "We have to publish this story. Report what happens when a team owner is negligent. No one should be going to games until your dad replaces the nets. I've called up and down the West Coast to get the standard height of nets at comparable ballparks for teams of the Spinners' caliber. Everyone else provides spectator protection as a matter of policy."

Shame burned the very tip of Linnea's tailbone. "It's too embarrassing to put in print. I should have kept my eye on the ball and tried to block it. I was stupid."

"What's stupid," Chelsea said, "is blaming the victim. Which is exactly what you're doing. Can't you see how self-serving your father is?"

"I can't even focus my eyes, Chels. How could I see something like that?"

"Don't turn this into a joke, Linnea."

Linnea imagined their readers waging a phone war, swamping her father's headquarters with concerns. Her head jangled as if a thousand telephones were ringing around her at once. She imagined Rick slamming down a receiver, cutting a citizen's call short, and then doing the same to their relationship. "Let's not do this."

"Let's not do what? Let's not tell the truth? You could have been in a coma forever because of his carelessness. I can't stand by and do nothing. *The Edge* has always been about exposing how mindlessness and selfishness hurts

our community. You would have been all over this if anyone else had been injured. What if we stay quiet and
someone else gets whacked in the head?"

She flinched reflexively. "God forbid."

"It could happen."

It would be awful, especially if someone was even
more severely injured. "I know. But I just can't…I can't
start a fight right now. I don't feel…steady…like I used
to."

Chelsea sighed in exasperation. "You are not the only
one getting hurt here. I don't care that Dad forgot to bring
me hot chocolate, but it proves he's is being worn to a
frazzle. And, I've got to go now. He has a doctor's
appointment in twenty minutes, and I want to find out
how bad his blood pressure really is."

* * *

By Wednesday afternoon, Linnea's pupil was back to
its normal size. She tried to work on her strike article. It
was important news that needed to make this week's
paper, but she had to stop typing. For some reason, she felt
guilty asking Chelsea to finish the piece for her. As she
pondered this, Rick stopped by on his way to the stadium.
"Would you like to come in my car? It has a smoother
ride."

Linnea glanced uneasily at Dan. He stood by the sink,
eating the purple-week grapes Chelsea had left behind
when she stomped out the door Tuesday. Her scalp was
purple, too. "I wasn't planning to go to any games for
awhile."

"Why not?" Rick sounded sorely disappointed.

"Because I have a bruise as big as a salad plate on my
head. I don't feel like going, and I don't want Megan to go,
either until you replace the high nets. It's too dangerous."

"But I reserved the best spots in the whole stadium for you." He stuck his lower lip out like Megan did when she didn't get her own way.

You're too old to pout. "So sell them to fans who want them."

"Come on," Dan urged. "This isn't about the fans. This is about family. We want you to be there. Don't be so paranoid. What are the odds of being struck by lightening twice?"

"Twice as many as being struck once."

"Silly." Rick reached out and tapped the tip of Linnea's nose, lightly.

The suddenness of his move startled her, and she jerked her head away. Her neck spasmed as she calmed her racing heart, reasoning with her reluctant self. *Don't be such a spoilsport. You don't have the right perspective on this because of the trauma. And you can't work anyway.*

So the Perraults went to the Spinners game. Despite Megan's protests, Linnea made her put on a neon pink bicycle helmet when they left the coffee booth, heading for their seats behind home plate. While Dan served up espresso, just the way his customers liked it, Megan whined, and several spectators raised their eyebrows at the child's protective gear. Most of the fans didn't notice, however.

Doggedly waving stuffed spiders, mini Spinnys on sticks, they cheered while the team's mascot performed slap-dash antics in center field. Rick stood on the baseline, using an air gun to shoot promotional hats and t-shirts up into the stands as Pilchuck's baseball community celebrated the Spinners' unprecedented weekend of victories.

"Yes, indeed, ladies and gentlemen," the announcer

proclaimed, "this team is three for three in its first week of the season."

"Take this." Larry offered her a well-oiled glove. "Keep your eye on the ball, and if it comes anywhere near you, block your head with it."

"Thanks." Linnea quelled the sudden urge to bolt toward the exit. "I don't want to go through that again."

"You won't." His eyes were soft. He smiled at her kindly.

"How do you know?" She not only wanted the informed opinion of an experienced team manager, but also the reassurance of a fatherly man. Rick hadn't been comforting at all.

"You are the first fan in over fifty years of playing here to be carried out of Spinners Stadium unconscious. Consider the odds of a reoccurrence."

She slipped the glove on. *Odds again? Why are all these men so willing to gamble on my head? And they've always had nets before.*

A tiny black form flew inches from her eye. She started like a tightly swaddled infant whose wrapping comes undone.

"What's the matter, Mommy?"

Anything coming toward her head was too much to take. "A mosquito," Linnea answered, shaken.

"Oooh, oooh! My bats are gonna *eat* him tonight." She tugged at her chinstrap.

"Good. Keep your helmet on."

"It's squeezing me."

Larry kneeled so he was at eye level with Megan. "Wear it tonight," he cajoled, "for your mommy. I'll get your grandpa to put higher nets up before the next game."

Linnea trusted Larry, but had her doubts that he could

deliver on his promise. He left for the dugout. Megan glared at her beneath the hard plastic brim.

She's definitely not scarred by my being carted away. Linnea was gratified that Shane and Jeff had seen to that. Dan had had his hands full with her, literally, and Rick had been too busy chasing down the implement of her injury. *Where is my father? He should be here guarding me against another foul.*

The catcher missed a fastball. It slammed into the backstop with a bone-aching thud. Linnea cringed, hoping no one, Megan included, had noticed her cowardice. *Don't be such a wimp. Just watch the ball.*

Even with the thick leather wrapped around her hand, she grew increasingly anxious as Spinny stepped onto the mound for the first pitch. His legs became the spokes of a black spinning wheel. She watched them whirl, her terror rising as the crowd cheered him on. *Forget it. I can't force myself to stay here.*

She stood suddenly, taking Megan by the hand. "Let's go help Daddy sell coffee. The concession area is covered. I won't make you wear your helmet down there."

Chapter Thirteen

Dan hurled himself onto the mattress beside her. The bedding bounced. The cold compress fell onto Linnea's tender, bruised scalp. She caught her breath sharply. Pain sloshed through her cranium.

He grimaced at her ice pack as if was the source of all discomfort. "Do you still need to bring that thing in bed with us? I rolled onto it last night. I almost got frostbite."

"Too bad for you. I still need it. And I don't care what you or Dad say, I don't want to go to any more baseball games. Every time I hear the bat crack or a glove snap, I tense up. Why hasn't Dad put the nets up yet?"

"He's distracted. Be patient with the guy. The Spinners are starting this season way ahead of the rest of the league. Every red-blooded American boy fantasizes about being part of story like this. His childhood dreams are coming true."

A soft sigh emanated from the baby monitor perched atop the Hans Christian Andersen book on Linnea's dresser. Dan jumped. "Why's that in here?"

"I'm babysitting Serengeti. Clary Sage is on a date with Pete. She's obviously desperate for a night out because I told her not to get involved with such a hard-hearted man." Linnea gingerly placed the ice above her brow.

He eyed the polka-dot pack suspiciously. "How do you know he's hard-hearted?"

Isn't it obvious? "He's had a whole week to apologize to me, and he hasn't done it yet."

"It was an accident. I can't believe you expect him to apologize to you. He's probably been hit by the ball a hundred times. It's no big deal to him."

"Well, it's a big deal to me. I haven't had a decent night's sleep since my concussion. I can't stand to rinse the shampoo out of my hair. I can't bear bending over to tie my shoe. I can't turn my head to back the car out of the garage."

Serengeti rolled over in her crib. Through the intercom, blankets rustled like pages turning. Linnea glanced toward the sound. "I feel like the *Princess and the Pea*, but no amount of mattress can keep me from feeling this bruise on my scalp and this hard lump in my neck."

"You've got to develop more machismo if you are going to inherit a baseball team someday."

The suggestion was alarming. "I don't want a baseball team," she said, but from Dan's expression, she was pretty sure he'd been caught up in every red-blooded American boy's dream.

* * *

Unswept walkways surrounded June's empty house. Weeds reveled in the debauchery of blooming inside her chain link fence. In case she returned soon, they let their leaves grow spiky in a hurry, determined to resist the relentless uprooting with which she had cursed their ancestors.

Linnea felt guilty for letting Rick see the untidy place.

She'd been surprised when he had driven to her house that evening. He usually went to Dan's A.A. meetings when the Spinners had a night off. Still excited about the last game, he had nearly danced a jig on the doorstep. "Did you hear Pete was five for five?"

Linnea had barely nodded. She had a jackhammer of a headache. She'd spent the afternoon painfully scrubbing Megan's old airplane swing. Dan had stored it in the attic when Megan outgrew it, but she had dug it out for Serengeti. She probably should have watered the bleach down more when she cleaned the bat guano off the red plastic.

Rick returned her weak nod, mirroring her constricted movements. His eyes flickered with concern. "Is everything all right? Did you and Dan have a fight?"

She didn't even try to focus her eyes on him. "I just have a migraine, I'm stressed out about an article I need to write, and I still need to zip over to feed my mother's cats."

"I'll drive you to Mom's. I'd like to meet all the little kitties."

June had expended so much energy avoiding the man since his return to Pilchuck, Linnea felt like she was undermining her by showing Rick where she lived. But with pain sluicing her scalp, the last thing she wanted to do was drive.

Once they were inside the dim, dusty entry of her childhood home, Rick said, "Show me your room."

She didn't want him to see where she'd been so little, so helpless, so absolutely unsatisfactory to her stepfather. "But Dad, I haven't lived here for fourteen years."

"I want to see it."

Misgiving flooding through her, she led him to the

small room next to the master bedroom at the end of the hall. It was every bit as depressing as she remembered it.

An undersized window with a rusted aluminum frame offered the only light, and the 1970's dark wood paneling sucked up most of that. "I had a pink patchwork quilt, a dollhouse in that corner, and a desk to do my homework right there."

Rick took in the humid space, a brother's massive stereo speakers, and the many obscene posters that hung on the walls. He turned back toward the hallway as if eager to get out. "No wonder you're so content with the puny little place you and Dan have now."

Linnea's cheeks convulsed, still retaining the fear a little girl had felt cowering beneath the rose-toned patches of her security blanket when Gunter approached. Fluid within her head pummeled her from inside. She sandwiched her temples between her palms, pushing back. Trying to equalize the pain coming from within and without, she followed her father to the front room. The matted, brown shag beneath their feet reminded her how to subdue her feelings until they were as flat and as dull as the carpet. *At least there are no mice this time. Maybe it's a good thing I've been spotty about feeding these stupid cats.*

Rick crouched beside the sagging sofa. "Here kitty, kitty," he coaxed. "Aren't you a pretty one?" An orange cat crawled out, purring. As it sidled along his knee, he scratched it under the chin. "You could be Babe Ruth's sister." A second cat sauntered out from beneath the couch, ostentatiously digging its claws into the frayed fabric of the sofa.

"No! Bad kitty," Linnea scolded. The couch was trashed, but someone had to make a stand.

He comforted the cat. "You aren't bad."

Suddenly, the spasms in her scalp intensified.

He rose to his feet, chuckling at her scowl. "Don't be so uptight, my dear. Let them be. Last night, I watched little Babe Ruth tear up that brown leather couch in my den."

She gasped in acute pain mingled with agonized disbelief. It had been so much fun for her to sink into the thick umber cushions beside him and watch the other customers in the furniture store envy her while the salesman wrote up his receipt. The couch had cost as much as Dan's espresso steamer, and if there were anything she wanted to inherit from Rick, that piece of furniture would have been it. "Why did you let her do that?"

Surprised, he explained, "Because it made her happy. A few years ago, I took a workshop from a great guy who taught me to let my love objects do whatever they need to do to be happy."

Love objects? Was that workshop the prerequisite course to Relationships 101 – the cheat sheet to *The Clueless Guide to Caring*?

Disgust bubbled in Linnea's belly. She looked away, catching a glimpse of her mother's antique tea set. She could almost see June plunking sugar cubes into lukewarm Earl Grey. She nearly heard her mother's voice hovering over it: *Poor man. Come on, Linnea. Cut him some slack.*

She turned her back on her mother's ghost. Head trauma made her testy. "Why did you let Pete take Clary Sage out in your car?"

Rick's eyes widened, but he folded his arms across his chest. "What's that supposed to mean?"

His sharp tone was like a shard of china slicing through her skin. The knot in Linnea's neck contracted so hard that when she shrugged, her right shoulder stayed hitched up.

"I can do whatever I want with my Opulence. Driving it made Pete happy, so I let him."

Something about his permissiveness frightened her. "Is he one of your love objects?"

"I'm not even going to dignify that with a response. And don't go around saying he's dating Clary Sage. She'll mess up his career."

Linnea was flabbergasted. "That's mean."

A disturbing shadow fell across Rick's face. "He'd be quite the catch for a little hussy who lets herself get pregnant by a sand nigger, wouldn't he?"

His voice was tinged with hatred. The lack of circulation in her scalp made her dizzy. "Hardly. I think he's creepy."

Rick threw back his head and laughed. "Creepy? Oh, honey! I know what's going on here."

"What?" Linnea wanted a father who really did know.

"My little girl is jealous." He grinned. "I think that's sweet, honey. I really do."

"I'm not jealous." *Jealousy is useless. Debilitating, actually.* But surrounded by her brothers' messes, June's drooping plants, and spoiled cats, how could she be certain that she wasn't jealous of Pete? *Maybe my inner child is. Maybe I do want more from my father.* "My doctor referred me to an orthopedist. It's going to be expensive."

Rick nodded, receiving her information as if it were just another bid for paternal attention. He pet the cat for a moment and then adopting the veneer of a conscientious parent determined to divide his focus equitably between needy children, he stopped to focus on her. "Why did he do that?"

My neck." She tilted her head to the left in an attempt to emphasize her words, but the offending knot tugged back in response, determined to keep her right ear connected to her shoulder.

Rick stared at her doubtfully. "When did your neck start bothering you?"

She was floored he was so unaware of her constant pain. "After the ball hit me."

"Hmm." He knelt again to scratch behind the cat's ear. "I'm glad we got this jealously thing out in the open because now, I know why you never ask about Babe Ruth. Sometimes, it really hurts my feelings that you don't inquire about your little sister. Now, I understand. Let's take good care of all these kitties for your mom."

Playfully, the recipient of his affection grasped Rick's hand between its paws. He smiled. "You know, I want to take Babe Ruth to the old folks' home with me when I go. You'll make sure that's all arranged when the time comes, won't you?"

A surge of anger flared through her, shooting up her spine like a radioactive flume. In its wake, a fatigue as heavy as a lead apron cloaked her. Unlike Little Red Riding Hood's ruby cape, Linnea's exhaustion was a drab gray. Her neck and shoulders strained beneath the clinging drape of her lethargy.

She longed for Sleeping Beauty's one hundred year nap or the blissful unconsciousness of Snow White's coffin. "Let's not talk about when you're old. I want to go home now."

* * *

Her health plan's orthopedist was on vacation. Linnea made an appointment for when he would return and spent the next week striving to ignore her ongoing headache and the tightness in her neck and shoulders. She concentrated on work. Each time she saw Rick, she expected him to offer to pay for her ambulance, the CAT scan, her overnight stay at the hospital, and the emergency room visits, but he didn't.

Returning home from the bank one day after juggling funds from one account into another to cover these costs, Linnea and Megan found Chelsea lounging on the porch swing with her legs propped up on four large boxes. "The fairy tales came!" She was snacking on sweet corn, spooning it right out of a pull-top can.

Megan climbed up beside her, peering into the container. "Is it a yellow week?"

"Yep." Chelsea offered her a few kernels. "And let me tell you, corn tastes a lot better than spaghetti squash."

Linnea bent down to double-check the shipping labels. Sharp pain shot up through her skull as if a strand of barbed wire were entwined around the vertebrae of her neck. "Shit!" She bit her lip. With tears in her eyes, she glanced guiltily at Megan. "That's a bad word, honey. Mommy shouldn't have said it."

"Oh, Linnea," Chelsea grimaced in sympathy. "It's getting worse. Don't wait until your network guy gets back. Find another doctor. So, what if it's twice as expensive?"

Rick's black Opulence pulled up to the curb. Linnea was glad. The incessant throbbing in her head and the dipping balance in her checking account was enough to convince her it was time to make her father listen to her troubles.

Pete stepped out of the driver's side door, nodding coolly at the women on the porch, as if the car belonged to him. *That car costs more than any house on this block. How can my father let him drive it, but not offer to help me?*

Clary Sage clambered out of the passenger's side. "Pete

made four double plays last night, so Rick let him borrow the car again. Your dad is so cool!"

Linnea couldn't smile, couldn't share her cousin's enthusiasm for either man at the moment, but she said, "I'm glad you had some fun."

Clary Sage lowered her voice, ducking her head guiltily, "I'm sorry I forgot to tell you I was going. Sandy has Serengeti."

"I wasn't worried about her."

Pete kissed Clary Sage on the mouth, right in the middle of the street. She waved as he drove away. With a giddy smile, she nearly skipped up the steps to her apartment's entrance.

Chelsea whispered, "In all the years Dad has managed the team, I have never seen a player get the owner's car for a joy ride."

"I was hoping she'd meet someone else to get past Hommy, but Pete bugs me. Let's get to work."

When she tried to lift the boxes, the muscles in her arms tightened so much they wrenched on the knot in her neck. "Ow! How can they be so connected?"

"I'll move them." Chelsea picked up a box. "Don't hurt yourself any more. And I'll type for you while you dictate your article on the teachers' strike. It needs to go tomorrow. We can't wait until next week."

As Chelsea moved the boxes, the glorious summer sun broke through the Pacific Northwest fog. Linnea put a call into the president of the teachers' union while Chelsea filled Megan's wading pool. They settled on the patio, Chelsea with her laptop, Linnea with her notes. Megan and Dwarfy played with plastic dolphins in water up to their navels.

Later, when Sandy wheeled Serengeti and Susie into

the yard, Clary Sage came out to help unload the double stroller. Sandy grimaced looking at Linnea. "How's your head?"

"My skull feels crushed and my neck really hurts," she replied. As she spoke about needing to see an orthopedist, her jaws ached. "My shoulders and arms have been getting really tight, too."

Sandy listened to her so intently and with so much sympathy, Linnea found herself on the verge of tears.

Cautiously, Sandy said, "I've dabbled in massage therapy. May I look at your neck?"

Linnea agreed, lifting her hair.

Sandy placed her cool fingertips just over the hard knot without touching her skin. "Hmmm...what you've got here is a very densely packed energy cyst."

Linnea had never heard of such a thing, but she knew precisely what it meant. "Do you mean the ball hit me so hard that its energy stayed stuck inside of my body?"

"Is that what it feels like?"

"Yeah. It feels like heat and pain and constant friction in the center of rock hard bone and muscle."

"I've been around baseball players all my life," Chelsea said. "I've never heard of this happening before."

Linnea didn't want to buy into anything crazy, but the whole idea made perfect sense to her. "How do I get it out?"

"It's very dark in there," Sandy whispered.

"But you said the baseball was an angel." She couldn't help being a bit spooked about the idea of hosting a very dark angel's energy.

Sandy seemed amused. "I said I saw wings."

Clary Sage shrugged sheepishly. "I added the angel part. What else would it be?"

175

Sandy placed her hands on either side of Linnea's neck, covering the cyst with her palms. Linnea's neck throbbed, but Sandy's soothing touch seemed to soak up some of the pain. "We most definitely need to send some light to this."

Chelsea shifted uneasily in her seat, her eyes darting about rapidly as she tried to steer the conversation toward the mainstream. "I hear laser light therapy is very popular in Europe."

"That might do it." Sandy's brown eyes twinkled beneath her finely arched eyebrows as she stepped away. "Be sure to let me know when you're finished with the doctors."

Linnea's head seemed far too heavy without Sandy's support. She stared at her, feeling bereft, trying to articulate the question, what did she know that the doctor wouldn't?

The telephone in the kitchen rang. Their Tales for Tots liaison, the children's librarian, was on the line. "My father is seriously ill, Linnea. I'm flying home in the morning to care for him. I'm so sorry to put this off, but can we wait a few weeks to process and distribute the books?"

"Of course. I hope all goes well." Linnea hated to think of a deprived child waiting any longer for a story to enrich her life, but at least the delay would give her plenty of time to share all the books with Megan.

* * *

Two weeks after the initial referral, the orthopedist asked, "Which player hit you?" Dr. Orbital whistled when she told him. "That guy is having an amazing season. I bet the major league scouts will be snooping around any day now."

"That's the plan." Linnea kept her voice vague. She wanted healing her injury to be the focus here, not the stats of the player who had given it to her.

He asked her to stretch her arms overhead and out to the side. With her jaw convulsing in protest and her flesh inflamed from the strain, she stood against the wall, like Jesus on the cross. "This is so uncomfortable. I even feel pain in my jaw like this."

"It's no big deal." He didn't even lift her hair for a glimpse at the source of her pain. "You just have a trigger point."

"What's that?"

"Just a place where the muscle bunches up real tight. You must carry your tension in your neck. All you need to take care of this is some ultrasound treatment."

"How much does that cost?"

He pulled a pad from his white coat pocket and began to write. "You only need three sessions, tops."

She was perplexed that he could make a diagnosis like that. What if he were wrong? She couldn't afford to take any more time away from work or to pay for a treatment that might not be the right one. "Aren't you going to touch it?"

Dr. Orbital seemed amused by her question, but his pen continued to race across the paper. "Here's a prescription for the therapy. How are you sleeping?"

"I've tried every pillow in the house. I've finally resorting to sleeping on a rolled-up towel, but nothing is comfortable."

"A lack of sleep can make pain seem worse than it really is. Let's get you a prescription for a sleep aid." Almost gleefully, he touched his pen to the page.

"My pain *is not* from a lack of sleep." Linnea wanted him to stop writing so she could collect her thoughts, organize her questions. She'd be the first to admit that pain was making her brain fuzzy, but his no-touch approach was more disorientating than a lack of sleep. If he felt her neck, maybe he'd realize how much it hurt. He was so removed.

"You'll feel better after a good night's rest. Call me if you aren't back to normal after your third physical therapy session."

Her pain was intense, stubborn. This sounded too easy. "Wait. Could it be an energy cyst?"

Dr. Orbital's clinically cold blue eyes glittered over his icy smile. "I have never heard of an energy cyst."

Linnea left the doctor's office feeling stupid.

* * *

Rick agreed to let Linnea see the physical therapist the Spinners kept on retainer. Jay Yorke's office was in a run-down strip mall on the outskirts of Pilchuck. The team was on the road, so she was able to get an appointment with him late that very afternoon. She walked into the stark, white space and handed the acne-scarred young man the orthopedist's prescription. As she kicked off her shoes to sit up on his table, he turned pink. His eyes watered.

"Are you having an allergy attack?" she asked sympathetically.

"No. C...C...can you...you put your hair up?" His hands were shaking. "Sorry. I don't have anything for you to use."

Linnea deftly pulled the top of her yoga pants away from her body to retrieve an elastic band from the small inner pocket.

Jay stared at the white skin stretched over her hip bone, swallowing hard as the spandex snapped back over it. She gathered her hair into a ponytail and waited for instructions.

"Uh, good," he wheezed. "I mean I'm glad you had something because I usually only work on guys."

Beginning to feel as uneasy as her therapist seemed, Linnea lowered herself stiffly onto the tissue paper covering the table. She didn't know anything about ultrasound treatment, except that she'd had an ultrasound when she was pregnant with Megan. But that was to produce pictures, not ease pain. Could a physical therapist project an energy cyst on a screen or record it on a DVD to take home to share with friends and family? Would it be clear enough that even Dr. Orbital could see it? Perhaps if she got Jay talking he'd feel more comfortable. "Do you do any light therapy?"

"Noooo." The young man's fingers trembled while he uncapped a tube of gel. "I don't have that kind of machine. They're very expensive." Then, like a firefighter keeping his distance from a burning building, he squirted the cold gel all over Linnea's neck.

He grabbed his wand. "Let me know if this gets too h...hot." Breathlessly, he rubbed the bulge in her neck with the constantly moving tip.

"So how is this different from a prenatal ultrasound?" Listening to him cough and splutter behind her, she realized that Rick had obviously gone for the new kid on the block, the lowest bidder in the business. She dropped her line of questioning and after a few minutes, the tissue in her neck loosened just enough to give her the tiniest taste of relief. She moaned slightly. "It's working," she added to reassure him.

"That's it. Just let it all go." The boy wonder said eagerly.

Linnea couldn't help but giggle. It was so like a bad porn film.

"What?" he asked anxiously, drawing the phallic rod away. He examined the end as if he couldn't remember how to use it. "It's not supposed to tickle."

She turned around from the waist, so she could look at him. "Can you do something about the tightness in my shoulders and jaw?"

He swallowed so hard that his Adam's apple wobbled like the baseball bobblehead dolls on his desk. "I can't," he gasped, pointing to the prescription he'd attached to her chart. "I'm only supposed to work on the b...bump."

* * *

Five weeks after the baseball fell on her, she completed her ultrasound treatment. It hadn't worked for more than a few minutes at a time.

"I can't believe no one caught this so far," the chiropractor said, pulling the heating pad away. "Your cervical vertebrae are way out of alignment. Tuck your chin."

"No one has touched...," Linnea began.

Suddenly, he grabbed her jaw and jerked her head to the side. Her heartbeat lurched into runaway rhythm, but the bones in her neck and the soft tissue around them refused to budge.

"Sorry," he said, "It's stuck. I can't get it to move."

And so the lump on her neck became a vortex, greedily pulling the muscles of her scalp, her jaw, her shoulders, and her upper back into its hungry center, spinning the fibers together like a pastry braid. Inseparable layers of soft tissue stuck together as stubbornly as cotton candy. But there was nothing sweet about the incessant pain and the ever smaller range of movement her body allowed. She had to hold books up to her eyes because any inclination of her head drew pain.

After a series of unsuccessful visits to the chiropractor, Linnea sat glumly in her office, staring at the stacks of fairy tales scattered across her desk and strewn all over the floor, proofing one of Shane Carpenter's ads. Every time she ran one, she wished she could go see him, but the Knights weren't part of her insurance company's network.

Rick knocked on the screen door and let himself in, another box of unwanted chocolate in his hand. "I got an email from a major league scout this morning telling me he's coming to watch Pete play soon. I think he might even want to cut a deal before the end of the season. I'm going to see if I can lure in a few more scouts. It'd be a kick to have a bidding war."

"At least my orthopedist was right about the scouts."

Rick set the candy on her fax machine, scowling as if she were purposely trying to interfere with the triumphant proceedings of his life's plan. "Isn't your neck better yet?"

"No." Linnea sighed sadly. "And the doctor's bills are astronomical. Dad, is there any way you could help us out?"

"Did Dan tell you how much coffee he sold last night?" Couldn't he hear her?

"More than his wildest dreams. Of course, I don't have to tell you that his wildest dreams have always been far too domesticated."

Her pain was so obviously outside his perception. Her automatic adaptation to insensitivity kicked in, and she set aside the part of her being that needed a caring response.

"What do you mean by that, Dad?" His sudden dig at Dan didn't surprise her. She realized she'd been expecting it. Of course, she'd encouraged it. She never should have told Rick she liked Zoka's as much as any other coffee. "Dan has plenty of ambition."

"So sue me for wanting to see my little girl better off. Go ahead. Sue me for wanting to see my daughter a little more comfortable."

Her skin was short-changed, tugged in too many wrong directions. Her spine was strained. Her right shoulder was literally stuck, hitched up less than a hand span below her ear. "I'd be comfortable if I could find a doctor to help me and if I weren't so stressed about paying for it."

Rick untied the ribbon and opened the box. "Chocolate for you?"

Chapter Fourteen

One stormy evening in mid-August, Dan flipped through the bills cascading across the dining room table, cursing the unstable pile. "You've had physical therapy with ice, heat, electrical stimulation and stretching. You've had massages and acupuncture. A saline injection...and what's this bill from the dentist for?"

Linnea was slow to respond. "My mouthguard. In case I'm clenching while I sleep. I can't remember who suggested I have it made."

For weeks now, muscle relaxants had fogged her brain like breath on a cool window. The anti-inflammatory medication had dissolved the lining of her stomach as surely as the precipitation outside washed Megan's chalk drawing off the sidewalk. Reflecting the summer rain flowing through the drainpipe, the pain in Linnea's head and neck methodically flowed through her entire body. As the next muscle down the line attempted to guard against the discomfort from above while assuming duties it was never supposed to handle, it became sore and then rigid from the strain. Yet she had gone about her daily business, remaining cheerful.

Rick's return had reminded her so much of her own childhood, she found herself re-doubling her efforts to make sure Megan was protected from worry, especially any regarding her. Although most of the childcare fell to her with Dan so frequently away at his meetings, she willed herself not to snap at Megan even as the agony seeped into her arms, her torso, her hips, and her legs.

Dan had been watching the bills accumulate in an old napkin holder on top of their refrigerator, but he hadn't really noticed how much harder lifting, bending, keyboarding, driving, or daily living had become for her. He gathered up the envelopes and took a long look at his now crooked little wife. His eyes narrowed, raking her entire body with barbs of frustration.

Linnea felt herself flagging like the window box petunias beneath the summer squall. "Are you mad are me?"

"Yes, Goddamn it. All the profits from the stadium booth are going toward your medical care and I want to know why the hell you can't even get a decent diagnosis." He sucked in the side of his cheek, imitating Rick. "Are you sure you aren't just using this as an excuse to keep getting massages?"

The urge to shriek profanity seized her, but she didn't have the energy to follow through. Besides, Megan and Serengeti were in the family room and she wasn't up for any more unpleasantness after today's appointment.

Dr. Folger had stroked her bare legs with his naked fingertips, ostensibly evaluating her ability to perceive sensation. It hadn't felt like he was practicing medicine.

"I can't lift heavy plates out of the dishwasher," she had told him forlornly. "That tugs on my neck...and I can't pull wet blankets out of the washing machine, either."

Parking his hands higher on her thighs, Dr. Folger leaned closer. "Did you say wet blankets?"

"Yes, you know, how they get all twisted up with the sheets in the wash?"

"What else can't you do?" The doctor stepped away, grinning like she was a game show contestant about to answer the million-dollar question. His bleached teeth were as straight as the sides of a tongue depressor and even whiter than his lab coat.

Pay my medical bills.

"Are you still able to have sex?" He continued without waiting for her answer. "Do you feel his thrusting all the way up in your neck?"

Don't go there. You're supposed to be the expert. Help me. "Can you diagnose me if I say yes?"

He nodded approvingly. "You bet I can. Let's schedule you for a lower body MRI."

Shit! MRIs are really expensive. "Aren't you going to examine my neck?"

"Next time, my dear." Dr. Folger patted her leg just beneath the hem of her hospital gown. "I don't think your neck is the issue at all. The problem is in your hip." With his other hand, he squeezed her shoulder lightly. "I can't wait to sit down and go over your results with you."

On the way out past the nurses' station, Linnea longed to grab a surgical knife and lance his abdomen like an old-time woodsman. She wanted to see if cloaked little girls and grandmas in their nightgowns tumbled out of his belly. Instead, she had wept in the car, letting tears trickle out from behind her sunglasses all the way home.

Now that the late rain was overshadowing the city, she shuddered, glaring back at Dan. "I am *not* trying to get more massages. The girls I see at the massage school are so inexperienced, they don't help much, anyway." She stopped herself, wondering if that were part of the problem.

"What did the specialist you saw today say?"

She didn't want to discuss it. "I'm going to check on Megan."

Dan blocked her way. "Tell me what he said."

"Dr. Folger, the renowned psysiatrist?"

"A psychiatrist! Shit! Our medical plan doesn't cover counseling."

"Not a psychiatrist!" she snapped. "A psysiatrist."

"What the hell is a psysiatrist?"

"A physical medicine doctor."

"Aren't all doctors physical medicine doctors? Does our insurance cover him?"

"He's not part of the network." She shouldn't have gone, but Dr. Mescar had been so certain Folger could help her. Today's fifteen-minute failure was going to cost $250.00. Despair overwhelmed her. "But don't worry. I'm not going back to see him again."

"Why not?" He sounded cross, like he did when Megan didn't want to go to bed before sunset.

"He wouldn't even touch my neck," she wailed. "I know that's where the trouble stems from, but he ordered an MRI for my lower body. I'm not paying for that."

His nostrils flared with barely-contained fury. "I thought you just said this guy is tops in the field."

"Dr. Mescar said that. I think they just play golf together."

"Well, you can get a hell of a lot of massages for the price of an MRI." Dan rammed a Spinners cap on his head. "I'm going to AA," he bellowed, striding out the back door.

Linnea bit her hand to keep from screaming at him to stay home to help her make sense of all her pain. Yet, digging her front teeth into the flesh below her thumb, she reminded herself that he was suffering in his own way. He had to go to AA and she just had to deal with it. Instead of yelling at him, she took a muscle relaxant and crawled into bed with a scratch pad of paper and a box of colored pencils. She drew an outline of her body with sharp barbed wire in the center. It extended from the top of her head, down her neck, through her shoulder, into her hip and the length of her right leg. After marking all the scraped tissue with angry red streaks and purple bruising, she cried herself to sleep long before Dan came home.

The next morning he called the house while they were finishing breakfast. He sounded conciliatory. "Hey, the coach up at the high school came in for his daily drip. He referred us to a sports medicine doctor. That's the kind of doctor you need to handle a baseball injury, right? And he must be good. He doesn't have any appointments available until October."

Linnea was heartened by Dan's actually taking the initiative to help, but two months? "Do I have to wait until then?"

"Nope. Today's our lucky day. Coach is giving you his appointment. He doesn't really need to go in, and he wants to thank you for the time you sent a pound of C Night Special to his house when his son was sick. Dr. Perdue can see you in forty minutes."

Linnea slammed down the phone. She and Megan hastily brushed their teeth, slipped into flip-flops, and hurried to the medical center. Once there, she filled out a lengthy questionnaire about her health and donned another extremely short examining frock. She felt hopeful and then reproached herself for her optimism. *Don't get too excited.* Yet, she couldn't help it. Maybe she could get some answers.

She sat shivering in the air-conditioned office for fifteen minutes reading *Little Red Riding Hood* to Megan before Dr. Perdue dashed in. His graying brown hair was pulled back into a short ponytail.

He introduced himself, shaking her hand, "So what can I do for you?" he asked kindly, sinking onto the stool as if he had all the time in the world. Staring at his onyx earring, Linnea couldn't help wondering if he charged by the minute.

Her voice shook as she described how she'd been hit by the baseball. She pulled the tear-stained drawing she'd done the previous night from her purse and handed it to him. As he glanced at it, she dug her fingertips into her neck, trying to loosen the lump in her flesh.

Dr. Perdue's brown eyes widened slightly as he studied the disturbing image. "The areas you sketched in red burn. Right? The thicker black barbed wires show where you feel the pain, is that correct?"

"And pain is moving into where the lines turn gray." She wasn't a very good artist, but at least he wasn't scoffing at her work. He actually seemed to be taking her seriously.

"Sounds like MPS to me." Dr. Perdue spun toward the counter for a box of facial tissue and handed it to her. "Myofascial Pain Syndrome."

Tears of relief welled over her bottom lids: at last, a diagnosis. Maybe Dan would calm down. "What's that?"

"It's a condition that wrecks havoc with your musculoskeletal systems. See, a continuous sheet of fascia covers all of your muscles and your internal organs. It's like the slimy stuff you pull off chicken before cooking it. When people, and for some reason most of them are women around your age, get injuries or develop trigger points in muscle tissue, the surrounding fascia bunches up abnormally. This can pull on bones and joints and even affect your internal organs. From the look of things, I suspect it all started with a compression whiplash when the ball fell on your head. You probably have a damaged joint in your neck." He handed her back the drawing. "Nice sketch. MPS is pretty complex. Unfortunately, few people understand this dynamic."

Linnea wiped the tears off her cheeks. She never would have thought being diagnosed with whiplash could be so comforting. "What can I do to get back to normal?"

Dr. Perdue smiled sympathetically. "We do need to rule out any other possible causes of your pain."

No. She wanted it to be what he thought it was so she could get started on the cure immediately. "If it is MPS, what can I do to get better?"

"Are you willing to exercise?"

"I do exercise." Linnea thought about all the chocolate her father had been bringing to her. She'd been forcing herself to use the treadmill at the gym to keep it off her hips. "But working out makes it worse. The muscles in my back and legs are so tight that whenever I stretch I feel tissue burning, even tearing."

"We'll give you pain medication to deal with that, but you have to stick to your work-out. Let's schedule you for a full body MRI, neck X-rays, and a bone scan. I also highly recommend that you have a psychological evaluation." He nodded meaningfully toward Megan. She was concentrating quietly on a puzzle Linnea had brought along for her. "Raising children is a tough job."

For her daughter's benefit, Linnea refused to agree. "She's an absolute joy."

"Stress exacerbates this condition considerably."

"She doesn't stress me out."

"Shit!" Megan looked up, an uncooperative puzzle piece still in her hand.

Dr. Perdue smiled.

"That's a bad word. Right Mommy? I shouldn't use it."

Monkey see, Monkey do.

"I'll go schedule that MRI."

Ruefully, Linnea changed back into her clothes.

He returned with two plastic bags full of individually wrapped pills. "This will save you a pretty penny." He handed the first bag to her. "This is a brand-new pain reliever. It's as effective as narcotics, but not addictive. You can take these as needed, up to three pills a day. If you like them, I'll be happy to write you a prescription. This second bag is a higher dose of the muscle relaxants you've been on. You can take up to four of these a day."

"I don't think I should take a stronger dose of those," she said hesitantly. "I think my muscle relaxants make me depressed."

"You probably just need more time get used to the medication. I don't think your depression stems from the drugs. You may be down because you're in chronic pain or…because of other issues."

Linnea blushed. She was handling her ongoing life situation better than most people would be able to, except for the pain. "There aren't any other issues."

"Let's talk about this next time."

* * *

At dusk a week later, when the bats in the yard took to the wing, Linnea closed *The Princess and the Pea* and kissed

Megan goodnight. Chelsea was in the kitchen, cleaning up the herb salad she'd made them for a green-week supper. Linnea joined her by the sink, not just to dry dishes, but to get a glass of water so she could take another of the pills she'd been anticipating since mid-afternoon.

Her drug-seeking was suddenly shattered by insistent rapping on the front door. Squinting through the peephole, she saw Hommy on the doorstep, holding a mixed bouquet of red roses, while lilies, and pink carnations. With his shoulders hunched, his head hung down, he definitely didn't appear as hostile as usual.

"Please open the door," he begged. "I must see Clary Sage."

"Who is it?" Chelsea whispered.

"Hommy," she hissed. "He's got flowers." Linnea cracked open the door. The lovely fragrance of Hommy's alms washed over her.

Tears sparkled in his dark brown eyes. His chin quivered. He repeated, "I must see Clary Sage."

He looked so woebegone, Linnea felt a stirring of sympathy. "Sit down on the porch," she said gently. "I'll tell her you're here."

She hurried upstairs to the bathroom where Clary Sage was bathing Serengeti. "Hommy's on the porch. He needs to talk to you. He looks awful." June would have added, "Poor man," but Linnea refused to repeat her mother's refrain.

Clary Sage wiped her wet hands on a gold towel and disappeared. Linnea knelt beside the tub, sinking onto the soggy pink rug. She played peek-a-boo with the toddler using a sopping washcloth and a yellow ducky. Clary Sage did not return. Despite the tug on her crooked neck bones, Linnea hoisted the cheerful child out of the water, diapered her, and dressed her in a pink terrycloth romper.

Clary Sage stayed out with Hommy for a long time. Linnea got a bottle from the kitchen and rocked Serengeti to sleep, revising *The Edge* in her head, promising herself that she would take a pill after she had tucked the little girl in for the night.

By the time she returned from the apartment with the baby monitor in tow, the voices coming through the open window from outside were little more than anguished whispers. Trying to ignore the rigidity in her neck and shoulders, she wondered what Hommy wanted. The last time he called was right before she got hit by the ball. He had stopped by to see the baby once at the beginning of the summer, but hadn't even asked for her tonight.

When she was certain Hommy had gone, Linnea got up to peek out the window. They were sitting on the swing together. Hommy's head was cradled between Clary Sage's breasts and now-toned belly. She stroked his shiny, jet-black hair away from his tawny, dark skin. Her blonde hair had grown over the past few months. She'd pulled it into a ponytail to bathe the baby, but now a long tendril escaped, tickling his cheek. She ducked her head and kissed his brow.

An invisible rubber band around Linnea's temples squeezed so tightly, she could have sworn the top of her skull was about to pop off. The muscles at the nape of her neck pulled back in opposition. She spun away from the window and ran into the kitchen for an ice pack.

Back in her office, she typed furiously with her one free hand. If Clary Sage was about to throw her life away, Linnea would hold onto *The Edge*. Even a short article about the farmer's market gave her life a generative purpose. Chelsea didn't say a word as she sketched an ad.

Clary Sage finally tiptoed through the door, holding her bouquet gingerly. They looked up at her expectantly.

"His older brother just died. His parents and sister-in-law are a wreck. They want him to come home for the funeral. He really wants to go, but if he leaves the country now, he won't be able to return."

Linnea stared at the flowers. Was Hommy telling the truth? "How did he die?"

"He shot his gun up into the air protesting the U.S. and the bullet came down on his head. It's so sad. He and his wife have a baby boy Serengeti's age." Clary Sage buried her nose in the flowers. "His parents desperately want to see him and Serengeti. He wants me to marry him, so we can go to the funeral and he can come back here."

"Not so fast!" Linnea exclaimed.

"It would take forever for you to get a passport," Chelsea said.

"I already got one way back when I had the baby. He needs an answer in forty-eight hours. If I say yes, we'll fly to Las Vegas first, get hitched, and head overseas from there. I hate to leave before Megan's birthday party, though."

Linnea was panicked and astonished. "I thought you were through with him."

"I guess he told his family we were already married. He said he'll give me a divorce later, if I'm not happy."

The rubber band reverberated against her brain. Worriedly, she snapped, "Why on earth would you want to go through a divorce in a few months, just to be nice to him now?"

"We might actually like being a family, you know." Clary Sage tightened her jaw. "My mom called me today, and I've been thinking about what she said. Relationships are never perfect. Maybe it's worth a try, to give Serengeti a chance at having a real family."

Shit! I shouldn't have told my mother to make Jean call. Serengeti is doing fine the way things are. She's only seen him once in the past few months."

"You hardly knew your dad, but you still wanted him when he came back," Clary Sage spat.

That rubber band was one nasty slingshot. The tissue behind her right eye spooled around her optical nerve. Linnea tried to picture Rick's face the day he came back last January, but the only thing she could picture now was pressing her new pills through the foil on the back of the sample packets.

"Look, I've become really attached to you and Serengeti." Linnea struggled against the urge to collapse on the carpet and crawl upstairs to bed. "I want you to make the best choice for your future. I don't think Hommy is husband material. If he really cared, he'd have been giving you money all this time and making a point to see Serengeti regularly. Please don't be swayed by a bunch of beautiful flowers."

"It's a big decision to leave the country with him," Chelsea said. "Are you ready to make it?"

Clary Sage looked wistful. "I might be, after my date with Pete tomorrow night. He invited me over to his place."

"What if Hommy sees you?" Linnea asked.

"They don't live on the same floor, and he won't be home, anyway. He has to work the night shift."

"Don't go to Pete's," Chelsea was adamant. "Jeff told me people are complaining about the high-volume, short-term traffic going in and out of his place. He has people showing up at all hours of the day. Dr. Jafairi thinks he's into crank."

"What does Dr. Jafairi know? Pete's just popular."

"He's had a lot of girls there, too."

"I know he plays the field. He's a short-stop, after all." With an air of sophistication, Clary Sage laid her bouquet across her arm like a beauty queen and left the room, heading for her apartment, completely unaware of how self-denigrating her little joke was.

* * *

Linnea overslept the next morning, so she didn't have time to exercise before she left for St. Genevieve's. She scrawled *going to the gym* in the late afternoon slot of her kitchen calendar, as testimony to her intentions to do whatever it took to get back to normal.

At the hospital, she had a variety of X-rays of her neck, and then, wishing she were out enjoying the sun instead, hurried over to another wing for her MRI. As she nervously locked her wedding band, the fake ruby June had given her, and the locket from Rick in the small cabinet the hospital provided, she remembered Dwarfy holding her jewelry in her room on the night of her concussion. She sank onto the stretcher, continuing to see his comforting face as a dry cloth was placed over her eyes. The technologist left the room and Linnea felt herself being drawn into a huge tube. Struggling to breathe calmly with the overwhelming metallic hammering of the MRI beating around her, she staved off claustrophobia by imagining every detail of Dwarfy's appearance.

After the MRI, she had bone scan dye injected in her arm. It would take two hours to travel through her skeletal system, so she went to the cafeteria for a salad with watered-down dressing and a bland roll that tasted like its

195

plastic wrapping. The best part of the meal was one of the marvelous pain relievers Dr. Perdue had given her.

Across the crowded eatery, she saw Dr. Jafairi. He was obviously a good man, but she wished he'd considered compression whiplash when he examined her. *You missed something. Something pretty damn significant.* Instead, she pulled out some editing material and began to work. He probably wouldn't even remember her.

Evidently, he did. Dr. Jafairi came over to her table. "How are you?"

"Messed up," she replied, rubbing her jaw. "No need to beat around the bush, is there?"

"None at all, but may I remind you that Moses *looked* into the bush?"

Linnea stared at him, but she had no chance to question his English or interpret his reply. The intercom paged him STAT.

"Take care," he said, tossing his tray onto a cart. With his white coat streaming behind him like wings, he practically flew out into the hospital corridor. Something about that bizarre exchange made her wonder if he knew anything about energy cysts.

An hour later, she lay strapped to the table, having her skeleton read. She imagined the dye in her system as the artificial tropical punch June had raised her and her brothers upon. The shutter on the camera-like device kept readjusting, droning on like a bee in a hibiscus bush.

Pretending that she was on the beach in Kauai, she floated off into a state of semi-consciousness. She was building a sand castle with her dad and Megan, making love with Dan. She felt so light and dreamy, she could almost smell the gardenia over the hospital's pervasive antiseptic.

She was too tired to go to the gym on the way home. She checked her cell phone and found she had a message from Dan. He had taken Megan to The Mill with him after lunch. This was good news. Dan hadn't carved out father-daughter time all summer. Perhaps, he was getting his feet back on the ground. Maybe they could go back to the way they used to be, to the Happily Ever After, to before Dan succumbed to alcohol and before Rick returned to Pilchuck.

She parked their faded station wagon, giggling with the sheer pleasure of not feeling tension in her neck and shoulders. *Prescription medication is a gift from the gods.* She unlocked the bolt on the kitchen door.

The house was cool and dim, the shades drawn against the afternoon sun. The only sound came from the rhythmic sway of the battery-operated baby swing in the kitchen. Serengeti slept, buckled into her seat, with her chin slumped to her chest. Linnea set her keys down quietly on the countertop. She didn't want to startle the baby awake.

Tiptoeing, Linnea hung her lightweight sweater on a peg in the laundry room, noticing that the door leading to the staircase to the apartment was closed. That was odd. Normally, Clary Sage wouldn't have shut it while Serengeti was downstairs alone.

Linnea turned the knob. The second story air, fraught with hot unstable electrons, bombarded her and she realized Clary Sage must not be alone. The rusty springs of the second-hand mattress were squealing beneath pulsating weight. She knew she ought to shut the door softly, save herself some embarrassment, and figure out what to say later.

"Stop it." She heard Clary Sage gasp. "I can't do this now."

Despite the clammy humidity descending upon her, Linnea froze. June had said such things to Gunter, hadn't she?

"Come on, Miss America," the man panted. "You obviously didn't have any protection when you did it with the sand nigger."

That was Rick's epithet. Was it him?

"Oh, God! Get off me," Clary Sage cried, choking off a sob or a scream.

Linnea glanced around frantically. What did she have in the laundry room that she could use as a weapon? A sponge mop with a hollow handle? A flimsy plastic flyswatter? A box of detergent? The spray bottle of full-strength bleach she'd used to clean the airplane swing? She grabbed it, praying the nozzle would work, and ran up the carpeted steps.

Beneath a panoramic wall poster of the African savannah, Clary Sage lay with the ripped hem of her sundress twisted around her waist. Pete gripped her throat with his fingers, forcing her shoulder down against the mattress with his own. His knee pushed between her clenched thighs. He clawed at her panties. As the toned cheeks his teammates so liked to pat pulsed toward Clary Sage's exposed hips, his brutal movement pushed plush toy tigers and wildebeests to the wayside.

The barbaric violence in the air penetrated Linnea's spirit, calling up the mother lioness that Megan's birth had unleashed in parts of her soul. Instinctively, she roared and bounded toward them.

Pete turned his head, surprise widening his eyes. "You're supposed to be working out," he said, just as she sprayed the bleach right between his thick, curly lashes. His hands flew to his face.

Bellowing, he charged backwards off the bed, like a rhinoceros in reverse. Floundering in its tangled mat of black thatch, his protracted penis shriveled up into his groin.

Clary Sage leapt to her feet. She dashed behind Serengeti's crib, grabbing the cordless phone from the window sill. "I'm calling the police!"

"Call an ambulance," Pete screamed. "I'm blind. My eyes are burning." He ran past Linnea, pausing briefly at the foot of the stairs. "You're gonna be sorry for this!" he shouted. "I'm going to sue you. Your dad is going to sue you."

"You are going to jail!" Linnea screamed.

Guiding himself by the handrail with one hand, he descended into the laundry room and ran out the kitchen door. Linnea followed, spray bottle at the ready, bolting the lock behind him. She hurried through all the rooms on the first floor, verifying that the front door was still locked and slamming any open windows closed. Panting, she returned to the kitchen. Serengeti opened her sleepy eyes, smiling happily. "Nea! Dow!" she called expectantly, struggling against the swing's restraining tray.

Afraid that Pete would break a window and force his way back into the house, she lifted the baby with trembling hands. Despite the strain on her whole body, she ran back up to Clary Sage's apartment, shut the door, and flipped the brass lock.

Clary Sage lay sideways on the floor. Her knees were drawn up to her chest as she sobbed.

"Did you call 911? Are you hurt?" Linnea set Serengeti down next to her toy box and knelt beside Clary Sage. Tentatively, she reached out to stroke her spine. She wasn't sure if Clary Sage could stand being touched, but she did not recoil, so Linnea kept her hands on, instinctively comforting. "Did he hurt you?"

"I'm okay," Clary Sage moaned.

"We should call the police. He was raping you."

Clary Sage cried for a long time. Serengeti crawled over to pat her shoulder sweetly.

Finally, Clary Sage turned her head to the side and spoke almost numbly. "It's my fault. I'm so stupid. I invited him up here to see my apartment. He pulled me into his arms and kissed me. While he was still holding me, I told him I might be marrying Hommy soon. I wanted to see if he'd care, you know? If he'd try to keep me from getting married. If he'd ask me to go steady or something."

"Uh-uh?" Linnea made her voice sound like a lullaby.

"He said, 'How can you marry him after you've been kissed by me?' It sounds jerky, I know, but it didn't sound like that then. It sounded romantic. I just let myself melt in his arms. He kissed me again, and I kissed back."

Her anguish tingled in Linnea's fingertips. "So you wanted to feel loved and wanted. You wanted him to care enough to keep you from making a mistake."

"I'm such an idiot. We made out a little on the bed, but I said we had to stop because I don't have any protection. That's when things started getting out of control." She rolled over to look up at Linnea, mascara underscoring the trauma in her blue eyes.

"We're calling the police," Linnea said firmly.

"You showed up just in time."

Linnea nodded, glancing up at the bed. The indigo fitted sheet had gone as splotchy as her cousin's face. White bleach stains had bled into the fabric, spreading so the blue became gray, taking on the color of a seagull passing into adulthood.

Chapter Fifteen

"Lin-nay-uh!" Dan bellowed at the foot of the stairs. "The hose is unrolled on the patio. Someone is going to trip over it!"

Why did he have to get home so soon? "So roll it back up!" she shouted.

"Mommy?" Megan called.

The urge to hold her child close struck, but she was reluctant to leave Clary Sage. "I'm coming, sweetie."

Slowly, she rose to her feet. Clary Sage grasped her hand fearfully. "What about Pete's eyes? What are we going to tell Rick? And Dan?"

Linnea tucked a wisp of hair behind Clary Sage's ear. "Don't worry about his eyes. I suspect he'll see women with a little more respect after today."

On the patio, Dan was impatiently winding the hose back around the wheel beneath the faucet. She said, "Pete tried to rape Clary Sage." She stared her husband in the eyes, willing him to have an appropriate reaction, for a change.

"Rape?" He repeated the word as if he couldn't remember its definition. "Why would he do that?"

"I don't know. Why would anyone do that?"

Dan looked slightly nauseous. "Is she all right?"

"I guess so. We should get her to doctor just to make sure. I sprayed bleach in his eyes to get him to back off." She waited for him to congratulate her.

Perspiration appeared on his forehead. "How can he play ball if he's blind? You could have really hurt him."

Linnea's pride was suddenly pricked by heartsickness. "And raping Clary Sage wouldn't have really hurt her?"

He grimaced as if she were being obtuse. "The scouts are coming to town later this week. Your dad is going to be upset if Pete can't play."

Rage surged in the pit of her belly. She couldn't bear his presence a moment longer. "I haven't made any dinner. Go get yourself something at the deli on your way to AA."

Dan glanced toward Clary Sage's apartment. "Are you sure you don't need me around?"

"I've got it under control." *Just leave. You're no help, anyway.*

* * *

"You are never going to believe this!" Chelsea breezed through the front door with her laptop tucked under her arm and cell phone in hand. "Jeff's down in the emergency room at St. Genevieve's with a police officer who's having heart palpitations. The cop had just told him a young woman filed a date rape report against Pete this morning when Pete himself rushed in screaming about his eyes. Some woman he got fresh with must have broke into her pepper spray. Hey, what's up with you two?"

Linnea was glad she'd hurt him. "I'm the trigger-happy woman."

Chelsea gasped. "I can't believe he had the nerve to make a pass at you. After what he's already done to your head?"

"Not me. He tried to rape Clary Sage."

Chelsea nearly dropped her computer. She dashed over to Clary Sage, taking her hands in hers. "Did you report him? Have you seen a doctor?"

Clary Sage hung her head. Her chest heaved; unspent tears came to her eyes. She bit her trembling lip.

"She doesn't want to do either."

"Oh." Chelsea stepped closer to Clary Sage. "May I hug you?"

Clary Sage nodded. With tears welling up in her eyes, Chelsea hugged her for a long time. "You'll get over this," she whispered. "It will take awhile, but you will. I promise."

"I was so stupid," she sobbed.

"Don't blame yourself," Linnea interjected gently. "You are the victim in all this. We should report him."

Clary Sage's face crumpled. "I want to take a shower."

"I know," Chelsea said, "but wait until we decide if you are going to press charges."

Stretching her skirt down over her legs as long as it would go, she shuddered. "I'm done with guys. And I am definitely not going to marry Hommy. When he calls me tomorrow night, I'll tell him he can just get on that airplane, fly back home, and stay there forever, as far as I'm concerned. I'm not going to bail him out of trouble. He can just tell his parents that his American wife was too much of an infidel to stay with him."

Sandy bustled through the open door with her arms wrapped around a pot overflowing with delicate blue flowers. She stopped short on the welcome mat. She sniffed the air. "This is about Pete, isn't it?"

Clary Sage began to weep like Cinderella unable to

attend the ball. Sandy quickly set the pot down next to the sofa and sank onto the cushions, pulling her down beside her. "There, there." She stroked Clary Sage's hair for a moment before plucking a blossom from the plant. "Eat this," she urged.

While Clary Sage chewed obediently, Linnea opened her mouth to speak for her, but Sandy gave her a warm, staying smile. "Every woman needs to tell her own story. Here, here, fresh clary sage for everyone." Sandy passed sprigs of the herb to Chelsea and Linnea.

Hoping the herb wouldn't interfere with her pain meds, Linnea popped the blossom into her mouth. When Clary Sage finished recounting, she seemed completely relaxed, but Linnea made a beeline for the kitchen, dipping into her bag of pain pills hours ahead of schedule. She dished up double-malted chocolate-crunch ice cream for everyone else. Upon returning, she handed Chelsea one of Serengeti's baby bowls heaped with ice cream.

"Why are you giving me this?" Chelsea was bemused.

"Because we don't have any purple ice cream. You'll just have to make do with the lavender dish."

"It *is* a purple week," Sandy agreed. "Sixth chakra in full bloom. Right before I got off, Pete came in, blubbering something about trying to do laundry. He handed me the prescription for eye ointment that Dr. Jafairi wrote for him, mumbling something about needing a milder detergent. I knew he was lying through his teeth. His eyes will be better in a couple of days, but he is suffering now." She took a big bite of her ice cream. "Mmm! Mmm!"

"He should be kicked off the Spinners," Chelsea fumed. "Captain Pillar would never have allowed this kind of behavior from his players. Dad won't stand for it."

"Mine won't, either," Linnea said quickly, hoping it

was true.

"I won't what?" Rick strolled through the front door, chuckling about catching his impromptu cue. His happy-go-lucky, carefree grin made him seem as flat as the two-dimensional cardboard cut-out of him that now greeted fans at the stadium entrance.

Linnea wanted to knock him down. "Pete tried to rape Clary Sage this afternoon. Serengeti was here, and Megan could have been. Not to mention me." She was gratified to see a dark shadow fall across his face. Maybe he understood.

"Did you call the police?" he asked quickly.

"Not yet," Chelsea said.

Rick sucked his cheek in, sizing her up. "I'd appreciate it if you didn't," he said slowly. "I'd like to give him a chance to speak for himself first."

Linnea's heart fluttered wildly against her rib cage. "He has to be stopped. Another woman filed charges against him this morning."

"Those allegations are false. My attorney's been working on it all day, and they will be dropped by sometime tomorrow." He stared rudely at Clary Sage. She inched even closer to Sandy. Sandy returned Rick's bold stare on her behalf. He looked away, glancing from woman to woman. "Does anyone know where Pete is now?"

"At home, I'd say," Sandy snorted with satisfaction. "With bandages on his eyes."

"What's wrong with his eyes?" he asked anxiously.

Linnea trembled inwardly, but spoke up firmly. "I sprayed bleach in them."

"What?" he yelled. He looked at her as if she were bird droppings splattered on the hood of his Opulence. "You sprayed my prize player's face with bleach?"

His disapproval blasted her like a car wash pummeling a windshield. As a child, she'd always been convinced the spray would crack the glass, overflow the car, and carry her away from her mother.

Her scalp was clamping down, squeezing her brain like a sponge. The medication had only begun seeping into her bloodstream. She begged it to hurry, to take over quickly "Well, I guess I could have used a flyswatter on his bare butt. I just didn't think it would faze him, since he's so used to all you guys down at the ballpark slapping him there."

"That is so uncalled-for, young lady." He smoothed the front of his Spinners shirt. "But I imagine today's confusion is wearing on everyone. I'll be back tomorrow, so we can talk about this in a more civilized manner."

Linnea's legs threatened to give out beneath her. "Pete's the barbarian here, not me."

Rick held his finger up to his lips as if he were shushing a small child. Linnea felt herself choking on soap suds, but it was only the aftertaste of clary sage. Rick retreated, leaving her spinning in a clammy whirlpool. Car washes weren't safe enough for the finish on his Opulence, but apparently he had no qualms about leaving his daughter drowning in a deep drain. *I should have known better than to get in an Opulence with a perfect stranger.*

* * *

Dr. Perdue's receptionist called right after breakfast the next day, asking her to come in at lunchtime to discuss her test results. Such prompt medical service worried Linnea. "What's wrong?"

"I'm not allowed to tell you *that,*" the receptionist replied. Of course, that was office policy, but did the woman have to make it sound like she did something wrong by asking for information about herself?

She had woken up dizzy and felt quite dopey, but Dr. Perdue's pills were keeping the pain at bay, so she pushed herself to type an article on the Pilchuck city council's decision to incorporate an outlying neighborhood. After that, she drew a donkey on gray poster board for Megan's party the following day. As she sketched, she felt an automatic smile creep across her face. No one was in the room. She didn't have to pretend she wasn't overcome with anxiety about her condition, but she was afraid to let her facade of ease fall. She doubted whether or not she could recover her pleasant face if someone else came along.

Cutting the figure out with scissors made her jaw spasm. She was rubbing her tight arms when Rick came over, wearing his Spinners jersey and a pair of shorts printed with a spider web pattern. He asked Linnea to walk down to the beach with him.

Her entire body contracted, resisting the very idea of going anywhere with him. "I have to set up for Megan's birthday party."

"It won't take long," he wheedled. "Please come."

"No." She held onto the doorknob for balance. "I've got both girls. Clary Sage went to the college to get some more information on financial aid."

"Bring them. We can stop at The Mill while we're out and get the girls a treat."

He was being so nice. She was so befuddled. "I don't have time right now."

"I really need to talk to you."

Maybe fresh air could clear up her confusion about him. "Okay, but no treat." She was ready to listen, but he did not speak as they walked along the tree-lined streets, past hydrangeas, blooming purple and pale blue. Linnea pushed Serengeti's stroller. Megan pulled Dwarfy in her little red wagon. Each time she hit a rut in the sidewalk, he toppled out of his carriage. Serengeti squealed with laughter. Megan began to exaggerate the antics.

Linnea sensed her father was growing impatient, and instinctively aligned herself with Megan's slower, more playful pace. She even stopped to sniff stargazer lilies in her neighbors' yard. Finally, they parked the wagon and stroller by The Mill's back door. Straining to lift Dwarfy from his seat, she deposited him in her father's arms. "Megan can't hold onto him and manage going down the steps at the same time. They're too steep. And you have to go first, so you can stop her if she starts to stumble."

Rick nodded. "Trust me."

Not with her. In a sugar-sweet mommy voice, Linnea said, "Go ahead, Megan. Follow Grandpa down. Hold the handrail and go slowly." She slung Serengeti onto one hip, triggering far more tension in her neck, arms, shoulders, and hips than she'd ever imagined possible. As she looked down at the top of the stairwell, she was suddenly disoriented by dizziness. She clutched at the handrail, breathing as deeply as her tight chest allowed.

Once upon the gravel and sand, the little girls threw rocks into the sound. Linnea and Rick stood beside the wrecked *Aurora.* He said, "You seem really edgy today."

Linnea rubbed her upper arm. It was going numb.

Rick lowered his voice until it was almost seductive. "Honey, I want you to talk to me about the things that bother you. Don't keep it all inside."

She didn't want to share her feelings with him, but she knew it was the adult thing to do. "Okay. I'm worried because I have to go back to the doctor again today. Like, I've said before I can't afford all of these appointments and tests."

Rick sucked in the side of his cheek. She got the distinct impression that he thought she was trying to manipulate him "I'll help," he finally said. "But don't tell anyone."

Didn't he love her enough to profess it through overt financial aid? "Why not?"

"Because it says right on the tickets that fans must assume their own risk at the games. I don't want everyone who ever gets hurt to expect me to pay for their care."

She wondered if he ever intended to replace the nets, but she didn't dare ask now when he was about to help bail her out of crushing debt. "How much can you give us? I need to know, so Dan and I can plan."

"How much have you spent so far?"

"Thousands. Now, we're hard-pressed to make our payment on the new roaster."

"Do you have a diagnosis?"

"Myofascial Pain Syndrome."

Rick rolled his eyes. "That's what they thought my ex-wife had before they settled on fibromyalgia."

Linnea blanched. That was a horrible, mysterious, life-altering condition. "I don't want fibromyalgia."

"Then you won't get it. I'm sure hers was all in her head."

Linnea's drug-induced comfort eroded. "Well, my condition started in my head, too. With a baseball, I believe." She snorted, expelling air laced with agony. Every part of her body ached. "Something is really wrong with me." She couldn't keep from wailing, "The snobby woman on the phone couldn't tell me anything about my tests. And Sandy says we have to buy sage to smudge the apartment after what Pete did in there, and I don't know where to buy it, and I don't what that smoke is going to do to my paint job. It was a really hard color to match."

He stepped close enough for her to see the gray-tinged follicles on his chin and smell the early morning coffee still on his breath. He took her hands and smiled lovingly.

Ah ha! He knows he's been way too callous.

"I need you to do something for me, Linnea."

He's going to say, 'Relax. Daddy's here. Relax and get well.'
"What?"

He squeezed her aching fingers gently. "I need you to write a public relations story about Pete. When the scouts get here, I want them to pick up a copy of *The Edge* and see that the whole community is rallying behind him. Image matters."

Rick's features blurred; his face went fuzzy as if a deceptively gentle tide had suddenly rushed over them with tsunami strength. Linnea felt as if she were choking. Finally, she spluttered, "You can't party all the time, abuse women and expect people to praise you."

The water receded. He dropped Linnea's hands so abruptly she wobbled. "Pete didn't abuse anyone. He's an American hero."

Her upper lip curled back. She hadn't had the urge to bite anyone since Brutus pinned her to the garage floor, but she now wanted to sink her teeth into her father. She just might have to chew through his flesh to see if there was any warm blood flowing through it. "There's nothing heroic about him," she hissed. "He's a villain."

"The girl who pressed charges against him yesterday happens to be the daughter of Kari Delaney, that left-field liberal in the state legislature. Her uncle is the

Superintendent of Pilchuck School District. They're going to court to find a way to void the Spinners' stadium contract. We need to put a positive spin on Pete before they can get organized."

Linnea's muscles clenched. "Dad! You can't put a positive spin on something like this. I saw it with my own two eyes. He terrorized Clary Sage. He could have traumatized Megan and Serengeti for life."

"Oh, Linnea," Rick said, matching her mother's habitually exasperated tone. "You take things too seriously. Pete's just a young guy, sweetie."

"This is surreal."

"Please, honey. I need this. You have a lot of clout in this community."

At least he'd noticed that. "That's because my readers trust me to tell the truth."

"Your truth," he said. "The one based on your morals."

"Well, it's the truth they resonate with. You said I had good morals."

"But your readers aren't your flesh and your blood. Are they? Do this one thing for me. I'm your father. Help make my childhood dream come true."

She was shocked by his insensitivity. "I thought your dream was to own the Spinners, not to use your daughter to promote a jerk?"

Rick stared at her. "You don't understand what I'm asking you to do. Sweetheart," he crooned, "I have a lot more life experience than you do. I know that things seem to be a much bigger deal than they really are when you don't feel well, or...when you're on medication."

That might be true, but not in this case. "This would be a big deal even if I felt great."

"Let's wait until after your doctor's appointment to

continue this conversation."

As artificial, as condescending as his tone of compassion was, she wanted to replay it in her heart and pretend it was real. It was a relief, really, to have a physical ailment which allowed her to postpone dealing with his request. With her spine sinking into the *Aurora*, she looked down at the sand beneath her feet and nodded.

* * *

As soon as she entered the kitchen, Linnea began making paper tails for the donkey. Dan was in the laundry room, scrubbing hazelnut syrup off the front of his shirt. She wished both men would leave and let her focus on the party preparations. She regretted going to her shoreline sanctuary with Rick, hated that he'd tried to desecrate the integrity of *The Edge* in the very spot she'd always found solace and inspiration. Megan had been right to drag her feet, incessantly dropping her dwarf all the way there.

"People were meeting at The Mill this morning to organize a petition drive," Dan said. "Something's got them all fired up. They want to shut down the ballpark immediately and start building the new school."

Linnea was gratified, and then flushed with guilt. She should be rushing to the café to write an article, but she didn't want to. She didn't even feel like calling Chelsea to tell her to hurry down there.

"Thanks for letting me know right away, Dan." Rick patted him on the back. "I appreciate that kind of loyalty."

Suddenly, their camaraderie seemed dangerous to Linnea. She said, "He just doesn't want to lose his coffee contract."

Dan scowled at her, tucking his fresh shirt into his jeans. "That's not it. I believe in the team. Dad has really motivated them to do something special this year, and I'd like to see it continue. I think you need to remind people what a huge asset the Spinners are to our community. In fact, I think you should do a publicity blitz for Pete."

Rick nodded eagerly. "See, Linnea? Great minds think alike."

She looked from one to the other, wondering if they'd discussed this idea between themselves, even before anyone knew of Pete's propensity to force himself on women. "Okay, great minds. Tell me how a sex offender is an asset to the community."

"Don't be ridiculous. He's not a sex offender." Rick said.

"He didn't rape her," Dan added.

"Because *I* stopped him."

"Right," Dan said. "So he didn't do it."

Frustration and fear crackled in Linnea's tailbone. If they would defend a bully, they certainly weren't able to protect the weak, and she was feeling more and more fragile by the moment. "He's not innocent of the crime just because he was interrupted in the act," she snapped. "I just don't understand what your problem is with this, Dan. It's just like you think my head shouldn't hurt because I was hit by a pop fly instead of a line drive."

"*Two* emergency room doctors said you were okay."

"And what if some guy raped Megan, but two emergency room doctors said she was okay?"

Both men's jaws dropped. Linnea wanted to shove cardboard donkey tails down their throats. Instead, she quickly unbelted Serengeti from the high chair and hoisted her onto her hip. "Come on, sweetie," she called to Megan who was practicing her hot potato party game with Dwarfy in the family room. "We're leaving now."

As she stomped toward the alley with Megan dragging

Dwarfy in the gravel behind her, the pressure at the base of her skull simply detonated. Her neck became a funeral pyre, its crackling flames lashing her jaw like forked tongues of fire. A jarring electrical current formed a burning skull cap.

She wanted to lay down on the ground and cry, but she didn't want to scare the children. She knew she should drag herself back in the house, but it didn't feel safe to let Dan or Rick see her in such a vulnerable state.

After she'd buckled both little girls in the back seat of the car, her jaw begin to spasm violently. Glancing into the rear view mirror, she was horrified to see that the paroxysms were clearly visible. By the time she reached Dr. Perdue's office, she had to clench her teeth to appear composed.

Dr. Perdue rushed into the examining room. "Good news! Your tests results are normal."

The peculiar contraction of her cheeks continued right before his eyes. Couldn't he see it? "But I'm still in pain."

"Well, I do think you have a damaged joint beneath the trigger point in your neck. But those sorts of things don't show up on the tests we did. Radiologists don't count soft tissue injury."

Neither did Dad or Dan. Panic overwhelmed her. "But it exists!" she nearly wailed. "Can't you see what's happening to my face?"

He sighed gently. "All you have to do, my friend, is learn how to relax."

"I know how to relax," she snapped. "I had my baby without any pain medication. In fact, my OB nurse said I could star in the next natural labor movie."

Dr. Perdue raised his eyebrow. It was a mistake to mention childbirth. Now, he was going to dub her a hysterical woman. "Are you *really* in that much pain?"

That he would actually take this tack made her wonder if she were going crazy. "Of course, I'm in pain."

"But, I just heard you in here laughing with these little girls."

She lowered her voice, "Isn't it obvious that I would fake feeling fine for the children's benefit?" She stared at the stubble on his chin with horror. Who was he to hijack her pain?

"Hop up here." He patted the examining table. Suddenly, the gold hoop dangling from his ear made him look like a pirate. Was that a bandana beneath his lab coat? He brandished a flashlight like a scimitar. The tissue paper crinkled beneath her.

He sheathed his weapon. "This is all par for the course," he said reassuringly. "It's just a little neuralgia. I'll be right back."

She covered her overwrought eyes with her cold hands. When she looked up, he stood before her, pushing another bag of pills under her nose.

"Go ahead and take two, no, three of these per day."

"But you already gave me those other pills."

She might as well have said she'd eaten two pieces of toast that morning. "Take one of these now and another one tonight. I'm going to a convention in South America for a week. Call me when I get back if you aren't feeling any better."

"You can't just leave the country," she cried, clinging to his sleeve. Didn't he realize he was the only person in her life that had any semblance of a handle on what was wrong with her? She'd never felt so unstable, so overwhelmed by her body, so out of control of her mind. With a husband at AA every night, she was afraid to rely on drugs. "Tell me why I have to take this much medication."

"You want to get better." Dr. Perdue peered at her suspiciously. "Don't you?"

"Yes," she sighed, apologetically releasing his wristband. "But will these make me better or just mask the pain."

"They'll ease the pain while you strengthen your muscles. Have you been keeping up with your work-outs?"

Why would he doubt her? So, she skipped yesterday, but her fatigue had been a good thing. Otherwise, she'd wouldn't have been able to save Clary Sage. "Whenever I contract my muscles, they stay locked up."

"So, you have to stretch them," Dr. Perdue said impatiently.

"They won't stretch."

"*That's* why I gave you muscle relaxants."

"They still don't work. The tissue is stuck together."

Dr. Perdue glanced at the clock.

She knew she was almost out of time. "All these pills make me dizzy and…" She was ashamed to admit that she no longer had the willpower to keep cheerful, but she knew she needed to be truthful, "depressed."

"Clinical studies have shown them to be highly effective in resolving these sorts of issues."

The jangling continued in her jaw, singeing her cheek. *Why doesn't he believe me?* Her face trembled vigorously. "Making me do more of the same thing that doesn't work is abusive. It's like forcing me to have dark chocolate when I wanted white." She held her breath. That sounded insane.

His eyes narrowed. His upper lip curled back. "I'll be

right back," he muttered. "Don't go anywhere."

"I can't stay." She was scared. "I have…"

Dr. Perdue was gone.

I should be at home, stuffing candy into a piñata, instead of waiting for you to fill me with drugs.

Within twenty minutes, Megan had used every tongue depressor in the room to build a house for the one of the more harum-scarum of the Three Little Pigs. Serenegeti had blown it over many times. Twice, Linnea decided to get up and leave, but stopped herself. She was afraid to alienate the only doctor who seemed to know anything about MPS.

Finally, Dr. Perdue showed a bald man into the room. "I'm Dr. Beasley, the psychologist from next door," he said, offering her his hand. "Dr. Perdue thought it would be helpful if I asked you a few questions. It won't take long."

Who was this counselor? What were his qualifications? He was clearly on the verge of mandatory retirement. Was he current? "The girls have been in here quite awhile," she stammered. "I don't know how much longer they can stand waiting for me."

"They're fine," he said in a soothing tone. He opened a cabinet, pulled out a big skein of gauze, and handed it to Megan. "Here, young lady. See what you can do with this."

While Megan mummified Serengeti, Doctor Beasley ascertained that she loved her husband, took good care of their daughter, had a college degree, held a job, and believed in a power higher than herself. Beaming, he backed out of the room, thanking her for her cooperation.

His hurried hallway consultation with Dr. Perdue was not particularly discreet. She heard it all through the crack in the door. "It's not psychological," Dr. Beasley insisted. "It's very subtle, whatever it is, but I firmly believe there's a physical reason for her condition."

"It's got to be psychological." Dr. Perdue hissed. "She's young. She's in great shape. It can't be physical." He paused. "Unless it's hormonal."

"Her case is simply beyond me," Dr. Beasley swung the door back open so quickly, Linnea had to scramble backwards. "Don't worry about the paperwork." He saluted her like a military officer. "I'll get your billing information from the desk up front." He marched away.

"And don't worry about staying overtime, either," Dr. Perdue reassured her from the doorway. "It's no big deal for the girls up front to bill for two sessions at once, a box of tongue depressors, and a roll of gauze."

She wanted to shove a fistful of the oversized popsicle sticks up his nose. "You aren't really going to bill me for the time I spent waiting, are you? And the tongue depressors? How much can a roll of gauze cost?"

"You need to take that up with the accountants. If you have any *medical* questions while I'm gone, you can call my office or answering service. They'll know where to reach me." He handed her three prescriptions and another bag. "Get these filled ASAP. There's a little anti-depressant for you in there. I think you'll be happy with it. Until we meet again, good luck!"

With trembling hands, Linnea liberated Serengeti from the gauze and gathered their things. She secured the girls in the backseat and drove home with her face still spasming. She had MPS, the "cure" made her feel worse, and drugs were the only way to deal with it.

Chapter Sixteen

When Dan came to bed that night, Linnea was barricaded behind a large assortment of contour pillows. Wearing an expensive magnetic mask to steady her palsy, she'd donned earphones, the better to hear meditative music. But she couldn't bare her teeth like the wolf in Little Red's tale. Her silicone mouth guard was clamped around them. She lay stretched out on a heating pad, elevating her feet on a sleeping bag. An ice pack was lodged between her trigger point and shoulder.

Dan lifted one of the foam-covered microphones away from her ear. "What's that weird smell?"

"Essential oil. Lavender. For relaxation."

"I don't like it." He sat waiting for her to get up and remove the cottons balls from inside her pillowcase.

Like a tube of toothpaste squeezed from the center, her anger squirted through her guarded teeth. "You're acting like an asshole."

He sounded hurt. "You don't have to swear at me."

"You complain about the cost of my treatments, my ice packs, and now my lavender. I'm in pain, Dan. You feel great and you haven't offered to do anything to help me. I

219

think I'm entitled to a little profanity."

He tensed. "Did the doctor say when you'd be back to normal?"

I'm becoming a wicked witch and I can't stop myself. "Any dosage now."

"This bed is too crowded for me." With a long-suffering sigh, he let the earphone snap back against her TMJ. He yanked the sleeping bag out from under her knees and left the room. She was too tired to fight. A wife in pain has its perks for a man who would rather walk out on significant conversations than solve problems. She sure needed someone to help her solve this one.

Linnea took a neuralgia pill to settle her face. Then, she lifted a pain capsule to her lips and paused. There was so much substance abuse in her family, she wasn't keen on taking more of what she already knew made her depressed, not to mention, dizzy.

Overwhelmed and confused, she could barely hold onto a thought, yet an idea was forming. She'd always been able to use her mind, her work, to keep from feeling emotional pain. If, as the conversation between Dr. Perdue and Dr. Beasley implied, her pain was at least partly psychological, she could theoretically skip the pain meds and will herself not to feel the barbed wire of inflammation along her neck and in her upper spine. It was quite a trick to control physical pain, but she wanted to try it. She skipped the drug, drifting off into an uneasy daze.

Throbbing pain roused her early. Her mind seemed partially out of her head, but she had no idea where the externalized part had gone. Linnea sensed her cheeks still convulsing, but not quite as strongly as they had the day before. She took another neuralgia pill, got out of bed, mixed the cake batter, and put the cupcakes in the oven before Megan woke up so the birthday girl could breakfast amid the celebratory aroma.

As a sudden craving for a pain pill struck, she clenched, challenging herself to wait until she couldn't stand the incinerating friction in her neck a moment longer. Mind over Matter would be her mantra. Once the cupcakes were cooling on the rack, it was time to head to the village for party favors. She knew driving was risky while taking new medication, but her body ached too much to walk one overwhelming mile. She buckled Dwarfy's seatbelt, wishing he could drive.

She couldn't find her sunglasses in the car. The bright sunlight was nearly blinding. Squinting, tearing, she drove to the bookstore. The owner showed her the newly-arrived miniature books containing Hans Christian Andersen stories. She bought enough of the tiny books for each party guest to get one. He also showed her a collection of *Perrault's Fairy Tales*. She had an old tattered copy herself, but Linnea couldn't resist the rich, red leather binding. She bought the book for Megan immediately. No matter what happened at home now, Megan would have Charles, just as she'd always had Hans Christian.

By the time they left the bookseller's, she was dismayed by how much her meager energy had dissipated. She led Megan into the boutique next door to buy a pair of sunglasses for the drive home.

"Mommy!" Megan tugged on her hand and pointed to a white chiffon gown with a sky-blue sash, displayed in the children's section. "Dwarfy says I should get that dress for my party. It will make me look like a princess."

Linnea was startled to see double daughters when she looked down. "You already look like a princess." It took real effort to read the numbers on the tags, but she finally found Megan's size on the rack and tossed the gown onto the counter. The price the cashier announced increased her anxiety momentarily, but she already had other things to stress over. *A little girl only gets a few birthdays before party dresses and dwarves belong to a bygone era.*

* * *

By three o'clock, Linnea was ready to collapse. She was as dizzy as if she'd been twirling in place for several minutes, but even so, she managed to balance the rhinestone crown on Megan's head. The sparkle of false diamonds and the cheers of the other children triggered more tingling in her scalp. She squinted at Megan as she joyfully ripped wrapping paper from her many gifts.

By the time Linnea had gathered the cards in a pile for future thank-you notes, the vibrations in her head had dislodged an unending reel of random images. Her brain was hell-bent on producing a scintillating fireworks show of its own. She tried to stop it. She tried to resist her pain, but she could not control what was happening to her. No matter what Dr. Perdue thought, it was all absolutely independent of her mind.

In the kitchen away from the others, Dan watched her struggle to light the five pink candles on Megan's heart-shaped cupcake. "Are you okay?" he whispered.

Her hand shook so much she knocked two candles over. "I'm fine."

"What's going on with you?"

The venom in his question scared her. Her hand slipped into the pink frosting, destroying all her careful spreading. But eight little girls and a few of their mothers waited on the other side of the wall. Linnea picked up the butane lighter and squeezed the trigger. Even the scant finger motion increased the tension along her arm, accelerating the sensations in her head. She was too weak to sustain the flame.

"Let me do this." Dan grabbed the lighter from her hand. He righted the candles and lit them.

Linnea sobbed. "But I want to carry it out to her."

"Are you having PMS?" Dan whispered. "Are you pregnant?"

"How could I possibly be pregnant?" She wiped her sugar-coated hands on a damp dishtowel, blinking back the tears. "You shouldn't have left the sleeping bag on the couch this morning. Do you want Clary Sage to know we aren't getting along?"

Dan shrugged.

He didn't care. She shouldn't have asked. Now, to top off the pain, she had hurt feelings, too. Linnea sucked in her spasmodic cheeks and carried the flaming cake into the dining room, praying she wouldn't drop it and burn the whole house down.

Near the end, when all the smiling little girls and their charmed mothers were gathering their things to leave, Rick showed up with an extra-large pizza and a shiny pink bike for Megan. It glistened, half in and half out of the trunk of his Opulence.

"Thank you, Grandpa!" Megan threw her arms around him, showering his cheeks with kisses.

He straightened the crown their hug had knocked askew. "You are very welcome, Princess. It was about time you got an upgrade." He chatted briefly with the guests as they left, exclaiming over the lovely party.

Megan stuffed Dwarfy into the basket on her new handlebars. "We want to take a ride, Daddy. Walk with us?"

He glanced at Linnea. Was he thinking that leaving

was exactly what he wanted to do? "We'll heat up the pizza when we get back."

Once they were gone, Linnea sank into the porch swing, shivering. The crown of her head felt like a twirling top.

Rick scanned her twitching countenance. "I guess a kid's party can take a lot out of you, eh?"

You wouldn't know. You never hosted one.

"I wish my mother had thrown parties for me."

Through the open window, she could hear Clary Sage washing dishes after the party.

"I was going to call you last night to ask how your tests went, but I just couldn't get away from the game. Even with special goggles, Pete was four to four."

How could he expect her to care? "I have a damaged joint in my neck."

"Is it is permanent?"

"Hell if I know. I got new medication."

"Let's talk about Pete's article."

Damn. "Chelsea won't go for it." She hadn't dared to bring his suggestion to Chelsea's attention, but she was willing to wager on her attitude regarding it.

"She will, if you say so."

"I won't say so, and I would never make Chelsea do something against her will."

Rick pushed off with his feet, rocking the swing wildly. "There a subtler ways of persuasion."

By now, Linnea's equilibrium was irretrievable. She grasped a porch pillar. "I don't manipulate people. I need to go lie down for awhile," she gasped.

The instant her head hit the pillow, Linnea remembered Megan kissing Rick in front of all her friends.

As her heart lurched into palpitations, she succumbed

to a psychedelic scene of moldy tessellating bath tiles. She felt the cloying sensation of being smothered by wet sheets imprinted with rag doll candy hearts. She couldn't extricate herself and missed Megan's birthday dinner.

* * *

Clary Sage tried calling Dr. Perdue's answering service, but the switchboard operators said he wasn't answering his cell phone. Linnea was bedridden the whole weekend. On Monday morning, the bedside phone rang shrilly, jolting her to consciousness. A friendly woman's voice said, "I'm calling from Dr. Beasley's office. I see your insurance doesn't actually cover psychotherapy, so I need your zip code to send you a bill."

What a relief! Contact with a professional. Linnea's mouth was parched. She could only croak, "Is Dr. Beasley available right now? I need to talk to someone right away."

The receptionist put her on hold. Linnea sat up, noticing Dwarfy on Dan's pillow. *At least I've got you.*

"This is Dr. Beasley."

Linnea explained her hallucinations and weakness over the weekend, nearly wailing. "I missed my daughter's birthday because of whatever is happening to me."

"Sounds like your meds need to be adjusted. I'll see if I can track Perdue down," he promised. They hung up. In a few minutes, he called back. "I reached him in South America. He says you can take more or less of the neuralgia drug. It's up to you to decide what feels the best."

Linnea was shocked. "I have to pay him two weeks worth of grocery money *and* dose myself? He's the one who went to medical school."

Dr. Beasley sighed. "I really wish I could help, but I'm not a medical doctor. What do you want to do?"

"I want to quit taking it," she sobbed. "It doesn't feel right. I have never been so out of control in my entire life."

"Perhaps you should see a neurologist. I've got the name of a woman here."

She noted his referral, hung up, and donned a pair of the chenille socks Rick had sent her months ago. With Dwarfy in her arms, she padded stiffly downstairs to the kitchen. What had become of her domestic realm without her?

* * *

Always waiting. At least at Dr. Amani's office, Linnea could admire the neurologist's collection of Oriental art. She sat contemplating a man-size statue of Ganesha, the Hindu god of wisdom and literature. His elephant head hovered behind and above the doctor's chair. She peered into his merry eyes as though he were to provide the diagnosis.

Dr. Amani came in through a side door. The women shook hands over an ink blotter and an expanse of mahogany so obviously expensive that it made Linnea think of Rick's car.

Dr. Amani's stout but upright stature and unwavering grip suggested a soothing stability. The jet black chignon at the base of her neck not only kept the hair out her face, but seemed to promise she would allow nothing to obscure her professional vision. "I'm sorry to keep you waiting. I was with a patient upstairs. I didn't want to leave her alone while the nurses changed shifts."

Linnea sat back in the leather chair, reassured. *A caring woman doctor is just what I need.* She answered all of the neurologist's questions about her injury and recited her history of treatment and medication.

As Dr. Amani finished reading her chart, a brief knock

sounded on the outer door. A young medical assistant, as willowy as the physician was stocky, turned the knob without waiting for an answer. She minced into the room with a simpering smile, balancing a steaming cup of coffee on a small tray.

Dr. Amani grinned lasciviously. "Ah, here comes my obsession."

Her uncommon candor about her relationship with an employee was startling, but heartening too. Linnea supposed such a forthright person would be straight forward with her about her mysterious medical condition. Nevertheless, she blushed.

Dr. Amani laughed. "I don't mean Monique. It's the coffee. I get it locally at a charming little place called The Mill."

Linnea sniffed the air, attempting to move beyond her faux pas. "Spinning Wheel Bay Blend is always a good choice in the afternoon."

Dr. Amani corrected her. "Miller's Blend."

"Spinning Wheel Bay," Monique grimaced apologetically.

Linnea felt the need to explain her expertise. "My husband and I own the Mill."

"Hmm." Dr. Amani glared at her over the rim of her mug. She obviously didn't like being corrected. "I'd offer you some, but my first suggestion for you is to cut down on things that stimulate your nervous system." Monique slipped out of the room. The doctor sipped her misidentified obsession, eying Linnea suspiciously. "You say you got a whiplash from a ball falling on your head?"

"A compression whiplash."

She peered over the rim of her mug. "I hate to ask, but I have to. Has your husband ever beat you up?"

Linnea's legs twitched. Could something Gunter did have shown up on her bone scan? "No."

"Come on," Dr. Amani snapped. "Tell me the truth."

"He hasn't hit me." *He just doesn't seem to care I'm hurt…and he spends all his time at AA.* Disbelief was stamped on the doctor's face. No one trusted her perceptions anymore. She broke down in tears. "I'm sorry," she sobbed. "I…he…it's just that he's a recovering alcoholic and things have been…difficult between us lately."

"It runs in families." She scribbled something in her notes. "You are probably just like your mother."

Linnea stopped crying. "What?"

Dr. Amani closed her notebook. "You are co-dependent."

Linnea knew the statistics. It made sense the doctor would jump to conclusions, but still she bristled instantly. "I am not co-dependent. I'm the one who encouraged him to go to AA. Heck, I dialed the hotline for him."

"I'm sure you did." Dr. Amani stood abruptly. She snatched a box of facial tissue from a side table and plopped it down to the right of her. Startled by the sudden incoming object, Linnea winced. Her scalp convulsed. She grabbed her temples, trying to hold her head, her very self, together.

"Ah ha." Apparently, her fear of head blows made Dr. Amani feel triumphant. "Time for the examination."

In the next room, Linnea sat on yet another tissue-covered table having her knees pounded upon with a rubber mallet. Dr. Amani gripped Linnea's upper eyelashes, shining disturbing lights into her pupils for so long that she gasped, "That's too intense. Please stop."

Throughout the exam, Dr. Amani swooped in and out

of her peripheral vision, snapping fingers and poking at body parts. All the while, she exuded an impatience that bordered on anger. By the time it was over, Linnea felt as fragile as her mother's Old Country tea set, certain she would shatter at the next provocation.

Back in her private office, Dr. Amani asked. "Do you have a drug contract with Dr. Perdue?"

"What's a drug contract?"

"A promise not to seek medication from other physicians for drugs already prescribed."

"He never mentioned anything like that."

"The symptoms you described having over the weekend and your oversensitivity to stimuli today are classic withdrawal symptoms. When you stopped your pain pills because of the new neuralgia drug, you went into withdrawal. You've been abusing narcotics."

Linnea was stunned. "I only took them for a week. Dr. Perdue said they were non-addictive."

Dr. Amani looked incredulous. "And you believed him?"

Flabbergasted, Linnea struggled to come up with a good excuse for trusting her doctor to heal her. *My mother believed in doctors, so I do, too? Does that make me doctor co-dependent?*

Dr. Amani whipped her prescription drug reference book off the shelf and flipped through it. "It's like opium. You were only supposed to have one a day, not three." She shook her head disdainfully, as though Linnea should have known better. "Are you willing to give them up?"

"Of course, I'm willing to give them up. That's why I'm in withdrawal." *Why would Dr. Perdue do that to me? How could he be so reckless with my body...my mind?*

"We can get rid of your trigger point with Erasure

injections. In fact, I'd be happy to do it for you after my next appointment. I ordered a vial to use on a patient this morning, but she phoned in with a touch of the flu. If you'll wait here, I'll be back in twenty minutes. We'll take care of this thing once and for all."

Hope quickened in her core. Relief from the pain and enduring tension would be so welcome. "Is it safe?"

"Of course," Dr. Amani said haughtily.

"It's botulism."

"It's pharmaceutical grade." Dr. Amani left the room.

Don't be so paranoid. The voices of June, Rick, and Dan rang out in her jangling brain. Nonetheless, with a racing heart and trembling hands, Linnea dialed Chelsea on her cell phone. Chelsea went online to look up the use of Erasure for trigger points. She read several Internet articles to Linnea. One detailed some of the negative side effects to the treatment and there was even a class action suit against a neurologist who'd used it.

Dr. Amani returned. "I'll inject several places around your scalp and a few spots up and down your neck." She quoted the price.

When Linnea looked heavenward at the outrageous expense, she met Ganesha's gaze. The elephant head rolled his eyes wildly, showing her the whites. He waved his trunk from side to side.

She quickly masked her surprise. It didn't seem prudent to confess a real-time hallucination to someone who already thought she was her husband's doormat and a drooling drug fiend. "Can't I have just one injection? I don't want to use the whole vial if I don't need it."

The now animated Hindu winked at her. *I probably shouldn't sleep with Dwarfy anymore.*

Dr. Amani surveyed her coldly. "You have to use the

whole thing."

"I'd rather waste it than pump too much of something dangerous into my body. How is using more Erasure than necessary any different from abusing any other drug?"

Ganesha nodded at her approvingly, but Dr. Amani gave her the same disparaging look that June always did when she checked her fork for cat hair. "There are several studies that show Erasure is extremely safe. I'll have Monique copy an article while I'm injecting you."

Linnea leaned forward, squinting slightly at Ganesha. "Will the shots take care of my myofascial pain and all these spasms?"

"Yes. I'd also like you to continue taking what Dr. Perdue gave you for neuralgia, but you have to promise to build up to your maintenance dose slowly. You can't just start slamming them down for kicks, like you did. That causes seizures. You have to titrate up, according to the manufacturer's recommendations."

"I didn't do it for kicks. Doesn't Doctor Perdue know how it causes seizures?"

Dr. Amani shrugged. "It's well-documented."

"So really, the symptoms I had this weekend were not only a combination of opium withdrawal, but also a too-quick a build-up of the other drug?" Linnea was bewildered. "I can't believe my treatment laid me up even more than the initial concussion did. If the Erasure will stop the spasms, and presumably the pain, why should I keep taking the neuralgia pills?"

"I think you've become hyper-sensitized to any form of mild discomfort. You can stop taking the pills as soon as you stop focusing on your pain."

"Are you telling me that if I develop the ability to ignore my pain, I won't have to take the drugs anymore?"

The doctor nodded.

"Then you're saying that my pain isn't real. You think it's a figment of my imagination?"

"Not exactly. You do need the injections and the medication, but your brain is fooling you. The pain isn't really as bad as you think it is. Most of it is in your head."

The muscles around the base and the tip of Linnea's spine contracted. That's what Rick hinted at on the beach.

Dr. Amani shrugged. "You have a weak psyche. Admit it."

That felt like her first and only bikini wax patch being ripped away. "I do not have a weak psyche! I am a conscientious mother. I support my cousin and help her take care of her baby. I publish a paper that empowers people to make informed choices and give back to my community. On top of that, I keep my alcoholic husband stable. And, I've compassionately welcomed my heartless, prodigal father into my busy life, even though I spent my childhood cowering before my stepfather and comforting my mother.

"So how dare you tell me I'm creating my own suffering? I don't want it, and I don't want the debt it's bringing me. You say my mind is creating it. I say, since I can manage everything else in my life, I am certainly strong enough to control my mind if I want to. Well, I've tried and since I can't stop the pain, I don't believe my mind is making it. Something else is going on."

Ganesha shook violently. He nearly hit the doctor in the back of the head with his trunk. "That's right." His deep voice rumbled all the way through Linnea, down to her toes. "Your psyche is as strong as Atlas. It's using your body to let you know its time to shift the weight."

Instead of being concerned because she could hear a

statue talk, Linnea wondered, *Why would a Hindu god be so chummy with a Greek one?*

Dr. Amani's nostrils flared like Gunter's used to when he was losing his patience. "Are you ready for the Erasure?"

Ganesha trumpted. As the sound waves wafted over her, Linnea realized she'd had enough of other people's prescriptions and of their denying her the power of her own perceptions. "I don't see the point in treating my pain with poison."

Dr. Amani threw up her hands. "Then you've wasted enough of my time for today. Just tell me, if you aren't interested in medication and modern treatment, why are you seeing a Western doctor?"

Suddenly, Ganesha's entire head split into a million tiny comets with white, red, and black scarves for tails. They spun about wildly, as if caught in a tornado. Some fell away from the eye of the storm, realigning by color, and settling over the pharmaceutical reference text on the desk between the two women. The layers took on the appearance of three separate books. In them, Linnea recognized her collection of Andersen, Grimm, and Perrault stories.

Within the throb of Ganesha's headless heart, she heard the words, "Physician, heal thyself."

Jesus said that.

"I don't know why I'm seeing a Western doctor. It's a good question. Thanks for asking."

The whirling comets became an elephant's head once more. Ganesha winked at her as Linnea backed out the door without a prescription.

Chapter Seventeen

Dan sat on the bottom step, hastily tying his shoes. "Megan wants to come to the ballpark with me tonight. I told her she could, if she left Dwarfy here."

Dizzy and distraught after her appointment with Dr. Amani, Linnea felt comforted that he wanted to do a father-daughter outing. She'd have time to herself that evening. But she was also annoyed at him for excluding Dwarfy and worried that he wouldn't watch Megan closely enough. "You'll keep her in the booth, right? You won't let her go into the stands unless you're with her and you have your glove?"

He sighed loudly. "She's not going to get hurt."

"You can't know that for sure." She felt guilty for not trusting him.

"What did the doctor say?"

That I'm an opium addict. "It's not something a neurologist can help me with."

He sighed. "So we're back at zero?"

Anger at being caught between the medical system and his impatience flickered through all of her nerve endings.

"She likes your coffee."

234

"Great! Can I pay her in beans?" He actually looked hopeful.

Megan minced downstairs, carrying the dwarf in front of her. "Mommy, please keep him company while Daddy and I go out."

Who's babysitting whom tonight? "Sure thing. Dwarfy and I are really tight."

"Tell him the Rabia story."

"Which story?" Dan asked.

"The one Mommy told us." Megan looked up at him as if he should remember. "Dwarfy loves it. It goes like this. One day, the mystic Rabia from Basra and her best friend discovered they were out of onions. The maid was going to borrow one from a neighbor, but Rabia said no. She'd made a promise to only rely on God. Only God could give her the things she might need. Just when she said, 'Don't go next door,' a bird flew over their fire and dropped an onion into the frying pan. It was all peeled and sliced. And Rabia said, 'I don't think so because,'" Megan paused and chortled, "'The higher power is not an onion vendor.'"

Despite the tension between them, Dan and Linnea chuckled in unison.

"And guess what?" Megan went on.

"What?" Dan asked, obviously enjoying her recitation.

"They ate their dinner without an onion."

For a moment, it felt like it used to, before Rick returned.

Linnea sent her family off on lighthearted terms. When they were gone, she got her old Hans Christian and Brothers Grimm fairy tale books from her bedroom and the Perrault volume from Megan's. Her cheeks were so rigid she couldn't chew, so for supper, she chose a bottle of the guava juice she'd been rationing since Rick brought it back from Hawaii.

She had so much to sort through and figure out. She sat at the dining room table, sipping through a straw, trying to choose which book to open first. Rick's voice interrupted her. "Hi, sweetheart!"

Her neck hurt. Miserably, she peered through the open window at him.

He flattened his nose, pressing up against the dusty screen. "What's new?"

I have a weak psyche. "Dan and Megan just left for the game." *You go, too.*

"I had a little chat with Chelsea."

And I had a little chat with a Hindu god.

"Why didn't you tell me *The Edge* takes two weeks off at end of the summer? Now I only have a few days left to convince you to give Pete a positive spin."

She stared at the huge spider front and center on his baseball cap. Ever since his return, he had assured her that she could be honest with him. Well, now was the time. "I thought I made it clear already, Dad. I don't want to do it. So quit badgering me."

"I see." He sucked in his cheeks and turned away. Rick let himself through the kitchen door. She felt the urge to flee out the front, to head toward the water, but she was too stiff to move like that. Pain or no pain, it was time to face this head on.

Once inside, Rick spoke slowly. "You know, I've put a lot into this deal with Pete, and I stand to lose a lot if you won't do this for me. In fact, I'm not sure I can handle Megan's tuition or help out with your medical bills if I can't sell his contract this year."

She knew he was lying. His expectation that she would

believe him was humiliating. "I wish I could rewind time and erase what you just said. It's bad enough you asked me to compromise my integrity and my paper in the first place, but I can't believe you are threatening me and Megan."

"Hey, I'm only asking you to make up a little story for me, like the fairy tales you like so much." Rick modulated his voice so it flowed over her like sweet molasses, but his whole demeanor was hard-baked. He wasn't going to yield.

Neither was she. "Dad! You are asking me to lie, to deny everything I saw and felt, to protect a jerk from the consequences of his actions. You're asking me to pretend that brutality and selfishness are all right. I can't do it. And it's not good for your soul for you to ask me to. It's making me sick."

A not-unfamiliar dark shadow fell across his face. "You'd better enroll Megan in public school, then. Just be sure to stock up on bottled water in lunchbox sizes. You don't want her to get sick."

Most people think there's a big difference between a violent man who overtly hurts women and children and a cool, calculating power monger. But Rick's lack of compassion was dangerous. It was exactly what had made it so easy for him to leave her with an abuser. His abdication of emotional and social responsibility granted men like Gunter and Pete free license in the physical realm. Linnea had pretended to be his princess, but he was unqualified to be a king. "Please don't be like this."

He held his hand up, blocking her plea. A bolt of lightening flashed within her skull. Rick's face suddenly went awry, like a Picasso painting. His features fell away. Some blacked out before others, but what was left after the jagged illumination was simply negative space. Fascia in the center of Linnea's forehead contracted into a tightly clenched sphincter desperately trying to block her peephole into his deformed soul.

"Call me when you change your mind," he said turning to go.

Automatically, she carried Dwarfy upstairs to Megan's room. Megan's educational future wasn't clear, but no matter what happened to her, at least her child would have a comfortable nest to come home to. She pulled her daughter's comforter back on the bed and plumped the pillow.

Linnea could feel the shattering beginning deep within in her bones. Nevertheless, she picked up the plastic bat to drop it in the toy box. Some crumpled black fabric spilled out of the chest. Megan had been practicing echolocation, carrying the bat, wearing Clary Sage's burka.

When the phone rang, she thought twice about answering, but decided she'd better. Maybe Dan hadn't been paying attention and let a ball fall on Megan's head, too. It was Dan. Her heart stopped with fear, certain Megan was on her way to St. Genevieve's.

"Hey," he said, "I need you to call the new kid and ask him to open tomorrow. I don't know his number at the dorm yet, but his parents are in the directory. They'll know how to reach him."

"I'll call." She mumbled into the cordless receiver, mindlessly returning to Megan's room.

"What the matter?"

The fascia around her neck squeezed like a noose. It was physically and emotionally excruciating for her to say, "Dad says that if I don't write an article about Pete, he won't help pay for Megan's school or my medical bills."

Dan's tone was flippant. "It's not that big a deal, Linnea. Media serves the sponsor all the time. I've got to go now. There's a line all the way to the front gate. People are dying for my new iced cappuccino. That new orange twist did the trick."

Her lungs suddenly refused to expand. Her heartbeat shifted into a sporadic rhythm. She was afraid to be alone. She picked up Dwarfy. Carrying him and the burka downstairs, she zombie-walked through the laundry room and back up to the apartment heavily scented with the blue flowers hanging from baskets in all four directions. *I'm still okay. I'm tidying up. I'm being responsible. I'm taking care of things.*

"Stop it!" the dwarf said.

Oh, my God. He's like Ganesha. She dropped him on Clary Sage's bed, her body trembling.

Feeling as though she were about to rattle apart, Linnea pulled the burka down over her. She sank to her knees like a woman praying for salvation while already encased in her body bag.

She hadn't quite expected the pleasure of sensory deprivation, the somatic hush that darkness elicited. Invisibility could be a comfort to someone already overwhelmingly unseen.

How could Dan have taken her father's side? Now, she had no one supporting her. Beneath the black veil, she suddenly understood the need for wailing walls and professional mourners. Her tears scalded her eyelids as if they were infused with ill-gained onion peel. *The higher power is not an onion vendor. I thought my father was a gift. How can a baseball have wings?* She thought longingly of her drugs.

She must have fallen asleep. She did not hear the keys

jingling in the knob, or the opening of the exterior apartment door. But she felt rough hands grip her upper arms and jerk her backwards so that her already-compromised neck snapped.

A man said, "I see you're ready to go to the airport."

Startled and blind, certain a single muscle fiber was all that lay between her frightened present and future decapitation, Linnea froze beneath the heavy fabric.

He punched her in the jaw. "You'll never betray me again."

"Get away!" she screamed, struggling to escape.

His hands grabbed at her, seizing her shoulders. Trauma and neuralgia reverberated through her neck and skull, but she stiffened her whole body against him, knowing that she could not afford an inch of subcutaneous softness in the grip of a man like this. She'd learned how to become a rock whenever Gunter grew angry. As he shook her, Linnea lost track of time.

She'd been a few years older than Megan was now. She'd just gotten her first bike for her birthday. With no one to teach her, still unsteady on two wheels, Linnea had circled around and around the driveway. The smooth concrete was slick from the mist, but she only fell once, skinning her knee, but not minding, in her general triumph. Finally, she glided into the open garage.

A preschool-age, half-brother was in there, on his plastic trike. As she braked, Jaime veered inward, crashing into her shiny pink rims.

"No, no," she said in a gentle big sister voice. "Don't wreck this."

Laughing, he reversed and rammed into her bike again. He thought it was a game. "No! No! Be nice."

He backed up again, and this time, as he came toward

her, Linnea reached down, picked up his handlebars slightly and dropped them. "No! No!"

Comprehension flooded Jaime's face. The surprising jolt made him giggle. Linnea smiled. They had an understanding.

Over their heads, she heard a roar, the warning sound that would have sent her running for the beach if she hadn't been straddling her soft new banana seat. Gunter swooped, ripping at the snap on her jeans, pushing the denim down over her thighs. Heaving with vengeance for her offense against his son, he picked her up by the shoulder. With the fingernails of one hand digging into her armpit, he dangled her in the air, knocking brooms and shovels aside with his other arm as he grabbed a heavy wooden dowel off his workbench.

Her panties fell around her chafed, bloody knees. She kicked in sheer terror. He swung the pole at her bare bottom and thighs as if she were the piñata at her own party.

The impact cracked a layer inside her. She twisted wildly, trying to make him drop her so she could run away before all her shattered pieces scattered irretrievably. When he let her fall onto the oil-stained concrete, she sensed it would be wiser to head down the street, but she was too ashamed to run naked in public. He snatched at her, but she fled into the house, down the hall. Her lower body throbbed from the assault.

He loped behind her, wheezing with satisfaction. Since his strides were so much longer than hers, he easily ran her down. He pushed her from behind. She fell face-first onto June's freshly-raked shag carpet.

He tossed the dowel aside to grab ahold of her ankles. Linnea tried scrambling away on her bare belly. He yanked her to him, the friction against the rug burned her skin where her shirt had rolled up. "Mommy! Mommy!"

He snapped her to her feet, jerking her head toward to her shoulder. "Look at me!" he demanded.

Linnea tried to send him as much love and compassion as she possibly could. He was her daddy....he didn't really hate her. What was it that Mom said? Yeah, his job was stressful. That was it. In the split second that their gaze locked, she sent an extra burst of sympathy and forgiveness to him right through her pupils.

"Don't look at me like *that*. Smile." He raised his hand, waiting.

She just couldn't manage it. He slapped her jaw; her neck snapped.

Gunter fumbled for the dowel again. Linnea scuttled out of his reach and fled into the impossibly narrow space between her bed and the wall. He'd have to pull the bed away to get to her. Enough time to give June a chance to set the hamburger helping seasoning on simmer and decide to come save her.

Linnea held her breath, stilled her blood, nearly stopped her heart. *Quiet. Don't ripple the air.*

Gunter was winded from the hunt. He stood, huffing and puffing like the Big Bad Wolf, clearly wondering if beating her again was worth the exertion of pulling her heavy mattress frame out.

The hood was yanked down.

"You?" Hommy cried.

Linnea blinked. It wasn't Gunter.

Suddenly, Hommy seemed frightened by his mistake. "You shouldn't have let Clary Sage be with another man. My bride is defiled."

"Let go of me!" Linnea screamed. "She's not going to

marry you. Get out of here."

As she stood up to him, he panicked, pushing her toward the bed where Clary Sage had nearly been raped. Linnea fell onto the mattress beside Dwarfy. The statue bounced up and off the bed, landing on the fervid man's foot. He stamped his heel in pain.

She flew to the other side of the bed. A bat glided through the open apartment door, heading straight for his head, throwing him off balance. He clutched at the bedpost, but the bat beat its wings, swooping at him, shepherding him toward the exit.

This was the best hallucination she'd had yet. Linnea scrambled to her feet, with the black veil falling around her. "Rabia from Basra has something to say to you." Wild-eyed and trembling, she flapped the sides of the burka like a bat's wings. "Do not do what you do from the fear of punishment or for the promise of reward, but simply to serve Love itself."

Terror flashed in the whites of Hommy dark eyes. He backed out onto the landing, stumbling over a huge pot of clary sage bobbing in the evening breeze. Linnea slammed the door and dead-bolted it. He ran away and she pictured the bat chasing him down the stairs.

Prisoner-of-war grade barbed wire scraped the inside of her neck. Her scalp convulsed. Her arms ached as if she and Hommy had been engaged in a tug-of-war for months. In a way, they had: hadn't the last months been all about forcing her kin, Clary Sage, and herself, back, back to scary, powerless times, back to the inexplicable era when June married Gunter. The battle had been far more draining than Linnea had realized. As Hommy withdrew, the palm-chafing rope that she'd been balancing against since Clary Sage and the baby moved in released. She completely lost her precarious footing. Her spine slid down the length of the heavy door. And as she so often did as a child, she slipped into unconsciousness, prostrate on the hard floor.

Chapter Eighteen

In the emergency room, Dr. Jafairi cocked his head, silently studying Linnea's hunched form.

"What's wrong with her?" Chelsea frantically dumped the bags of drugs she'd found in Linnea's bedroom onto the cot. "She swears she didn't take any of these, but she cried hysterically all the way over here and won't say how she got that black eye."

Sandy stepped through the curtain. She spoke to the doctor. "Moses, this is a friend of mine." Gently, she took Linnea's hand and smiled.

Her warmth washed over her like gentle waves, making Linnea feel much less vulnerable. She sat up straight. "Hommy thought I was Clary Sage. He hit me."

"Mohammed did this?" Dr. Jafairi looked ill "I thought he would just go home to his mother after Mr. Andersen told him you found Clary Sage with another man."

"Rick's unbelievable." Chelsea scoffed.

Dr. Jafairi poked through the pills, frowning as he picked up the last batch Dr. Perdue had given her.

"I didn't take any of those," Linnea offered. "Something didn't seem right."

Dr. Jafairi's jaw pulsed angrily. "If you *had* taken this

anti-depressant with all these other drugs, you could be dead right now. Or in a coma for the rest of your life." He nodded meaningfully at Sandy, saying something under his breath that Linnea couldn't quite distinguish. "I've got to go report this. I'll be right back." He rushed away, disappearing behind the burgundy drape.

Chelsea sighed. "Thank God, you didn't mix those medications. I should have gone to the doctor's with you to advocate."

Guilt surged through Linnea. "But, you've been doing both our jobs as it is." Frustrated, she cried, "I'm so sick and tired of this pain. I wish I had taken all those pills together."

Chelsea tensed. "You aren't thinking about suicide, are you?"

The prospect was suddenly enchanting. *Yes.* "I would be if I didn't have Megan."

Sandy held out her open palm. "Quick, give me your necklace."

Too apathetic to ask why, Linnea gingerly removed the chain from around her inflamed neck. Sandy suspended the empty heart over her brow and waited. Nothing happened. The pendant hung as still in the air as a corpse lies in a coffin.

I want to die. Die. Die.

Sandy frowned, replacing the gold around Linnea's neck. "Listen," she whispered, "if Moses heard you breathe a syllable about wanting to die, he would be required to keep you under a suicide watch for seventy-two hours."

Three whole days? Linnea was tempted to confess to him. Yet, if she were committed, her loved ones would dismiss all the things that mattered most to her, her questioning, her advocacy, and her resistance to their ideas of how she should do things as evidence of mental illness. Could she sacrifice her legitimacy for a time-out?

"You need a break." Chelsea touched arm softly. "Don't you?"

Linnea burst into tears again. In a way, it was a relief to admit her life was too much. Maybe Dr. Amani was right. Maybe she really was weak. How often had her mother, Dan, and even Rick implied that she was paranoid?

Sandy cradled Linnea's chin, staring her in the eyes. "Clary Sage and Serengeti are safe now, in a way you and your mother never were. You need to take care of yourself now."

"What about Megan?"

"I'll watch her," Chelsea promised. "I will take her and Dwarfy to Dad's cabin in the mountains for a few days. We'll play. She'll be totally safe. Don't worry."

Sandy stroked Linnea's hair. "Dr. Jafairi is a dear friend. He may not speak English very well, but he can translate his own Rumi. He apprehends trouble with the eye." Sandy winked as though she expected Linnea to understand what that meant. "I could ask him to admit you to the psychiatric ward for observation, but if we move fast, you have another option."

She dug in her pharmacy coat for a ferry pass and a ring of keys. "Here, the bus outside the pharmacy entrance leaves for the dock any minute. Walk onto the Tower Island ferry. Once you get to the island, someone will be waiting for you. She'll take you to a quiet place where you can rest. Stay there for a few days. Relax. Get your head back on straight."

What a strange proposal. "What if I get lost?" *What if I decide to kill myself?*

"The Universe will not allow a single one of its own to be lost. If you can't find your way, call. A legion of angels will come from all directions to help you."

"What about the doctor?" Chelsea whispered. "Doesn't he have a protocol to follow."

"No worries," Sandy whispered. "Every culture has its visionaries. Poor man."

Rick's voice rang out from within the waiting room. "Where is she?"

Dan sounded breathless. "Receptionist said triage."

Beneath her rock-hard fascia, Linnea wanted to run. "Dan won't understand any of this. He'll be so angry at me for checking out. Oh, and I can't even deal with my dad right now. But I should say good-bye to Megan. I can't just run away and leave her."

Chelsea stepped in front of gap in the curtain as if to shield Linnea from Rick and Dan. "Yes, you can. Your black eye might scare her. I'll tell Megan your head hurts and the doctor said you needed to take a long nap right away. She'll understand that, even if your husband and your father can't."

Sandy pressed the keys into Linnea's hand. "Doctor Jafairi will tell them you checked yourself into the psychiatric center and aren't allowed to have visitors."

"What about my neuralgia medication?"

"Here." Sandy scooped up three of her pills. "This should be enough."

Chelsea backed out of the cubicle. "I'll get Megan and take her home to pack. Then, I'm calling the police. Hommy's visa is about to become non-renewable, no matter what he tries to do in the future. Don't worry about a thing. Just get some rest."

Sandy lifted the burka from around Linnea's shoulders

and veiled her face. She led her through the emergency waiting room. It was deserted, except for the two men. Instantly mesmerized by the major league game on the television, neither Rick nor Dan seemed to remember they were looking for Linnea. They didn't even notice the women passing beneath the mounted screen or the hem of the burka brushing over their toes.

Sandy guided Linnea through the drug-stocked shelves in the back of the empty pharmacy. When they reached the rear door, she declared. "All clear."

Linnea pulled the veil away. They were promptly doused with diesel smog emanating from the departing city bus. "Oh! I missed it!"

Imperiously parked in a *No Parking Zone*, with its right wheels claiming the public curb, a black car purred away, polluting the marine air. Sandy grinned mischievously. "Have you ever driven an Opulence?"

Linnea shook her head. "No, but my brother stole one once."

Sandy tucked a package under her arm. "So be his sister tonight."

"What if I get caught?"

"Tonight, St. Genevieve's Psychiatric Center is the worst thing that could happen to you. Come on, dear woman. Have a little trust in your angels." She dug a handful of latex gloves out of her lab coat, pressing a pair upon Linnea. Donning one herself, she reached for the silver handle.

"The door is open," the computerized sensor announced.

"Hurry!" Sandy urged.

Linnea tossed her parcel inside, put on the gloves, and slid onto the decadent leather. She did not take time to remove the burka.

"Drive fast."

Linnea sped to the shoreline. Continually glancing in the rear-view mirror for cops, she finally felt a twinge of kinship with her brothers. *I'm a former opium addict with a weak psyche. I may be crazy. I might have brain damage, but I can steal a car like this with the best of them!*

At the docks, she locked the keys inside the car and slammed the door as the last whistle blew. With the rumble of the boat's engine vibrating the metal beneath her feet, she loped up the plank for walk-on riders. Her legs burned from all the friction the ropey fascia generated while she ran. When the green and white ferry pulled away from the pier, she grasped the handrail steadying herself and catching her breath.

 Shrouded in black, Linnea stood in the shadows on the deck, clutching the parcel Sandy had given her. Fireworks skyrocketed over Spinners' stadium. The home team had won again. The searchlight on St. Genevieve's helicopter pad was on, lighting up Spinning Wheel Village, but Linnea knew no one was looking for her.

* * *

A fine mist ringed the perimeter of Tower Island. When the captain cut the engine, a chorus of frogs serenaded the ferry from watering holes in the dark interior. Linnea's fellow passengers disappeared quickly into the cars they'd left in the lot. Wondering who would greet her, she watched the ferry crew hastily power the boat down for the weekend.

"Ha-lo!" a voice called from below the weathered dock.

Linnea peered over the splintered rail. A wiry, winkled fisherwoman was standing in a small rowboat just beyond the pier. Her face was as pale as bone. She held a lantern, beaming the light through the mist. "You look like the right person. Ready for your trip to the tower?" She illuminated the grassy descent. "Come on."

As if drawn forward by a mystical thread, Linnea practically floated to the water's edge. She stepped aboard; the boat swayed.

"Easy there," the old woman said. "I don't have any life jackets."

"Don't worry about that." Linnea wondered if Sandy had notified the guide of her self-destructive fantasy.

Her escort chuckled, patting the bench opposite her.

"I'd help you row," Linnea said, taking her assigned seat, "but I've been having trouble with my neck and shoulders lately."

"There's no need for you to take an oar tonight. The body is the soul's manuscript and I can read yours. No matter what your doctors tell you about exercise, you should not be bearing weight now. You most definitely need a break from any repetitive or resistance work. But," the old woman eyed her cagily, "if you come out of the tower intact, you'll row for someone else another day."

Linnea settled into her seat, wondering what on earth she meant. Why wouldn't she come out of the tower intact? Clasping the parcel Sandy gave her, she simply said, "My name is Linnea."

"We met briefly at your auction, dear. I chair Pilchuck's Friends of the Library. I'm Serendipity Pillar."

"Of course." Linnea hadn't recognized her in the dark garb. "And you sold the Spinners to my father. He says we're related."

Serendipity smiled knowingly. "Yes. We are kin. And I saw you coming from a long way off." The lantern cast such an eerie glow across the old woman's face, Linnea was transfixed. "I'm not really a fisherwoman, you know." Serendipity rowed away from the dock. "I got this get-up from a mail-order catalog. I call it my Baba Yaga costume."

Baba Yaga, the witch from the Vasalisa fairy tales? The frightening hag who lived in a house with chicken leg pilings that could walk and twirl? The crone who posted the skulls of imposters on her picket fence – who created her own barriers with human bone? Suddenly, Linnea relaxed. If anyone knew anything about the fire inside of her cranial plates, Baba Yaga would be the one.

Very soon, the rickety rowboat ran ashore on rocky beach. Serendipity pointed to the top of a vine-covered embankment. "The entrance to the tower is at the top of the path."

She was afraid of trespassing. "Who owns the tower?"

"My mother left it in a trust, to be used in times like this. I'll be back when it's time for you to go."

"You're leaving?" Was her neuromuscular system destined to short circuit without a single witness? "But how will you know when that is? What if I need you sooner? Is there a telephone in the tower? Do you have a cell phone number?"

"There's no phone service of any kind here. Run along, dear. I need to get on home. My joints pretty much call the shots these days, and it's time for my nightly tincture. Start climbing."

Linnea looked inland. Beyond the beach, all she could see were the outlines of dark cliffs and the shadowy tops of cedar trees. Slowly, she disembarked. The sharp stones of beach poked through the thin soles of her shoes. Fog obscured the moonlight.

"Go on, now," Serendipity urged. "Don't be afraid of

what's in the dark. You need to crawl into it and stay awhile."

Obediently, Linnea picked her way over the rocks, inching toward the path. She heard the scrape of the boat being shoved back into the water. She spun around to watch the figure in black step aboard and shove off with her oars. She was being abandoned on a pitch black beach in the dead of night. A child's panicked scream built in her chest, but the boat disappeared before she could push it up through her throat.

With burning muscles, Linnea made her way to the earthen path and trudged up the incline. By the time she reached the thickly-hewn, wooden seaward door of the lighthouse, she was winded. A dull bulb, too small for its lamp, lent barely enough light for her to insert the key into the lock.

She pushed the door open slowly. As she slipped within, she kept one hand on the knob, leery about locking herself in with the unknown. Ghostly fingers formed by lunar light stretched through a trio of tall, narrow windows. With their assistance, Linnea finally found a lamp made of amber glass and turned it on. A warm, golden glow illuminated the round space.

The whole tower was hushed. Carved out of muted stone, it felt empty, absolutely peaceful. Flanked by two battered stools, a ship's steering wheel was mounted on the end of a massive table, balanced by an anchor attached to the other end. A full tub of pellets to fuel the fire and a bale of straw were stacked beside a stove. A portable bed, looking a lot like a massage table, stood in front of the windows. The thick fleece blankets piled upon it made Linnea want to lie down.

A flurry overhead made her jump. A bat hanging from

an outcropping over the bed opened its wings and then wrapped them back around itself as if in greeting. *Bats aren't bad. Gunter lied.*

Using the book of matches on the table and straw for kindling, Linnea lit the pellet stove. Although her hips hurt, she gingerly climbed up the ladder and poked her head into the loft. The space was empty, except for some sleeping bags. Huge windows served as walls. A strobe light to guide ships was mounted on the sea side.

After descending the ladder, Linnea rummaged through a swaying antique sideboard for provisions. She found a basket of white tea, a dented box of strawberry toaster pastries, and a dark chocolate letter, an S, in its own telltale golden box. *So Sandy or Serendipity spend time here, too.* Linnea set the tarnished tea kettle to boil and popped pastries into an old toaster.

She found several sets of scrubs in Sandy's parcel and changed into a white top and drawstring pants. Taking one of the pills, she climbed beneath the blankets on the narrow bed and nibbled at the chocolate. Staring up at the bat in the moonlight, she scolded herself for leaving Megan without saying goodbye. Why hadn't she remembered to ask Chelsea to look in the dryer for Megan's favorite sweatshirt before leaving for the mountains? The bat rustled softly, somehow assuring her that Megan was fine. She had Chelsea and Dwarfy.

Listening to the rollicking lap of the sea, drifting in and out of consciousness like the tide rolling in and out of Spinning Wheel Bay, Linnea felt safe, hidden away from her father and Dan. In the deep dark, Linnea felt her shoulders let go, just enough to lure her into the softness of the mattress and lull her to sleep.

* * *

Thirteen hours of dreamless slumber later, a seagull pecking at its own drab reflection in the center window awakened Linnea. Drenched in the gray-white light of a socked-in stormy day, she watched the bird. Her neck ached horribly. Turning her head slightly in a futile effort to stretch skin that could not give, she found herself eye-to-eye with a bearded man, sitting cross-legged on a stool.

Shane Carpenter grinned at her. "Somebody has been eating my chocolate. And sleeping in my bed. Are you Goldilocks?"

"Hi," she said sheepishly. Despite the pinching sensation in her neck, she wondered if this was a dream. "Why are you here?"

"I'm staying here."

A strange sense of relief seeped through her unrelentless spasms. "Sandy made it sound like I would be out here all alone."

He smiled wryly, shaking his head. "Oh, Sandy."

"I could leave." Linnea studied his kind face, hoping he wasn't annoyed by an unexpected visitor.

Shane didn't seem angry at all. In fact, he seemed pleased about the mix-up. He reached out to touch her hand. "Don't leave. I'm sorry if I scared you just now. I didn't want to wake you."

Linnea smiled gratefully. "That was very thoughtful of you. I needed the extra rest." The comfortable tingling where his fingers met hers told her she wasn't a dreaming this encounter.

Slowly, he withdrew his hand. "I camped on the other side of the island last night, but the rain brought me back early this morning. Good thing I stopped by the market on my way in. I'm sure you are hungry."

"Sorry. I ate your chocolate."

"Don't worry about that. I'm glad there was something for you." He searched her face. "How do you feel about me being here?"

"I'm not afraid of you." As that truth resonated deep within her bones, uncontrollable dry heaves shook Linnea's whole body. She couldn't stop them.

Shane stood, stepping to her side instantly. He laid a gentle hand upon her upper back. "Now, now. I know I'm not the most handsome brute in the Pacific Northwest, but I'm not that bad to spend some time with."

A stray twig was stuck in his brown hair. Mud caked Shane's jeans. A splotch of chlorophyll on the leg looked like the handprint of a green giant. The hole in his tweedy sock and the hair on his big toe were soothing. "How long are you staying?" he asked softly.

Linnea's stone-hard shoulders twitched beneath his touch. "I'm supposed to stay for seventy-two hours."

"Exactly?"

"Well, as long someone would stay under observation at St. Genevieve's."

"What kind of observation?"

She didn't want to confess it. "I'm on a...suicide watch."

"But who's watching you?" he asked.

"Me, myself, and I. Isn't that crazy?"

He sank back to the stool beside her with a sad sigh. Did he really care? She told him what had happened in the emergency room, how she'd gotten to the tower, how none of the doctors had listened to her for weeks. Linnea's hands wrung the wooly fleece of her blanket with a will all their own. "The neurologist wanted to inject me with Erasure. She said I have a weak psyche."

Shane's serious eyes crinkled merrily. "A *neurologist*

diagnosed you with a weak psyche?"

"Yeah," she sobbed.

He pulled a box of tissue out of a brown paper grocery bag and handed it to her. "It must be scary when all the experts who are supposed to help you, can't or won't."

Shane sank back onto his stool. "This reminds me of the story about the three blind men who tried to describe different parts of an elephant. One man had an ear, another, the tail, and the last, the trunk. But since they couldn't see the whole, none of them were able to identify the elephant. Do you think you have a weak psyche?"

"No."

"And what makes you think that?"

She lifted her eyes to his. "I have never taken any of my stress out on Megan."

Shane nodded. "What else?"

Playful amusement and a bit of daring swirled through her as she blurted, "Ganesha told me."

"The Hindu god with an elephant head?" Like an ember reconstituing a wild fire, the comforting glow in his eyes blazed, momentarily unbridled. "Where did you meet Ganesha?"

She told him. "He almost hit Dr. Amani with his trunk."

Laughed warmly as if they were sharing a private joke, Shane pulled a jute string out from under the collar of his Knights Physical Therapy T-shirt. A clay figure of Ganesha was centered over his collarbone.

Chapter Nineteen

Outside, the late summer rain pummeled Tower Island. Shane grinned when she reentered the room after a warm shower. "You have to feed a broken heart," he said. Hearty waffles with maple syrup waited for her on the table, piled high on a chipped plate beside a cracked bowl of small, ripe blackberries. Chewing was difficult. Nevertheless, her first bite was delicious. "I'm really sorry to crash your vacation."

"Actually it's a vision quest."

Linnea didn't know what to say. Her jaw muscles were so tight that she could barely tilt her chin to sip the pomegranate juice he served, but she took a sip. She hoped the scrub top she was wearing was loose enough. Her bra was still wadded up in the pile of clothes she had tossed onto the straw last night.

"I think I might have the paternal version of empty nest syndrome. I came out here to do some processing around it. My daughter just graduated from the University of Washington in June. She's amazing at linguistics. Last week, she went overseas to study Arabic in Egypt."

I've never heard of men getting empty nest syndrome. Of

course, I'd never heard of myofascial pain before, either. "It sounds like you raised her yourself?"

"I did." His eyes softened.

"So that's why you knew what to do with Megan. I feel bad that I never thanked you properly for keeping her distracted while the paramedics were carting me off. She handled it all really well. Thank you."

He passed her the bowl of berries. "It was my pleasure."

She hadn't thought he was old enough to have a daughter out of college, but he did have crow's feet at the corner of his eyes. There was some gray at the temples, but Shane wasn't old enough to be her father. He was the right age to be a lover. She bowed her head to hide the blush. The pain in her neck quickly curtailed any more romantic musings.

They finished the meal in companionable silence. They tidied up, joking about the makeshift kitchen.

"Why do you think the original Mrs. Pillar mounted a ship's steering wheel on the end of her table?" Shane spun it.

"It must be from the *Aurora*," Linnea said. "When it broke, it brought her true love to her."

He didn't argue. He didn't say anything snide. He simply smiled, making her feel as if she were sipping a cup of soothing tea. He excused himself to clean up after a night of roughing it in the wild part of the island.

Linnea continued to scrutinize the spinning wheel. Could it be the one that originally brought her Andersen ancestors to the area? Was it the severing of *this* wheel by the hand of Fate that Rick had resented all his life, the breaking of *this* wheel's chain that he blamed for all his unhappiness?

Linnea spun it gloomily. Even if it would make Rick happy, she couldn't force herself to write the words he wanted. How could Dan expect her to betray the truth? Just as once verdant grass had become kindling straw for the stove, Linnea felt her own flesh shrivel into fibrous twine. She moaned as the knots tightened.

From the other room, Shane rushed to her aid.

"I'm okay," she gasped. "Nasty spasm."

In his hurry to reach her, he seemed to have forgotten that he was grasping a dusty wine bottle by the neck. Shane didn't seem to be the type to spring liquor on a woman in her condition. Though her tight fascia resisted any such extraneous movement, Linnea nearly arched an eyebrow.

Shane shook his head slightly, holding up the amber glass. "Someone sent a message in here."

Linnea recognized the vehicle of her dearest and most distorted childhood desire. Horrified, she wanted to stop Shane from extracting the note with the tweezers on his Swiss Army knife, but her cry congealed deep within in her constricted throat. *It was a mistake.* He grasped the tightly furled page inside the bottle, gently rocking the paper back and forth until it nestled in the neck. Patiently, he coaxed the scrap up and then through the open mouth. *I don't want to go back anymore.*

"Oh...don't read it," she cried.

Like cells sloughing off skin, the weathered message flaked apart upon his palm, but it did not disintegrate before he saw the childish magenta handwriting: Daddy, please come back for me.

It was wrong to want him.

Fear detonated within every cell of her body, her overwrought nerves arcing as freely as if the stabilizing functions of her flesh had failed. Her muscles clamped down, struggling to subdue the frantic spasms, but to no avail.

Shane scooped her off the hard floor and led her to the narrow mattress. He pulled back the sheets for her, grabbing a pillow to slide beneath her knees. Quickly covering her with a blanket, he pulled one of the stools to the head of the bed. "Easy, now," he crooned. "Close your eyes." He placed his steady hands beneath the firing knot at base of her head. "Take a breath."

Linnea couldn't. Parting her lips was petrifying. Drawing air in through her nostrils suddenly seemed dangerous.

Almost imperceptibly, Shane began to move her head from side to side, like a mother using hip motion to comfort a crying baby. "Slow it down," he whispered. His even steady breath provided a rhythm for her to match.

Haltingly, tentatively, she inhaled and exhaled. Settling into the subtle rise and fall of his open palms, she was buoyed by the ebb and flow of his chest. She heard air coursing through the weathered spokes of the old ship's wheel. Had she set it in motion by collapsing?

"I will help you," he whispered.

A second wave, one of absolute self-loathing, exploded inside of every already terrified cell. Icy cold impatience at herself chilled Linnea's body to the bone. She shivered. "Don't you despise my...helplessness?"

"Linnea, there's nothing wrong with needing assistance." He sounded truly puzzled. "Or taking it." As the old wheel spun, he repositioned his hands, placing his thumbs upon her temples. "Let this space open." The unbearable electrical energy tormenting her slowed. Instead of randomly whipping about inside her cranial tissue, it formed a spiral in the center of her forehead.

"A little more," he coaxed. His tone was hypnotic. Like Hansel and Gretel moving in to nibble on the witch's sugar house, the frenzy behind her brows gravitated toward his fingertips and began to lift.

"What are you noticing?" he asked.

Relieved and exhausted, she began to relax. "I hear the turning wheel…and I smell the straw. The gold on my clavicle is cold."

"Ah!" Shane moved his hands down to her shoulders, lifting the chain with his thumbs. "What does that remind you of?"

Mesmerized by the force flowing between his warm hands, she whispered "Rumpelstiltskin." Images from the old fairy tale wafted through her memory. Like the needle of an old-time record player sliding into a groove on a vinyl disk, her mind latched onto the story, "A girl who had to spin straw into gold."

Shane pressed on a knot in the ropey tissue binding her neck to her shoulder. "Who would ask a girl to do such a thing?"

"Her father told the king she could it, so His Royal Highness locked her up in a tower with straw and a spinning wheel." Linnea sighed as the knot softened between his fingers. He worked better than any ultrasound wand.

Shane gently stretched the spasming muscle. "What if she couldn't do it?"

"She would die…but…a little man got into the tower and helped her."

He snorted. "I'm not that little."

He seemed so calm, so capable. Could he really heal her? "Can you spin straw into gold?"

He laid a fingertip on her troublesome trigger point. "What will you give me if I do?"

Fireworks ricocheted through her scalp. For a split second, Linnea worried about how Dan would feel if he knew she was with Shane. Her body was intrigued by his confident touch, cooperating as if it already understood the sacred contract they were negotiating. She closed her eyes. She felt truly safe with him. Her anxiety flowed right out the opening he'd created at her temples. She floated in exquisite relief.

"Would you give me your necklace?"

"I didn't want it in the first place." How odd. It was true, and yet she'd worn it everyday since Rick gave it to her. Why?

"What's inside?"

Grief in her sternum seeped up like carbon monoxide in a mine. "Nothing," she gasped. "My father gave it to me a few months ago, and it's absolutely empty."

"Take it off."

Painfully, Linnea lifted her head enough to slip the chain over it. She watched Shane shove it into his shirt pocket and closed her eyes again.

"You could lose the scrubs, too," he said evenly, "unless you prefer to wear clothes when you get a massage."

This part would make Dan very nervous, but Linnea found herself surprisingly comfortable with stripping beneath the blanket. Although the muscles in her shoulders seemed glued to her ribcage, she lifted her arms enough to ease the shirt over her head. She let it drop to the stone floor. With difficulty, she removed her pants and tossed them aside, all the while hoping he was adept at draping. There hadn't been any panties in Sandy's bundle.

Shane lifted her right arm out from under the fleece and jostled her stiff limb until it began to relax. "It's always a good idea to get warmed up before unwinding. Tell me the story Rumplestiltskin from the beginning."

Her biceps were melting between his palms. The long forgotten sensation of being soft was delicious. She was in danger of forgetting the fairy tale altogether. "I don't know if I can remember it."

"Just tell me what comes to you. Let whatever wants to happen happen. There's no right or wrong in the tower."

Linnea drew a deep, shuddering breath. "Once upon a time, a poor miller and his wife had a baby girl. When her parents held her, they felt as if a magnet were tugging at their own hearts. The feeling made the miller uneasy, for if the truth be told, he had very little heart himself, and what he did have he'd already pledged to the king. He wasn't willing to let his baby take any more away from him."

Shane laid his hand on her left bicep. Coagulated layers of soft tissue began to separate. "When the little girl laughed, her joy spilled out like rich golden honey flowing over warm buttered biscuits. People who weren't afraid of getting a little sticky liked to listen."

"That sounds nice."

"But it wasn't." Her chest contracted. "One day, the king summoned the miller. The miller left his wife and child, without provisions, an explanation, or even a goodbye, and never returned."

Shane's hands moved to the muscles just below her collarbone. "How did the little girl feel about that?"

"Bewildered, mostly. Especially since her father hadn't been gone very long before a man from a neighboring town came a-calling. He wanted the miller's wife and his mill. He didn't seem to mind taking a child, too. He knew nothing of children, but, at first, he thought having a little girl would be like having a pet, a rabbit, maybe, that he could lock in a cage if she got too out of hand."

"Did he lock her in a cage?"

Goosebumps surfaced on Linnea's flesh. She was grateful Shane's hands were warm. "Not a real one, but his jealousy of her joy drove it inward. Her happiness huddled in her heart. Her honeyed laughter crystallized deep within."

"What did her mother do?"

Sadness filled Linnea's sigh. "She got so busy tending to babies she didn't seem to realize how stiff and quiet her daughter had become. The girl worked hard at home and at the mill. She seemed to be content. She had to. The miller punished her if she ever seemed ungrateful."

Shane approached Linnea's right hip, but her muscles there tensed. He skipped to her calves.

"One day, just before her eighteenth birthday, the king himself stopped by the mill, to request an especially fine flour. Since the miller wasn't very good at it, he called the girl to sift and measure out the best they had. The king admired the stepdaughter's grind, and the miller, swept up in the euphoria of royal praise, blurted, 'I taught this girl everything she knows. I saved her and her mother from the streets.'" Linnea's lower body stiffened. "The miller said, 'Because of me, she can spin straw into gold.'

"At that, the king demanded the girl be turned over to him. She ran into the kitchen, begging her mother for help. The miller's wife threw up her hands. 'I cannot help you. You must go if he wants you.'

"The girl wailed, 'I don't know how to spin straw into gold.'

"Her mother shrugged. 'You'd better figure it out.

Once you leave here, you can't come back. You won't be welcome if you fail.'

"The miller bellowed for them to hurry. The mother dug a golden heart-shaped locket out of a dented tin in the back of the pantry. She slipped it around her daughter's neck. 'Your real father sent you this from afar.' Then, with young ones mewling and tugging at her skirts, she pulled a golden band from her finger. It was deformed from years of toil. 'This is a family heirloom. You have it.'

"The anxious young woman arrived at the king's castle with a dusting of her stepfather's flour across her brow, a chain from an unknown father clasped around her neck, and an ill-fitting ring from her mother tight upon her finger."

Linnea paused.

"Did your mother ever give you a ring?" Shane prompted her.

She sighed, slipping the fake ruby from her finger and handing it to him.

When Shane reached for it, their fingers met. The tingling sensation that she'd felt when he'd touched her hand that morning revived, magnified. Something magical was really happening between them. She launched back into her story quickly.

"The king led her into a tall tower filled with straw. 'Spin this into gold by morning,' he commanded, 'or you'll be out on the street before breakfast.' He locked her in the room with a spinning wheel and went away.

"Left alone, the young woman tried to do as she was told, but straw is straw. Staring at her surroundings, she sank to the floor, anxiously twisting the gold locket around her neck and staring at the ring on her finger. She wanted to cry, but her whole chest had become so constricted and so heavy, she could not even heave it high enough to sob."

The bed jostled as Shane adjusted something. "Roll over now and put your head in the face cradle."

Linnea complied, careful to keep the blanket over her naked body. He laid his hands on her upper back, seemingly asking rigid spinal muscles just how much freedom they were ready for. He slid his hands beneath the blanket, pressing into her shoulder blades. "Go on."

"She sat up all night. Between the damp chill of the tower and the fear for her future, she was nearly frozen by dawn."

In Linnea's mind, Rumpelstiltskin popped out of the center of the spinning wheel. "Then an ugly little man came." She stopped talking. As the image came into focus, she recognized the obsidian eyes, the white beard. "He looks like Megan's dwarf. He was at the ballpark the night I got hit."

"Yes, and at the Mill when we met."

She was surprised. "You remember that?"

"I remember recognizing what an old soul Megan is the second she gave me part of her cookie." He chuckled softly. "Besides that, you make a pretty indelible first impression, Linnea."

That seemed inaccurate, somehow. "I've felt invisible lately."

"Even with your name and picture plastered all over the most popular paper in town?"

Maybe she really was losing her mind. Her pain had drawn her away from reality.

Shane rolled her skin between his fingers down the entire length of her spine. "So what did our Dwarfy say to the young woman in your story?"

"He said he'd spin the straw into gold in exchange for

her ring." Linnea watched Dwarfy hold up a false ruby ring and bite into it, grimacing as it stung his tooth. "He tossed it over his shoulder into a heap of straw and mounted the stool by the spinning wheel. The whirl of the wheel quickly lulled the girl into a trance. When she came out of it, the sun was high and the king stood over her, grinning at the gold skeins. She was astonished and pleased.

"A cloaked servant silently served the miller's daughter a fine breakfast and drew a lovely bath for her afterwards. For the first time she could remember, she wasn't caked in flour.

The servant led her to a magnificent bedroom where she napped the afternoon away. Just before supper, the cloaked woman returned with a midnight blue dress from the tailor. After she had clothed herself in the luxurious velvet, the veiled figure led her to the king's private dining room."

"What does the king look like?" Shane whispered.

"I don't know." Linnea panicked. "There's a tall bouquet in the center of the table. I can't see his face very clearly."

"You saw Dwarfy. Use your inner eye to see the king."

Suddenly, Linnea realized what Dr. Jafairi and Sandy had meant when they indicated her problem was with her eye. "I can't," she said desperately, "but I can hear him laughing. He's so pleased with her beauty."

"Oh, so she was pretty?"

Linnea felt depressed, realizing how long the heroine's loveliness had been obscured by flour. "Of course. It is a fairy tale."

"Did she look like you?"

Her cheeks felt tight, but his indirect compliment made

her smile in the face cradle. Suddenly, seeing His Royal Highness wasn't so urgent. "The king was polite, almost kind to her throughout the meal. But once they'd finished dessert, he led her to the room with the spinning wheel and said, 'Spin this into gold by morning, or you will die before breakfast.'

"He locked her in and gestured for the garbed servant to guard the door. The miller's daughter saw that the whole tower was filled with straw, so much that she was afraid to pull any from the bottom of the heap. She knew if she did, it would all collapse and bury her."

"How did that make her feel?"

The sorrow in the center of Linnea chest drew her upper torso into its vise. "Like she was going to suffocate."

"Bring your breath into here," he urged, pressing lightly on the rebar that was her backbone. "What did she want to have happen?"

"She wanted the little man to come again. Anxiously, she twisted the locket around her neck. On the fifth twist, Dwarfy emerged from the spinning wheel." Shane's thumb moved in a circular motion against her vertebrae.

"He untwisted her chain. She unclasped and handed it to him. Dwarfy tried and tried to pry the sides of the locket apart. It was very difficult, but when he'd finally opened it, he said, 'You don't have anyone's picture in here.'"

Shane pushed into the tiny muscles between her ribs, his hand behind her heart. "How did she explain that?"

"She said, 'I didn't have time to put anything in it. I've been too busy smiling.'"

"Oh, that's right. I think you already mentioned something like that." Shane's voice was soothing, but he was stepping away from the table. Prone, her body pleaded with him to stay. The release in her back was beginning to free up her neck.

She heard him take a sip of water. "When did you get the locket you gave me?"

"January."

He rummaged through the duffle bag he'd dropped by the door, sounding nonchalant. "Close to nine months, and no photos?" He twisted the cap off something.

It had not seemed right to put Rick's digitized picture into the locket before she had his face ingrained enough in her brain to recall what he looked like when he wasn't around. Now she could only picture him from her hallucination, like a Picasso.

"So what did Dwarfy do with the necklace?"

"He tossed it over his shoulder into the tightly-packed straw. Once again, the girl was lulled into a trance while he worked. When she came to, the king stood over her, chortling."

Shane sprinkled fragrant oil across the shell of her skin. Linnea's subcutaneous tissue spread eagerly under the essence. She wasn't even sure if he was actually touching her, but her flesh undulated beneath the ointment. She inhaled the serene, masculine, sandalwood scent, drawing it into her lungs. "That morning passed like the first." Linnea sighed contentedly.

After a few minutes of her silence, Shane said, "And later?"

"In the afternoon, when she was napping, the king came to her chamber." Intense, irrational fear welled within her.

"What did the king look like?" he asked again.

The agonizing electrical charges within her scalp resumed firing, overwhelming her ability to articulate. The barrage whipped the almost-relaxed tissue in her upper body back into spasmodic frenzy.

He pushed her spinal muscles down toward her hips. Her heart began to race. She was swept up in an adrenaline rush. As Shane's hands approached the curve of her buttocks, her hips and thighs tightened, resisting his touch. "He praised her. Profusely."

Shane's hands lingered at the top of her hips, "You are holding something in here."

Linnea struggled for an answer, a plausible reason for her panic attack. "I...I don't know what it is."

The seagull landed on the outside window pane, squawking madly, as if urging them to grab digging sticks and hurry to the beach before the rising tide covered the meaty clams. But Linnea didn't care what the scavenger was trying to tell them. She could only focus on the tremors between her neck and her hip joint. "I feel like my body is trying to tell my mind something it doesn't want to know," she said at last.

Shane drew a deep, remember-to-breathe breath and took his hands away. "What does your body feel like doing right now?"

"Running," Linnea gasped. "I want to run as far and as fast as I can...but I can't. I can't exercise at all, because my muscles get too tense. It's like my body wants to keep me stuck until I figure out what its trying to say."

Shane was silent for at least a minute, letting the information she'd blurted sink into her own awareness. He patted her kindly on the shoulder. "That's enough for now. I'm going to go outside while you get dressed. Get up slowly."

He left the tower. Linnea lay on the table, wondering if he'd stopped the session because he realized there was something wrong, really wrong, with her psyche. Maybe he was trying to figure out how to handle a nut case like her. Perhaps, he was dialing his useless cell phone now, desperately plotting how to get her back to St. Genevieve's on the next ferry

The vivid pictures that had appeared in her mind while she retold Rumpelstiltskin and the somatic communications she was still receiving were spooky. Could it be that her unconscious and her body were working together? Were they stridently taking the upper hand? Were they purposefully cracking through the tough shell around her brain, forcing her out of her usual life until she figured out whatever the hell they wanted her to know? Linnea sighed, stepping back into the blue scrubs a wise woman had stolen for her.

Chapter Twenty

Shane stepped back inside, closing the heavy door on the unseasonably cool wind and rain. Linnea blushed. "I'm so embarrassed. I guess I lost touch with reality."

He smiled kindly at her. "Consensual reality, perhaps. You were doing your work in your own way. I think you are very brave."

She hadn't felt brave. She'd felt compelled, but she nodded. "I really appreciate all you've done for me today, but I don't want to impose on you. I really should find a hotel room for tonight."

He chuckled. "That's the beauty of Tower Island. There are no hotels here. Don't run off, Linnea. There's plenty of bedding in the loft for me. We can both stay here."

Dan would be beside himself if he knew. "Maybe I should just catch a ferry and go back to Pilchuck."

Shane shrugged. "No ferries until Monday morning."

What a wonderful excuse to remain exactly where she was. "So I really am locked in the tower?"

"But we have provisions. I bought a big tub of the best clam chowder to be had, some delicious bread, and organic salad for dinner tonight. We've got a chessboard to keep us busy, too."

She'd played chess with Dan once, back when they still lived under The Mill. She'd captured his rook. Playfully, he'd pounced on her, trying to pry it from her hand, and then all of a sudden they were making love on the coffee ground-laden rug next to the space heater. Linnea remembered squeezing into the shower together afterward. Lathering her in soapsuds, Dan had washed Sumatran off her back.

She smiled coyly at Shane. "I'm pretty good at chess."

* * *

As she placed the white king beside his dark queen on her side of the board, the bat swooped down from the loft. It startled her so much that she dropped the piece. It rolled to the floor. She stretched down to pick it up. The bat re-roosted in the rafters, but Linnea's adrenaline was pumping. A hissing refrain rushed through her triggered mind. Her neuralgia resurfaced.

Shane placed a steady hand on her trembling arm. "What?"

"I keep hearing a voice in my head, saying 'Die, die, die.'" She sank back down onto her stool, propping her elbows on the spinning wheel table and covering the nape of her neck with her hands.

Instead of touching her, he went to his duffle bag and pulled a tattered book from an interior pocket. "Do you like poetry?"

"I think it's the only way to save the world," she mumbled. She lifted her head to meet his gaze, spasming. "Maybe not the verse itself, but if people can think metaphorically, they won't read their holy tomes so literally."

He opened his book. "The Prophet Muhammad said,

'Die before you die.'

Linnea felt trickling between the inflamed tissue in her cranium. Something was moving in there. "Are you suggesting the voice in my head is metaphorical?"

Shane shrugged. "Let's see what else it has to say." He nodded toward the narrow bed and turned away so she could undress.

She'd been so angry at Dr. Perdue and Dr. Amani for assuming that there was a psychological aspect to her pain. It felt as if they were accusing her mental and emotional being for creating the mayhem in her body. She'd been so relieved that Dr. Beasley had dismissed the notion. What part of her was marauding behind the metaphorical? She sank onto the table.

"You might like the other poems in my book," Shane said, once she'd covered herself with the blanket. "I read them when I'm down in the dumps." He slid his palms beneath the back of her head.

"When I was a kid, my fairy tales always made me feel better."

"I gathered that," he remarked. Carefully, he probed the worst knot in the tissue around her trigger point.

As he loosened and soothed, Linnea saw a cold, wet, wrinkled bed sheet hanging on the back of her eyelids. In the center of it, a rag doll's exposed candy heart pulsed. She tensed against falling into the clamminess and the cold, moldy cavity she knew the threadbare cloth concealed.

Why was she so scared? There was nothing for her to be so worried about. In an almost defiant rush, she whispered, "He climbed between her sheets. When the king went to the young woman's chambers, he climbed between her sheets."

"Was she scared?" he asked in a low tone.

"Not then." Linnea felt jittery all over. "That evening, the cloaked servant brought her an even finer dress to wear to supper. She spoke for the first time, whispering, 'You are with child,' before leaving the girl alone to dress herself.

"The miller's daughter knew the mysterious servant had spoken the truth, and realized that it would be no small honor to bear the king's heir. By the time she reached the dining room, a little of the frozen honey in her heart had softened and was already oozing down toward the center of her body, making its way to her womb. As the king touched her shoulder, she thought about their afternoon behind the bed curtains. He loved her. She wouldn't have to spin straw into gold anymore. She was free of the impossible.

"She smiled, thinking of the little man who had come to save her. The king grinned, gesturing for her to follow him. Believing more romance was in the offing, she was greatly dismayed when he led her to the tower room.

"'You have pleased me greatly,' he said. 'If you spin the straw in this room and the straw in the tower next door tonight, there will never ever be a need for you to spin again. If you fail, I will give you the choice between life on the streets or death.'

"'But I am with child,' she told him. 'Your child.'

"He shrugged and left, once again locking the door behind him."

Shane stretched her crimped neck muscle. "What a jerk," he muttered, more to himself than to her.

His affirmation of her unspoken feelings made Linnea feel safe. He pulled her soft tissue apart like taffy. "So she knelt before the spinning wheel and peered into the center shaft, willing the little man to come out.

"Dwarfy climbed out of the spinning wheel, craning his neck to see the top of the straw. He peeked through the door to the adjoining tower and then sat on the stool, mopping his brow. 'This is beyond me. You'll have to give me something really special to make it happen by morning. What do you have?'

"'I have nothing left to give,' she said, 'but my desire to live.'

"'Then promise me your first-born child. It's going to be a beautiful little girl, and I will take incredibly good care of her.'"

Linnea considered his deal. She trusted the magic the little resin statue had wrought for her daughter. She was willing to cooperate with his likeness in her imagination. Besides, she already knew how the story would end.

"Now, nine months seems like forever when someone is young," she told Shane. "The miller's daughter figured she'd be queen by then, and three quarters of a year seemed like plenty of time for her to figure out how to keep the baby, so she promised. Dwarfy sat at the spinning wheel and began to spin. He was so delighted by the possibility of getting his own little girl to love that he chortled the whole time. He forgot to tell the woman not to watch. This time, she paid attention as he worked."

Linnea felt the thrill of tasting forbidden fruit as she watched Dwarfy squeeze handfuls of straw together. He teased the end of a single strand out from the cluster. As he ran it through his fingers, it softened and stretched. He fed it into the spinning wheel. As the piece wrapped around the core, it was transformed into shimmering gold. Shane's hands pressed into her, urging her to keep talking. "In the morning, Dwarfy was gone. The king was delighted.

"They were married within the week. Nine months later, when the queen held her newborn daughter to her breast, she was happier than she could ever remember being. Though there were servants to do it, the queen chose to care for her child on her own, day in, day out and, of course, night after night. In those first few days, all the joy that had been frozen in her own heart since childhood flowed out as freely as her milk.

"The moment the princess bestowed her first angelic smile upon her, the queen's long-suppressed, sticky laughter welled up and slid out of her throat. The baby cooed a lovely sound in return. Instantly, the door to the queen's bedchamber opened. Dwarfy stepped inside and bolted the door behind him.

"'I've come for your child,' he announced. To the queen's eyes, the little man was ugly once again.

"She shook her head furiously. 'I had no idea what I was promising you. I can't let her go. She is a part of me. She needs me, and I will die of a broken heart if I lose her.'

"'Give her to me.'

"'My husband is the king. He won't allow you to take her.'

"'Ha!'" the dwarf snorted. "'How can you trust him protect your child when you don't even know his real name? You still call him Your Highness.'"

Linnea realized she was crying. Her entire body surged with the sense of hopelessness that she had felt when first Rick and, then Dan had pushed her to write the article about Pete. She was focusing so hard on her fairy tale that she barely noticed what her body was doing. She knew Shane was still working on her, over her, around her, but she was barely aware of his touch.

"'I'll give you anything,' the queen promised frantically. 'My horse, my secret grinding methods, my health, but not my beautiful little girl.'

"'Tempting,' the dwarf said, 'but I haven't the slightest interest in any of those things. What I want is what makes that lovely sound slide out of your throat. I'll give you three days, and if you can guess your husband's name by the time I return, I'll let you keep the babe.'

"The little man went away. When the king came to her that night, she said, 'Your Highness, I notice you have never once asked for or called me by my birth name. Do you know it?'

"'Of course I do,' he lied snappishly, 'but I don't care to use it. Your title is best, queen.'

"She tried again. 'I do not know your real name. Will you tell me what it is?'

"'You don't need to know what it is,' the king replied. 'As your title fits you, mine suits me. I wish for you to call me Your Highness.'

"The queen was frantic to protect her beloved child, but said calmly, 'But, if I am to raise your offspring, and do it really well, I need to know your true name."

Linnea stopped. Lightening strikes hammered the interior of her skull, walloping her consciousness with unbearable bolts. This wasn't a fairy tale at all.

"Just slow this down, Linnea," Shane whispered in her ear.

As if she could modulate her own dose of awareness! She turned her head from side to side, trying to escape her fear and the pain.

"Tell me what he said."

Linnea could barely whisper the words. "He said, 'I'll tell you *after you spin more straw into gold.'*"

Shane drew his hands up, hovering over Linnea's shattered heart as the king's broken promise hung in the air of the tower. He drew a deep breath. He seemed uncertain about how to proceed.

Tears ran down Linnea's cheeks. "But I can't spin straw anymore." she cried.

"'I won't reveal my name until you spin all the gold I want." He backed away, double-bolting the door.'"

"She must have felt pretty helpless," Shane said softly. "She was about to lose the most precious thing she'd ever had because an ill-informed promise. Have you ever felt that?"

Linnea barely heard him. In her vision, the Queen flung herself against the unyielding locked door, sobbing, "I don't have enough energy. The baby wakes so often in the night. And now, even my savior wants to make me give up my little girl."

As if awakening from a dream, Linnea opened her eyes to look up at Shane. He wasn't looking down at her face, but out beyond her feet. As if he had felt the questioning in her gaze, he glanced down. His eyes twinkled. "Anything you say here is okay."

She told him how Rick's return to Pilchuck had triggered memories she'd long forgotten and created a lot of trouble at home. He lightly traced a wide path around her black eye. "I thought you might be having some present day trauma."

With a burst of anxiety, Linnea's neuralgia reasserted itself.

Gently, Shane took her temples between his palms. "When a small animal escapes a predator, it hunkers down somewhere and trembles until all the adrenaline is worked out of its system. You've carried a lot of fear within you since you were too young to know what to call it. When the baseball hit you, your body said, 'Enough, already.' And Hommy…well that was more than too much." Her face continued to tremble as she took in his words.

He cradled her head for a long, long time, whispering what might have been mantras until slowly, in fits and starts, the palsy simply petered out. Held that way, she felt nurtured in a way she had never known before, as if she was really and truly worth someone else's undivided attention. She giggled, opening her eyes, catching the satisfaction in his.

"Sweet," he said warmly. "That's what I like to hear."

Realization rose up and out of her. "When I got hurt, all the pain in the past came back up and mixed in with what my dad and Dan have been doing. The doctors and therapists didn't know how to handle that. Shane, don't you see? Sandy must have known you were here. She sent me to you because she can see what others can't or won't, and she knows you can, too." Happily, Linnea stretched her body the length of the table. "I want to finish my fairy tale. It needs a bat."

"You're in charge."

Linnea drew a deep breath, settling back into her imagination. "So the king wouldn't reveal himself and the queen was a wreck. Dwarfy reappeared. 'Do you know your husband's name yet?'

"The queen guessed several times, but after each of her suggestions, the little man shook his head. 'That doesn't sound right to me. I'll be back tomorrow night.' The queen lay in bed, holding back her tears, so as not to frighten the baby.

"She guessed forty-three names on the second night, but once again, Dwarfy shook his head and said, 'That doesn't sound right to me.'

"On the third day, the sleep-deprived queen put on the dress she'd originally worn to the castle, smudged her face to look like a beggar woman, and wrapped her baby in a blanket. With the babe in her arms, she ventured out into the village. She walked up and down the streets and in and out of businesses all day long. From the alchemist all the way down to the tinsmith, she begged everyone she met for the true name of their king. The people she solicited stared at her blankly before simply replying, 'His name is His Highness.'

"As dusk fell, the queen trudged home, planning to retrieve the baby's layette and flee before the little man could find them. On her way past the king's counting room, however, she paused outside the heavily-fortified door to peer through its small, barred window. The king sat at a massive table, gleefully counting the skeins of gold the little man had spun a year ago. Although the man with her husband looked unfamiliar to her, the queen felt as if she knew him.

"The stranger examined a skein of gold, pulling a heart-shaped locket from the bundle. 'Your Highness,' he said with a frown, 'this is the very necklace I sent to my daughter a year ago.'

"The king replied, 'How odd! My wife was wearing it when she came to the castle to spin.'

"The stranger said, 'That's my girl.'

"'Her stepfather takes all the credit,' the king informed him wryly.

"'He's a usurping son-of-a-bitch,' the stranger said, 'but obviously it is a very good thing that I left her to him, because it spurred her to develop this rare talent. I'm pleased she has served you so well. Perhaps you will permit her to spin a skein of gold to delight and benefit her true father?'

"'I can command her to do it, if you wish, my loyal one,' the king said grandly.

"'And perhaps,' the miller said, 'the baby can be ordered to do the same when she comes of age?'

"The queen's heart nearly ceased to beat, and her breath became so shallow that her lungs began to shrivel." Suddenly, nearly quivering with excitement, Linnea exclaimed, "I see the bat!"

"Where?" Shane sounded curious, fascinated, actually.

"In the story, she's the veiled servant. She's taking the princess away for a short while."

"Is she saying anything?"

Linnea focused hard, feeling deeply comforted. "She says, 'Don't worry, I'll bring her back when the time is right.'"

"Does the queen trust her?"

"Yes...because she doesn't say much, but when she speaks, what she says is true. She's really a wise old woman."

The crimped vertebrae in her neck spread apart between Shane's fingers. Linnea shuddered with delight.

"You are doing an amazing amount of work," he said softly. His fingers hovered over her flesh as blood rushed into starved tissue. "Don't hurry what happens next. Just soak up how good it feels to be safe, relaxed, and stretching."

He moved his fingertips in a subtle, counterclockwise motion over the trigger point in her fascia. The knot became a spinning wheel, swirling in reverse. A long, long time seemed to pass before, he whispered. "Ah, yes. This is the fruitful spot."

Something substantial sprang out of the unwinding fibers. Large as life, nearly as tall as Shane, Dwarfy stuck his face so close to Linnea's that she could smell sage smoke in his beard. Gingerbread cookie breath blasted her cheek.

"Why so comatose?" Dwarfy asked.

Linnea realized that she must be in a trance, much like the miller's daughter was when Rumpelstiltskin spun straw into gold. Within her own little bubble of altered consciousness, Dwarfy was absolutely real, as real as the hands upon her body. With Shane touching her, she felt safe enough to converse with an apparition. "I'm afraid of becoming the little match girl. If I can't spin all this straw into gold, I'll end up on the streets."

Dwarfy snorted. "I'll spin it for you, but you have to give me something of yours."

"You already have my daughter. Megan loves you. All I have left on me is my wedding ring."

Dwarfy pointed toward Shane with his elbow. "Give it to him."

Linnea pulled off her wedding ring. "Here."

Shane stopped the massage. "I don't want to take your wedding ring," he said nervously. "How are you going to explain that to your husband? The guy's already on the apoplectic side. He must drink a gallon of coffee a day. He'll freak if you go home without your wedding ring."

"No. He won't. Please," she begged, "just keep touching me."

"Linnea, you're vulnerable right now. I don't want to give Dan more fuel for his fire. You're under too much stress as it is."

She watched the little man incline his head toward Shane. "But Dwarfy insists that I give it to you."

Shane cleared his throat. "So you see him again?"

"He's not just in my head. He's real. He's like a dream, but he's inside and outside of me. You have to take my ring." She pressed the band into his hands. "Just for now."

"Okay," Shane said soothingly, "but you need to talk to him out loud, okay? So I can hear you?"

Linnea nodded. He laid his hands across her breastbone. *Mmmm...yes.* "Why aren't you with Megan?" she asked the dwarf.

"Because *you* called me up," he explained. "Like Vasilisa's doll, I always show up when someone needs the truth. Every century or so, I have to reclaim what really happened from those who keep spinning it to serve their own petty selves."

Dwarfy threw his pointy red cap onto the stone floor. He jumped up and down upon it in anger. "I hate this story. It pisses me off that nobody ever questions the motivations of the girl's parents. What the hell was your father thinking, just taking off and leaving you? And why didn't your mother just run the mill he left behind by herself? Women ran mills all the time in those days. Speaking of idiocy, why don't the storytellers ever explain why grown men would expect a young girl to figure out how to do something they couldn't do, let alone threaten her life if she failed? Why would they expect her to take something as lifeless as straw and spin it into riches for them?" Dwarfy spread his arms, raging at the ceiling. "Can somebody please tell me WHY storytellers screw this one up so much?"

Shane whispered in her ear, "Good job, Linnea. Something's shifting."

As the deepest layers of her skin began to stretch apart, Linnea's body trembled so much she felt she might quake into bits. "I feel the opening."

"Is it scary?" Shane whispered.

"Yes, but there's more than fear."

"Are you angry?"

"Not exactly."

"Yes, you are!" Dwarfy stuck his face between Shane's mouth and Linnea's ear. "I am a funnel cloud of rage, finally wafting up to the loom of your consciousness where you can acknowledge me. I am the fully-fermented, frustrated desire of a little girl wanting a father's love from a man who cannot get deeper than or beyond his own shallow skin. I am fury at a mother who imprisoned her little girl inside in the misery of her own marriage instead of protecting her from an ogre. I am a destructive power wishing to obliterate a cruel stepfather from your childhood memory, from your life path, from the journey of your soul. I am a maiden's grief at discovering the man she gives herself to can't or won't support her as she changes and grows. Oh, yes. You are angry, and I AM YOUR RUMPLED STEEL SKIN!"

Dwarfy began to whirl, over and around her bed, howling like a dervish. His wails intensified her heartbeat until the organ associated with love pounded against her ribcage like heels skipping rope on hard asphalt. Linnea felt her whole body being sliced by mendicant knives.

Her trigger point felt like a lump of burning coal. Shane stretched the faschia around Linnea's neck. If seemed as if he were coaxing a tiny glow of sparkling life energy from her ignited flesh.

Linnea whimpered. As the energy and light expanded, it pushed her pain and pent-up emotion out. As her agony lifted through Shane's hands, her flesh melted, softening. In the release, her desire to be one with the divine force moving through her pulsed to an intoxicating peak.

Suddenly Gunter was there, shouting. "Look at me when I talk to you!" His bellow drove the loveliness back beneath her skin. "Smile."

Rick stood beside her as well with his ever-shifting face holding up a pornographic poster of a bikini-clad teenager. A turkey feather protruded from his ear. "Spin me a story about my party boy," he wheedled. Linnea's buttocks clamped down hard where her father had groped her.

"Better do it." Dan said, stepping up to link arms with Rick.

Holding her breath, Linnea squeezed her eyes shut as tightly as she could. The lovely energy was gone.

"Breathe," Shane whispered. "Come on. Breathe now."

All the flesh in her pelvis clenched, determined to stick to her tailbone. "I don't want to see it," she gasped.

"You don't have to look at anything you don't want to," Shane said, "but I invite you to use this time to get the dark energy to leave your cells."

Serendipity Pillar's hooded form lifted from the backs of Linnea's retina. As she spiraled to an upright position beside Dwarfy, she drew her head covering aside. It wasn't Serendipity at all, but the real Baba Yaga with warts and patches of wiry hair scattered across her face. She peered curiously at Linnea. Opposite her, Gunter bellowed, "Look at me when I talk to you, little girl."

Baba Yaga drove the bony tips of her clawed fingers into the clenched knot along Linnea's jaw. She used her cold palm to lift Linnea's chin, to turn her farther away from her fathers and Dan, to turn her toward Dwarfy.

"I am not just your frustration," Dwarfy whispered urgently. "I am not just your fury or your desire to have had your life go differently. I am not just the dammed-up grief that you weren't allowed to express. I am not just your confusion about your father coming back and trying to mess up all that you've created for yourself. I am not just your outrage that he'd ask you to use your voice to spin a horrifying lie. What I am is pure love, clinging to its source. I AM YOUR RUMPLED STEEL SKIN."

"Step through the fear." Baba Yaga bent, cheek-to-cheek, eye-to-eye with Linnea. "Look at them with me one more time."

With the crone's cooler flesh against her face, with Baba Yaga's head supporting her skull, Linnea fixed her eyes on Gunter. The witch's nearly imperceptible pulse arced from her aged temple through Linnea's bruised tissue. The inflammation just above her brow burst into flame. Under her fiery gaze, Gunter shrunk into a piece of red-hot coal no bigger than the spider logo on a pair of Spinners socks. She felt a surge of pure, cauterizing power. She incinerated Rick and Dan next. Baba Yaga cackled with glee. "Good work!" she hissed into her ear, making the infinity sign over Linnea. The fire in her skull extinguished, leaving a pleasant tingle in its place.

Baba Yaga stepped aside for Shane.

He moved quickly, freeing Linnea's congealed tissue from all her rattled bones.

She'd never felt so much peacefulness and joy. To her relief, she realized she hadn't been suppressing fear, shame, anger, and abuse as much as she had been suppressing a love so shiny it was simply unrecognizable to the daily onlooker, average therapist, or standard physician. Indeed, as she acknowledged her rumpled steel skin, Shane was able to tease the heavenly golden light energy from her neck down to the end of her tailbone until it shimmered through and beyond her entire body in the most ecstatic waves. With his magic fingers, he was spinning her whole being into gold. She was enveloped in sweet, honey-colored light. She could see it all around them. *Thank you. I love this.*

"There you go," Shane whispered.

Linnea's fascia released. She was wide open. No joints were jammed. No bones tethered by short tendon. Not a single bit of her flesh felt pinched. Her blood flowed freely. Her organs resonated. Her illuminated nerves hummed, gleefully. Joy radiated from her heart, circulating through her head and down to her tingling toes. "What are you doing to me?" she gasped.

"*You* are doing it." Shane sounded both incredulous and pleased.

Dwarfy used his shovel to scoop up the soot that had been the men in her life. "I'm taking this dark energy back to Gaia. She can take these guys." He paused on the threshold, winking back at her before disappearing.

Baba Yaga tapped the center of Linnea's relaxed forehead. "Be mindful of that fire, my dear. It has been known to burn a house down now and again." With that, she was gone.

Shane smoothed the last bit of sticky tissue as gingerly as if he were unwrapping the gauze from a healed wound. He dropped down on the stool behind him, wiping his brow like a marathon runner and grinning in the glow of a miraculous triumph.

* * *

Linnea sat bolt upright on the massage table. Someone or something was just outside the door. Her first impulse was to run to Megan, but as she struggled with the overwhelming dizziness sitting up so suddenly caused, she fell back in her story. Reminding herself that the baby was safe with the veiled servant, she skimmed across the cold stone to check the lock with only a blanket across her chest. Horrorstruck, she watched the bar across the tower door slide open of its own accord.

A bearded man lunged through the doorway with stunning velocity. As he crossed the threshold, his facial hair disappeared to reveal a handsome face. He lay his hands firmly upon her shoulders, kicking the door closed behind them. Locked in intense eye contact with his woodland brown irises, Linnea was petrified to hear the deadbolt slide back in place.

"I'm here to take the princess," he said. He nodded at the ebony fleece barely covering her breasts. "Why are you wearing black?" he whispered.

So we have to finish the story after all. "I'm wearing black," she answered angrily, "because I'm in mourning for my child. You're here to take her away, and there's nothing I can do to stop you."

"Don't you know your husband's name by now?"

"No one will tell me," she snapped. "Even he thinks it is Your Highness."

He nodded admiringly. Amusement sparkled in his eyes. "That's it. Now that you know, you may keep your baby."

"What?" Linnea was flabbergasted. "I racked my brain, broke my heart, and begged on the street for no real reason?" Even as she frowned at him, she noticed how much she liked his musky scent, his wild essence. "But Your Highness is no name for a human being. There's just no compassion in it."

"You're right." The man traced her collarbone with his fingertip. "But just because that's who your husband is, doesn't mean you have to strangle your own soul."

With the manual skill of one who can spin straw into gold, he loosened the knots marital bonds had made in Linnea's heart, transforming her sense of captive commitment into a ball of dead straw. Blowing a spark from between his lips, he ignited it, and tossed the burning mass of pain into the air. It flared like a falling star and then simply, completely dissipated into the chilly night air.

"Who are you?" she asked. "What is *your* real name?"

"I am the Doer of Impossible Tasks."

Baba Yaga has left her poised to seize the only power worth having, the power of seeing the hidden, feeling the unfelt or forbidden. "Why did you come?"

"I've been here all along, waiting for you to wake up."

Linnea's laugh slid out of her throat. His rich earthy one merged with it. She opened her arms to him, and he stepped into the embrace of her blanket. Carefree and deliriously happy, they whirled hand-in-hand toward the ladder, blending dualities, masculine and feminine, shadow and light, concrete and astral, integrating body and soul, consummating self.

Linnea paused at the first rung. All of a sudden, she was a single body again. The Doer of Impossible Tasks had set her free. She was ready to live to the fullest, express herself, and feel pleasure wherever she found it.

She climbed to where Shane lay awake in the moonlight. He was stretched out on top of a red sleeping bag, wearing a pair of shorts. He sat up quickly when she appeared. With concern knit across his brow, he asked, "Do you need something?"

She sank onto her knees beside him, pressing her bare thigh against his. She could feel the hardness of his quadricep against the softness of her flesh. "I want to make love," she announced, allowing the blanket to slip below her shoulders.

His leg tensed. "No."

Linnea reached up to cradle his cheek with her hand. The scents of sandalwood oil and sage shampoo mingled in the narrow space between them. She stroked his beard. How glorious it felt to reciprocate his gentle touch. She let the black sheepskin fall away completely. Her breasts were luminous in the moonlight.

Shane cleared his throat. "That was therapy down there," he whispered hoarsely. "I don't want you to do something you'll be sorry for later."

"I won't regret a thing," she whispered. "It is right to want this."

He smiled slowly. His eyes flickered with passion and glowed with good humor and admiration. "So, you're the energy vortex I've been looking for." He pulled her into his arms. Her honeyed laughter bubbled up, filling the lighthouse with joy.

Chapter Twenty-One

Wrapped in the woolly fleece blanket, Linnea sat near the shoreline, watching sunlight dance on Puget Sound. Now that her energy cyst had been released and her vertebrae coaxed back into its rightful space, her neuralgia was gone. No medication necessary. Although many of her muscles were still sore and much tighter than the average person's, there was a lot less restriction in her movement. She felt hopeful and happy, grateful for the smooth slab of solid granite against the soles of her bare feet.

Shane handed her a steaming mug of coffee.

"Thank you." She smiled shyly, wondering how on Gaia's green earth he'd guessed she took cream.

"So how did your story turn out?"

"How do you know I finished it?"

"Just a hunch." He stepped out of his heavy Jesus-type sandals, moved her socks aside, and sat on the stone beside her.

Linnea studied his profile, surprised at how bashful she could be after being so brazen last night. *He knows me better than Dan.* "Dwarfy came back, and the queen guessed that her husband's name was His Royal Highness.

She was right, so she got to keep her baby."

Shane appeared puzzled. "What does that mean to you?"

Linnea took a sip of the coffee. *Red Sky at Morning.* "His Royal Highness can't believe in a power higher than himself, so he assumes that he's the highest power there is. And its so heady for him. He wields his power over and over again, forcing or charming or manipulating others to do what he wants. He never considers what it costs their souls, because he's so out of touch with his own and so unaware of its source. The way he gets what he desires doesn't matter to him, just as long as he gets it."

Shane cocked his head. "So the dwarf didn't take the little girl?"

"He took the queen, instead." She smiled coquettishly, glancing down at the book he was balancing on his lap. With golden sunrays upon her face, she closed her eyes, letting the words rise from a daring place deep within. "So while the king and the millers slept in their own separate beds that night, each benefiting in his own way from the queen's ability to do the impossible, the silent veiled servant brought the lovely baby back to the queen. They left the castle with the magical little man."

"That's quite a twist."

"Well, who wouldn't want a man with the power to make himself smaller or larger as needed? Who wouldn't go with a guy who could bypass a locked door to free a living woman from rigor mortis?"

"Some women wouldn't go for a guy like that," Shane remarked ruefully.

She smiled at him, certain in her wisdom on this matter. "But a queen would."

"Thank you," he said, coloring slightly. "You would

know."

Tears came to Linnea's eyes. "How is it that you know what I need to hear? You make me want to climb into your lap, lean my head on your shoulder, and cry like a little girl."

Shane chuckled, wrapping his arm around her shoulder. "That's not exactly the effect I want to have on women."

"No wonder your daughter is brilliant at languages. She has a daddy who let her have a voice."

Shane squeezed her into him slightly as she laid her head on his shoulder. "You're no slouch with words, either. You can spin a quite yarn. Hey, isn't that your sock in that seagull's mouth?"

Linnea nodded, barely registering the bird's theft. "I'm not going to publish a lie about Pete Stealer in my paper. My father never should have asked me to do it, and Dan should have supported me."

"He has a choice to make now, doesn't he?"

Linnea watched the bird drop its burden in the water. "And I only have *one* sock."

"And now you know to wear study shoes when you come to rocky beaches. You have to shield tender soles."

The sock floated out to sea. "We can learn a lot from seagulls," she remarked.

"Some people call them the rats of the bird world."

"Because they are scavengers. But I think scavenging is highly underrated. All my life, I've sifted through the good, the gifts, and the garbage to sustain myself."

Shane took her hand in his. "Body, mind, spirit. You've created a whole woman that is far more radiant than the sum of all your parts."

Linnea smiled shyly. "And bats. They're considered

creepy, too, but like the bat in the tower, I had to shut myself off, wrap my wings around myself so I could rest. You know, bats are really amazing. They are the most mistrusted mammals in the world, but they are the ones who keep insect and vermin populations under control."

"So," he said, "you are the embodiment of a divine scavenger. You know it's okay to seek out what you need to be truly alive."

Ease undulated through all the pathways in her body. "Thank you, Shane. I've never been this open with anyone before."

"And I've never been with anyone who was able to do what you did with her own story. You are very powerful, Linnea."

She blushed. "I couldn't have done it with anyone else, just you. Thank you for being my knight in shining armor...my Jedi master."

"It's an honor."

She looked into Shane's eyes. In them, she saw a trusted friend, a life-giving, guiding father, a caring brother, a passionate lover, and, most of all, a man truly at peace with feminine power. In his eyes, she saw sacred masculinity. He was the very elixir she'd needed to mend the cracks in her own shattered soul.

She struggled to convey her intense gratitude. "Thank you for touching me, for *really* touching me, for bearing the intimacy and being so generous. I didn't know how much I needed compassion and care. I'm sorry I interrupted *your* vision quest."

"You didn't interrupt it all."

Linnea peered at him quizzically. "What do you mean?"

He opened his book to a marked place and read,

We never know how high we are, till we are called to rise.
And then, if we are true to plan, our statues touch the skies.
The heroism we recite would be a daily thing
Did not ourselves the cubits warp
For fear to be a king.

"Emily Dickinson," he said. "I've been working on my healing, what Sandy calls my magic, for a long time now, but I didn't know how truly responsive I could be to a soul in need until you gave me an occasion. And then, later, I...well, you just made me feel like I was in heaven, dancing with the stars."

Shivers of delight ran up and down Linnea's spine. She hugged her knees to her chest. The universe was still good.

* * *

Linnea napped most of that day while he was out hiking. They went to bed early that night and slept in, awakening on the same pillow. With the mid-morning sun languidly caressing their entwined arms, Linnea opened her eyes to find his lips against the hollow of her breast bone. With a delightful new ease, she found she could arch her neck without moving her head so that his tongue could trace its way to her ear.

As they ate leftover waffles at the spinning wheel table that afternoon, she glanced out the window to see Serendipity row her rickety boat toward the shoreline. Still dressed in black, Baba Yaga's stand-in stood motionless inside her craft, letting it bob on the water while she stared up at the tower, summoning her passenger with a steadfast gaze.

"My ride's here." Linnea stood up sadly, smoothing the dark red capris she'd worn to the island. "I guess I'd better pack up my burka and go." Shifting uneasily from one foot to the other, she studied him. She wanted to remember every detail of his appearance.

He stepped around the spinning wheel. Standing face-to-face with her, he gently took her hands and turned them upward. He placed his palms about an inch over hers. The pleasant tingling between their hands wasn't far different from the electrical jolts that had been tormenting her before she came to the tower, but now, it was much less frightening and quite a bit more mellow.

Linnea felt the force within him connecting with energy inside of her. "You have given me the most beautiful gift I've ever been given. You didn't hurt me when I was weak, and you kept me safe until I found some inner strength again. And then...you...celebrated my well-being."

Shane lifted her hands to place her palms against his heart. Huskily, he whispered. "In this Universe, Love does not let Love die."

Linnea stepped back, almost ready to face the real world again. As their hands lost contact, she felt as if, instead of being knighted with a light saber, she'd been inducted into a secret society by loving touch.

Shane handed her the small brown paper bag he'd stashed on the sideboard. "Along with your jewelry, my business card is in here, in case you decide to visit Sedona in the near future."

Images of him wearing a felt cowboy hat trimmed with turquoise flashed through her mind. Could she possibly go? What about Megan? Oh, shit! What about Dan?

"If you don't make it to Arizona, I'll be back next summer."

Reassured that they would be together again, Linnea

threw her arms around him, hugging him whole-heartedly.

"Peace be with you," she whispered.

Shane returned the hug. "Amen."

She gathered her things in her arms, threw him one last longing look, and hurried to the boat. As she settled on the hard wooden bench opposite Serendipity, she wondered why Cinderella ever went to the ball. *Why would she rush away from where the magic actually happened?*

The old woman dipped her oar into the water. "Your sadness is welcome here, but no one can stay in the tower long."

"How does everyone associated with this little trip know what I'm thinking all the time?" Linnea asked, already missing him. "How do they know what I need next?"

"We've all been on similar little trips ourselves. But to answer your first question, Cinderella was given the magic *so* she could go to the ball, *so* she could influence the monarchy. She wasn't given the gift just to attend a hoity-toity party or marry into a life of leisure. Of course, storytellers leave that part out these days."

Linnea felt herself smiling. How delicious to be able to do that spontaneously without pain. "And they neglect to mention that the fairy godmother was actually a handsome dwarf."

"To each her own story, Missy. I thought you'd make it through. I had a vision of you rowing others here someday."

Not if Shane's here.

Serendipity threw her head back with a great belly laugh. "Don't you worry, my dear. Only once a kalpa are two people allowed to share tower space." She nodded, sagely. "Once they do, they can reclaim what they had there whenever they are together."

For the first time in her life, Linnea understood what the term soul mate meant and she wanted to think about it, but, she had a job to do. "First, of all I'm going to take on the Spinners."

"I expect you will!"

She didn't want Serendipity to take her attack on the team personally. "I know your dad started it before my father took over and you might be somewhat attached to..."

"I'm not attached. It is time for the divine feminine to reweave our world and reclaim our culture. When I was about forty-five, I had a dream about Spider Woman, not the pop cartoon character, you know, but the Native American goddess. She was awfully offended that my father had co-opted the spider for his team logo. She'd been mad about it since day one, but she had to wait until she could access a person who could hear her. She told me that I would inherit the team someday and that a man with enormous mandibles would offer to buy it. She said I should let him have it. Now, I get what that prophecy was all about. I can't wait to tell all my Sisters-In-Her-Name why we've been having spider dreams this summer." Serendipity adjusted her Baba Yaga cloak, and looked at Linnea intently, "Gaia speaks through many avatars."

Linnea was surprised to find that they were already at the dock. She walked aboard the ferry and stood against the railing on the lower deck. Serendipity gave her a comradely wave, turned, and rowed the boat away. Linnea put on her sunglasses so the other passengers wouldn't see the tears in her eyes and opened the paper bag Shane had given her. She tucked his business card into her purse and she stared into the sack of jewelry.

Each piece now represented how stifling her spirit to preserve her connection with the givers had actually corrupted and damaged the connective tissue within her body. She couldn't bear the thought of wearing that same metal against her soft skin again. Now that she had strayed into wide-open spaces and the mystic wilds, forcing herself to stay within the bands of awareness and constraints of her original clan was unpalatable.

As the ferry sailed toward Spinning Wheel Bay, she took out the ring her mother had given her and dropped into the deep blue grayness below. Automatically, she thought, *I'm sorry if this is not very good for the environment,* but that now even that seemed too detached. She whispered, "I'm sorry, Gaia."

She dangled the heart locket Rick had clasped around her neck, watching it flutter in the breeze for a long moment, and with more apologies to the Great Mother, let it go, too. The sparkling chain glistened for a second before being sucked down into the Sound. Linnea took out her wedding ring and held it over the edge for a long time. Then, she slipped it into the coin compartment of her wallet.

She went inside the ferry and slid onto a vinyl bench. Using the pen from her checkbook to write on the bag Shane had given her, Linnea doggedly drafted an article for the next edition of *The Edge* while the unsteady angular table wobbled beneath the crinkled brown paper.

Clary Sage and Sandy were waiting outside the dockside chowder bar at the end of her ride. Clary Sage flung herself at Linnea as soon as she stepped beneath the awning. "I'm so sorry you had to go through all that with Hommy because of me."

301

"Because of *him*."

As Linnea pushed her sunglasses up in the shade. Clary Sage gasped, "Oh, my God! Your eye!"

"Yeah. It looks just like yours did after you bumped into Hommy's door jamb."

For a split second, Clary Sage appeared stunned, but she grimaced apologetically. "I'm sorry. I should have told you the truth about that, but I was too embarrassed. I swear I never gave him a key to my apartment, though. I don't know how he got one."

Linnea nodded. "He won't bother us anymore."

"You're right about that," Sandy said. "He's gone. One of my friends works for an airline and she confirmed that he got on a plane heading to the Middle East right after he assaulted you. He won't be able to get back into the States again. Moses and Chelsea both filed a police report against him."

"So that's that," Clary Sage looked sad. "No daddy for Serengeti."

"That's okay." Linnea bent to kiss the toddler in the stroller. "Depending on the daddy, sometimes none is better."

She realized as she was saying it that this, and not ethnicity had been the whole point of the piece on cross-cultural relationships that she hadn't been able to write. Culture provides the most comforting explanation for cruelty. Otherwise, the universe is far too random and scary, with just a bunch of bad people bumping into good ones and knocking them off course. But she and a mystic named Rabia had chased Hommy away. The beaming little girl before her would not come to age cowering beneath a callous man. There really was progress.

"Dan was pissed," Clary Sage said.

"He was livid that you'd checked yourself into St. Genevieve's without giving him any warning. But I told him that was bullshit," Sandy said. "I told him you've been giving everyone a heads-up for a long time. Your father was equally brusque, but I told him to quit being such a pain in the neck, literally." She placed the side of her open palm against her heart, using her other fist to punch the air beside her. "Nia move," she explained.

"Actually," Clary Sage blocked the empty air with an uppercut fist and kicked imaginary butt. "She told him to quit being a pain in the ass, literally."

Tears came to Linnea's eyes. "Shane helped me a lot," she said, in a low voice quaking with emotion. "And Serendipity explained some things. Thanks for everything, Sandy. It feels wonderful to be in the club."

Sandy winked. "Shane is one in a billion. He's a true king of hearts, but I know a few other healers who can guide you until you get your own feet back on the ground."

* * *

When they arrived home, Dan was on the porch swing, brooding over a steaming cup of Miller's Blend. The air around him hung heavy with the expectation of a volcanic eruption. Clary Sage hurried to her apartment, carrying Serengeti on one hip and banging the folded stroller against the other while Sandy sped away. Linnea approached him slowly.

His accusing blue eyes bore into the tinted lens of her glasses. "How could you commit yourself to an insane asylum without telling me first?" He demanded. "And then, when I get home from the hospital where I wasn't allowed to see *my wife*, I find a note saying that your friend has taken *my daughter* away.

"I wasn't in an insane asylum." Linnea modulated her voice, cuing him to be quieter. Already, Mr. Smith next door had ceased deadheading his dahlias to listen. "I was simply under observation. Chelsea's only keeping Megan for a few days, so I could rest and get my head back on straight."

"Why couldn't you just rest here?" Dan evidently hadn't noticed Mr. Smith, or didn't care.

"Because I was suicidal." Somehow, that no longer seemed like a shameful admission. It seemed like a statement of fact.

"Shit, Linnea. How could you consider killing yourself? What would I do without you?"

Linnea found herself wondering what she would do without Dan, and suddenly, the picture did not look so terrible to her. How hard she'd been working to hold their relationship together in her mind without receiving much reward in reality. "The usual stuff, I suppose. Of course, you'd have to make your own dinner, do your own laundry, shopping, and pay the bills. Oh, and you'd have to drive Megan to school sometimes, and continue to work and go to AA. You could handle it, Dan. The only real problem I see is that you'd have to budget carefully to be able to afford a babysitter for all the hours you spend with your support group."

"Fuck babysitters. If you died, I'd just start drinking again."

Fury rose, swelling her hair follicles. So he would abandon his daughter, just as Rick had skipped out on her. "You'd do that to Megan?"

His eyes narrowed viciously. "Are you accusing me of being selfish?" he spat. "Because if you are, you'd better think twice."

She stared back at him, trying not to look guilty. Could he sense she'd slept with Shane? Did he realize that she'd made the first move, the second, and several others before they'd lost track of who initiated what in mutual desire?

"It was selfish of you to check out on me this weekend. I almost went out and bought a six-pack." He stared at her smugly, clearly waiting for her to apologize.

"You have no idea how much pain I've been in lately, do you?"

He shrugged. "You can always take medication for that when you want to, but I can't have a drink, even when I need it."

Stunned by the vindictive jealousy in his tone, she heard preschoolers chanting as if from far away. *Peter, Peter, Pumpkin eater. Had a wife and couldn't keep her. Put her in a pumpkin shell and there he kept her very well.* Only Dan wasn't playing a child's game. This wasn't a boyish prank. This is how he perceived life.

"Quit trying to pull me down into your pumpk...pity pot," she snapped. "*That's* selfish. You might want a drink because you don't like how you feel, but I don't want to take medication because my father expects me to lie about a party boy. I don't want to take drugs because you can't support me in what I believe is important. I don't want to take drugs because I'm so hurt ..."

He folded his arms, eyeing her triumphantly. "So what you're saying here is, all of your headaches and stuff have all been in your head? They haven't even been real?"

A few days ago, his accusation would have reduced her to tears. "I had whiplash and head trauma, Dan. My pain is real. Feelings are real, too. And guess what? I actually have some. Physical and emotional pain are connected, and I have to take care of my whole self. I may have to take some medication, but if I can, I want to avoid it."

"It must be nice to have a choice." Dan snickered nastily.

Linnea felt Shane supporting her head, gently stretching her neck up, freeing the voice caught between crumpled vertebrae. She felt him massaging her jaw so she wouldn't have to mince words. "You have choices, too."

"Hah! What are they?"

"One, choose between me or my dad. I've written an article telling the truth about Pete and how my father's plans to sell his contract are the real reason the new school had to be sacrificed. It's coming out in our next edition."

"I never thought you'd be so stupid," Dan hissed.

The way he set his mug on the porch railing and faced her full-on reminded Linnea of how Gunter used to posture himself before pummeling her. For a moment, she hesitated. But Megan wasn't home and, to hell with the nosy Mr. Smith. She chose to escalate. "Two, choose which of the drug and alcohol counselors in the phone book you are going to see. Just make sure they are absolutely current in the field. I don't want you hanging around with people like Rick Andersen at AA meetings anymore. Just because a person doesn't drink doesn't mean he is free of whatever dark energy made him want to in the first place."

Dan threw his hands up as if he were completely disgusted with her. "Hey, you're the one who said I should go to AA. You can't just change your mind now."

Baba Yaga fire flickered in her skull. "Yes," Linnea said firmly. "I can change my mind. Three, you'd better hurry up and give me input on which marriage counselor we are going to. After you've done your fair share of research, of course." She was panting. Now that she'd done it, she could scarcely believe she'd thrown ultimatums at him.

Dan evidently couldn't believe it, either. "Wait just a minute Linnea. We need to stick it out with your dad because of your medical bills and Megan's school. How can we pay for therapy and the goddamn second roaster I bought on top of all that?"

"We'll figure it out on our own."

"And what about trips to Hawaii and the car you were going to get for your birthday?"

"They aren't worth it."

"But I need AA. Damn it, Linnea. You are acting like I'm having an affair with my Twelve Step program."

The color rose, prickling her face like Shane's day-old stubble had chafed her naked breasts, but she was done with guilt and shame. "What you need is a power greater than yourself, Dan. You need to stop waiting for someone at AA to serve it up to you and generate it yourself."

"What the hell are you talking about?" he cried. "Am I supposed to pull power out of thin air? Manufacture it in my own internal organs?"

Images of Dwarfy, Baba Yaga, Rabia, Jesus, Ganesha, Atlas, Muhammed, and Spider Woman swirled around her. "Something like that."

He scowled. "Come on, Linnea. Alcoholism is a disease. I'm sick. I have to go to AA. What else can I do?"

She wanted him to understand, for his own sake. "Do your own impossible."

"Ha!" Dan snickered. "And beyond that?"

"Be respectful of Dwarfy."

A malicious gleam came into his eye. "And they let *you* out of St. Genevieve's?"

"They sure did."

The cordless telephone on the porch railing trilled. Dan

answered the call immediately as if he were grateful to make contact with another human being in the face of her insanity. His tone was dead-pan, but merriment replaced the malevolence in his gaze when he handed the receiver to her. "It's your mother."

Linnea drew a deep breath. If June knew what she was asking of Dan, she'd accuse her of being cruel and crazy. June would say that he was a good provider, that she was lucky to have a man like Dan, that it was her duty to concoct good excuses for why he was failing her heart and disappointing her spirit. June would be wrong. "Hello?"

"What happened?" June snapped. "I thought you were going to come over here and get everything ready."

Linnea didn't want a *Welcome Home* banner like the one June hung over the pantry each time the boys made parole, but she couldn't keep the injured resignation out of her voice. "Dan didn't tell you that I was in the hospital?"

"I haven't had time to talk to Dan. I've been cooking and *cleaning* since I walked through the door. Jaime's home, and he wants a roast with all the trimmings for supper. They don't serve good food in the slammer, you know. Why didn't you come over and get the house ready for us?"

"I wasn't available, Mom. Even if I had been, I wouldn't have done it because I didn't feel like it. It's not fair for you to ask me to."

"Life isn't fair," June snapped. "It doesn't matter how you *feel*. You have to do what has to be done."

For the first time, she realized just how crazy June sounded. No wonder Linnea had so automatically ignored her own feelings, and let Rick and Dan do the same. Her mother hadn't been able to teach her how to acknowledge them. "*I* don't have to do what *you* think has to be done."

"Well, I'm sorry to see that hanging out with your father has affected you so strongly." She began to cry. "Your brother needs me now. His trial is next week, and I really can't handle you acting like this when I'm under so much stress."

Although she was nearly spent, Linnea made her voice firm. It was taking an inordinate amount of energy to transform herself in front of her husband and her mother at the same time. "You have to." She hung up.

June did not hit the redial button, for a change. Mr. Smith had crawled behind a hydrangea and was now squatting so close to her that Linnea could smell his sweat. Wondering if she could call him out of the bushes by walking away, she headed into the house, removing her sunglasses as she went.

"Oh, my God!" Dan screamed suddenly. "What did they do to you at the hospital? You've been beaten."

She didn't try to strain the sarcasm out of her voice. "I get a reaction now because you can *see* the bruise? How inconsiderate of me to have months of injury invisible to the naked eye. This didn't happen at St. Genevieve's. Hommy did it."

"No one told me he hit you. Jesus Christ! What possessed you to let him in the house?"

Naturally, it must have been her fault somehow. "I didn't. He had a key." She held up her hand to quell Dan's spluttering. "Clary Sage says she never gave him one, and I believe her." She frowned. "You are the one that let him in. You are the one that let him get to me."

Dan seemed bewildered. "What are you talking about?"

"You gave him your key ring when he parked the car at Claudio's. He must have recognized me and had a key made while we were eating dinner."

Dan sank onto the steps, burying his face in his hands. When he looked up, his eyes were moist. "I've been an asshole on auto-pilot for a long time, haven't I? I'm sorry. I want to change."

Linnea sighed. Damn, if he still couldn't get to her by showing a little emotion, but she knew better now. "I'm not going to hold my breath while I'm waiting. And if you don't hurry up, I'll be taking a little trip to Sedona. I won't be coming back."

He appeared perplexed. "Isn't that in Arizona?"

"Yeah." Linnea's eyes twinkled. "And in my soul."

* * *

Cool, pleasant evening air wafted through the screens. Crickets and the frogs sang farewell to the pink light on the horizon. Moths clung to the porch lamp, fanning their papery wings. Rick sank onto the sofa. He leaned forward, his elbows on his knees. "Did they prescribe antidepressants for you while you were in the hospital?"

Linnea settled into the rocking chair opposite him, inhaling deeply. "I don't want to talk about medication. I want to discuss the article you asked me to write about Pete." She folded her hands demurely in her lap.

"Oh." He smiled warmly. "I'm so glad you are going to do it, sweetheart. He's a damn good baseball player. He deserves a chance to make it big."

"I don't think you care about Pete. I think you wanted to see if you could make me betray my integrity."

Rick appeared stunned. Outside, darkness crept into the void left by the vanishing sunlight. When he did not answer, she elaborated. "You wanted to force me to spin straw into gold to make yourself feel more powerful."

Rage pulsed beneath Rick's skin. "What the hell are

you talking about?"

"I'm hurt, Dad." Linnea watched a bat dart from its home in the backyard cedar tree. "And it's your fault." With that, she knew there was no going back.

"Hey!" He jutted her chin toward her. "You assumed your own risks when you came to the stadium that night."

The hot pink fushias hanging in baskets outside the kitchen door waved in the mosquito hunter's wake. It was time to test the bottom of blood sucking; time to dredge her father's depths. "Did I assume my own risks when I went to live with Gunter? I was only four years old when you handed me over to a man who beat and humiliated me for being *your* child."

Rick crossed his arms. "Hey, your mother should have..."

"I grew up and I got away. I assumed my own risks and did pretty damned well for myself. And then you came back, and I welcomed you into *my* family. I let *my* little girl love you, and then you grabbed my butt in plain view of my husband and God only knows how many other spectators at your little game."

Rick sat back, entwining his legs. "I don't know what you're talking about."

"I have a witness."

"Dan?" His tone was derisive, but there was fear in his face.

Linnea stared at him levelly. "I think you did it to see what you could get away with. To see how much power you had over me."

Arrogance curled his lips. "I did it in front of Dan on purpose. I wanted you to see what a weak ass-wipe you married. He didn't do anything to defend you, did he? Can you believe he'd let something like that happen and not intervene?"

Like a geyser dissolving sediment, disgust surged from within her skin. "You are some piece of work. I don't need or want you to save me from Dan. You should have saved me from Gunter."

"Cheer up," he snapped. "You managed to come out of your childhood with good values. My leaving you with Gunter gave you the chance to develop some scruples. What I did was essential to your spiritual evolution." He smiled like a prosecutor resting an invincible case.

Linnea was stunned by his self-acquittal. "Are you telling me that you don't have any regrets about what happened to me? That the ends justify the means? That abandoning your daughter is ultimately good karma?"

"Something like that."

Now that she was healing, she realized how wounded she'd been. "Gunter could have destroyed me."

"But he didn't, and you forgave me."

"That doesn't give you a lifetime pass. And this isn't a baseball game. You don't get to run home without interference just because you stole second base."

"See! I'm stuck in the role of prodigal cad for the rest of our lives, and you get to play Ms. Nobility. You are the lucky one in all this, sweetheart."

"No," she insisted. "You are the lucky one. I forgave you for the past and welcomed you into my family. But you weren't satisfied with that base. You tried to manipulate my paper, mess with my marriage, incite Hommy to kill Clary Sage, and deny my daughter a safe school."

Calmly, Rick said, "I'm sorry you feel that way."

Linnea vomited words. "You are not sorry. You don't have any compassion for me. You talk to me like you've cut and pasted parts of *Relationships for Self-Serving Assholes* into your memory bank. Whenever things get dicey, you just click copy."

"St. Genevieve's Psychiatric Center was good for you, I see. I'm so glad we're finally sharing our real feelings and having a relationship." He stood up, spread his arms and shouted, almost joyfully, "You piss me off, too!"

Linnea's mind went blank. Black, primordial, pre-language consciousness simply obliterated his grip on her.

"You didn't let me come to your wedding!" Rick yelled belligerently. "God, how good it feels to get that out!"

"Is that why you are trying to ruin my marriage now? Denying me a family when I was a little girl wasn't enough? You want to take away the one I created as a woman, too?"

He suddenly appeared frightened and confused, his chest heaving. "I am your family, Linnea. Who will take care of me when I'm old?"

"I don't know." Linnea once again felt the heavy gray cloak of fatigue fall across her shoulders. "Maybe the children you send school supplies to in Mexico. Or your housekeeper in Hawaii. Pete might do it."

He blanched. "Not you?"

"No." Linnea's whole body trembled with grief. "I can't."

"But I'm your *real* father."

Those words tugged at her heart, but they were as hollow as the empty locket, now adrift in Spinning Wheel Bay. "A *real* father wouldn't let any one like you near me. A *real* father would tell you to hit the road. You're so disintegrated, there's no part of you I can hold onto. I can't even remember what you look like when you're not in front of me."

"How can you say these awful things to me? It's so unbelievably selfish of you."

She was getting dizzy. "*I* was the abandoned child. You were supposed to support me. I was supposed to lean on you. But, I managed to stand on my own two feet without any help. How dare you come back and try to topple me, for any reason?"

Wrath quickly replaced the fear in Rick's eyes. He enunciated so that his words cut like a razor across the rose on her ankle. "You wanted my help, and you know it. Your husband wasn't going anywhere until I came along, and it's your choice to continue wasting your writing talents on a community service rag. You could make big money if you weren't so damn uptight about your *truth*. You are messing up your life, honey, not me."

A community service rag? "Dad, are you sure you aren't crazy?"

"You're the one who just spent seventy-two hours in the loony bin. Maybe your *issues* have more to do with your condition than with me. I can't believe how much time I've wasted since I quit drinking, pining away for you. If I had raised you, you wouldn't be such a strike-out now. If Gunter failed you, it's because he didn't discipline you enough to make you respect your elders."

His words hit her nearly as hard as Pete's pop fly had, but Linnea felt Shane's light touch on her elbow, lifting her spirit from the cold stone floor, freeing her from the last remnants of filial fear. "There is one quality I wish I'd inherited from you, Dad."

Curiosity apparently quelled his need to continue assaulting her emotionally. "What's that?"

"The ability to say 'Fuck off" to people and not feel an ounce of remorse."

He smiled, a victor's grin. "Separation. It's the key to success."

"I'm still working on the remorse part, but fuck off, Dad, and don't come back."

Rick considered her for a moment, sneering nastily. "I never wanted you in the first place, and I certainly never owed you a thing. I wish your mother had had an abortion."

The trigger point in her neck began to pulse, causing all her muscles along its circuit to spasm. Linnea picked up her old Hans Christian Andersen book, open to *The Emperor's New Clothes* and flung the heavy volume at the stone fortress around her father's heart.

He fumbled, catching her beloved book by the binding and strode toward her. Though her neck and her knees threatened to buckle, Linnea held her head up straight, bracing herself for a Gunter-like blow. Rick surveyed her as if he were amused by the fear her flesh betrayed.

Baba Yaga cackled, "Made you see." And suddenly, Linnea was not afraid. He could hit her. She'd survive and then she'd call the police. In fact, his arrest would be a particularly dramatic way to end her article. He thrust the white leather into her hands. "Keep it," he sniffed, and sauntered out the door.

She couldn't tell if he meant for her to keep the book, or her newfound ability to reject what didn't serve her soul. It didn't matter. She knew his cat would inherit the Opulence now. She tasted Babe Ruth's orange fur as if it were on a fork stuck to her lips, imagining it plastered against the smooth mahogany of the dash. But at last, Linnea had gained something of true value from her father. She'd earned it the hard way. Keep it she would.

Chapter Twenty-Two

Dan finished reading the proof about Pete, tossing it onto the kitchen counter, next to the spluttering coffee pot. "Your father will never forgive you if you publish this."

It was mid-morning. She'd skipped breakfast; her belly shriveled. Up since four, she'd been typing in her office while he snored away on the couch. She'd kicked him out of their bedroom, giving him space to consider his choices.

"Chelsea and I want it in the stands when the scouts arrive."

With sleep still in his crow's feet, Dan stared past her as if he couldn't bear making eye contact. "I never thought you could be so vindictive."

Linnea's abs clenched. She couldn't help being anxious about how the community would receive her whistle blowing and longed for the support a stable marriage was supposed to offer in times like these. "You need help, Dan."

"Right," he muttered, rummaging through a drawer for the Pilchuck phone directory. He was naked but for the tropical print boxer shorts she'd bought him for their trip to Hawaii. She watched him thumb through the business pages, biting her lip, thinking of Shane in jet-black briefs. He could still be out there on Tower Island. She wanted to hop a ferry and go back, but she had a lot of dirty laundry to do, and a paper to get to the printers. And how could she go when the man she'd pledged to stand by until death did them part was skimming the ads for a marriage counselor? She watched him jot down several phone numbers. She wouldn't question him about it now; she'd wait until he'd done the research and approached her, ready to talk.

* * *

Linnea vacillated between feeling numb and excited as she and Chelsea delivered *The Edge* to shops and home subscribers late that afternoon. The Mill was their last stop. Looking forward to a mocha and balancing a huge pile of newsprint, she struggled to unlock the basement door. Chelsea followed her, burdened with her bundles of papers.

Chatter and laughter from the crowded café wafted down the stairs. A brand-new double bed was positioned next to Dan's second roaster. Linnea was nonplused. "He's moving out? I thought he was calling a counselor."

Chelsea sighed. "It looks like he was calling the furniture store."

Linnea felt her face contorting. "How can he just skip out? What about Megan?" She threw her papers onto the coffee-stained carpet and kicked the air angrily. Linnea no longer felt the need to maintain her composure or keep her feelings secret around her friends.

Chelsea had seen her at her worst, and stuck by her. She'd listened to her confession about Shane, too. "Do you really want him to come home? After everything that happened in the tower?"

"I don't know," Linnea answered honestly. "It's just that my father tried to break up our marriage. I can't bear giving him the satisfaction of prying my family apart."

"You've been holding it together since long before Rick showed up," Chelsea reminded her gently. "Can you live with him just being the straw that breaks the camel's back?"

Linnea sucked in the side of her cheek, surveying shopping bags of mismatched towels and jarring plaid sheets. Her eye fell on a check, casually tossed onto the bare mattress. It was dated that day, written to Dan, and signed by her father. The amount was well over what was needed to pay off the new roaster. On the memo line, Rick had scrawled *For your moving-out expenses.*

She blanched. Attorneys, judgment, shame, single motherhood, child counseling, poverty, grief: everything she'd been afraid of was now on her horizon, but she didn't allow her soft tissue to knot itself into a tourniquet. She allowed sorrow and agony to spurt through her body, down to her feet. She felt it cramping in her toes.

"I know it's Dan's turn to step up to the plate. I just can't believe he's going to bench himself." She shuddered. "And damn all this baseball lingo!"

She pictured herself dropping onto the concrete outside the bus station. The boot-clad foot of a man, drop-kicked a little girl into the dirty space beside her. "Who are you?" the child asked her.

In her mind, she whispered, "Linnea."

"I know Linnea," the little girl said matter-of-factly, as if she'd overhead a multitude of adult discussions about the person in question. "She's beautiful. She's smart. She's very talented. And she's," the child lowered her voice, as though she were about to utter profanity, "selfish."

Fear prickled Linnea's spine just before Baba Yaga's ghastly face popped up over the child's shoulder. The old witch was playing a game, but instead of the usual peek-a-boo, she cackled, "Cracked Bat!"

Linnea was so startled, she couldn't help laughing. "Yes, she *is* selfish," she said, her heart full of tenderness for the little girl and the old crone. "Would you like to beg here at the bus station, or come away with me?"

"I want to stay with you, Cracked Bat."

Linnea took the child's hand and stood up. She opened her eyes, no longer seeing Baba Yaga or the little girl, but her real life and her real best friend. "I need to get out of here."

Chelsea seemed worried. "Where do you want to go?"

Linnea drew a deep breath, inhaling all the support her real and imaginary friends had to offer. "To Robin's class, with Clary Sage. It's time for me to start dancing now, no matter what happens."

* * *

The following spring, Chelsea and Jeff were married in a small brick chapel across the street from the demolished stadium. School construction materials were staged on the perimeter of the property. Megan was the flower girl, strewing rose petals all the way down the aisle. Dwarfy rolled along behind her on a flatbed wagon laden with daisies, bearing the rings on a white satin pillow discreetly duct taped to his torso.

After the ceremony and photographs, Linnea hurried outside to *The Edge's* van to transport large flower arrangements full of clary sage to Claudio's. Wearing an elegant gown with a black velvet bodice and full taffeta skirt of shimmering gold, she was obliged to step over the plaque in the sidewalk that read, "This is where the baseball landed when Pete Stealer hit his final home run for the Spinners." Local baseball aficionados, including the orthopedist, Dr. Orbital, had insisted the epitaph be placed there last September, after Rick sold Pete's contract to a major league team for an undisclosed but substantial sum. The hasty deal was made while villagers were reading the special edition of *The Edge*. With the immediate public outcry over Pete's suppressed indiscretions and the team owner's negligence regarding audience safety swirling about Spinning Wheel Bluff, Rick quickly dissolved the team on the day of the big deal. And while Linnea was delighting in her first Nia class, he stuffed a yowling Babe Ruth into a cat carrier and gassed up the Opulence. He and his love object left town that night, leaving the waterfront mansion in the hands of real estate brokers.

It had taken months and a lot of haggling, but a local neurologist was finally moving into Rick's swanky home. The first thing Dr. Amani unpacked was a coffeemaker.

Linnea carefully tucked the herbal altar decorations between large boxes of white chocolate Ls in the back of *The Edge*'s van. Crinkled papers emerged from beneath a seat. One was a half-completed *Consume Your Colors* log. Chelsea had gone back to a regular diet the day Jeff had slipped the engagement ring upon her finger. The second sheet, stamped with a dusty child-sized shoeprint, was a newsletter from the kindergarten teacher requesting that parents donate tissue and snacks. Linnea shrugged. She'd already given quite a bit more than her share.

Her exposé on the Spinners had won the Puget Sound Small Press award, a prize that came with a check. Chelsea had gladly donated her half of the prize to the good cause of covering Megan's private school tuition until the new, non-toxic school building could be built. She called it the

Serendipity Scholarship, a title that had positively confounded Dan. He still lived at The Mill, contentedly hosting AA meetings several nights a week after closing. It was a great way to use up the last of the afternoon's brew and get rid of the day-old pastries.

In a gown matching Linnea's, Clary Sage shepherded Serengeti, Megan, and Dwarfy through the side door of the van. "Your mother stopped me on the steps to tell me she is coming to the reception after all. Jaime didn't make parole this morning." She breathlessly buckled the little girls in on the bench seat, tucking Dwarfy between them. "Did you really give her that overpowering perfume?"

"It's mostly lemon balm." Linnea slid into the driver's seat, smoothing her skirt and adjusting the black plastic bat hanging from the rear-view mirror. After her award-winning article came out, she'd received a package in the mail. Inside, she'd found a heart-shaped heating pad and a wooden box of essential oils just like the one she'd come across in the closet at Rick's house in Kauai. There had been no return address, but the attached note read, "His second wife started this little tradition. You'll get over him. Pass it on. Love #4, the Hypochondriac." She had given the whole bundle to her mother, hoping to bring the healing full circle.

On Evergreen, Linnea swerved to park, her right wheels up on the sidewalk. "I'll be right back," she told Clary Sage and the girls. She quickly retrieved three gold boxes from the back of the van. Wondering why the parade of honking reception-goers had halted behind her instead of going around, Linnea practically flew across the lane in her higher-than-usual heels. Avoiding oncoming traffic and trying not to twist her ankle, she leapt over residual rain puddles. Earning her Nia white belt last

January had certainly helped strengthen her body. Perfectly balanced, she stopped in the median where three burly men in orange jumpsuits were picking up trash.

"L stands for love," she told her brothers. "I wish we had had more of it."

As she drove past a tall brick building downtown, she smiled fondly. After Rick left town *Tales for Tots* had set up a booth on the sidewalk outside the bus station so she could joyfully dispense fairy tales to needy children. And thanks to the generosity of the German deli's owners, they'd held another auction in February. It had been just as successful as the last one, even without Rick Andersen or Peter Stealer on the guest list. The Universe is good.

At Claudio's, Sandy and Dr. Jafairi helped carry the plants and a huge basket of white chocolate L's into the reception hall. Once they had unloaded everything, Linnea and Megan moved the van to an overflow lot alongside the water. Rosebushes just beginning to leaf out after the long winter lined the walking path to the restaurant. As Megan darted ahead, Linnea noticed a long train of white trailing behind her. "Oh no, sweetie, is your lace unraveling?"

Startled, Megan stopped and looked down at her patent leather shoes. She shook her head and lifted her skirt. "Chelsea said brides have to wear something blue. This is all I had."

A troll doll with blue dreadlocks was laced to Megan's calf with the white gauze she'd gotten from Dr. Beasley, billed for by Dr. Perdue. With his wrapping coming undone, the troll hung upside down, his head bobbling against the cobblestones.

For a moment, Linnea was enchanted by her little girl's ingenuity, until she remembered with horror that Rick had given Megan the troll doll the last time they'd come to

Claudio's. Her face began to tremble with superstitious fear.

Somewhere, he and Pete were on warm beaches, congratulating themselves for getting away with soft tissue crime. Downtown, Dan was still luxuriating in his sad story, fueling it with his stimulating brew. Old grief swelled in Linnea's heart. The trigger point in her neck clamped down, clenching her jaws, squeezing her scalp. Her hands trembled so much that she wondered if she could fulfill her duties at the reception. Then, she drew a deep breath and let her sorrow lift, releasing it to the sky, letting it drift away with the cirrus clouds.

"Don't worry, Mommy." Megan stepped out of the cloth binding, slipping her hand into Linnea's. "I'm not really hurt. I had to use these bandages because Dwarfy took all the duct tape."

Behind them, a seagull landed on the van with a thud. Linnea turned around. The plastic bat beneath the rearview mirror swayed beneath the subtle impact. The bird nodded and flew away.

"You're caught in the thorns," a man said behind her. "Don't move."

Linnea recognized his voice instantly. She twisted around as Shane disentangled her taffeta skirt from the scratchy bramble.

He straightened up, smiling happily. "Go on ahead, flower girl. The ring bearer is on the dance floor, waiting for you."

Megan wrinkled her nose at him as if they'd been friends for eons. She skipped toward the entrance of the restaurant, paying no heed to the unraveling gauze or the troll scraping against the stone behind her. Linnea nearly stopped her for safety's sake, but Megan unknowingly hopped right out of the fray as Larry opened the door for her. Neither noticed the troll skidding into the mud beneath a silver shrub.

Shane took Linnea's hands in his. "Sorry I missed the ceremony. My flight was delayed."

Linnea trembled with joy. Chelsea had never mentioned inviting him, but there had been days when, despite meditation, yoga, hot tub, a muscle relaxant, bodywork, Nia class, wise women's counsel, and her fascination with fairy tales, Linnea's whole being still begged to go back to the tower, to be with him. There were times she wanted to go digging around Sedona, craving Shane's presence, touch, and healing alchemy. She'd poked around the Internet looking for flights, but she'd hadn't let herself go beyond that.

After all, she'd told herself, Shane could have had a drooling Saint Bernard who slept at the foot of his bed. Perhaps he had cats and let them tiptoe across his kitchen counters. Maybe he held season tickets to local baseball games. He might even have had a girlfriend. And she'd been busy adapting to the dynamic changes taking place in her core to pine too much. Since the day Dan took up residence back in The Mill, she had stepped right into her role as a single mother. She was strong and successful. The divorce had been final for three months. She smiled happily at Shane. "Your timing is impeccable."

"I couldn't wait until summer to see you again," he whispered, "so I came to town for a seminar on Earth consciousness, healing energy, and opening to love. Would you like to go with me? "

Linnea laughed softly. "Would you like to go with *me*? *The Edge* is sponsoring the program."

Shane squeezed her hands lightly. "I'm not surprised."

A tingling charge traveled up her arms. Linnea shivered as it coursed through her spine. A sparkling mist glittering with all the colors of the rainbow emanated from them as their hearts reconnected. It felt as if they were in the tower once again, as if they'd never left.

He drew her into his arms. Linnea's high heels made her the perfect height. Heart to heart, they accepted synchronicity with a kiss.

Odd, but abandonment can be a blessing in disguise. Every woman who has seen her illusions shatter, felt her consciousness crack, gets to come up to bat again. Cracked bats become all-star players in new paradigms. Every day, perfect strangers are kinder than spoiled fathers are cruel. Healers soften flesh turned to stone. Divine scavengers spin straw into gold. Every day, when Love relieves a body, it liberates the story of a soul.

Acknowledgements

Thank you to my editor, Anne Mini. I am deeply grateful for the insight, guidance, and expert attention to fine detail that you so generously devoted to this project.

Also, many thanks to Melinda Peeples for the original cover art and to Rhonda Dicksion for the design. I truly appreciate how adeptly each of you honored my vision while imbuing it with your individual flair.

I am indebted to the friendly people at Seattle's Zoka Coffee Roaster and Tea Company for answering all my questions about coffee roasting.

Blessings to Deb Lambo, and all of my Yaga Sisters, especially Treena and Grace for their careful reading and heartfelt encouragement. Many thanks to my Nia friends at the Monroe Wellbeing Center and the many myofacial release experts who keep me moving.

The crew at Ten Pentacles has been awesome. Thanks for your support, guys.